Praise for the

OUT OF THE LIGHT, INTO THE SHADOWS

New York Times Bestselling Author
LORI FOSTER

"Foster writes smart, sexy, engaging characters."
—Christine Feehan

"Foster writes about real people you'll fall in love with."
—Stella Cameron

"Known for her funny, sexy writing, Foster doesn't hesitate to turn up the heat." —*Booklist*

National Bestselling Author
L. L. FOSTER

"Unique and fascinating."
—Elizabeth Lowell, *New York Times* bestselling author

"Entertaining paranormal romantic suspense that grips readers." —*Midwest Book Review*

National Bestselling Author
ERIN McCARTHY

"Intriguing, entrancing, and enrapturing!"
—*The Romance Readers Connection*

"The writing is seamless, the story a page-turner, and the romance is one to defy all odds." —*Romance Reviews Today*

OUT OF THE LIGHT
INTO THE SHADOWS

· LORI FOSTER ·

· L. L. FOSTER ·

· ERIN McCARTHY ·

BERKLEY BOOKS, NEW YORK

THE BERKLEY PUBLISHING GROUP
Published by the Penguin Group
Penguin Group (USA) Inc.
375 Hudson Street, New York, New York 10014, USA
Penguin Group (Canada), 90 Eglinton Avenue East, Suite 700, Toronto, Ontario M4P 2Y3, Canada
(a division of Pearson Penguin Canada Inc.)
Penguin Books Ltd., 80 Strand, London WC2R 0RL, England
Penguin Group Ireland, 25 St. Stephen's Green, Dublin 2, Ireland (a division of Penguin Books Ltd.)
Penguin Group (Australia), 250 Camberwell Road, Camberwell, Victoria 3124, Australia
(a division of Pearson Australia Group Pty. Ltd.)
Penguin Books India Pvt. Ltd., 11 Community Centre, Panchsheel Park, New Delhi—110 017, India
Penguin Group (NZ), 67 Apollo Drive, Rosedale, North Shore 0632, New Zealand
(a division of Pearson New Zealand Ltd.)
Penguin Books (South Africa) (Pty.) Ltd., 24 Sturdee Avenue, Rosebank, Johannesburg 2196,
South Africa

Penguin Books Ltd., Registered Offices: 80 Strand, London WC2R 0RL, England

This is a work of fiction. Names, characters, places, and incidents either are the product of the authors' imagination or are used fictitiously, and any resemblance to actual persons, living or dead, business establishments, events, or locales is entirely coincidental. The publisher does not have any control over and does not assume any responsibility for author or third-party websites or their content.

OUT OF THE LIGHT, INTO THE SHADOWS

A Berkley Book / published by arrangement with the authors

PRINTING HISTORY
Berkley edition / August 2009

ISBN: 978-0-425-23052-7

BERKLEY®
Berkley Books are published by The Berkley Publishing Group,
a division of Penguin Group (USA) Inc.,
375 Hudson Street, New York, New York 10014.
BERKLEY® is a registered trademark of Penguin Group (USA) Inc.
The "B" design is a trademark of Penguin Group (USA) Inc.

PRINTED IN THE UNITED STATES OF AMERICA

10 9 8 7 6 5 4 3 2 1

CONTENTS

Have Mercy
LORI FOSTER
1

Deal or No Deal
ERIN MCCARTHY
89

Total Control
L. L. FOSTER
161

Undead Man's Hand
ERIN MCCARTHY
251

Have Mercy

Lori Foster

ONE

THEY'D been together six months now. Not super long, but for Mercedes Jardine, it was long enough for her to irrevocably lose her heart to Wyatt Reyes. Since their first date she'd loved him, and every day since then the feeling had grown more powerful. When she was with him, she felt complete, fuller and happier, and more like a woman.

Only with Wyatt did she move out of the shadow of her impressive big brother.

Only with Wyatt did her insecurities melt away.

What she felt for him was forever.

Now she had to know how he felt.

The thought of declaring herself, of laying her heart on the line, gave her twinges of anxiety. But if she left it to Wyatt, she figured they'd be together for years before he took their romance to the next level.

Marriage.

It was what she wanted now. What she *needed*.

A lifetime with Wyatt would be so wonderful. He was the most amazing man, solid like her brother, responsible and caring. He worked hard, respected others. And for

Mercedes, he was the sexiest man alive. Six feet, two inches of hard, labor-inspired muscle enhanced with dark blond hair and clear green eyes—he epitomized the rugged man's man, but he had the confidence and charisma to be a ladies' man, too.

The concrete construction company he owned had grown even in the months she'd known him. He put all his revenue into building it bigger and better, and he had a sound reputation for quality work. The last thing she'd ever wanted to do was interrupt his five-year plan. But if he'd let her, she could help him with that.

Today, she'd start the conversation with that proposal—and then move on to another.

Taking a deep breath, Mercy got out of the fancy sports car her brother had bought for her birthday, and headed for the front door of Wyatt's modest rented home. Though she had her own key, his truck was in the driveway, assuring he was home. She opened the unlocked door and stepped into warm air circulated by a fan.

Even though spring in Ohio was especially warm this year, Wyatt rarely used his air-conditioning. Like her, he enjoyed the fresh air more, but unlike her, he was also conserving money wherever he could.

Sometimes the differences in their financial standings made her feel guilty. After all, he worked hard for his pay, but thanks to her brother, Mercy hardly worked at all. Most wouldn't label her artistic jewelry more than a hobby. She was good, and her custom pieces brought high-ticket sales. But she only worked when she felt like it, or when something inspired her.

As soon as she closed the door, she heard the shower running. Her confrontational plans faltered; knowing Wyatt was naked had the effect of obliterating her best intentions.

Biting her lip, Mercy considered things for only a moment before deciding first things first. Even though she'd carefully dressed for her objective today, she hurriedly

stepped out of her strappy sandals and stripped away her
ultrasoft camisole tank as she went down the hallway to
the bathroom. By the time she reached him, Mercy wore
only her summer gauze skirt, panties, and jewelry.

She stepped out of the skirt before opening the bathroom door.

"Wyatt?"

"Hey, babe." He pushed aside the shower curtain, saw
her standing there, and his gaze did a slow, nearly tactile
scrutiny of her body.

Without a word, he held the curtain wide for her to get
in.

Showing ridiculous haste, Mercy pushed down her
panties, removed her watch and earrings, and stepped into
the narrow bath. As quick to urgency as her, Wyatt pulled
her into a long, tongue-twining kiss that curled her toes
and had her locking her fingers in his wet hair.

"Until I saw you," he whispered against her throat, "I
was so exhausted, I just wanted to eat and sleep."

"And now?"

"Now I'm fully alert, believe me." He leaned back to
see her face, and a roguish smile curled his sexy mouth.
"A nap holds no interest, but eating . . ." He covered a
breast with one hand, and with the other, he explored between her thighs. "I like that idea a lot."

Her eyes closed, her head fell back, and her heart
nearly punched out of her chest. With Wyatt, she stayed so
sexually attuned that a mere look had her primed and
ready. When he said things like that, when he implied
what he'd do, it drove her wild.

Carefully, he pried her hands from his hair and folded
them behind her. "Leave them, sweetheart."

Oh God, she loved it when he took control like this.
He'd torment her, make her crazy, but in the end, he always made it worthwhile. This time, however, she didn't
know if she could take it.

"Wyatt—"

"Shh. No talking. But feel free to moan."

Shaking all over, she put her hands to his shoulders to stall him. "Wait."

"No." With a chastising look, he caught her wrists and held her hands behind her with one loose fist. "You're only making it harder on yourself, Mercy. You came in here naked, full of invitation." He treated her to a deep kiss to emphasize his control. "Now be still, and let me do what we both want."

The long, shuddering moan escaped without her permission.

As he turned her with her back against the tile wall, he bent to her left breast. He licked, held her nipple captive between his teeth and tongued her roughly before sucking hard.

Mercy arched her body, and he accepted the temptation, pushing his free hand between her thighs. But he only cupped her, giving her the heat of his palm, a slight pressure, without any real stimulation.

"Wyatt . . ."

His teeth nipped, making her jump and sending a jolt of pleasure curling in her womb. She bit her lip to remain quiet.

He licked his way to the other nipple, circled with his tongue, and then sucked lightly, a direct contrast to what she'd expected. She couldn't predict what he'd do next, or how he'd do it, and the unknown kept her on a razor's edge of need. She tried grinding her mound against his palm, but he laughed and eased the pressure.

In no way did he seem exhausted to her.

She opened her legs more, a silent request for him to explore, to touch her, to *penetrate*.

"You want my fingers in you?"

Because he'd told her not to speak, she nodded.

He came up to kiss her ear, her throat. She felt his erection against her, long and solid, and she felt his smile against her throat. "Soon."

He enjoyed this game even more than she did. If she

could ever keep her head about her, she'd one day pay him back in kind.

And thinking that nearly pushed her into a climax.

"Now, Mercy?" As if he sensed her readiness, he stroked between her legs, parted her lips, and began pushing two fingers into her. It was a tight fit, and she squirmed in mixed pleasure and urgency as he worked them deep—and then again, stopped moving.

She felt herself contracting around him, needing him, and she saw him smile. He was such a dominant personality—but he only applied that dominance to her in bed. Outside the bedroom, he was so courteous and deferential that she felt like a princess.

He went back to her breasts, alternately licking and sucking her nipples, sometimes tugging with his teeth until she cried out, then lapping gently. She couldn't take much more, and he seemed to know that, too.

"You are so damned hot, Mercy. I love playing with you."

Love. God, how she hoped that word had real meaning to him.

Those thoughts were obliterated when he brought his thumb up to her clitoris and lightly stroked.

She gasped, stiffened.

"You're all swollen and ripe," he said against her temple, nuzzling her ear, her throat. He teased her clit more, and her legs started to tremble. "So close already. But Mercy . . ." He stilled the movements and leaned back to look at her.

Noooo. She needed release so badly, she was ready to plead with him, but he touched her lips with his fingertips, quieting her.

And he explained, "I want you in my mouth when you come."

Oh God.

He released her hands, sank to his knees, and cupped her derriere in both big palms. "I love how you taste, Mercy."

Love again. The dual assault of what he said and what he did proved too much. The second his mouth closed over her, her tremors started. She covered her own aching breasts and closed her eyes against the pleasure of his tongue languidly moving over, in and out of her most sensitive flesh. He licked once, twice, then closed his lips around her and sucked.

Just that easily, she exploded.

Holding her upright with his grip on her bottom, he kept her pressed tight to his mouth, relentless in his assault, dragging out her climax until she did beg, until she was totally spent. "Stop, please."

In a heartbeat he was before her again, one arm around her waist, the other shutting off the water.

"Hold on to the towel bar."

She managed to do that, just barely. He watched her with burning green eyes while he dried himself, and then quickly dried her, too. When the soft terrycloth towel touched between her legs, she gasped, still too sensitive to bear it—and that seemed to turn him on, too.

Now he was the urgent one, and they were both still damp when he lifted her in his arms and strode out of the bathroom to his bedroom.

At five feet, nine inches, she wasn't a dainty woman, but Wyatt carried her as if she weighed nothing. Along the way, he kissed her forehead, the bridge of her nose, the corner of her mouth. Her back had barely settled on the unmade bed when he pushed her legs wide, settled over her, and entered her with one powerful thrust.

They groaned together.

At the feel of him inside her, Mercy's body reignited and she was ready for round two. After all, with Wyatt, there was always a round two, and sometimes a round three or four. He was such an amazing lover, ensuring her pleasure before ever taking his own.

Eyes closed, head back, Wyatt stilled for several heartbeats. After two deep breaths that seemed to compose him, he looked down at her. High on his cheekbones, dark color showed the level of his arousal. The green of his eyes darkened, grew more intense. His jaw clenched tight.

Slowly, his gaze locked with hers; he pulled out, and sank back in again. He took interested note of her sharp inhalation, studied the signs of pleasure on her face. "Damn, Mercy, it feels incredible being inside you."

To her, too. She loved feeling him, and only him. After they'd been together three months, they'd given up condoms. She'd been on the pill awhile, and they knew each other well enough to trust on all health issues.

Little had she known how easy it was to render the pill ineffective.

A little dazed by the overwhelming chemistry between them, she rested her hands on his chest, pleased to feel his galloping heartbeat against her palm.

His chest hair was darker than the sun-streaked hair on his head, and it drew her fingers. Following his body hair as it angled down to his crotch, Mercy coasted her fingertips over his flat brown nipples, his muscled abdomen, then over the lighter skin of his narrow hips.

Emotion filled her, making her almost weepy. She met his gaze, saying softly, "I love the way you love me, Wyatt."

He froze, searched her face, and then the words seemed to ignite him beyond some invisible restraint. Growling, he hooked his arms through her legs, drawing them high and wide, holding her in a way that left her completely exposed and vulnerable to anything he wanted to do.

That suited her fine, because everything he did was for her pleasure.

Giving her his weight, he pressed her legs wider still and sank in so deep that she caught her breath. He opened his mouth on her throat. She felt his teeth just before he began a frantic rhythm that pushed her quickly toward another orgasm. As she started to come, he rose up to his elbows to watch, and without deliberate decision, Mercy said, "I love you, Wyatt."

His eyes flared, but he didn't stop thrusting into her. If anything, he drove harder, deeper, and she said again, "I love you."

He took her mouth, smothering the words and kissing her deeply as he, too, gained his release.

Mercy clutched at his back, loving him so much that it hurt, so immersed in mind-numbing pleasure that she couldn't even imagine the repercussions of her declaration.

Not yet.

WYATT slowly came back to reality—and knew the lingering euphoria burning through his blood had more to do with what Mercy had said during her orgasm than the incredible carnality that sizzled between them.

Did she mean it?

Women often said things during sex that they didn't mean. But he didn't think Mercy was like that. She wasn't careless that way. She was never indiscriminate, in speech or action.

He'd never known a woman like her. Quietly independent, sweetly vulnerable, so sexual and hot that she burned him up whenever they made love.

Did she love him?

For six months, he'd felt himself sinking further under her spell—and he didn't care.

He didn't want it to end.

Yet . . . she didn't know everything about him. She didn't know the past that influenced him, the past that would forever dictate his future.

If that future was to include her, she'd need to understand a few things. Not that he'd bare the deep scars of adolescent hurt. Never that.

Those wounds were fifteen years old, but at inconvenient times, they still bled as if just inflicted. Too many nights they burned his subconscious, waking him from a sound sleep to find himself drenched in his own sweat, his brain exploding, his throat tight with acidic regret.

No, he wouldn't dredge those up for anyone. But maybe he wouldn't have to.

Untangling himself from Mercy's sweet body, he moved to her side. Long damp lashes rested on her cheekbones, and her lips, rosy and full, parted to accommodate her deep breaths.

His heart swelled. She was so pretty, so innately female. He moved a heavy lock of sleek, midnight hair from her forehead. "Sleeping?"

Her slender throat flexed as she swallowed and shook her head. "No."

She didn't open her eyes, the little coward, and that amused him. Did she hide with regret at the hasty words, or shyness from their truth?

He bent and kissed her slack mouth. "Stay put. I'll be right back."

Now she came alert, and her startling hazel eyes filled with alarm. Starting to rise on one elbow, she said, "Wait. Where are you going?"

Pressing on her shoulders, he got her flat on her back again. "Damn." He looked at her breasts, slightly abraded from his whiskers. "I was about to shave in the shower when you showed up."

Such an inane comment helped her relax. "I'm fine, Wyatt. You'd never hurt me."

Not intentionally. But he knew better than most that there were all kinds of hurts. Some that lasted a lifetime.

He touched a red spot on her belly, another at the inside of her thigh. Sitting up, he moved her legs apart again to check for more beard rash.

Modesty had her sputtering in protest. "Wyatt . . ."

"With you," he told her, staring at her soft, pink sex, "I don't think I'll ever get enough." He put his fingers on her, slightly in her, and closed his eyes at the pleasure of it.

She flinched. "Wyatt."

He had to get a grip. Just because a woman claimed love was no reason to ravage her. At least, not again, not so soon.

"Stay put. Just like this, Mercy." He lightly stroked her inner thigh. "I like looking at you. I'll be right back." And without more explanations, he left the bedroom and went to the hall bath. So fast that he nearly cut his own throat, he shaved. After rinsing, he dampened a washcloth and went back to her.

It satisfied him to see that she was just as he'd left her, sideways across the bed. Her long hair hung over the edge of the mattress, her arms rested limp at her sides, and her legs were open, one knee bent.

His heart started punching in his chest. He looked at Mercy, and he wanted her. Hell, he thought of her and he got so hard he ached. Spending a lifetime with her, if she could abide by his requirements, would be as close to heaven as he'd likely ever get. It'd definitely be more than he deserved.

As he eased down beside her again, her gaze turned watchful. It was a fascinating combo, for her to trust him completely, but remain wary of what he might do to her sexually. It excited them both.

Without air-conditioning, the house was warm, and that combined with their vigorous carnal activity left little dots of sweat over the bridge of her nose. He used the cloth to stroke her face, then her throat.

Those amazing hazel eyes watched him. They were the first thing he'd noticed about her when they first met. The contrast of striking golden eyes and pitch-black, silky hair distinguished her from other women. But it was every-thing else about her, everything beyond the physical that kept him entranced.

"I don't understand you."

Wyatt smiled. "What's to understand? I'm a man who adores your body and sexual appetite." He bathed her breasts and saw her soft nipples tighten. When he slowly dragged the cool cloth down her body to her belly, she squirmed.

Spurred on by her response, he pressed it between her

thighs and held it there. "Don't fret, sweets. I'll give you a few minutes to rest before we continue."

Her eyes widened. "But . . . I thought you were exhausted!"

Knowing he confused her, that she wanted to know what he thought of her declaration, Wyatt laughed. "Before you flashed your beautiful body at me, I was. I pushed hard today to meet the deadline on a big job, and then I had a meeting. I'm pretty sure I nailed the contract for a new deal that'll put me a lot closer to my goals. I'll even be able to invest in another truck and some other equipment I wanted, and I can give the crew a much-deserved raise." If things worked out right, he'd soon have four cement trucks and two dump trucks.

Eventually he wanted twice that many—but for now, progress was good. He and his men managed with what they had, and they always did top-notch work for a reasonable price. In the contractor business, being reliable and on time was a major plus. Most didn't expect it, and were blown away when they got it.

Showing a familiar habit, Mercy worried her bottom lip with her teeth. "You know, I wanted to talk to you about that. About your business, I mean. I've been thinking, you really should let me talk to my brother—"

"No." They'd had this conversation once already. He didn't want to talk about her wealthy brother, or how he could expedite Wyatt's plans. He would accomplish his goals on his own, under his own terms, and in the end he'd owe no one.

His tone must have been more curt than he'd intended, given how Mercy's expression pinched into a frown.

"Don't look at me like that." He caressed her thigh. "You already know how I feel about a loan from your brother."

"But it doesn't have to be a loan. It could be an investment."

"I'm not taking on investors."

"Not just any investor, no, but this is my brother. You don't know him yet, but he's wonderful, I promise. Okay, a little intimidating, maybe, but you could trust him not to—"

"I said *no.*" Never would he give up control over any aspect of his life, not even to her doting brother. He'd lived too long with no control at all to risk losing it for any reason. "I mean it, Mercy. I don't want to hear any more about it."

Though she didn't move, he felt her emotional retreat and hated it. Her lush lips trembled until she tightened her mouth to still the telltale sign.

Well, shit.

After kissing her nose, he said, "I don't want to do business with him, but I wouldn't mind meeting him."

That perked her up. She'd been after him to meet her brother for some time.

"Really?"

For too long he'd kept women at an emotional distance, doing his utmost not to get too involved, blocking any hint of feeling. But with Mercy, it proved impossible.

He really didn't have any choice in the matter; he was already in over his head, and not being with her would hurt a hell of a lot more than loving her ever could.

He sat up and, with a casualness he knew left her off balance, cleaned away his semen from her sex. Her ragged moan was both embarrassment and interest.

Mercy might turn wild when he made love with her, but outside the bedroom she was a gentle woman with impeccable manners and lofty standards.

He adored the contrasts.

Belying his previous stance on the issue, he said, "Of course I want to meet your brother." He tossed aside the cloth and settled between her thighs. "It's only right to meet the family of the woman who loves me."

Her eyes widened.

She was still wet, swollen, and sensitized. He eased

into her, going as deep as he could, slow this time now that he'd taken the edge off his need.

He cupped her face in his hands and kissed her. "Tell me again."

"I love you."

"One more time."

She wrapped her legs around his waist. "I love you, Wyatt Reyes."

"I'm glad." He kissed her again. "Because I love you, too, Mercedes Jardine."

TWO

FIFTEEN minutes after another amazing climax, excitement still made Mercy giddy.

Wyatt loved her.

He was finally ready to meet her family.

That should have been enough, and she did hate to push him, but really, what choice did she have? Now, after he'd proved so receptive to her emotional declarations, seemed like the best possible timing.

Shoring up her nerve, she turned to her side and rose on one elbow.

Lord help her, but the man was fine. He had the most gorgeous body she'd ever seen. It had been his body that had first drawn her, but his personality that had stolen her heart.

She put her hand on his abdomen, touching the layers of muscles there, and his eyes opened.

His mouth didn't move, but she saw the smile in his green eyes as he looked at her. Before she could say anything, he asked, "You hungry?" And just that quick, he sat up and left the bed. "Because I'm starved. Let's go figure

out something for dinner. Or better yet, you can nap and
I'll come get you when I have stuff ready."

Two seconds later, Mercy watched his sexy backside
disappear out the door.

Well.

Insulted, frustrated, and a little hurt, she sat there and
tried to decide what to do.

Did he suspect her intentions? But that couldn't be.
Wyatt was not a man to run away. If he didn't want to talk
about certain things, he said so—just as he had refused
any discussion on her brother financially assisting him in
any way.

Her hands knotted in the now-rumpled sheet. Damn it,
Braxton had more money than he knew what to do with.
Why shouldn't he help the man she loved?

But Mercy knew it was in part Wyatt's independence
and stubborn streak that made her love him. If he weren't
so proud and sometimes arrogant, if he were anxious to
partake of her brother's wealth . . . well, he wouldn't be
nearly as appealing.

Too many times to count, she'd met gold diggers who
considered her greatest appeal to be her relationship with
her wealthy brother.

Pushing aside the sheet, Mercy got out of bed. Better
that she be fully attired to have her showdown with Wyatt
anyway. She'd feel more secure and in control that way,
and Wyatt would be less likely to distract her with sex.

After sneaking around the hallway to retrieve her hast-
ily discarded clothing, Mercy dressed and even fixed her
hair and touched up her makeup. The final result was ade-
quate. Except for the glow in her cheeks, no one would
guess she'd just been thoroughly loved.

As she slipped into the hall, she could hear Wyatt whis-
tling in the kitchen as if he hadn't a care in the world.
That thought was interrupted with the delicious scent of
sizzling bacon.

Maybe she was hungry after all.

She smoothed her clothes, bit her lips to add a little color to them, and headed off to her confrontation.

She found Wyatt standing at the stove in unfastened jeans and nothing else. The jeans rode low on his hips, displaying plenty of sleek, tanned skin. She took in the sight of his wide back, the deep groove of his spine, and tight, narrow hips.

Mercy sighed. Even his big bare feet looked beautiful to her.

"How can I help?"

Glancing over his shoulder at her, he gave her a once-over and raised a brow at seeing her fully dressed. "You can slice a tomato if you want." He went back to forking the bacon.

Stubborn jerk. Forcing a sugary sweetness to her tone, Mercy agreed. "All right."

Wyatt set out pickles and chips, grabbed some lettuce leaves, and then put bread in the toaster. "I hope BLTs are okay. I was too hungry to start the grill."

"It smells wonderful. So . . . when do you want to meet Brax?"

"Your brother?" He shrugged. "I don't care. Whatever's convenient."

"How about over dinner?"

"Here?"

She would love for Brax to see Wyatt's home. Not that it was anything fancy, but it reflected the type of man Wyatt was—organized, tidy, promising . . .

He didn't look thrilled with that idea.

Mercy cleared her throat. "Or we could go to a nice restaurant."

Nodding, he said, "You pick a place and time, and then give me a little notice so I can clear my calendar, and I'll be there."

"Thank you."

When he set the platter of bacon on the table, he also bent and put a kiss to the back of her neck. Voice low and husky, he said, "Want to say it again?"

Being a little stubborn herself, Mercy said, "Thank you."

"No." He gave her a disgruntled look. "You *know* what I mean."

Why couldn't she stay annoyed with him? It was too bad that he got past her temper so easily. "I love you."

He laughed.

"What's so funny?"

"Oh, I don't know. Hearing you say that while you're frowning at me like you want to kick my ass just struck me funny."

Mercy couldn't help but smile. "I do sort of want to bludgeon you."

He feigned confusion and affront. "After I made you scream in pleasure three times? Damn, Mercy, you're a hard woman to please. No wait. That'd be a terrible contradiction, wouldn't it? You're easy for me to please." His smile turned smug. "Maybe because you love me?"

Her face went hot in a flash. *"Wyatt."*

Mimicking her scandalized whisper, he said, *"Mercy."*

He even looked charming while teasing her. Not that a little charm would get him out of a chastisement. "The dinner table is no place for talk like that."

"If you say so." He pulled out her chair. Once she'd seated herself, he asked, "What do you want to drink?" And then, back to teasing, he added, "Your throat has to be sore."

Mercy swatted at him, but he ducked out of reach and didn't come back until he had two cans of cola and a glass with ice for her.

They ate in silence until Mercy couldn't take it anymore. Wyatt had just taken the last bite of his loaded BLT when she decided she might as well just say it and get it over with.

She sucked in a huge breath and blurted, "Will you marry me, Wyatt?"

The second the words left her, she cringed. She'd almost shouted them at him. And she was so tense that she had to look like she might pounce on him at any minute. She took another breath and tried to relax.

And waited.

Wyatt glanced at her, but he didn't choke. He didn't even look all that surprised by her proposition. He just . . . chewed. And swallowed. And sipped his drink from the can.

Mercy threw a pickle at him. "Well?"

He sighed. "I do love you, Mercy, when I never thought I would feel that way about anyone."

Anyone—not just any woman? Her heart squeezed tight, but she didn't interrupt him.

"I love being with you. God knows I love having sex with you. You keep me entertained, and when we're out together . . ." He considered his words. "It might sound dumb, but I'm . . . I don't know, *proud* to be seen with you. You're this great class act, so pretty and intelligent, and you always dress great."

The praise warmed her clear to her bones. She started to relax.

He gave her a startling, megadirect look. "But I don't want to get married, honey. Ever."

The contentment drowned beneath a surge of hurt; her heart sank. "Why?"

Pushing his plate away, Wyatt sat back in his seat. He looked aggrieved and put out. "Marriage . . . muddies things."

"What *things*?" Oh God, she had to stop screeching at him like that. Hadn't he just called her a class act? Class acts did not screech. "Explain that, please."

One big shoulder rolled. "The second a woman gets married, she starts wanting ridiculous things. Picket fences and mortgages." He slanted her a look, and his voice hardened. "Kids."

Now her heart pounded so hard it hurt. But she wouldn't give up on her dream just yet. She couldn't. "That's silly, Wyatt. I have more than enough money of my own to handle a mortgage—"

His hand lifted, cutting her off. "And you already know

how I'll feel about that." His stern frown didn't bode well for her cause. "Unless I can contribute at least half, preferably more, I won't be saddled with a mortgage. And you know I can't contribute jack shit until I get my business financially sound."

Very slowly, Mercy licked her lips. "Okay, so you don't want a mortgage."

"Or kids."

What should she do? What could she say in the face of that implacable tone?

Praying his reservations were about money and not something more insurmountable, Mercy said, "If you wait to start a family until you think you're financially ready, you never will—"

He shook his head. "You misunderstand, Mercy. One day I'll get myself a house, and I might even throw up a damned picket fence. But kids? They're not for me. Not now, not ever."

Her stomach hurt. He sounded so final about it. Mercy desperately wanted to understand his reasoning so that she could maybe find a counterargument to dissuade him from his stance. "You don't like children?"

"Other people's kids, sure. Nothing wrong with little people. But I'm not going to be a father, Mercy." He didn't touch her, didn't reach for her. "If you love me, if you want to be with me, you might as well get the idea of kids out of your head."

Numbness rolled over her, broken only by a slight queasiness.

Finally Wyatt left his chair and came to crouch before her. He took her hands in his. "I do love you, babe. And you say you love me." His stark expression broke Mercy's heart. "Why can't that be enough?"

What could she say? The truth?

No, she couldn't. Not right now. Not with Wyatt on his knees.

She smoothed her hand over his hair, then rested it on his shoulder. "Yes, it's enough."

Relief stole his frown. He caught the back of her neck and drew her close for a long, deep kiss.

She didn't lose her head this time. Not only had she recently been sated, but worry kept sexual thoughts at bay.

"Hey?" He nuzzled against her throat. "As long as we're taking things to a new level, you want to move in with me?"

Desperation influenced her better judgment. "You want me to?"

"I would love waking up with you each morning, and going to bed with you each night."

It was a start. "Yes, I would love that, too." And then maybe while being in such constant close proximity she could change his mind on marriage and children. What did she have to lose? She had nearly eight months before reality forced a final decision on her, so she may as well spend it working on him.

THE noonday sun loomed high in the sky when Mercy drove down the long cobbled driveway to her brother's home. Over and over again in her mind, she rehearsed what she'd say to him, and what she wouldn't say—if she could keep control of the conversation.

Her brother had an uncanny knack for picking apart her best intentions.

She parked beside a large fountain that funneled water into a beautiful stream. The stream ran beneath glass flooring in the foyer of her brother's home. The extravagances of her brother's creativity never failed to amaze her.

There were new trees in the lawn, new cut-glass panes in the front windows. But today, Mercy had too much on her mind to be in awe of the many changes that greeted her every visit.

At the enormous double doors, she didn't knock. Braxton would have a fit if she ever did so. His home was her home, or so he repeatedly insisted. She opened the door and stepped into the foyer.

Immediately, Cameo Smithson, her brother's longtime assistant, came to greet her. No doubt Cameo had seen her pull up on the security cam.

Arms out in welcome, Cameo said, "Mercy, I didn't know you were coming by today. I'd have had lunch for us."

"I know I'm unannounced," Mercy said after they broke away. "Sorry about that."

As always, Cameo looked impeccable. A low ponytail held back her light-brown hair, showcasing her high cheekbones and the soft baby blue of her eyes. Her white silk tank top fell loose over tailored black slacks and black pumps.

If Cameo ever let herself, she'd be a knockout. But because she chose to be understated, she looked merely pretty.

"You do not have to announce yourself, Mercy. You know that." A very take-charge woman, Cameo hooked her arm through Mercy's and led her into a study. "Can I get you something to drink? Tea? Lemonade?"

"No, thanks." At the moment, her stomach was unaccountably jumpy. She sank onto a plush sofa. Caught between conflicting emotions, she asked, "Is the lord and master in?"

"For you, you know he's always in."

Mercy almost winced. She did need to tell Brax of her plans. But if he'd been out somewhere, she'd have had a reprieve.

Cam, maybe recognizing her dread, squeezed her hand and then started out the door. "Give me just a minute to get him for you."

Mercy shot back to her feet. "Is he busy?"

One slim hand, unadorned, waved away that concern. "Just making business calls."

She rushed after Cameo. "Then don't disturb him. I can wait."

Cameo turned to her with mock horror. "Do you *want* me to lose my job, Mercy? Of course you don't. But that's what would happen if I didn't immediately tell Braxton you're here."

"Baloney." Cameo might enjoy playing that game, but Mercy knew the truth. "Brax would never fire you because he can't get by without you. You're his . . . everything."

Cameo's smile showed a hint of melancholy. "Under any circumstances, with or without any assistance, your brother would more than get by, he'd succeed impossibly, and we both know it. He is by far the most capable person I know."

Truthfully, he was the most capable person Mercy knew, too. "True enough, I guess. But it's wonderful that you free up so much of his time by taking care of all the pesky little details in his life."

"Perhaps. Now sit and relax and I'll be right back."

Like she had a choice? Mercy listened to Cameo's heels clicking on the marble floor as she headed down the long hall.

Mercy was alone again.

One hand to her stomach, she watched the water streaming under the foyer. Maybe she even saw a gold-fish. She wasn't certain.

Above the foyer in the high ceiling, a skylight released sunlight to shine down on the spotless glass of the floor, decorated with a multitude of large potted plants. Natural marble tiles framed the glass and carried on through to the long hallway.

Her brother was . . . decadent. But he was also gener-ous, financially funding many charitable organizations and scholarships and selflessly donating his time to worth-while causes.

He overwhelmed her, so how would Wyatt feel around him?

Mercy faded back into the study. Bright, fragrant flow-ers decorated the corner of a desk and a small curio table. Original artwork hung on the walls. Carefully arranged furniture gave an air of cozy comfort. Everything in the room was beautiful and very, very expensive.

It was also all new from the last time she'd visited. Her brother had a thing about changing décor often. His mind was so quick, his energy level so high, he grew bored with most things familiar.

Except Cameo. She'd been with him for five years now.

Without making a single sound, her brother was suddenly there. "This is a nice surprise."

Mercy jumped at his voice, then turned to him with a smile. Unlike most multimillionaires, Brax dressed for himself rather than to impress. Today he wore chinos and a black polo. His midnight hair was mussed, his big feet bare.

Before she could scrutinize him further, he had her in a warm bear hug, lifting her right off her feet.

He smelled familiar and safe, and she hugged him back, allowing herself just a minute of sheer comfort. "I'm sorry to interrupt your day."

"You're never an interruption. In fact, I've been thinking of you today." He set her away from him but held on to her shoulders. His golden eyes, so like her own, stole into her soul. "How are you?"

Mercy knew that look only too well. Depending on how he used it, it could make women melt, or scare grown men half to death.

On her, that look meant he was already on to her and questions were just a formality. Braxton had the most uncanny intuition, especially where she was concerned. He knew when she was happy, when she was sad. And he always, without fail, knew when she was afraid.

Trying for an enthusiastic smile, she said, "I'm great."

He gave her a disconcerting and measuring look and came to a different conclusion. "Don't lie to me, Mercy."

"I'm not!" Not really. Well, maybe just a little. "I'm fine, really." At least she would be as soon as she got past whatever brick walls Wyatt had built around his heart.

Brax wasn't buying that. He wrapped his long fingers around her wrist and stared at her palm before narrowing his gaze on her. "You're nervous. Why?"

Jerking her hand free, Mercy flattened her lips and crossed her arms defensively. "I'm going to be changing residences."

Frowning, Brax crossed his arms, too. "Tell me why moving is such a big deal."

She'd lost her parents so long ago, she struggled to remember them. Details about them escaped her, more so every year.

But what she never, ever forgot was that an eighteen-year-old Braxton had taken over raising her, and never, not once, had he failed her in any way. "I'm moving in with Wyatt."

He didn't even blink. "This is the man who has resisted meeting me?"

"Yes, but it wasn't just you. He was . . . resistant to meeting any of my family."

"I'm your *only* family, Mercedes."

"Well, I sort of consider Cameo family now, too—"

Rather than deny that, he said, "Don't try to change the subject."

"Fine." There was no point anyway. Brax was impossible to distract. "Wyatt didn't want to meet you because he didn't want things to get too . . ."

"Personal?" Brax supplied with a heavy dose of derision.

This wasn't going well at all. "Maybe. I'm not sure." In many ways, Braxton was old-fashioned and very overprotective. "But now we're going to rectify that."

"How so?"

This time her smile was real. "Just last night, he said he'd like to meet you over dinner. I'll make the plans just as soon as you tell me when is good for you."

Braxton narrowed his eyes—and steered her toward a chair facing his desk. "Pick a place and time, and I'll be there."

Funny that he'd give the same response as Wyatt. Men. They were helpless unless a woman made the plans. "I thought I should clear a time with you first because your schedule is so busy . . ."

"There's nothing I can't rearrange for you. You know that."

She did know it. Always, even before her parents died in that awful plane crash, Braxton had been there for her. She dropped down into the wing chair. "Fine. I'll make the reservations and then be in touch."

Settling into his seat behind his desk, he looked at her in a familiar way that told Mercy the interrogation had only just begun. "Tell me about him."

"Wyatt?"

He rolled his eyes. "Who else?"

Easy enough. "He's wonderful, Braxton. Gorgeous and sensitive, and hardworking. Fair. Kind. Sexy. I love him, everything about him."

Steepling his fingers together and tapping them to his chin, Brax considered her. "What does he do for a living? Have you met his family? Are they close?"

A good opportunity if there ever was one. "He owns his own construction company. He started it himself and built it from the ground up. He pours most of his profits back into it. He pays his crew well."

"You've met his employees?"

She nodded. "I've gone to his job sites to meet him for lunch a few times. They all tease him, as men like to do with each other. But I could tell that they like and respect him. His foreman told me that Wyatt has a reputation for being honest and hardworking, meaning he finishes on time and within budget."

Cynicism tilted his mouth. "Sounds like a regular saint."

"Far from that. But then I'm not perfect, either." Mercy locked eyes with her brother. "You know, I was thinking that his company would be a good investment for you, and with added revenue, he could reach his goals a lot sooner."

The tapping stopped. "If that's what you want, I'll check into it."

Again she smiled. "Don't bother. When I mentioned it to Wyatt, he flatly refused."

Brax's left eyebrow went up. "I can see that you're dying to tell me why."

She did feel a little smug about Wyatt's independent streak. She wanted to help him, but at the same time, knowing he wasn't after the family fortune made her feel all warm and fuzzy inside. "He doesn't want to be indebted to anyone. When he gets the company where he wants it to be, it'll be his and his alone."

Nodding slowly, Brax said, "And his parents? He doesn't want them involved either, or do they not have the means?"

"His parents are deceased."

Brax stilled. Maybe he was empathizing, having lost his own parents so long ago, or maybe it was just deference to the situation, but his tone changed, became less challenging. "Any other family?"

"I don't think so. None that he ever mentions."

"How did he lose them?"

Mercy shook her head, as frustrated in her inability to explain to Brax as she was with Wyatt's lack of disclosure. In some ways she knew Wyatt better than she knew herself—and in others, he was a complete enigma. "He doesn't like to talk about them."

"Hmm."

Oh, she knew *that* look, too. She sat forward in her chair. "Don't you 'hmm' me, Brax."

He said nothing as he jotted down a short note on a piece of paper.

"Just stop it!" She reached for the paper, but Brax folded it into his palm. "I know what you're up to, and I forbid you to do it."

At her raised voice, Brax's hazel eyes glowed. "You *forbid* me?" Amusement brought out a deceptive dimple. His laugh was short and mocking. "You must be in love to think you can order me around, especially when it comes to ensuring your safety."

"Of course I'm in love! I already told you that."

He stood. "Unfortunately, as much as I admire your spunk, this is not up for discussion. If you think you're moving in with him before I know all there is to know about him, you need to think again."

"Damn it, Brax—"

"Cursing, too?" He pushed a button on his desk. "Cameo, I need a thorough background check on Wyatt Reyes. ASAP, please."

Naturally her brother would remember Wyatt's last name, even though she hadn't mentioned it in weeks. "I won't allow this!"

Paying no mind to her anger, he said, "Now that that's done . . ." He pulled her chair around to face him, knelt down in front of her, and studied her with unnerving intensity. His voice gentled when he asked, "What else is going on, Mercy."

Damn him, how did he know?

"You can always talk to me, honey. You know that."

She resented his calm. He made her feel small and insignificant, and ten years old again. "I am not a child, Brax."

"No, but you are my sister and nothing will ever change that, I promise. So please, tell me what's bothering you."

Mercy eyed him. "It's downright creepy how you do that."

"Do what?"

"Read me. It's just not natural."

Startled, he leaned back for a moment, but quickly recovered with a scowl. "You mean how I know when something is bothering my sister? My closest relative?"

She may as well stick to her guns. "Yes, exactly. You figure things out before I even say anything."

"There's nothing creepy in me caring about you and for you."

Mercy let out her breath. Yes, Brax made her feel ten, but he also loved her more than anyone she knew. Probably more than Wyatt, since Brax would move heaven and earth to make her happy, and Wyatt didn't even want to marry her.

Suddenly worried about disappointing him, she lowered her head. "You won't like it, Brax."

His big hands tightened on the arms of her chair. "Try me."

Maybe she should. Even if he wasn't happy about it, it would be nice to have someone to talk to. Her mind made up, Mercy nodded, choked up the words, and admitted, "I'm pregnant."

For only a moment, he stared at her. Then his mouth quirked. "Is that all? God Almighty, Mercy, you had me scared."

THREE

WHEN Brax stood and turned away from her, Mercy quickly followed. She grabbed his hand before he could touch that blasted buzzer on his desk. "This is *private*, Brax."

Looking happier than he should, he laughed. "I'm going to be an uncle and you want me to keep it secret?"

Oh God. Why couldn't anything be simple anymore? "It's not . . . it's just . . . Wyatt doesn't know yet."

That wiped the grin off his face. That blasted brow went up again. "Assuming he's the father—"

She slugged him in the shoulder, and only managed to hurt her hand. Her brother was solid granite. She glared displeasure at him. "Yes, of course he is."

"—then is there any particular reason you haven't told him?"

Covering her face for only a second to gather her wits, Mercy said, "Yes, there's a reason." She dropped her hands and summoned up some composure. "I wanted to do things in the proper order."

His mouth quirked. "Too late for that, isn't it?"

If her hand weren't still throbbing, she'd have punched

him again. Her eyes narrowed. "I doubt you want the nitty-gritty details about the conception."

"I'm a big boy, sweets. I can take it."

Her chin came up. "Fine. I was on the pill, so we skipped condoms."

His brows came down. "And?"

"You remember when I had that flu?"

"Nasty stuff. I remember."

"Well, according to the doctor, I probably barfed up a few pills before they had a chance to take effect."

"Huh." Brax thought about that. "Makes sense, I guess. I have no idea how long you'd have to keep one of those pills down to make them efficacious, but from what I remember, you threw up off and on for three days. Bad timing with the nausea and voilà—you're pregnant. Surely you don't feel responsible for that."

"It wasn't anyone's fault. I just hope that Wyatt will understand that."

Something dark and dangerous changed Brax's expression. "You think he'll blame you?"

"No. I don't know. I . . ." She threw up her hands. "Before I could tell him about the baby, I wanted to tell him I loved him."

Brax crossed his arms and nodded. "I get it. You wanted him to know that the baby didn't influence how you feel."

"Exactly."

"So how'd he take your declaration?"

Her heart hurt, remembering how Wyatt had reacted. "He said he loves me, too. And he wants me to move in with him."

"So far, so good. I see no reason I should kill the bastard, so why are you a jumble of nerves on this topic?"

She turned away. She couldn't face her brother while telling him the rest. "I asked him to marry me."

For several seconds, Brax was silent. When he spoke, he was right behind her. "His reaction?"

She closed her eyes and whispered the awful truth.

"He said marriage is out for him, because the minute a woman gets married she wants kids, and . . ." A lump of hurt made it difficult to swallow. Mercy shook her head. "He . . . doesn't. Ever."

She waited for Brax to react, to say something. Knowing his temper, especially where she was concerned, she expected the worst.

His quiet explosion—which she considered the worst and most lethal—didn't happen.

Instead her brother put both hands on her shoulders. "Mercy, you have to understand men. They dig in on something and can't find a way out. Wyatt said all that without having the facts in hand, so you can't hold him to it."

"I don't know, Brax." Could her brother be right? "He sounded pretty dead set on not being a father."

Brax turned her to face him. "A lot of people think they never want children until they find out the kids are on the way. Then they realize they're ecstatic."

"I don't think that's the case with Wyatt. There was just . . . something, something dark and absolute in the way he spoke." She looked up at Brax for understanding. "I'm afraid he'll never want the baby."

"If that's true, then he's not good enough for you, anyway. But listen to me, Mercedes Jardine. You are a wonderful judge of character, and I trust you. So I find it hard to believe you'd fall in love with a man who wouldn't want his own child."

Put that way . . . "I hope you're right. One thing's for sure. I'm not giving up on Wyatt yet."

"What are you going to do?"

Done exhibiting her self-doubts, something she knew was foreign to Brax, she straightened her shoulders. "I'm going to move in with him, and hopefully change his mind."

Doubtful, Brax gave her *the look*. "I'm not sure that's a good idea. The longer you're with him, the more hurt you'll be if he doesn't come around."

Hearing him voice her own concerns made his pep talk less encouraging. "I love him, Brax, so I'll be devastated whether I'm living with him or not. At least if I'm there, I might be able to figure out *why* he feels the way he does."

"I'll put my money on you." His smile lacked assurance. "But if things don't work out? What about the baby?"

In her mind, that wasn't even an issue. Feeling a stroke of protectiveness, Mercy folded her hands over her belly. "I love the baby already, Brax. I'm keeping him or her, no matter what."

Relief showed in his amber eyes. "Who needs a husband anyway, right? Between us, the little one will get more than enough love."

Tears welled in her eyes. "You're going to be a great uncle."

"Or more, if it comes to that." He rubbed his hands together, already planning ahead. "In fact, I'd love to have you living here, you know that. I have more than enough room to set up a nursery, and we could hire a nanny, and—"

Laughing, Mercy put her fingers over his mouth. "I'll remind you again: I'm a big girl. I can handle everything. But Brax?"

"Yes?"

"Thank you for always being here for me."

This smile was as sincere as they came. "There's nowhere else I'd rather be."

B Y that evening, Mercy felt more tired than she should have. She hadn't yet heard from Wyatt, and that made her maudlin. True, he didn't call every night, and the lack of a call had never stopped her from going by his place when she knew he was getting off work.

But now everything was different. Now she'd laid her heart out there, asked him to marry her, and been rebuffed.

If he wanted to see her, he could damn well call.

She went to her place, dropped her purse, kicked off her shoes, and fell across her bed to sleep. Perhaps it was the baby, or maybe it was pure emotion, but she felt exhausted. Within minutes she was sound asleep.

A tickle on the back of her neck woke her. Bleary-eyed, she looked at the clock on her nightstand and saw it was only seven. She'd been asleep for two hours.

The tickle on her neck turned into a gentle love bite. "'Bout time you woke up, sleepyhead."

She rolled to her back and found Wyatt stretched out beside her, propped on a forearm. "I didn't hear you come in."

"You were dead to the world." He smoothed her hair. "Why didn't you come over to my place tonight?"

Her stomach felt unsettled and her head hurt. "I wasn't sure what to do."

He bent and kissed her gently. "We agreed you'd move in with me. That's not cause to suddenly not show up—especially when I'm expecting you."

"I worried you?"

"Yeah." His gaze went from her eyes to her mouth, then to her breasts. Slowly, he started unbuttoning her blouse. "I called, but you didn't answer."

"I left my phone in my purse in the other room."

He parted the blouse and put one big hand over her right breast, caressing her through the sheer material of her camisole and bra.

Mercy caught her breath. Already her breasts were tender, and though Wyatt didn't seem to notice, she'd gone up nearly a cup size.

His gaze came back to hers. "Tell me you love me."

"I love you." Her stomach started to churn a little more, and her mouth went dry. "Wyatt, I need to get up."

His brows beetled and his hand on her breast stilled. "Are you angry with me?"

"No, of course not." Oh God, please don't let her throw up. The doctor had told her that morning sickness didn't stick to mornings. So far she hadn't had much nausea, and now would not be a good time for it to start.

She turned to her side, away from Wyatt, hoping that would help.

He spooned her and started kissing her neck again. "I'm free this weekend," he whispered in between soft, open-mouth kisses to her sensitive skin. "We can get you all moved in—"

Mercy caught his hand when it moved to her belly. "Wyatt . . . I'm not . . . Now's not a good time."

He stalled, then sat up. "You are pissed, aren't you?"

She shook her head. "No." Talking wasn't easy with her growing queasiness.

"Bullshit." He leaned down to her ear. "You have to be mad, because I've never known you to turn down sex before."

Anger didn't help the situation any. "Don't you curse at me, Wyatt Reyes."

He caught her chin and turned her face toward him. "Then just admit it. I said I didn't want to get married, so now you're getting even with me in the best way known to women."

Mercy saw red. She half sat up to confront him. "How *dare* you accuse me—" Her stomach pitched, revolted, and she knew she had to leave the bed. Now. "Damn you!"

Scrambling free of his hold, Mercy rushed from the room.

Wyatt, the jerk, followed her. "Wait a minute! Where are you going?"

"Go *away*, Wyatt." She raced for the hall bathroom—away from him.

"The hell I will. We have to talk about this."

She tried to slam the bathroom door.

His hand flattened against it and it clattered open again. Too late.

She was already on her knees, already heaving.

Wyatt drew up short. "Ah, hell."

Mercy clutched the toilet. "Out, or so help me I'll kill you."

"Right. Sorry." He backed out and shut the door. "I'll . . . uh, go make tea."

So miserable she wanted to disappear, Mercy hung her head and waited for the awful sickness to pass. Knowing she'd have to face Wyatt and the inevitable questions didn't make it any easier.

It was a full ten minutes later before she felt poised enough to venture out of the dubious security of her bathroom. She'd rebuttoned her blouse, combed her hair, and cleaned her mouth.

Mortification smothered her, but hiding wouldn't solve anything.

Wyatt was in the hall waiting for her. He had his back against the wall, his head dropped forward. The second he saw her, he straightened.

"Feeling better?"

"Yes." Miraculously, she did. Still a little washed out, but no longer sick. "Sorry about that."

Cautious, he held back. "I'm the one who needs to apologize. I had no idea you were sick. I acted like an asshole, accusing you of—"

"It's okay."

Tentatively, he reached for her. "No, it's not okay." When he had her in his arms, he cradled her close and rested his chin on the top of her head. "I guess everything is just so new and different now. I've never been in love." He leaned her away and tried a smile. "Will you forgive me for being an idiot?"

Astounded, Mercy stared at him. Wyatt wasn't a stupid man, but he obviously wasn't going to put two and two together. "You're forgiven."

The charming smile she loved so much didn't quite reach his eyes. "If that's true, then why are you looking at me like I'm a two-headed toad?"

"Am I?"

"Yeah." He put a hand to her forehead. "You don't feel

feverish. Do you feel like eating? I made the tea the way you like it, but I can heat up some soup or something, too."

How could a man so considerate and caring be so dense? "Actually, I'm starving now. How about we order up a pizza?"

"You're sure you're up to that?"

At the moment, she felt like she could eat three loaded pizzas all on her own. "Positive."

His smile spread, more genuine and filled with relief. "Well, alright then. I'm glad you're not sick. Maybe it was just something you ate earlier." He took her hand and they went to her kitchen together. Wyatt pulled out a chair. "Just relax and drink your tea while I put in the order."

Now that the nausea was gone, needs beyond food presented themselves. She thought of what Wyatt had been doing earlier, while he used the phone. After he hung up and joined her at the table, she smiled.

Judging by his expression, her smile confused him. "Food should be here in twenty minutes, they said."

"Great." Mercy turned her head to study him. All of him. "After we eat, I'd be more than willing to pick up where we left off."

He stilled, but not for long. "Well hell, woman, I just said we had twenty minutes." He rose from the chair and scooped her up. "But after we eat, I'm game to go again if you are."

WYATT was unaccountably relieved when Mercy didn't protest his stopping to get cardboard boxes. They'd need them to pack up her stuff, but after what had happened yesterday, he wasn't sure she still wanted to move in with him.

She'd said she did. And once he got her in bed, she'd been as enthusiastic and giving as always. But . . . something felt different about her.

It worried him.

Loving her scared him shitless.

But the thought of losing her was worse than anything he could have ever imagined.

He didn't know jack about love, not how to accept it, not how to give it, but for Mercy, he was determined to figure it out. Showing her how much he cared physically was a piece of cake. Hell, he loved that part.

When they were alone and naked, Mercy turned him inside out and upside down, and it blew his mind. Never before had he realized the immeasurable differences between sex and making love. But now that he knew, he never wanted to give it up.

She hadn't mentioned his promise to meet her brother, so he figured he should. Surely a willingness to meet her family would prove . . . something. If not love, then at least commitment.

He hoped.

Glancing over at her, he noticed how her profile had changed. Not her face, but her body.

She looked more lush than ever. Maybe love did that to a woman. If so, he'd love her so silly, she'd stay as sexy as she was right now.

"The next couple of weeks, my work schedule is going to be crazy, but I think I can get done early enough for dinner if you want to go ahead and set something up with your brother."

She looked startled, as if he'd interrupted some deep thoughts. "I was thinking about that."

"You were?" Did it worry her, the idea of him meeting Braxton? If so, why? Did she think he wouldn't measure up in her brother's eyes? Would that matter to her, what her brother thought?

"How about tomorrow night? It's a Sunday, so you aren't working, and Braxton, who always works, said he'd make the time whenever I wanted."

So soon. "Whatever you want, honey."

Her beatific smile gave him pause. "Tomorrow it is. Six o'clock okay with you?"

Dread filled him. "Sure." He clutched the steering wheel. "I sort of thought we'd use the weekend to get you moved in."

Mercy laughed. Today she had her glossy dark hair in a high ponytail. A bright pink silk halter top and designer jeans made her look like a relaxed model.

Damn, he was lucky.

"I don't need the whole weekend for that." She glanced back at all the collapsed boxes he'd put in the back of his truck. "I won't really need all those either."

Wyatt didn't understand. "You have a lot of stuff in your apartment, Mercy."

"But I'm not bringing all of it."

Whoa. He flexed his hands again, doing his best to fight off the invading alarm. If she didn't move everything in, then she wasn't really living with him.

Was this all just temporary for her? A trial run?

Hard as he tried, there was still an underlying edge to his tone when he spoke. "I'm not sure I understand."

"I'm keeping my apartment." Though she sounded relaxed and happy, she stared out the passenger window instead of looking at him. "My lease isn't up for almost a year, and I have a ton of furniture. Your place isn't big enough to hold it all, and I don't want to sell it."

He pulled into the parking lot of her apartment building. "So . . . you're not really moving in."

Her hands folded in her lap. She dropped her head, and he could almost see her thoughts churning.

When she looked at him, her eyes were filled with resolve. "You don't want to marry me, Wyatt. That's fine," she said before he could speak. "I understand your sentiment on it. But for me, nothing is truly settled without marriage. *I love you*. I want to live with you. But I'm not going to leave myself without options for a man who doesn't want to fully commit to me."

Son of a bitch. He shoved the truck into park and turned toward her. "I told you I love you."

"And I believe you. I see it in your eyes. I *feel* it in the way you touch me." She reached over and took his hand. "I am so looking forward to this. We'll go to bed together at night, we'll wake up together in the morning. We'll share everything. And Wyatt, I promise you, I'll be with you one hundred percent—unless you change your mind. And if you do, I want to know I have a place to go."

Urgency clawed at him. "I won't."

Her eyes darkened with sadness—but the resolve remained. "You must not be sure of that yourself, Wyatt, or you'd go ahead and marry me." She opened her car door. "And if you're not sure of how you feel, you can't expect me to be either."

She left the truck, and Wyatt sat there, feeling hollow, sick—and wishing he could make it right.

But marriage . . . Just thinking about it soured his mood and made him tense. Kids always followed marriage, and with kids, everything changed. He knew that better than most.

Mercy was right. He wasn't willing to risk that. He couldn't.

He also couldn't tell her why. Doing so would mean dredging up a past long buried.

Why couldn't love be enough for her? It was more than he'd ever offered before; it was all he had to give.

The truth slammed through his brain like an annoying drumbeat.

What he had wasn't enough.

It never had been, and probably never would be.

FOUR

WYATT couldn't remember the last time he'd been so uncomfortable. Mercy had told him to wear whatever he wanted, that her brother didn't dress for dinner, he dressed for himself.

And that meant . . . what? Was Braxton Jardine likely to show up in a tux, or jeans? The restaurant Mercy had chosen was nice, but moderately priced, likely a concession to him since she knew he tried not to indulge extravagances like fancy meals at five-star restaurants.

Mercy never seemed to care about things like that, but what would Braxton think? The man was richer than Midas and had to be used to the best dining around. Would he consider Wyatt a cheapskate? Would he think him unfit for Mercy?

Damn it, he was not a man with insecurity issues. Through his adult life, he'd made a point of not giving a fuck what others thought. He did things his own way, lived by his own moral code, and was the best man he knew how to be.

If that wasn't good enough for Braxton, then . . .

Mercy's arms slipped around him from behind. "You look awfully brooding, Wyatt. Please don't tell me you're already regretting dinner."

Never in a million years would he admit such a thing. "Not at all." He turned to face her and managed a smile. "Why should I?"

Too serious by half, Mercy stared up at him. "I know you never really wanted to meet my family. I sort of twisted your arm—"

Wyatt bent and kissed her. "No, you didn't. We're moving in together, and I want you to be happy." He hoped she believed him, because he meant it. Short of marriage, he'd do what he could to see that it was true. "It's important to you that I know your family, so it's important to me, too."

Looking too tired for his peace of mind, Mercy nodded, and a small smile appeared. She straightened the collar of his beige-and-blue-striped button-up oxford shirt. "You look very handsome."

Frowning, Wyatt rolled the sleeves up to his elbows. "I have a suit I wear when I have important meetings, but I wasn't sure it'd be right for dinner."

"Your khakis are perfect, I promise." She held out her hands. "How do I look?"

Her sleeveless, ankle-length sundress hugged her body in all the right places. Black with a beige-and-gold floral design, it brought out the golden hue of her eyes and made her smooth skin look especially creamy. The scoop neck showed just enough cleavage to make him a little nuts.

Staring at her breasts, which lately seemed to be all but bursting out of her clothes, Wyatt said, "If we had time, I'd show you how incredible you look." He sought her gaze with his own. "You're damn near irresistible."

Her chest lifted on an inhalation of pleasure. "Thank you."

Wyatt cupped her face. "But babe, you do look tired."

Every time he saw the strain on her face, guilt took another bite of him. He measured her expression and saw no hope for it. "Is it stressing you to move in with me?"

Her brows pinched down. "Stressing me? What do you mean?"

So she'd make him spell it out? Well, he supposed he deserved that, since he couldn't give her what she wanted most of all. "I love you. I don't want you to feel like you're compromising yourself."

"How so?"

Damn it. He released her and took a step back. "Does it bother you to live with me when we're not married?"

Her brows smoothed out, but her expression stayed neutral. "I love you, Wyatt. If the only way I can have you is on your terms, then for now, that's how it'll be."

That *for now* had him gritting his teeth, but what he said was, "My *terms*?"

Her bare shoulders lifted. "You won't marry me, so I'll settle for cohabitating." She smoothed a hand over his chest. Nervousness emanated from her in waves. "The thing is . . . someday it won't be enough."

He couldn't think about that day.

"Someday I'm going to want the storybook ending."

His guts knotted. He put his hands on his hips and looked away with defeat. His desolation emerged as one whispered word: "Fuck."

A flash of pain filled her eyes before the resolution returned. She dropped her hand and took a step back.

There was so much distance between them, it killed Wyatt. "Mercy."

"I want my happily ever after, Wyatt, complete with babies, *our* babies, that I can hold and love."

He had no idea what to say. "I'm sorry."

She patted his chest. "Don't worry about it, Wyatt. For right now, here with you like this, I'm fine."

He wanted her better than fine. He wanted her one hundred percent satisfied and happy. The problem was, he had no idea how to manage it.

His doorbell rang, taking them both by surprise. Glad for the reprieve, Wyatt started around her.

She rushed after him, asking, "Were you expecting anyone?"

"No."

He heard her grumbling before she said, "If that's Braxton, I'm going to smack him."

He gave her a quick look, glad to see her looking like herself again. "Why would it be your brother? I thought we were meeting him at the restaurant."

"That was the plan, but you might as well know right now that Braxton has a mile-wide overprotective streak. I told him I was moving in with you, and so he'd want to see where you live."

Wyatt stopped before he reached the door. It'd be best if he knew what to expect. "What did your brother think of you moving in here?"

A heavy fist knocked impatiently.

Mercy rolled her eyes and stepped around him. "He wanted me to come live with him instead."

Before Wyatt could react to that, she opened the door, and sure enough, there stood her brother and a woman.

Even though he'd never met Braxton Jardine, Wyatt knew him on sight. He had the same jet-black hair and bright hazel eyes as Mercy.

Mercy had told him what a formidable presence Braxton had, but she hadn't stated that strongly enough. The man stood damn near six and a half feet tall, towering over them all. Unlike his sister, he had darker skin, and though Wyatt knew him for a rich businessman, he had a body used to physical labor.

His black slacks and white T-shirt reeked of money, but they weren't overly dressy. The woman with him wore a blouse, pencil skirt, and low-heeled pumps. She looked like the quintessential secretary.

Only half under her breath, Mercy remonstrated her brother. "Braxton! What are you doing here?"

Beside Braxton, the woman nodded. "He knew good

and well that we were to meet at the restaurant, Mercy. I told him not to do this, but you know how he is. He wouldn't listen to me."

Braxton showed his teeth in a predator's smile. "I always listen to you, Cameo. Sometimes I just don't obey."

The tension in the air crackled, prompting Wyatt to take control.

"It's not a problem." He clasped Mercy's arm and edged her aside so she no longer blocked the doorway. "Come on in. We have some time before we have to head to dinner."

The woman entered.

Braxton didn't.

Instead, her brother lounged on the door frame, filling the entrance and eyeing Wyatt with some lethal intensity, almost as if he planned to dissect him and wasn't sure where he wanted to start.

His pose was casual enough, but it didn't fool Wyatt. The man looked capable of attacking at any moment.

Provoked, Wyatt narrowed his eyes. Braxton might be big, but his size didn't intimidate him. He had confidence in his own abilities, and if he needed to, he'd more than hold his own.

But this was Mercy's brother, so Wyatt was determined to keep things civil—if he could.

"Introductions first, huh?" Lacking a smile, Wyatt held out his hand. "Wyatt Reyes. And I take it you're Mercy's brother, Braxton."

Expecting a formidable contest on who had the strongest grip, Wyatt was surprised when Braxton merely shook his hand and stepped inside.

"Nice to finally meet you, Wyatt. Call me Brax." As an aside, he said, "Only the women call me Braxton, and only when they're pissed about something."

Both women glared at him.

Brax slipped his arm around his date's waist, which, judging by her expression, took her off guard. "Cameo, meet the long-elusive Wyatt Reyes." His smile mocked them all. "Wyatt, Cameo Smithson."

"His assistant," Cameo said.

"Actually, she's more than that." Braxton made no pretense of looking around his home, checking out everything. "Just ask Mercedes."

Flustered, Mercy stammered, "Yes. Of course. Cameo is like family."

"Not precisely like family, but close all the same." Brax smiled that wicked smile again, but this time Wyatt knew it wasn't directed at him.

Wyatt nodded at Cameo. "Take a seat." When it came to entertaining, he lacked skills, but he could manage the basics.

Cameo sat.

Braxton did not.

"Would either of you like a drink?"

"No thanks." Brax headed for the kitchen. "Mind if I look around?" He didn't wait for an answer.

"Braxton," Mercedes wailed, running after him.

Wyatt couldn't help it. He grinned.

Cameo let out a long sigh. "They squabble like this incessantly. Of course, it's usually Brax's fault. He does like to tease her."

Leaving Mercy to trail her brother, Wyatt sat in a chair opposite Cameo. Talking with her seemed a safe way to find out what he was in store for with Braxton. "It's nice that they're so close."

She tipped her head. "Yes, isn't it?"

A little subtle prodding wouldn't hurt. "Mercy told me that Brax raised her?"

"After their parents died, yes."

"That had to be rough." He shifted, uncomfortable with meddling. Unfortunately, he'd set the tone with his own rigid privacy, and couldn't very well grill Mercy about her own past. "It was just the two of them?"

"They have uncles from their father's side, but the

men in the family are always off to God knows where, doing God knows what. From what I understand, they're somewhat eccentric, adrenaline junkies with Brax's good looks. A troubling combination, if you know what I mean."

"I suppose so." He thought of Mercy as a little girl, feeling lost and alone. That image struck an uncomfortable chord, and he mentally switched tracks.

Seeing Braxton Jardine now, it was hard to imagine how he could have ever been a young vulnerable boy. But when his parents died, he would have been at an age where he wanted to sow wild oats and test his independence.

Instead he'd taken on raising a child.

Wyatt knew only too well that many parents balked under that kind of responsibility. With more sincerity than Cameo could know, he said, "Mercy was lucky to have him looking after her."

She sat back and crossed her legs. "He was only eighteen at the time, but as you can tell by how Mercy turned out, he did a fabulous job."

"I agree."

"He dotes on her still, sometimes to the point where he almost smothers her." Her smile hinted that she found Brax's smothering tendencies an endearing trait. "It's because he loves her so much, you understand."

Wyatt nodded. "Mercy is an easy woman to love."

She sat forward with sudden purpose. "Brax is a gifted, highly intelligent, and giving man, and Mercy is his top priority. He always has her best interest at heart, so I hope you won't take offense if he . . . meddles a little."

Wyatt could hear Mercy and Brax talking in his kitchen, and raised a brow. If meddling meant taking a self-initiated tour of his house, then no, he didn't mind too much. The intrusion was only a small inconvenience, and he could easily overlook it to keep Mercy happy.

But if Brax thought to invade his personal privacy, then yeah, he'd have something to say about it.

The discussion in the kitchen dwindled to a barely audible whisper. Whatever they discussed, they didn't want anyone else hearing.

Wyatt turned back to Cameo. "Define *meddling* for me."

She frowned in thought. "He means well."

The way she kept cautioning him, Wyatt was starting to expect the worst. "So you've said."

Her smile flickered. "You'll find out soon enough that Brax is not the most tactful man around. He's built an empire by making sure he gets his way in all things." She glanced toward the kitchen, and then back again. "All I can tell you is that it's best not to cross him."

Alarm bells went off in his brain. "Is that a warning?"

She flapped a hand. "Nothing so dire. Just know that he always finds out what he wants to know anyway. Being up-front and honest with him is much easier than digging in and fighting what will ultimately be a losing battle."

Wyatt didn't like the sound of that at all.

Cameo studied him. "If you want to build a life with Mercy—"

"I do."

"Then you'll want to keep in mind how close they are. Mercy knows Brax isn't perfect, but she loves him every bit as much as he loves her."

Meaning he was fucked no matter what he did? Was he supposed to roll over for Brax, regardless of whether he got out of line?

Wyatt stood, ready to find Brax and lay down a few ground rules of his own. That proved unnecessary when Brax came striding back into the front room. Mercy was right on his heels, grumbling low, but Brax ignored her as he addressed the room at large.

"I'm starved. We ready to go?"

Wyatt crossed his arms. "That depends. Are you done poking around?"

"Not really, no." Brax threw an arm around Mercy, pinning her to his side. Next to Brax, she looked especially small and delicate. Her expression showed hostility, annoyance—and resignation.

Cameo stood with a sigh.

Nettled, Wyatt asked, "Did you want to see my bank statements, too? My utility bills? Maybe talk to my barber?"

Brax shook his head. "Not necessary. I already looked into your company. You're a good businessman showing sound financial planning."

Flummoxed, Wyatt stared at him. "What are you talking about? What did you do?"

"Nothing illegal, so uncurl those fists."

Wyatt hadn't realized his fists had clenched until Brax pointed it out. He looked at Mercy and saw the worry in her golden eyes, her bottom lip caught in her teeth.

Deliberately, he relaxed his stance and drew a breath. "How exactly did you get access to my private business?"

Brax scrutinized him as if fascinated with his reaction. "I checked you out the same way any potential employer would—all upright and legitimate. And before you go all hostile again, understand that I liked what I saw. You can judge a lot about a man by how he does business."

Wyatt had always believed the same, but he'd be damned if he'd agree with Brax. Tamping down the hostility as much as he could, he growled, "We won't be doing business together so I'd appreciate it if you stayed out of my personal affairs."

Squeezing his sister a little closer, Brax said, "That's not going to happen."

Cameo sighed again.

Distracted, Brax frowned toward her. "What's the matter with you?"

"You're being impossible, Braxton, that's what." She came around the coffee table to face off with him. "For God's sake, turn your sister loose. You're forcing her to choose sides, but then not even giving her a choice."

"I wasn't—"

"And why pick a fight anyway? What in the world do you think that'll accomplish?"

He released Mercy, and when she just stood there, he said, "Well, go on to him before Cameo flays me."

Instead Mercy poked him in the chest. "Stop it right now, Braxton. I mean it."

Brax glanced at Wyatt with an indulgent smile. "See? They always call me Braxton when they're pissed off."

Wyatt almost grinned. True, he was annoyed, but seeing the large and imposing Braxton Jardine surrounded by feminine fury struck his funny bone.

Braxton didn't seem particularly put off by it. He shoved his hands into his pants pockets and affected a bored expression.

Mercy's second poke was harder, prompting Brax to grab her finger. He appealed to Wyatt. "Come on, man, take her away before she bores holes in me."

The man was certifiable, that's all there was to it. Wyatt didn't move. He wasn't about to ask Mercy to come to his side; she could damn well make her own decision.

"Thanks for nothing," Brax told him. And then to Mercy: "Men have their pride, sweetheart. You know that. Don't you think you should switch sides here?"

Mercy jerked her finger free of his loose hold and planted her fists on her hips. "I don't have to declare a side because Wyatt knows how I feel about him."

Unconvinced, Brax asked, "Is that right?"

Mercy glanced back at Wyatt, did a double take at his undoubtedly sour expression, and seemed to ignite. "You should go, Brax." She shoved at him. "I don't think Wyatt or I, either one, is in the mood for dinner now."

Brax sent him a *Do something* look.

Well, fuck. Her damned brother was too important to her for things to start off this way. Neither of them could know why he was so private. They couldn't have a clue what hid in his past.

Not that any of that mattered right now. Wyatt didn't

want to come between them, no matter what. He loved Mercy, and as Cameo had claimed, Brax meant well.

He couldn't marry her, but he could give her this, and if certain sacrifices had to be made, so what? Brax could dig into his company business all he wanted.

He'd never find anything off the mark there.

Drawing another deep breath to help alleviate his irritation, Wyatt stepped forward. "Actually, I had an early lunch, so I'm starving."

Mercy's eyes widened. She stopped trying to shove Brax out the door.

Cameo smiled in pleasure.

But Brax, damn him, wasn't in the least fooled. His nod was serious and accepting. "Putting Mercy's feelings first—not a bad start."

And with that, he turned and led the way out the door.

M ERCY stared at her plate and knew she'd made an error in judgment. The grilled chicken had been delicious and she'd eaten every bite, along with her salad and potato. She'd thought she had room for dessert, but now that the rich and creamy cheesecake had been placed before her, her throat burned and her stomach started to pitch.

Why did they call it morning sickness if it came all the damn time?

Always attuned to her, Wyatt touched her hand. "Everything okay?"

"Oh, yes, I'm fine."

Brax, damn him, watched her like a hawk—and she could almost swear he had anticipation in his gaze.

Did he want her to be sick in front of Wyatt?

So far, after one inauspicious morning when the baby had thwarted Wyatt's plans for early lovemaking, she'd managed to get up before him. By the time he awoke, she'd already sipped tea and nibbled crackers and settled her belly the best she could.

The nausea had hit a couple of times in the evenings, but she'd found a variety of excuses to stay out of range of Wyatt when it happened.

Wyatt squeezed her fingers. "You're not eating your dessert?"

No, she wasn't. She couldn't. Laying her napkin over her plate in the hope that not seeing it would somehow help, she smiled at Wyatt. "I guess my eyes were bigger than my stomach. I'm not really hungry after all."

Like a doting husband, he put the back of his hand to her forehead.

Mercy felt very conspicuous. "Wyatt, really, I'm fine."

"You eat like a bird lately." His hand slid around her nape. "And you always look tired."

"Imagine that," Brax said.

Oh God. Her stomach roiled—and she shoved back her chair. "I'm going to run to the restroom." *Run* being the operative word. She waved Wyatt back to his seat when he started to rise. "I'll be right back."

She fled the room with as much dignity as she could muster under the circumstances. Luckily there was no one else in the john when she got there.

But as soon as she started throwing up, Brax sauntered in.

Appalled, Mercy glanced back at him, groaned, and hung her head over the toilet again. Finally the sickness abated and she stood, went to the sink, and washed her hands.

Brax handed her a dampened towel. "You look like hell, hon. I take it the baby is kicking up a fuss?"

"I'm so damned sick." She groaned, not all that surprised that Brax was as comfortable in the women's restroom as he was in the boardroom. "Why did it have to happen now?"

He smoothed back her hair. "You're worried about things, and I bet you're feeling guilty."

Her startled look prompted him to say, "Keeping secrets isn't your way. You're more honest and up front than that."

Usually, but not with this. Not with her happiness on the line.

She bent to swish out her mouth with water, spat in the sink, and rinsed again. "Make yourself useful and let me know if Wyatt comes looking for me."

"Cameo's on it. She'll keep him entertained. No worries." He lounged back against the counter. Thrusting an icy glass of something under her nose, he said, "Here, drink this."

Mercy curled her lip. "What is it?"

"Clear soda. It's supposed to help settle things."

She'd barely taken a sip when he said again, "You need to come clean with him, Mercy. He's not an ignorant man. Pretty soon he'll figure it out on his own, and then how will he react?"

Feeling very unsure of herself and her plan, she whispered, "I don't know."

"He'll be furious—and I won't blame him. Getting pregnant was an accident, but keeping it from him is on purpose."

Needing a moment to think, she drank the rest of the soda. It helped more than she could have guessed. "The thing is . . . I don't want him to feel trapped."

Her brother didn't give an inch. "That's not for you to dictate. And who knows? Maybe he'll surprise you and be overjoyed."

She snorted at that.

"You can't know until you tell him."

With her stomach more agreeable, Mercy used the towels to blot her face. "Am I presentable?"

Brax crossed his arms. "Avoiding the subject isn't going to make it go away."

She knew that, but for right now, she just wanted to get through the night. "So you're saying that I'm not presentable?"

He must have seen something in her face, because he allowed her the change of topic. "You look fine."

Relief brought out a smile. "Thanks to that soda. What was it, anyway?"

"Sprite."

"I'm buying a case of it and carrying it with me everywhere I go." She hooked her arm through his. "Now let's get back before Wyatt comes to find me."

Brax pulled her up short. "I'm good at reading people, we can agree on that, yes?"

He'd made his fortune by being an astute judge of everything and everyone. Mercy didn't know quite how he did it, how Brax stayed so infallible, but she couldn't deny the truth. "Yes."

"I like him, Mercy."

Pleasure expanded outward, giving her a huge grin. "I just knew you would!"

"He's a good man. But," he added when she started to speak again, "he's got some very dark secrets."

Her jaw loosened. No, surely he hadn't, not after she'd forbidden him to. Shoulders back, mood grim, Mercy demanded, "You *dared* to go snooping into his background?"

Unfazed, Brax frowned at her. "You're looking green again. All this excess emotion and worry isn't good for you or the baby."

She threw up her hands. Leave it to Brax to be so cavalier over such a breach of privacy. Wyatt was waiting, so she couldn't have it out with her brother right now. But first thing tomorrow she'd give him a piece of her mind.

Disgruntled, she glared at him, then swept a hand toward the door. "Shall we go, preferably before someone comes in and finds you here?"

The corner of his mouth twitched. "I'm ready. But Mercedes, think about what I said. I understand your perspective, but being a man, I can also anticipate Wyatt's take on things. A lie, even a lie of omission, is never the way to get things off on the right foot." He touched the end of her nose. "Okay?"

"Yes." As she considered Wyatt's reaction to full disclosure, she put a hand to her stomach—a protective instinct that she couldn't quell. "I'll . . . think about it."

"You do that." Brax straightened with a smile. "I'll head back first. Wait another minute or two before returning. You don't want him to know that we were in here together, holding counsel in the ladies' room. I'm sure he wouldn't like that very much either."

As soon as her brother left, Mercy turned to the mirror and faced her own shortcomings. She'd never before been a coward, but she desperately needed to hang on to the dream of a happily ever after.

If she didn't confront Wyatt with an ultimatum— accept her *and* their child—she wouldn't be forced to face his likely rejection.

But her brother was the most judicious man she knew. Eerily so. Never had he given her faulty advice. If he suggested she confess to Wyatt now, then that's what she should do.

Tonight. She'd do it tonight and damn the consequences. He either wanted her, all of her, or he didn't.

Having made the decision, she was *almost* relieved.

She was also so afraid of losing Wyatt that she nearly got sick again.

FIVE

A S Cameo droned on about everything from the weather to corporate planning, Wyatt tossed back the last of his wine. It was delicious and outrageously expensive, and it didn't help one freaking bit. He wasn't much of a drinker, but it'd take more than a glass of wine to numb his misgivings.

Where the hell was Mercy?

And for that matter, where had Brax gotten off to? It was damned suspicious that they were both gone, had been gone for so long.

Were they together? He sensed a conspiracy, and damn it, he didn't like it.

Maybe Brax was trying to persuade Mercy to walk out on him. Mercy's brother was such a hard man to read that Wyatt didn't yet know if he'd been accepted or not. In the normal course of things, he wouldn't have given a shit one way or the other.

But this was Mercy's brother, a man with great influence over her, so unfortunately it mattered.

In some ways, Brax appeared to respect him. He'd discussed business with him as an equal, though Wyatt had remained distracted with Mercy's emotional distance throughout dinner. She'd sat right beside him—but it felt like she was miles away.

At other times, Brax seemed to be just waiting for an opportunity to take Wyatt apart. He'd look at his sister, and some barely veiled emotion electrified the air. Cameo didn't seem to notice. Neither did Mercy.

But one man seldom missed the protective instincts of another. The unspoken warning was there: Brax blamed Wyatt for making Mercy unhappy.

But then, Wyatt blamed himself.

Dinner might have appeared relaxed to the casual observer, but for Wyatt, juggling emotions and protective urges of his own, it had thus far been excruciating.

Mercy had planned the damned dinner, so why was she so quiet and withdrawn? Hell, she'd been too damned quiet everywhere lately.

He didn't like it. He wanted his fun-loving, teasing, sexy woman back. God, he missed her.

"Don't you think?" Cameo asked.

Wyatt glanced up, knew that she knew he hadn't been listening, and said, "About what?"

She laughed, and the amusement in her face turned her from mostly plain to downright stunning. "My God, Wyatt, you have the whole ominous bad-boy thing down pat." Coyly, she added, "But then, I'm sure you know that."

Wyatt shook his head in confusion. "Bad boy?" What the hell was she talking about?

"Oh come on. You have the edgy good looks, the super-buff build, and the aloof I-don't-give-a-damn personality to pull it off. Add that thunderous scowl and you ooze dangerous appeal. I'm sure the women who like that sort of thing come on in droves."

Sitting back in his seat, Wyatt crossed his arms and leveled a look at Cameo. Her smile never wavered; she propped her chin on a fist and waited.

"I don't play that game."

"Ah, of course not. You *live* it." She feigned a delicate shudder. "Authenticity is important, right? And Mercy apparently likes the edgy persona—to a degree."

Wyatt had to concentrate hard not to ratchet up his scowl. She poked fun at him, all the while wearing that innocent grin.

But why? If she was any other woman, he'd think she was coming on to him. But with Cameo, he sensed it was something else entirely.

It almost felt like mothering concern . . . for Mercy. "The only woman I'm interested in is Mercy."

"Of course." The smile got replaced by in-your-face candor. "But that interest has limits, now doesn't it?"

Ice ran up his spine. Had Mercy told her that he wasn't the marrying kind? Had she gossiped about their very personal conversation?

Or was Cameo just that shrewd? "You care as much for her as her brother does."

"Oh, no." She shook her head with emphatic disagreement. "Not possible. *No one* could love her more than Brax."

There was no missing the implied insult. "I might challenge that."

Thoughtful, she looked down at her plate, then swung her gaze back up to his. "I hope so, Wyatt, I really do. But it appears to me that you're going about it in the wrong way."

Prepared to demand answers, Wyatt leaned forward— and Brax pulled out a chair, halting whatever he might have said.

With a hint of humor, Cameo told Brax, "Propitious timing."

"Is that so?" Brax looked from Cameo to Wyatt and back again. "Judging by the crackle in the air, I'd say I've missed some scintillating conversational tidbits. Anyone care to fill me in?"

Not in this lifetime. Wyatt dropped back in his seat and looked beyond Brax, but didn't yet see Mercy. "Where is your sister?"

"She hasn't returned? What do you suppose she's up to?" A rhetorical question, given that he turned to Cameo. "Any ideas?"

And just that quickly, Cameo pushed back her chair to leave the table. "No, but I'll go see what's holding her up."

Brax stood, said, "Thank you," and continued standing until she'd gone.

Knowing that he had arranged the private moment, Wyatt tensed. Would her brother now read him the riot act? Give him all sorts of dire warnings? Lecture him?

"So." Wearing no expression at all, Brax reseated himself. "You're madly in love with my sister."

Not a question at all, but Wyatt confirmed it all the same. "Yes."

Brax nodded slowly. "No doubt you've noticed, but she's very special to me, too."

Accepting that as truth, Wyatt said, "You raised her."

"Yes. And for that reason, we're closer than most siblings."

Did he miss some subtle meaning there? "Mercy values your opinion." What did he think of Wyatt?

"Not as much as you might think." Brax declined more wine when the waitress came by. As she departed to get the bill, they both noticed Mercy and Cameo on their way back to the table.

To Wyatt's jaundiced eye, despite fresh lipstick and a steady smile, Mercy looked distraught and pale.

Brax said, "Yeah, I see it, too." When Wyatt showed his surprise, Brax smiled. "A man in love is easy to read. And because I believe you love her, here's a word of advice, man to man."

Expecting the worst, Wyatt locked his jaw. "I'm dying to hear it."

"Mercy is more independent than you can imagine. She knows that I'm always here for her, but she doesn't need me." He leaned a little closer, his posture forceful. "She doesn't need you either, Wyatt. She wants you, for now, but we both see that she isn't happy. A smart man would figure out how to get her happy and quick, and then he'd tie her to him, legal and otherwise, before it's too late."

Wyatt stiffened. That was certainly in his face and to the point.

Brax held up his hands when Wyatt started to speak. "Just a friendly observation, that's all. No insult intended."

Obviously Mercy *had* discussed their private business with her brother and Cameo. Maybe that was the norm; what the hell did he know of siblings? He'd never had any.

Hell, he'd barely had parents.

Knowing that Brax and Cameo were privy to the dealings of his personal relationship with Mercy burned his ass, but he'd be damned before he said so.

"I'm keeping her." Somehow he'd make it true.

"Because that's what she ultimately wants, I hope you're right." Brax pierced him with a stare. "But you better shake off the past and get with the future. Quick."

The opportunity for conversation ended when Mercy and Cameo reached the table. Wyatt and Brax both stood, but it was her brother Mercy turned to.

"I've had a wonderful time, but I hope you don't mind if I beg off early."

"What's wrong?" Wyatt asked.

At the same time, her brother said, "Still not feeling well?"

As Mercy glanced at both men, the smile didn't reach her eyes. "A little tired, that's all."

"Probably the big move," Brax teased. "You two go on, then. Cameo and I will hang around for some coffee."

The waitress returned with the check, and Brax snatched it away before Wyatt could get hold of it. "I'll handle this."

Like hell. Wyatt pulled out his wallet. "Thanks, but I've got it."

"This is the first time I've had Cameo out on a date." Brax draped an arm around Mercy. "I'm not ready to take her home just yet."

Both women seemed surprised by that. Wyatt didn't care one way or another. "I'll give my credit card to the waitress."

"Never a good idea." Brax kissed Mercy's forehead before releasing her and realigning himself next to Cameo. She looked a little wary as Brax put a hand to the back of her neck, beneath her hair.

The hold was more possessive than intimate.

"Assuming you'll be around long enough," Brax said to Wyatt, "and assuming I can talk Cameo into accompanying me to dinner again, why don't you just get the next one?"

Through his teeth, Wyatt said, "I'll be around."

Brax turned to Cameo. "Well?"

"Oh . . . I, uh . . . sure."

"Great." He saluted Wyatt with the bill in hand. "The next dinner is on you."

Mercy stood there, wide-eyed and slack-jawed, staring at Cameo, who stared back. Brax remained as nonchalant as ever.

Short of wrestling him for the damned bill, what could Wyatt do? "Thank you."

"Anything for Mercy."

The words felt like a jab. Anxious to get her alone so they could talk, Wyatt sighed and put his arm around her. With a verbal nudge, he asked, "Ready to go?"

She nodded, but it took her a moment to get her attention off her brother and his assistant. "Yes, I'm ready. Brax, thanks for dinner. Cameo, it was great to see you again."

Cameo's stiff lips formed a vague smile. "You, too. Drive safely."

As Wyatt led Mercy away, he saw Brax bend down to whisper to Cameo, and he saw her cheeks flush—with embarrassment or pleasure?

Cameo was more than an assistant—or soon would be. Not even a blind man would miss Brax's interest in her, but Wyatt had a feeling that until now, Cameo and Mercy had both been unaware.

"That was *so* weird," Mercy whispered.

"Dinner? I'll say."

"No, I meant Brax hitting on Cammie."

Wyatt noted her use of a less formal name when discussing her friend now, almost as if with her worry, the pet name had slipped in.

Mercy turned her face up to him. "He's never done that before. Not once that I know of in all the years she's worked for him."

Curious about her reaction, Wyatt gave her a small squeeze. "Does it bother you?" Did she prefer to keep her brother all to herself?

"Only because I love Cammie and because Brax . . . well, he does tend to go through women."

Wyatt led her out the front doors and into the humid evening air. "Women like Cameo?"

"Oh no. In fact, I've never known him to be interested in anyone like her. Usually he favors . . ."

"Bimbos?"

Acting more like her old self, she elbowed him. "No, Brax is always discriminating, even in his social life. He enjoys intelligent, independent women. But so far they've all been more outgoing than Cammie. She's . . . reserved. Classy."

"And his usual partners aren't?" Wyatt opened the passenger door of his truck for her.

"That's not what I mean at all." Rather than get in, she turned and leaned on the truck.

Moonlight shone on her ebony hair and made her eyes

more golden than ever. She was the most beautiful woman, inside and out, that he'd ever known.

"Whenever I've met one of my brother's dates, and it's always a different woman each time, the thing I noticed most was that the women were affluent and openly sexual."

"Take-charge women?" Wyatt put one hand on the truck beside her head, leaning in closer to her, enjoying the feel of her body heat, inhaling the scent of her skin and hair.

"Maybe, but it was more than that. Cammie is the take-charge type. It's why she's so perfect as his assistant. Not everyone can put up with his demands for perfection."

"No kidding." He really didn't want to talk about her brother. He wanted . . . Mercy. All of her. Right now.

"Most of the women I've seen him with make no bones about admiring him. They hang on his arm and his every word. And the clothes they wear, their makeup and perfume, are always meant to entice."

"Looked to me like Cameo enticed him, too, whether she meant to or not."

"And that's the weird part! Never have I seen her treat my brother with anything other than respectful deference for their business association."

Teasing her, Wyatt said, "Maybe she has carnal depths she's hidden from you."

Mercy scoffed. "You saw her."

"She's very pretty when she laughs, but yes, otherwise, she's the epitome of an upscale and businesslike assistant."

"Exactly." Mercy put a hand to his chest. "I can't imagine her putting up with my brother's domineering ways—outside the office—for a single heartbeat."

"Speaking of domineering . . ." Wyatt's heart pounded. Tie her to him? Yeah, he wanted to tie Mercy to him, and he would.

With sex.

She was the perfect bed partner for him, a willing and

anxious participant in everything they did. He wouldn't let her forget it.

Her smile warmed. "What did you have in mind?"

Wyatt bent his bracing arm, caging her in, letting his body brush hers. With the fingertips of his other hand, he lifted her face. "Much as I enjoyed meeting your brother—"

She laughed. "Fibber."

He ignored that. "I've been dying to get you alone."

"Hmmm." She smiled. "Is that so?"

"Damn right." Tracing along her jaw to her throat, and down to her cleavage, he said, "You look beautiful tonight, Mercy."

She touched her hair and said again, "Fibber. I look terrible."

"No. Just tired, that's all." But that acknowledgment redirected his thoughts. "You're always sexy as hell, but if you need to rest—"

"I'm never *that* tired, Wyatt. Not for you." Cupping his jaw, she brought his face up and whispered, "Never for you."

Damn, but his blood rushed, his muscles tightened. He took her mouth and kissed her with all the need raging inside him.

Mercy might deny it, but he felt her slipping away. It seemed the minute she claimed to love him, everything went wrong.

Somehow he had to make it right again. Mind-blowing sex would be a good start.

MERCY practically raced Wyatt into his home. She knew she should discuss things with him first, tell him that their situation was about to change in a very big way, but she wanted this, him, without added pressures for possibly the last time.

She made it to the bedroom before he caught her wrist and spun her around toward him. His mouth was on hers, his hands on her backside, before she could take a breath. He devoured her, almost as if he sensed the same urgency to steal this special moment.

When he started to catch her wrists together, Mercy stopped him. "No."

He breathed hard, and his eyes were diamond bright with lust. "No?"

God, she loved him so much it hurt. Licking her lips, Mercy stepped back and said, "Take your clothes off. Tonight I want to take the lead."

His left eyebrow shot high; his lips parted. A bulging erection strained his slacks above the fly.

"Take off your clothes," she repeated, "and stretch out on the bed."

"Damn." He hesitated only a moment before yanking enough buttons free that he could jerk his shirt off over his head.

She loved his chest, the chest hair, the muscles, the sleek skin. She curled her hands into fists to keep from reaching for him.

After toeing off his shoes and sliding his belt free, he shoved down his slacks and boxers and took off his socks as he stepped free of the clothes.

Challenging her, daring her, he stood there naked and watched her.

"On the bed, Wyatt."

Pleasure curved his mouth. "Alright." He lay down on his back and put his arms behind his head, bent one knee. "Now what, baby?"

"Now you stay like that." Watching him, she removed her jewelry and sandals, taking her time, enjoying the way his eyes tracked her every movement.

His relaxed posture didn't fool her. She'd played the supplicant for him too many times not to know just how tense with anticipation he was right now.

Her gaze went over his body, scrutinizing him, enjoying the sight of him. "I love your arms, Wyatt. Your biceps." Her breath faltered on a shaky inhalation. "And the sexy muscles on your abdomen."

Those muscles tightened, fascinating Mercy. Wyatt had a delicious body that only got better each time she saw him naked.

She wanted to see him like this for the rest of their lives.

Lifting her dress off over her head, she placed it across a chair. Wearing only a demi-bra and thong panties, she moved closer to the bed. Would Wyatt notice her thickening waist? Her plumper breasts?

Lately, her nipples had become supersensitive. Just thinking about his mouth tugging on her made her damp with need, achy with lust. Now, with her body's changes, she needed gentleness—at least at first.

She crawled onto the bed and straddled his lap, carefully settling on his rigid erection.

His jaw clenched, but he managed a smile. "Damn, you're hot."

"Burning up, actually." Reaching behind herself, she unhooked her bra and let it droop off her shoulders. Wyatt stared at her breasts. She cupped them in her palms, keeping the bra cups in place. "I want your mouth on me, Wyatt."

His eyes flared, he started to reach for her, and she said, "Unh-uh. Be still." Teasing him with a smile, she whispered, "I'll come to you."

Heat flushed his high cheekbones. He settled back, his biceps bunching even more with his restraint. Voice rough, he said, "Whatever you want."

"I want you to suck on me, but gently. Very gently."

His chest rose on a deep breath. "Bend down here."

With the expectation of how hot his mouth would be, how it'd make her feel, Mercy's nipples tightened and she almost moaned.

Breathing hard and fast, she dropped the bra over the side of the bed.

"Come to me, Mercy."

Even in this, he tried to take control. She had to get a grip. Tonight was for him, a memory they'd both cherish.

Deliberately sliding along the length of his shaft, Mercy adjusted her position and felt him stiffen more.

She put her hands on either side of his head, arms straight, so that her breasts hovered over his mouth. "Well?"

"Tease." Wyatt lifted his head and licked at one nipple.

Everything deep inside her tightened. She bit her lip and forced herself to stay still.

He licked again, circling her before closing his mouth over her and suckling softly.

Oh, God. Her thighs clenched on his hips. She closed her eyes and curled her fingers into the bedclothes.

Wyatt moved to the other breast, giving it the same tender treatment, and just that easily, she was ready, already wet and pulsing.

Determination kept her from changing her plans. She wanted this to last. She wanted to physically show Wyatt how much she loved him.

Eyes burning, Wyatt challenged her. "You need me, Mercy."

Never did she want to be a burden. She wanted his love and respect, his affection and fidelity, but not his sense of obligation. "For this, yes, I need you."

His brows came down in a fierce frown. "So it's only mind-blowing sex you need? Well, babe, I can give it to you."

"Oh, trust me, Wyatt, I know you can." The exchange of words helped her compose herself. "I'm counting on it."

"Then . . ."

"Shhh." What she wanted to prove was that she could give him the same wild satisfaction. "Just be patient."

As she moved to Wyatt's side, his expression darkened more. She rose to her knees and pushed down her panties, then sat back, stretched her legs out, and took them off completely.

In the process, she made sure to give him a show. It worked, given his rapt expression and the narrowing of his eyes.

Using her silky thong, she teased his cock, sliding it around him, stroking him. His legs shifted on the bed; he made a low, growling sound of mixed frustration and pleasure.

While still playing with him, Mercy sought his gaze. It startled her, even unnerved her a bit, to catch the dark intensity of his direct stare.

To compose herself, she looked back at his erection. A drop of fluid showed on the head, tempting her and filling her with satisfaction. She blindly tossed aside the underwear, curled her fist around him to hold him steady, and slowly leaned down.

Wyatt's feral groan matched her descent until she reached him. He held his breath. Mercy squeezed him tight. She closed her eyes—and opened her mouth around him, taking him deep into her mouth in one move.

His breath hissed out and he strained beneath her. When she started to pull back, his hips lifted, keeping his cock buried deep in her mouth.

Mercy teased him as far as she could, then pulled away and straddled his hips again. She was shaking all over, his lust inspiring her own. She held him again and ever so slowly eased down to take him inside her.

Wyatt's riveted gaze took in the slow penetration even as his chest bellowed and his muscles clenched.

"You're killing me, Mercy."

She didn't reply. She couldn't. Tipping her head back, she took more of him. It was so deep this way, and her body was so different now, more sensitive, needier. Riper.

"*Mercy,*" he warned, lifting his hips again to speed up her progress, pushing up into her until he couldn't go any farther. "Spread your knees."

Done with her game, she did as he asked, and felt herself slip down another inch. She gasped.

"Wyatt?"

His jaw worked. "Yeah?"

"You can take over now."

So fast that she didn't have time to catch her breath, he sat up and pulled her closer, covering her mouth with his own, kissing her hot and deep. His fingers tunneled into her hair, holding her skull as he raped her mouth.

She loved every second of it. So close to the edge that she couldn't take it, Mercy started to move.

Wyatt stopped her. "Oh, no you don't." His hands slid down her back to clasp her hips. "If you start that, I'll come and it'll all be over."

"I want you to come."

He shook his head. "Not just yet." Bracing an arm behind her back, he arched her forward and bent to her breasts. His mouth was hot, damp, but now the gentle tugging wasn't enough.

Mercy tried to encourage him with small sounds and movements, but he only released one nipple to move to the other.

"Wyatt . . ."

"Shhh." He met her gaze. "Open your knees as far as you can. Let me look at you."

Mercy didn't hesitate. She saw his eyes darken and narrow, and then he put his fingers there, touching her so lightly, teasing her.

Caught so close to a climax, her breath strangled in her throat.

"Look at you, all stretched around me, wet and slick."

She should never have tried to play this game with him. He was too good at it.

"I need—"

"To come, I know." He kissed her slack mouth. "Tell me you love me."

"I love you."

His fingertips moved over her swollen clitoris, found a rhythm, and that combined with his erection filling her was more than enough. As the orgasm rolled through her, she felt his mouth on her nipple again, sucking, tugging, and she lost total control. Her hands dug into his shoulders, and she cried out.

The waves of pleasure were barely starting to recede when Wyatt dropped back with her, rolled, and put her beneath him. Still a part of her, he rose over her on stiffened arms.

"Look at me, Mercy."

It was an effort, but she got her heavy eyes open.

"I love you."

She smiled. "I love you, too."

He started thrusting, hard and fast. The muscles of his arms corded with his rising tension. His face darkened, his jaw locked.

He put his head back on a deep groan and shuddered with his release.

Watching every nuance of pleasure over his face, her heart full with emotion, Mercy stroked his chest.

When he dropped down onto her, she squeezed him tight and kissed his shoulder.

It was fifteen minutes later when she realized he'd dozed off. A tender smile caught her by surprise. He worked so hard, but still he'd made time for dinner with her brother.

With a nudge to his shoulder, he rolled to his back and sighed. "You okay?"

"I'm fabulous." She started to get out of the bed.

His hand settled on her thigh. "Where you going?"

"To clean up and remove my makeup, brush my teeth. I won't be long."

He sighed again, stretched, and sat up with her. "I need to do the same." He gave her a long look. "God Almighty, you're beautiful."

Mercy laughed. "You like that just-tumbled look, do you?"

"When it's you, and I'm the one who did the tumbling, yeah." He left the bed and, buck naked, strode into the bathroom.

Her heart softened. She owed him the truth. Now. Tonight. But she couldn't do it like this, in the bed they'd just wrecked.

She'd shower first, and then . . . Well, whatever happened, she'd deal with it. She was Brax Jardine's little sister, and that meant she could deal with anything.

SIX

"WYATT?"

He was still repairing the bed when Mercy stepped out of the bathroom. Smiling, he glanced up and found her freshly showered and . . . dressed. He glanced at the clock. It was damn near midnight.

Uneasiness clawed through him; he straightened. "Going somewhere?"

Her fingers laced together. "I hope not."

His mind raced. He wanted to go to her, to hug her, but she wore that distanced expression again, as if she guarded herself so she wouldn't be hurt. "This is your home now."

She nodded, took a deep breath. "There's something I need to tell you."

If it was another man . . . But no. Mercy wouldn't do that. He couldn't believe that. "What's wrong?"

"I'm hoping nothing is."

Wyatt frowned.

"That is, I'm hoping you won't think anything is, because I don't."

"You're not making any sense, honey."

She nodded again and squeezed her hands a little tighter. With an effort, she put her shoulders back and met his gaze. "I'm pregnant."

For one dizzying moment, the world closed in around him. Things from his past erupted into his future, hateful comments, murderous gestures that he'd long buried in an effort to forget them.

Unseeing, he stared at Mercy. "How?"

Her laugh held no humor. "The usual way."

"You told me you were on the pill." It wasn't so much an accusation as an effort to assimilate what she'd said, to come to grips with it.

Pregnant. A child. *His* child.

God, he'd never thought—

"I was on the pill, but—"

"Was?" He could see her now, and it tore at him. She looked lost, sick. His throat burned, making his voice rough. "When did you go off them?"

"When I found out I was pregnant."

He shook his head again. She wasn't making any sense.

Taking one step toward him, Mercy rushed into speech. "You remember when I got sick? Well, I was throwing up a lot and the doctor thinks it's possible that for a few nights, my body didn't have the chance to absorb the pill, and . . . I got pregnant." She ended with a shrug.

Wyatt looked at her breasts. They were bigger, he knew that. He'd noticed it, but he hadn't thought . . . And her waist, it was a little thicker. She looked tired all the time, and she'd thrown up—

His head went back with disbelief. "How long have you known?"

"For only a little while."

Things her brother had said, Cameo had said, reso-nated anew in his brain. He caught the bedpost for support. "You told your brother and his assistant? All through dinner, they knew?"

Now she took a step back. "I never told Cameo. I guess Brax did."

She thought that made it better? His hand tightened on the post. "You told your brother, *but not me*?"

Tears welled in her eyes, but she blinked them away. "I share everything with my brother."

What could he say to that? He wanted her to share everything with him—but she hadn't. Maybe she never would.

His heart punched hard against his ribs. He needed a minute alone, a little time to bend his mind around the impossible. No words came to him, so he said nothing.

Feeling as if hell chased him, he turned away from her and left the room. All through his house he now saw signs of her presence in his life, his heart. He went to the back door and stepped out into the yard.

The moon hung low in the sky, surrounded by glittering stars. He dragged in a breath, but still his lungs ached with tightness.

A child.

His child.

How the fuck could that be?

And more important, what would he do about it?

The sound of his front door closing jerked him around. No. Fuck no. He ran around the house to the front just in time to see her headlights bounce off the driveway, hit the road, and start moving away.

"Mercy!"

She kept going—not speeding, but leaving him all the same. Chasing her barefoot, in his boxers and nothing else, would be insane—but that's what he wanted to do.

Prodded by panic, he ran back into the house and grabbed up the phone. He dialed her cell, but she didn't answer.

Damn it.

He closed his eyes and again saw her desolate expression. No, he didn't have any answers. God knew he'd never, ever expected to be faced with this particular situation. Statistically, he was probably the very worst candidate to be a father.

But he knew with a bone-deep certainty that he couldn't lose Mercy. He loved her far too much.

Everything else could be fixed. *Somehow*.

Driven by new resolution, he pulled on a shirt and jeans, grabbed his truck keys, and raced out the door to find her.

IT was just beyond dawn when Mercy gave up and pulled into Brax's driveway. She felt like death warmed over and probably looked pretty close to that, too.

She'd left Brax's house in a T-shirt dress and flip-flops, her hair a mess, her face devoid of makeup . . . and damn it, she was going to cry again.

Sitting in her car, she struggled to get herself together. It was bad enough that her face was blotchy, her eyes swollen. If she walked in sobbing, Brax would want to kill someone. From the time she was a child, it crushed him to see her upset and he went overboard to "fix" things to make her happy again.

Resting her head on the steering wheel, she drew in slow, steady breaths.

When a tap sounded on her driver's-door window, she screamed. It so took her by surprise that everything in her jolted.

"It's me, Mercy. Cameo."

Mercy squinted her eyes to see in the early-morning twilight. Man, even at the crack of dawn Cameo looked very pulled together.

She rolled down her window and, feeling like an idiot, said, "Hi."

Cameo's mouth flattened and her eyes rolled. "Give it up, honey. I can see you're a mess, and no, you don't need to explain. Come on, let's go inside."

Grumbling to herself, Mercy relented. She opened the car door and dragged her sorry behind out. "What are you doing here so early?"

"Brax starts his day at five A.M."

"You're kidding."

Cameo put her arm around her and started her toward the entrance. "Sometimes he has very important business that can't wait, and when that happens, I'm here."

"What kind of business needs to be done at this ungodly hour?"

"I have no idea. It's not my business. I just ensure he's ready to go by six thirty A.M."

At the door, Mercy balked. "Is he still here?"

"He's working out in his gym. Even when business intrudes, and sometimes especially then, he works out first to get his day going. He claims a good sweat kick-starts his brain."

Mercy thought about retreating. It was obvious her brother was very busy today and didn't need a weeping sister intruding on his day.

Cameo shook her head. "No way, Mercy. He'd string me up if I let you leave now." She patted her shoulder. "You can have a few minutes, maybe a cup of coffee to help you feel better, and then I have to let him know you're here."

Desolation closed in on her again. "I don't think coffee is going to help much."

"Ah, honey." Cameo reached for her, but Mercy backed away and held up her hands.

"Sympathy only encourages me to excesses of emotion, believe me." She drew in a deep steadying breath. "I'll be okay." Maybe if she said it often enough, it'd be true.

"Of course you will be." Again, Cameo got her moving inside. "Brax Jardine didn't raise any wimps. And you know what else?"

As soon as Mercy stepped inside, she smelled the coffee. Cameo had it in the den, but she didn't head that way. Instead, she tugged Mercy along to the massive stainless steel kitchen. "What?"

"No matter what has you so upset, I personally think you'll work things out with Wyatt. That man has got a bad case for you. Take my word for it. Sure, he's got his hang-ups like all men, but he truly loves you, so it's going to be okay."

"I don't know . . ."

The front doorbell rang, followed quickly by a hard knock.

Mercy's eyes widened.

Cameo smiled. "Well, speak of the devil."

In a ridiculous whisper, Mercy said, "You think that's Wyatt?"

"Who else would it be? Brax was planning to leave, so I'm sure he didn't invite anyone. And as you know, people are not comfortable just dropping in on your brother."

"Ohmygod." Mercy looked down at her badly wrinkled cotton dress. She put her hands in her hair and felt numerous tangles. She'd sniffled so much that her nose was surely red, her eyes, too.

Panicked, she locked eyes with Cameo. "He can't see me like this!"

Full of take-charge confidence and admirable calm, Cameo started toward the door. "Quick, go downstairs with your brother. I'll buy you some time."

With her brother? "But—no!"

"Brax has an extravagant bathroom down there with everything you'll need to do some repairs."

But she'd have to face Brax first. "No, I don't want to . . . Cameo, wait!" Never slowing, Cameo waved a hand over her shoulder. "Damn it," Mercy grumbled.

Left with no choice but to do as Cameo said, Mercy practically leaped for the door that led to her brother's private sanctum.

She'd been downstairs only a few times. His house was big enough that he didn't need use of the area for entertaining.

Bright lights kept the ornate metal staircase well lit, but still Mercy held tight to the handrail. She imagined if anyone fell down those hard stairs, they'd suffer quite an injury. Perhaps that was why Brax never invited anyone down.

Or maybe the stairs were meant to keep people from venturing there on their own.

The entire house was wired for an intercom system, so when Cameo needed Brax, she could call down without trespassing. He'd only had Mercy down there to show her the security measures and instruct her on how to use them "in case of an emergency."

What emergency she'd ever have at his house, she couldn't imagine, but Brax insisted she learn to use everything. He also insisted that if the need ever arose and she needed sanctuary, she should come to him.

As Mercy reached the bottom of the stairs, she saw the numerous security screens, all of them on and showing various areas of the grounds, the house, and beyond, all the way to the street.

Loud music played, but even over that Mercy heard the *thump, thump, thump* of leather on leather. She bypassed the state-of-the-art theater room for the fully equipped gym.

Before she reached the door, Brax stepped out, already frowning. He wore only black boxing shorts, and most of his body gleamed with sweat. To Mercy, he looked somehow larger than she remembered, definitely menacing.

"Mercy?" He took one look at her and his scowl smoothed out. He lifted a white towel off a stand, dried his face and chest, then tossed it around his neck. "I take it Romeo let you down?"

Restraining her tears made her hiccup. "I don't know," she said in a broken whisper. If she cried in front of Brax, she'd go back and find Wyatt and smack him a good one.

Brax urged her to sit on a low wooden bench outside the gym door. "I'd hug you, but I'm sweaty and I know how you hate sympathy anyway." He crouched down in front of her. "Now tell me, what does 'I don't know' mean?"

Feeling like an utter fool, Mercy again reached for composure. "I told him I was pregnant and he was . . . furious."

"About the baby?"

She lifted one shoulder. "Maybe, but he was definitely enraged that you knew before he did."

"Ah." Brax gave her an *I told you so* look. "You might have kept that part from him."

"Somehow he already knew, and lying didn't seem like a good idea." Using both hands, she shoved her hair away from her face. "I wanted to be totally honest with him, like you said."

"So he was angry—justifiably, I might add—and then what?"

She dropped her hands. "He went off by himself. All the way outside in the backyard."

"That far, huh?" Brax shook his head. "And what did you do?"

To keep them from shaking, Mercy clutched her hands in her lap. But there wasn't anything she could do about the awful quaver in her voice. "It broke my heart to see him turn away from me like that."

"Honey, a man going off to think is not a rejection."

"It certainly felt like one."

Brax sighed. "You can't expect men and women to react the same way to things. But we can go over that later." He straightened to stand before her, hands on his hips, bare feet braced apart. "There are some things you need to know about Wyatt. Important things." He shook his head. "Awful things."

A little afraid of what she might learn, Mercy blinked up at him. "What?"

"Things happened to him long ago that are likely coloring his reactions today." Brax rubbed the bridge of his nose and his voice lowered. "I knew it, I saw it whenever I looked at him, but even I was shocked by what I learned."

Mercy was wondering what Brax was talking about

when from behind them, Wyatt said, "I'd like a moment to talk to Mercy, please. Alone."

Mercy jumped and leaned to see around Brax.

Wyatt stood there in jeans and an open shirt, beard stubble on his face, his blond hair spiky as if he'd run his hands through it too many times, his green eyes burning as he stared at her.

God, he looked haggard, worse than her maybe.

Brax stepped in front of Mercy. "You made her cry."

Mercy heard the lack of patience in Wyatt's tone when he said, "Not on purpose."

Brax crossed his arms over his chest. "If I thought it had been deliberate, you'd be on the floor right now."

Wyatt made a sound like a snarl, and then repeated, albeit in a growl, "I'd like to speak to Mercy. *Alone*."

The last thing Mercy wanted was for Wyatt to be coerced in any way. She stood and put a hand to her brother's shoulder. "Brax, please."

He turned his back on Wyatt and bent to her. "Remember what I said, Mercy. The man is due a break, okay?" He touched her chin. "He needs you."

Surprised by the encouragement, when she'd expected just the opposite, Mercy nodded. "Okay."

"You can always trust in love." Brax turned and sauntered toward Wyatt. "No one," he said in an authoritative tone, "is supposed to be down here. Wrap this up quick and get the hell out of my basement. Understood?"

Wyatt had eyes only for Mercy. He took a step forward. "Whatever."

Brax rolled his eyes, must have decided that was good enough, and headed for the stairs, bellowing, "Cameo!"

Wyatt stopped in front of Mercy and then . . . he just stood there, watching her face, looking hard and fierce and somehow afraid.

Her nerves jangled and she said, "Sounds like Cameo might be in trouble for letting us down—"

Wyatt leaned down and kissed her. Though he didn't

touch her anywhere else, it was not a sweet kiss. It was one of possession and exploding need. When he pulled back, he put his forehead to hers. He swallowed once, twice, then said, "God, Mercy, I looked everywhere for you. At your place, back at mine, up and down the streets, before I finally realized you'd come here."

"I didn't at first. I wasn't sure where to go or what to do so I just . . . drove around. I only got here a few minutes before you."

He let out a breath, then said, "So I'm going to be a father?"

He didn't quite look at her, and Mercy's heart started breaking again, but this time, for different reasons. "And I'll be a mother." She put a hand to his jaw. "Wouldn't it be best if we did that together?"

She felt him breathing, felt his tension growing. His arms came around her and he hugged her in tight. For the longest time, that's all he did. She was starting to worry again when he suddenly picked her up and went to sit on the floor, his back to the wall, with her cradled in his lap.

"My father killed my mother. He tried to kill me. He thought he *had* killed me. Then he shot himself."

Mercy's throat closed, her heart raced. Forget warding off tears; they poured down her face. She couldn't get a single word out and could barely breathe.

Wyatt squeezed her closer. "I was twelve. For years Dad had blamed me for a lot of things, mostly for ruining his marriage. He said that before me, my mom loved him. But after me, she just stopped caring about anything."

His hand tangled in Mercy's hair, curled around her skull and kept her face tucked in close to his throat. She felt each swallow, each difficult breath.

"He told me Mom didn't love me either, and I believed it." His laugh was a sad sound of acceptance. He kissed the top of her head. "She blamed me for a lot, too, for my dad drinking and gambling. Before me, she was able to go with him everywhere, but she was stuck home with me, and that's why he wandered."

Mercy knotted both hands in Wyatt's shirt and held on tight. Devastated by what he'd said, what she felt in his explanation, she wished for a way, any way, to comfort him.

"One day Mom gave up on the fighting and filed for a divorce. Dad went nuts. I was in bed when I heard the first shot, and then I smelled the smoke."

His heart pounded against Mercy's cheek. She slipped a hand into the shirt, over his skin.

"The second shot sounded before I managed to get moving. I tried to open my door, but it was jammed."

Dear God. She tucked in closer, and he let her, cradling her as if he wished to protect her from his awful truths.

"I don't know if he couldn't bring himself to shoot me, or if . . . if he thought the fire would be worse. But he tried to burn me to death." He slumped back against the wall and his touch became gentler, as if automatic as he recalled devastating memories. "I broke a window and went outside. Neighbors who'd heard the shots were already showing up, and right after that, the police."

She couldn't stand it. Mercy turned, straddling his lap and rising to her knees. "Thank God you escaped." She kissed his brow, his temple, his mouth. "Thank God."

His hands dropped to his sides. "I spent a shitload of time in therapy, Mercy. Psychologists told me all about mental abuse—and how it can be hereditary."

"No." She shook her head hard. "You are the finest, most wonderful man I know."

One corner of his mouth lifted, but his eyes remained sad. "Brax might not like hearing that."

"I love you, Wyatt. I need you. More than anyone."

"No. You don't need me, honey."

She gripped his shoulders. "I do. Tonight, without you, oh God, I kept trying to picture my life and it was miserable."

Wyatt curved a hand over her belly. "You'd have made it a happy life. For our baby. I know you would have."

Sensing he needed something from her, Mercy settled

back, sitting on his thighs, and nodded. "I would protect our child no matter what, Wyatt. But then, so would you."

He lifted a finger and traced her jawline. "Children of violent or abusive parents are always at higher risk of being violent or abusive. Even though I lost my parents young, the association is still strong." He threaded his fingers through her hair. "Compared to kids with average parents, I'm four to seven times as likely to be abusive."

Mercy got mad. "Why would a psychologist tell you such a horrible thing?"

"To help me understand that a lot of abuse is genetic. It wasn't me as a kid, it was them as parents. They had the problem, not me." He brought his other hand up, so that he held her face. "I never wanted to do to a kid what was done to me. You can't know what it feels like, your parents hating you like that, hating you enough that they'd rather be dead."

"They . . . they were sick."

"Exactly. But I made a vow early on to never fall in love, to never put anyone at risk, and to never, ever have a child."

Her hopes started to sink—and then Wyatt said, "But now I am, and . . . I can't help it. I'm fucking *overjoyed*." He closed his eyes, as if disgusted with himself, and dragged her in close again. "God help me, Mercy, I don't know that I deserve you or a baby, but I want you both so much, I can't even think straight."

Mercy squeezed him so tight that it hurt her.

"It scares me shitless, but losing you or my child scares me even more."

She nodded, choked back her tears, and hugged him some more. Finally, after several minutes, she was able to speak. "I am so sorry for what you went through, but Wyatt, please trust me on this. You are not an abusive man, not in any way."

He set her away from him. "If you believe that, then will you marry me?"

Joy blunted some of the hurt she felt for him. "Yes."

His mouth twitched into a smile. "You didn't think about that very long."

"I've thought of nothing else since I found out I was pregnant." She drew in a breath. "But Wyatt, I swear to you, it's not just about the baby. I'd have wanted to spend my life with you, with or without a child."

Again, he touched her belly. "I'm glad it's with."

Mercy covered her mouth with a hand, and nodded. "Oh, Wyatt. Me, too." She threw herself against him again.

They sat there a long time, holding each other, whispering about weddings and a nursery and names.

Brax, fully dressed and looking more lethal than ever, came to loom over them. "Now that we've worked out the kinks, can you two find somewhere else to cuddle? I have business to attend."

Wyatt stood with her still straddling him, and let her feet slowly drop to the floor.

Mercy, determined to protect Wyatt from any other hurt, turned to her brother. "We're getting married."

"I figured as much. I'd like the honor of throwing the wedding, but—" He glanced at his wristwatch. "We'll have to discuss it later. Dinner tonight? I think Wyatt owes me one."

Mercy shook her head and hugged closer to Wyatt. "No, I want a quiet night at home. We have a lot to talk about. Next week?"

Brax nodded. "Set it up and give Cam the details." He turned to Wyatt, looked at him down the bridge of his nose, scrutinized him, and then seemed to give up.

"I'd appreciate it if you didn't ask too many questions, or act too freaked out, if you just tried to go on faith here, but . . ." He glanced at Mercy, then back at Wyatt. "You're going to be one hell of a dad."

"Thank you."

"It's not a compliment, Wyatt. It's a fact. I wouldn't let any of this happen if I didn't know it for sure already."

Wyatt cocked a brow. "So you're a psychic as well as a financial genius?"

"I'm neither. I just have hidden talents that are . . . very hidden." He slapped Wyatt on the arm. "Now you two go figure out your lives, but I'd appreciate it if you keep me posted."

WYATT rested with an arm around Mercy, his hand curved low on her belly, where his baby grew. His mind buzzed too much to let him sleep. The wonder of it all kept bringing a ridiculous smile to his mouth. Twice, his eyes had burned, but no way would he cry about it.

When Mercy turned to him, displacing his hand to her bottom, he realized that she didn't sleep either.

"Hey."

He smiled. "Hey yourself. Not tired?"

"I'm too in love to be tired." She kept doing that, kept reassuring him as if he were that needy adolescent kid again.

And damn it, he liked the reassurances. They fed his soul, made it all so real, so believable.

So possible.

She kissed his chin, then scooted until her head rested on his shoulder. "You might have doubted yourself, Wyatt, but I swear to you, I never did. I feel like the luckiest woman alive, just because I have you."

An invisible fist squeezed his throat. Her love was more than he'd ever dared hope for, but Mercy had given beyond that.

She'd given him back life. Trust. Hope.

For the first time in fifteen years, contentment and peace settled over him, sank into him bone deep, and chased away the darkest shadows, obliterating the most wretched memories.

Used to be, those memories colored everything. Now they were where they belonged, in the past. Not forgotten, but put to rest.

He made a new vow: If need be, he would give his life to protect Mercy and his baby.

It amazed him, but he knew he'd beat the odds. It wasn't that he believed Brax had the ability to foretell the future or any nonsense like that.

It was the love swelling inside him, the protectiveness, the determination to ensure that his child knew so much love, felt so secure and cherished, that he or she would never suffer a single moment of doubt or insecurity.

As usual, Mercy was right: he would never deliberately cause harm to another. Most especially, he would never harm his woman or child.

He was a better man than that.

With her or without her, he would have broken the legacy of abuse.

He'd spend the rest of his life showing her how happy he was to have her with him.

"We are going to be wonderful parents, Wyatt."

He curved her close and spoke the truth she'd given him. "Yes, we are."

DEAL OR
NO DEAL

ERIN McCARTHY

ONE

"YOU can't just throw that away! What's the matter with you?" Katie Stolin looked at her brother, Peter, in consternation and snatched from him the necklace that he'd been about to dump in the trash.

Of course, asking what was wrong with Peter was a rhetorical question. There was a lot wrong with him, and Katie had to admit, after a hundred years in his presence, she was more than ready for a little alone time. But that would leave Peter in the care of Nick, and Katie wasn't sure she could toss him that hand grenade and walk away.

"Who cares?" Peter said, rolling his eyes as he flung his thirteen-year-old body down onto the couch. "It's ugly and it reminds me of being weak . . . I hate those memories."

"But it was from Mom. It's a symbol of how much she loved you. I didn't even know you had this still." Katie held the necklace up in the air as she stood next to the coffee table in Peter and Nick's suite. It wasn't a beautiful necklace, being clunky and overly gilded. Then again, back in the Russia of their youth, when they had lived as a prince and princess, gold had been much in fashion.

The more detailing, the bigger, the flashier, and the more expensive, the better it had been. That had been their mother's philosophy.

But she hadn't bought this particular piece for prestige or pleasure. It had been a gift from her holy advisor to protect her son, Peter, from the terrible effects of hemophilia. How ironic then that the same son had wound up a vampire, trapped forever in his underdeveloped preadolescent body.

"Mom was a nut and you know it. I didn't even remember I still had the necklace, and I don't want it. If you want the piece of shit, you can have it for fifty bucks."

Katie glanced over at her brother. She was used to his adult language and mentality housed in a boy's body, but she still didn't like him. He'd been a spoiled brat of a child, and he was still a brat at a hundred.

"I'm not paying you anything. You were just going to throw it away."

"Fifty bucks or it goes in the garbage disposal."

"Careful. Your sentimental side is showing again," she told him ruefully.

"Screw sentimental. I need the cash. I would have preferred some actual money from our parents instead of a crappy necklace."

"And I would have preferred that they weren't shot in front of me," Katie snapped at him, sick of his callousness.

Peter just rolled his eyes. "Let it go. It's been almost a century. And it's not like either of them could have ever qualified for parent of the year. I'm serious. Fifty bucks or I'll trash it."

"I'm the one holding it," Katie reminded him, undoing the clasp. Let the little punk try to make a grab for it. She'd wrestle him to the ground if she had to; she was not about to be blackmailed.

The necklace was shaped and detailed like a Fabergé egg with a starburst of gold around it. At one time there had supposedly been some kind of medicine sealed in the egg portion of the necklace, but Katie didn't know what it was. Hell, there had probably never been anything in there. It wasn't like her mother would have checked—she had been willing to believe anything if she thought it would help her son.

Looking into the mirror above the console table in the entryway to Nick's suite, Katie watched the necklace dangle in the air as she held it up to herself. As a vampire, she couldn't see her own reflection, but the piece of jewelry shone vibrantly. Katie put it around her neck, ignoring her brother's diatribe of complaints from behind her. Peter always had something to whine about, and she had learned to tune him out. The cool metal settled against her flesh as she managed to hook the clasp.

Staring at it was pleasing, a wave of nostalgia washing over her. Despite what Peter said, their parents had loved them and cosseted them as children, and Katie was entitled to still miss them, along with her three sisters, who had also been killed in that tiny room in Ekaterinburg. Nick, the guard who had saved her and Peter and turned them to vampire, was the closest thing she had to family now.

Suddenly afraid that she might cry, which she hadn't done since that awful time when her family had died and she'd found out Michael had betrayed her, she forced a joke. "I look damn good, don't I?"

As if she could see herself.

For once, Peter didn't have a snarky remark. He just shrugged when she turned back to smile at him. "I've seen uglier women than you."

That was a serious compliment coming from him. Katie laughed. "Gee, thanks."

"But it's making a red mark on your neck."

"Really?" Katie tried to look down at her chest, nearly going cross-eyed. She couldn't see very well, but she did see a red line when she shifted the necklace. "Great, I'm allergic to it."

"Told you it was trash."

Katie made a face at her brother and told herself she

was not feeling itchy, even as her hand reached up and scratched her skin.

THE vampire formerly known as Rasputin was walking across the main room of his apartment, where most of his business operations were generated, when he drew up short. His hand flew to his neck, where the snakehead necklace he'd been wearing for more than a hundred years suddenly was tingling. Reaching under his black T-shirt, he pulled it out and gripped it tightly, caressing the vial that was encased in the snake's mouth.

Well, who would have guessed?

A grin split his face, and he turned to the irritating young man who did all of his computer work for him. Sergei was sitting at the desk Rasputin had stolen from an office-supply store, typing away at the keyboard diligently, his glasses slipping down his nose. Rasputin had often thought that it was no wonder Sergei wanted to work for the largest Internet porn operation in Russia— the kid was clearly not getting laid.

But Sergei's lack of sex life meant nothing to Rasputin at the moment, not when the necklace was heating from the inside out so intently it was burning his flesh.

"Sergei, I need you to do some research for me. Whatever the hell you're doing will have to wait."

He had long suspected that not all of the royal family had died in that room, and two bodies had never been found.

Now he had confirmation that someone still lived.

Only the tsarevitch or his sister could cause such a reaction from the vial around his neck.

One of them had put the necklace on, the one that Rasputin had given the tsarina for her son to wear, to sustain him during his illnesses.

The one that was filled with the drops of blood of every ancient vampire still walking the earth.

The one that Rasputin needed to increase his own strength and stave off gradual aging.

"What do you need, sir?" Sergei asked, swiveling in his chair.

"I need you to find a boy and a girl for me."

"For a video, sir, or for you personally? How old?"

Sergei's face was impassive, and Rasputin grinned. For being such a sweet-looking lamb, Sergei certainly never blinked in the face of any perversions Rasputin threw his way.

"No, for neither. This is more of a family matter. My niece and nephew have been missing for several years."

Rasputin held the necklace tightly and closed his eyes, to focus, to let the energy pass over him. He could see bustling crowds of people, bright flashing lights, poker tables, and . . . the Eiffel Tower? "Where is there gambling and a fake Eiffel Tower?"

Sergei frowned. "Perhaps that would be Las Vegas in the United States, sir."

That might be it. "What is Las Vegas like?"

"Very flashy. Hotels built on themes like Paris and Venice and the Colosseum. Lots of lights. Surrounded by desert. Beyond that, I am not sure. Would you like me to investigate it?"

"No, no, that sounds right," he murmured, eyes still closed. "Book us passage to Las Vegas and find us a hotel. Leaving tomorrow."

"Tomorrow?" Sergei asked in surprise.

"Yes, tomorrow . . ."

And then there it was—the names he had been hoping would come to him out of the energy of the person wearing the necklace.

"And see if you can locate Nick, Katie, and Peter Stolin in this Las Vegas."

It was time for Rasputin to pay a visit to some old friends.

MICHAEL St. Markov was eyeing the massive display of biscuits at Harrods and wondering how it was he could still crave the sugary sweetness after all these years as a bloodsucker when his cell phone rang.

It was Sergei. "Hello?" Michael glanced around out of habit for anyone who might be a threat, but there was no one in the department store, minutes after it had opened, who cared that he was talking on his cell phone.

"Do the names Nick, Katie, and Peter Stolin ring any bells?"

"No." Michael frowned, picking up a tin and shaking it absently. "Why?"

"Because he's on the move. We're heading to Vegas for no other reason than those three are living there and he just figured it out. They're from Odessa—a security guard, his twenty-something niece, and his thirteen-year-old son."

Michael paused in his abuse of the biscuit tin, the light from the fluorescent department store fixtures reflecting off the colorful metal. His grip tightened. He didn't quite dare to verbalize his desperate hope, so he just said, "And?"

"And it seems very likely that this is them, Michael. Nothing else would send him all the way to Las Vegas on twenty-four hours' notice."

Closing his eyes briefly, Michael took a deep breath. "Alright, I'll meet you there then."

Tossing the biscuit tin back on the shelf, he strode out of the department store, only vaguely aware of his surroundings. He had to pack, and then tomorrow, if all went well, he would see the woman he loved for the first time in a hundred years.

TWO

KATIE dealt the cards and watched the faces of the
trio at her table. It was a slow night. August wasn't
the peak season of tourism in Vegas, and it was nine
P.M., when the live shows Vegas was famous for were in
full swing. They would have an influx of fresh gamblers
after midnight when the shows let out, but for now it was
quiet.

And she was bored. Fondling the necklace she had per-
suaded Peter to let her keep, she tried to ignore the fact
that it made the flesh beneath the chain itch as she did her
job absently. She was scanning the room repeatedly, not
even sure what she was looking for, but wishing for something else, something different, something more than the
same old routine night after endless night. They had been
in Vegas only a few months, and it felt like an eternity.
Not good, considering she did actually have an eternity to
live.

"So how does a nice little girl like you fall into this
kind of work?" the good-looking guy in his thirties with
the Southern accent asked her, sticking his cigar back in
his mouth.

And how did a man that young fall into such a cheesy pickup line? Katie gave him a shrug and a smile, amused at the fact that he probably had no idea he'd made her sound a bit like a prostitute. "Oh, you know how it is. Life throws curves at you."

"You're not from here, are you? I hear some kind of accent."

Turning the cards, Katie efficiently collected them as the house won yet again. The man kept going over, yet he seemed in no hurry to leave or to change his strategy. He looked content to sit in his chair and lose money hand over fist.

"I'm from Russia."

"Russia? Well, hell, that's a long ways away. What made you come here?"

Keeping her tone light and conversational, she said, "The current job market for Russian princesses sucks. So I gave up my tiara and headed to the States." All true, in a roundabout sort of way. Katie had found that if she joked about the truth, no one believed her, and she didn't have to deal with the discomfort of lying. No lies, no way to slip up either. It made everything easier.

"A princess? You're telling me you were a princess?" He cocked his head and gave her an amused stare, his dark eyes sparkling. "Alright, then. That sounds like quite a story. *Story* being the key word."

"Shocking, lurid, and true. Royalty to blackjack dealer. It happens to the best of us. And if you want to get technical, I was actually a Duchess."

"You're sassy," he said. "I like that." Ignoring the other two players, he continued, "Can I buy you a drink after work? You can tell me all about the path from princess to poker."

There it was. Part of the biggest problem in her life, and no doubt part of the reason she was feeling such malaise. Here she had an attractive and friendly male asking her out, and she couldn't work up one ounce of interest. Not one. She hadn't been on a date since shoulder pads were in style, and she hadn't had sex since the infamous summer of love, which practically didn't count because everyone breathing had had sex that summer. Yet she had no desire to say yes to the man in front of her.

Something was totally wrong with her that she was still ruined for other men when it had been a goddamn century since she'd had her heart broken. It was pathetic, lame, weird, and unnatural to be unable to move on from a failed relationship, and it felt somehow like if she stayed celibate and alone she was letting Michael win.

So despite having more interest in watching people sweat and starve themselves on TV for prize money than going out with the good ol' boy in front of her, Katie nodded. "Sure."

"Well, alright then." He smiled at her. "What time do you get off of work, darling?"

Katie dealt the cards to the players and said, "Four in the morning. I don't know if you want to stick around that long."

"Why not? I'm on vacation. So I'll meet you here at four, then. It's a date."

"Actually, the lady has plans."

Katie froze, the timbre of that voice rolling over her like the soft caress of a lover's touch, the sound so long unheard but instantly recognizable. How many nights she had delighted in that voice, whispering endearments and declarations of love to her as she giggled and sighed and drowned in the passion and bliss of youthful love.

The voice that had meant everything to her. The voice she would have defied her father and mother for.

Gaze snapping up, Katie took in the sight of Michael, standing casually in front of her as if an entire century hadn't passed, as if they weren't half the world and a million lifetimes away from St. Petersburg. He was wearing jeans and a blue shirt, his caramel-colored hair shorter than it had been, carelessly tousled, the air of the rich and privileged still securely around him.

"Hello, Maria," he said in French, the language of her

youth, a small secret smile on his beautiful face. "I've missed you."

The voice, the face, the words, the man . . . all of these she had loved and her heart still trembled at the thought of them, let alone the reality. He was here, in the flesh, in front of her, using the name she'd been born with, and telling her that he missed her.

It was everything she had dreamed of, longed for, prayed for, and cried into her pillow over.

So she took a deep breath, looked the man she had intended to marry straight in the eye, and said, "Drop dead, Michael."

MICHAEL had been awake nearly thirty-six hours, no small feat for a vampire. After packing and making sure he had the small box he intended to give Maria, if she was in fact alive and living in Las Vegas, he had headed to the airport. The plan had been to sleep on the plane, his head under a blanket, to pass the long flight and the daylight, but he had been too keyed up to actually fall asleep.

It had felt like too much to hope for that he could have actually found Maria after all these years. He had known in his heart that she was alive, logical or not. He would have felt it if the woman he loved, the better half of his very self and soul, were no longer walking on the earth.

But he had been unprepared for the sight of her standing there in a white shirt, hair pulled up in a messy knot on top of her head, smiling as her fingers efficiently dealt the gambling cards.

It had hit him like a tsunami, a century of love and longing and grief. Regret.

She was more beautiful than ever, the young girl grown into the woman, her stubborn chin now more regal and confident than obstinate. Michael had stood at the edge of the casino floor, hidden by the row of slots, and watched her interacting with the players at her table. She hadn't sensed his presence, but then again, there were vampires crawling all over the casino. His scent wouldn't draw notice to her if she were inured to the quantity of undead around night after night.

When being content with watching had no longer been enough, when he had wanted desperately to hear her voice, to see the love for him bloom in her eyes when she spotted him, Michael had moved forward and taken up position at the edge of her table.

Intellectually he knew it was possible her feelings had dimmed over the years. That perhaps she had met another man, one who had claimed her heart. But he didn't really believe it, nor did he think that even another man in her life would diminish a warm reception for him. Her first lover.

So he was more than slightly unprepared for her to tell him to drop dead.

The strong words, the venom in them, made his mouth drop open. "Excuse me?" he asked, stunned at the icy stare she was giving him. Somehow he had to have misunderstood what she'd said. Her French accent had sounded a little rusty.

"You heard me," she said, slapping down gambling chips with more force than was necessary. "I hope you die. I want you to turn around, walk away, and drop to the floor cold and dead on your way out."

Well, there was no misunderstanding that. But it bewildered and scared the shit out of him. This was not the way this meeting was supposed to go. "I can honestly say that is not how I expected you would greet me after all these years." Michael reached out and put his hand over hers, stroking the skin. "What time do you go on break? We need to talk, Maria."

She yanked her hand out from under his. "One, do not call me that. My name is Katie now. Two, we have absolutely nothing on this planet to talk about. Three, I hate you and I'm going to scream if you don't leave right now."

Her cheeks were flushed and her eyes were flashing.
Her behavior was so irrational, Michael lost some of his
fear. Clearly, this was some ridiculous misunderstanding.
Maria had always been feisty and prone to dramatics, and
he just needed five minutes with her to calm her down.

"I'm not going to leave. I need you to explain to me
why you're so upset."

She gasped. "You need me to *explain* it? Are you *jok-ing*?"

The man who was playing cards shifted on his chair.
"Is there a problem here?" he asked Maria, or Katie as she
clearly preferred to be called. "Do you need me to get rid
of this guy?"

Like Michael needed some yahoo with a cowboy hat to
interfere in his relationship with Maria—Katie—whoever
the hell she was now. "Mind your own goddamn business," he told him in English.

"It's fine," Katie said at the same time. "He's leaving."

"No, I'm not." Michael stubbornly stood his ground.
"Not until you explain to me why you're so angry."

Her head tilted, her green eyes flashing. She abandoned the discretion of French and spoke in English. "You
have exactly five seconds to get out of here."

Michael crossed his arms. "I'm not going anywhere."

"Suit yourself." Katie shifted behind the table.

Although Michael wasn't familiar with casinos, he had
been in enough dicey situations to know when an alert
had been sent. She had pushed some kind of button, he
was certain of it. Looking behind him, he already saw a
security guard moving toward them.

"You didn't," he told her, in disbelief.

The corner of her mouth turned up. "Oh, yes, I did."

"Call him off, Maria. Katie." Michael gave her a stern
look, one that would have made her quail back in their
youth.

It didn't have the same effect. She actually leaned
around him as if he hadn't spoken and told the approach-

ing guard, "This customer needs to be escorted out of the casino. Cheating," she added.

Oh, now that pissed him off. He had traveled halfway around the goddamn world on no sleep to give her a cache of family treasures and personal mementoes, and to tell her how much he'd loved and missed her, and this is what he got? Hauled out of a casino that proclaimed itself a bedazzled version of Paris by a mindless security guard, and nasty words from the woman he had pined—literally *pined*—over for a freaking century?

"I don't think you meant to say that," he said carefully, even as the security guard nodded for him to follow him off the floor.

Katie stared back, her lip suddenly trembling, giving away more emotion than she had probably intended. "Oh, yes, I did."

Michael hesitated, wanting to argue, wanting to wait for her to become reasonable, wanting to rewind and do this differently, but the security guard touched his arm to urge him along.

He gave the man an impatient glare. "Get your hands off of me." Then he turned back to Katie, but she was already preoccupied again with the deck of cards in front of her.

"Katie."

She looked up and said sarcastically, "So nice seeing you. Let's do this again, like, I don't know—never."

It was that last verbal kick in the nuts that had Michael losing all control over his dignity. He had waited years and years for this moment, to see the woman he had cherished and loved and vowed to marry against all familial protests, to know that she was well and truly alive and healthy and his.

And she might as well have spit in his face.

Instead of walking out with his head held high under his own recognizance, Michael had the insufferable man grabbing his elbow again to escort him out.

"Come on, buddy, out, or I'm going to get rough with you."

Oh, really? Michael felt the rising anger melding with his heartache and shock, and he flashed the guard a look, one that in the briefest of moments, allowed the man to see into his mind, to feel the thirst for blood, the painful depths of eternity, the loneliness of an oftentimes violent, frequently restless life. The guard's eyes widened, and he backed up, dropping Michael's arm.

It gave him the briefest of satisfactions until he heard Katie whisper so low that no mortal could hear, "Shame on you, Michael St. Markov."

The fact that she was chastising him should have been jabbing to his already wounded heart, but the sound of his name on her lips, in a voice he knew so well, and so long silenced from his life, brought immense comfort and pleasure. This wasn't over. He wouldn't let it be. Not until he had answers.

"I'll be back, my love," he told her.

She bristled. "And I'll have you thrown out again. And don't call me your love. I'm not your anything."

Michael gave her a small, sly smile. "Then I'll come back again and again until you agree to speak with me. We have things to say to one another."

And he walked out ahead of the guard before she could even respond.

THREE

KATIE'S hands trembled as she cut the deck. Oh, my God, she could not believe Michael was there, in Vegas. Standing in the Paris casino smiling at her like nothing had changed. Like he hadn't betrayed her and her family, contributing to the confinement and the eventual deaths of her entire family, save herself and Peter.

He looked the same, just as beautiful and charming and sexual as he always had. Though maybe with a little more of an edge to him. A touch harder, a tinge more cynical. She'd never known him as a vampire, either him or herself, and that gave both of them a glossier, surreal quality. Everything about him was slightly improved, smoother and shinier, yet lacking in that warmth she had remembered for all these years.

Of course, that might not be vampirism. That might be either his true character or the toll of all the ensuing years. God knew she was far warier than she had been at eighteen.

In those days, when Michael walked into a room she felt as soft and sweet as a bag of cotton candy, ready to dissolve with one touch of his tongue.

She had loved him with all the naïveté of her young and caring heart. Her family had lived in isolation, her parents doting and indulgent, surrounding her and her siblings with a happy, loving home and family. She hadn't known anything about the true depth of evil and the depravity of men.

All that had changed when her family had been imprisoned, and Michael had been a part of that betrayal, a fact she was never going to forget or forgive.

Was she bitter?

Hell, yeah.

Sometimes that scared her, the scathing cynicism that seemed to have settled into the marrow of her character. But even scarier still was the realization that when she had seen Michael, a tiny portion of her heart, long contained with lock and key, had opened up and leaped for joy.

"Is there room at this table?" a deep, gravelly voice asked.

Distracted, Katie glanced up, her finger going to hit the security button again in a strange subconscious gesture that startled her. She stopped herself from actually pushing it, but when she saw the face staring back at her, she wished she hadn't exercised the restraint.

Her mother's so-called holy advisor looked different, his beard shaped more like a goatee, his hair long and in dreadlocks, but there was no mistaking that nose, those eyes. That voice. "Well, well," Katie said, squeezing her fists behind the table so he wouldn't see the tremor left from her encounter with Michael. "Look what the cat dragged in."

Rasputin grinned. "It's delightful to see you *alive* and looking so well. I had no idea you were in Las Vegas. You should have sent a Christmas card with your new address."

"I wasn't aware Hell had door-to-door postal service."

He laughed, leaning to the man in the cowboy hat parked next to him. "We're old friends. We go way back."

"Seems to be a lot of that going around tonight," the

man said, starting to show exasperation that he was no longer the center of attention.

Katie couldn't believe she had been saddled with a visit from Rasputin mere minutes after encountering Michael. Were there any other assholes from her past who wanted to join in the fun? Maybe the guard who'd shot her in cold blood or her pervy uncle who used to try to cop a feel?

Gather them all up and she could throw a People Who Suck party.

Then again, maybe it was better to not tempt fate.

At least Rasputin wasn't dangerous, he was just irritating. He also had questionable hygiene and enjoyed anything that smacked of sexual deviance. Even as an adolescent Katie had pegged him as a total creeper, but her mother had believed in his dubious mystic powers.

Now, ninety years later, he looked even more the dirty old man to Katie's mature mind, though not nearly as frightening. It was a remarkable coincidence that two men from the royal palace days of her youth would show up across the world in her casino and approach her. So maybe it wasn't a coincidence at all, though she couldn't imagine what the sudden interest in her would be.

"So, *Katie*," Rasputin said, emphasizing her fake name with zero subtlety. "How is your brother these days?"

Irritation increased. What the hell did he want with Peter? "He's fine. And in case you haven't noticed, I'm working. I do not want to get fired."

"Of course, of course. I'll stop by later so we can catch up on old times."

"Great. Can't wait." She had no desire to talk to him, but she was curious to know how both he and Michael had found her. Neither had just stumbled across her—they had both approached her with the confidence of someone who knew she would be there.

She supposed it had been inevitable. In the modern world of electronic information, it was damn near impossible to stay hidden. It was probably a miracle she and

Nick and Peter had remained anonymous as long as they had.

But two unfortunate blasts from the past in one day? Seriously, it was more than any woman should have to tolerate. It was like gaining ten pounds and getting a bad haircut all in one two-hour stretch.

Rasputin leaned over the table and smiled, displaying teeth that were elongated and pearly white, a vast improvement over the crooked sallow smile he'd had in the past. Did he have vampire veneers? That must have cost a fortune, so clearly whatever he was up to in the present, it was profitable.

"I was always most fond of you," he told her. "I'm looking forward to renewing our very special friendship."

Eew. Lecher alert. "Don't be," she said. "I'm not good company. I'm bitter and bitchy and tend to whine a lot."

The move surprised her, but in retrospect, she supposed he had been hitting on her back in the day, too, she had just been too naïve to fully understand it. She had only known then that he made her uncomfortable. Now there was no mistaking the leer in his eyes. Old Ras wanted a little somethin' somethin' and there was no way he was ever getting it from her.

Scratching her chest where the necklace was irritating her skin again, she shot him what she hoped was a threatening glare.

Rasputin just laughed, not looking the least bit concerned. "I'll see you later, Katie."

Twisting the silver cross earring in his lobe, he gave her a sly smile and left, the back of his black trench coat billowing out behind him. He wore combat boots to complete the look, and Katie had to give him credit. Somehow he had managed to stay exactly the same, yet modify his look to the modern interpretation. The dreadlocks on him were the epitome of attention seeking, an attempt to give credence to his mystical left-of-center lifestyle.

Freak then and a freak now.

How comforting to know some things never changed.

Allowing herself an eye roll at his retreat, Katie refocused on the players in front of her. "I'm so sorry about that," she told them.

They grumbled their acceptance of her apology, and then Cowboy Hat stood up.

"I'm going to move on along," he told her. "I think we can skip that drink later."

"Really? Why?" Not that she had wanted to go at all, but hell, she didn't want to be rejected either.

"Honey, a blind man could see the sparks flying between you and that man."

"Him?" she asked, pointing at Rasputin's back, using hand gestures to indicate his dreadlocks. "Absolutely not! Yuck, no, never."

"Not him. The first one."

Shit. He had to go there.

"Nah. Old news. Nothing special."

If giving Michael her virginity, vowing to defy her family, and planning a secret elopement was nothing special.

"Maybe you ought to talk to the man. Nobody lives forever, you know. Might as well enjoy it."

Except that she *was* going to live forever, with a bitter heart and a nonexistent sex life.

Now there was a cheery thought.

MICHAEL paced the lobby back and forth, trying to collect his thoughts. His emotions, on the other hand, were just uncollectable. They were rattling around, strung out and panicked, winging out in all different directions. For years he had pictured the moment when he would see Katie again. It always started with him drinking in the sight of her as she gasped in surprise. Then tears of happiness, confessions of love to one another, and a happily ever after. The way they had left off. The way it was supposed to be.

For years he hadn't even been certain she was still

alive, and now he knew. He had total blissful confirmation that she still existed on this earth, yet she had rejected him. Told him to go away.

It hurt worse than anything he could have ever imagined, and he needed to hear why she was so angry with him. It had to be a misunderstanding, it just had to be. This wasn't a case of a woman whose feelings had faded over the years of no contact. That kind of angry emotion radiating from her led him to believe she thought something had happened, or something had been said that in fact hadn't.

Approaching her at the casino had been stupid, but he had been so eager to see her, to connect, to see the love for him shining in her eyes.

Which made him a total dumbass.

His cell phone rang in his pocket, and he pulled it out. It was Sergei. "Yeah?"

"He's going up to her in the casino. Did you confirm that she is the one? She's Maria?"

Michael's chest tightened. "Yes, she's Maria. No question about it."

"Okay. So what does he want with her?"

"I don't know." That was the question. Michael had spent a lifetime watching Rasputin's movements, out of concern for Katie and her brother. That was why he had Sergei working on the inside of Rasputin's porn business, to monitor his activities.

At the time, back before the revolution, it had made sense that Rasputin wanted to ingratiate himself to royalty, but with the passage of decades, why would he care about contacting Katie and Peter? They didn't have anything Rasputin could possibly want.

Or did they?

The thought made Michael's vampire blood turn even colder than it already was. "Is he still with her?"

"No, he's walking away."

Good. "Can you follow him?"

Michael couldn't, since Rasputin knew who he was.

He would be recognized as one of the Russian princes who had tried to murder Rasputin when he was influencing the tsarina. It would be suspicious if he were spotted in Vegas with no apparent purpose.

"Sure. What are you going to do?"

"I'm going to leave Maria, or Katie, a gift."

He was patient, a skill learned over the years as a vampire with eternity to while away. Katie had to be entitled to a break from her job, and when she left the gambling floor, he would be ready.

RASPUTIN tossed back a shot of vodka in the bar at the edge of the casino floor and felt it warm his insides. It was almost as satisfying as the jolt of lust he'd experienced when he had leaned forward and felt the exchange of energy between his necklace and Katie's. It had warmed his flesh, trailing down his chest to his cock. He hadn't thought about bedding Katie, but now that he'd seen her again, observed how she'd grown into a sassy woman instead of a moony girl, he might have to reconsider.

He could take the necklace by theft, force, or seduction.

All held their own appeal, but pleasures of the flesh were and always would be his personal weakness.

The mother had been creative and enthusiastic, though prone to emotion and incessant chatter.

Perhaps the daughter would have her mother's positive attributes, and none of the flaws.

The woman sitting next to him at the bar tapped his arm.

He glanced at her casually. Middle-aged, attractive, showing an impressive amount of quality cleavage.

"Hi," she said, even that simple word slurring under her intoxication. She grabbed his wrist for balance.

Rasputin smiled. Drunk and touching him. It was just too easy.

"Hi, beautiful. Are you enjoying yourself tonight?"

He conjured the power of the vial on the chain around his neck, a millennium of ancient vampire blood mingling together and giving him the ability to pick through any mortal's mind and alter their mood, their thoughts.

Maybe it was too soon to take Katie, but he could have this woman with no more effort than ten seconds of concentration.

She blinked up at him, tottering on her heels. "I would be doing better if you would fuck me."

"I would be happy to," he told her with a smile, letting go of his necklace. "Lead the way, babe."

FOUR

WHEN her lunch break came around, Katie told her boss she was sick and needed to go home. She couldn't take the strain of wearing a fake smile and pretending she was perfectly fine for one more second. He wasn't happy with her, but he let her go when she feigned retching sounds and slapped her hand over her mouth.

Hurrying to the elevator, Katie bit her fingernail and thought about calling Nick. Nick would have advice and would calm her down. He was like a big brother to her, and was responsible for saving her life when she had been shot and almost killed during the Russian Revolution. He had turned her to vampire and provided for her for many years.

But he was at work himself, since he was a night bodyguard for Roberto Donatelli, vice president of the Vampire Nation. Which meant that Peter—who was at best a brat, at worst mentally unstable—was up in their suite of rooms with Kelsey Columbia, his loosely termed babysitter. Kelsey wasn't all that bright from what Katie could tell, and Peter was more insane adult than thirteen-year-old child, but Katie suspected that the babysitting arrangement kept them both from getting in trouble.

In any case, she didn't want to encounter either one of them, so while she decided she would go to her own room, she hoped like hell that Peter wouldn't sense her presence next door and decide to drop by for a chat. Pushing the button a second time for the elevator, she waited impatiently, wanting to be alone.

God, why did Michael have to show up? Why did he have to be as beautiful as he'd always been? Even more so than that, why did he still have any effect on her? Her words may have been repellent, but her miserable, lonely little heart had wanted to fling her arms around him and kiss the snot out of him.

"Going up?"

Katie jumped. Shit, the bastard had just walked right up next to her while she'd been lost in thoughts about same-said bastard. "Not if you are."

"Maria." He held up his hand as she opened her mouth to protest the use of her former name. "Sorry. Katie. I just want to talk to you. I've been looking for you for nearly a century. After everything we shared, can you at least give me five minutes?"

That made all thoughts of his cuteness and the taste of his sexy lips flee. Was he freaking serious? She knew precisely what they had shared, and it had obviously meant way more to her than it had to him. "Excuse me? I don't owe you jack shit, buddy."

The elevator door had opened and a couple exiting glanced at her curiously as her voice rose in agitation, but Katie ignored them. She moved forward, intending to go up in the elevator and into her room, slamming the door in his face if she had to. She could not deal with this, not knowing that he was the one who had alerted the Bolsheviks as to her family's location, which had resulted in their imprisonment and death. Not knowing that he had also been responsible for the theft and sale of her family's most prized possessions to line his pockets and protect his sorry ass from the new regime wresting power from them.

Michael's eyes narrowed, his chin set. "Oh, no? You don't owe me a thing? How about a goddamn explanation as to why you're so clearly angry with me when as far as I knew, even when we were separated physically we were still together emotionally. We never broke off our relationship, you were just taken away from me."

Yeah, when his henchmen came and collected her and tossed her in prison. Anger coursed through her as she turned around to face the front of the elevator.

"Don't play stupid with me, it's totally unattractive on you." Katie hit the button for her floor, patting her pocket to make sure she had her room key.

"Did something happen that I'm supposed to know about? Because I'm totally in the dark here." He hit the pause button, and the elevator ground to a halt.

"What the hell?" Katie hit the button to start it up again. "You're psychotic."

"You're the one acting insane."

The elevator opened at her floor. "You're not following me to my room," she informed him.

"Yes, I am."

Somehow she had known he was going to say that. "I'm going to call security again. How did you get back into the casino anyway?"

Following her down the hall, Michael said, "I have two talents—I move quickly, and I'm very charming."

Katie made the mistake of glancing over at him. Oh, she knew he was charming. It was the very first thing she'd realized about him after she'd finished drooling over his looks and had first spoken to him all those years ago. He could charm the skin off a snake. Or in her case, the panties off a princess. Bastard. She just couldn't use that word enough to describe him.

"Well, why don't you move quickly and charmingly back to the elevator and get the hell out of my life?"

She stopped in front of her door, and Michael ground to a halt beside her.

He put his hands on her shoulders and gave her a little

shake. "Explain this anger to me. What happened? The last time I saw you, we were dancing in the garden at the summer palace. You looked stunning that night, your skin and lips and hair perfect, your smile and eyes filled with love for me. I kissed you good night under the moonlight, do you remember that?"

Katie crossed her arms across her chest, her heart beating unnaturally fast. She wanted to run, wanted to smack him, make the flow of words from his mouth stop, but she just stood mute, immobile.

"I had just given you an orgasm behind the copse, do you remember that? I slid my hand under your gown and when you came, I covered your cries with my own mouth, and it was the most amazing feeling to give you that pleasure, to share that night with you." His hand reached out and brushed her hair back, his dark eyes mesmerizing. "Please tell me you remember, my love."

She remembered. She remembered everything between them, every glance, every smile, every word. Every kiss. Every touch and every sigh of pleasure he had coaxed from her. After all this time, she remembered. She had been in love, hopelessly and passionately in love, and he had betrayed her.

"That was then, this is now," she said, striving for flippant but sounding more than a little hysterical.

Pulling her room key out of her pocket, she tried to insert it in the lock, but her hands were shaking too badly to align it correctly.

Michael hadn't responded to her words, but he was still standing there, watching her fumble. Wanting more than anything to get into her room and be alone to scream or cry, whichever came out first, Katie finally got the key card in, only to pull it out and see that the light was red, not green, and that the door was still locked.

"Shit." She must have pulled it out too quickly.

"Let me help you." Michael reached for the key card.

Katie yanked it out of his reach, irrationally irritated with the fact that he would just step in now, over something as stupid as a key card, when she had needed him all those years ago, damn it. Needed him there when she was terrified to die, grieving for her lost future, and nursing a broken heart. Where the hell had he been then?

"No, I've got it." She stuck the key card in and had the same negative result.

"Just let me help you." Michael touched the card, intending to take it out of her hand.

Katie held on to it. "No."

Michael pulled harder and they engaged in a ludicrous tug-of-war over the stupid room key.

"Let go!" she yelled.

"No. Let me help you, goddamn it."

"No." They were both pulling so hard now that their arms were springing back and forth like a saw. They narrowed their eyes at each other, neither intending to give in despite the ridiculousness of it.

With their vampire strength they could yank incredibly hard, and when Michael gave an extra hard tug, he pulled the plastic from her hand. The freedom from her resistance sent his elbow catapulting back into the wall, sinking a solid three inches into the drywall.

He couldn't get it out.

Katie watched him turn around and remove his elbow with his other hand, swearing the whole time, and she bit her lip.

Now that was funny.

Considering the glare he shot her, he obviously didn't agree.

Which made Katie actually laugh out loud.

Too bad vampires couldn't be captured on film. She'd love a snapshot of this for posterity.

Michael in Wall, from the Bastard series.

She laughed even louder.

MICHAEL had no idea what exactly was so riotously funny. He had his elbow stuck in the hotel hallway wall, and for what? So he could claim possession of Katie's room key?

They were both acting insane, and he had no idea how they had gotten to this point or how to get them back out of it.

Katie knew, or thought she knew, something, and as a result she was angry with him. Unfortunately, he had no clue what it was he had allegedly done that had made her this upset with him, and it was infuriating that she wouldn't just tell him.

After he retrieved his elbow, he crammed her key into the slot, relieved to see the green light blink on. He shoved the door and held it open for her.

"Feel free to enter whenever you're done laughing at me."

Her laughter cut out. "You're not coming in."

Michael sighed. He didn't know what else to do or say. "Fine. I guess I can't make you tell me what's bothering you."

She didn't answer, but her hand went to the necklace she was wearing, and she pulled it out from under her shirt, moving the gold piece back and forth on the chain in a subconscious gesture.

Michael did a double take. He knew that necklace. "How long have you been wearing that?" he asked her.

"Huh?" Katie glanced down at her chest. "Oh, a couple of days. My brother found it with some old stuff of his and he was going to pitch it, so I rescued it. It was my mother's, you know."

The softness that came into her voice when she mentioned the tsarina made Michael's heart break all over for her. Maybe that was where the anger came from, even if directing it at him was misplaced. Katie had watched her family die. Maybe she was afraid to love, afraid she would lose him again, like she had lost her parents and her sisters.

"I know," he said softly. "I remember."

Only it was more than just a showy piece of jewelry.

Its appearance around Katie's neck a mere two days earlier explained the sudden movement of Rasputin. That was no coincidence.

Michael now knew why the former holy man had come to Vegas, and he needed to talk to Sergei about what they should do about it, and how to protect Katie.

But first he would leave the woman he loved with another reminder of her past.

"I brought something for you," he told her. "I've been saving it for when I would see you again." He ran his thumb over her cheek, swallowing hard at the feel of her softness beneath his touch-deprived fingers. Michael dropped his hand and reached for his pants pocket.

"If you whip out your penis, I'm screaming," Katie said.

That made Michael laugh. "No, that's not what I had in mind, but I can arrange that if you'd like." His cock would gladly leap out of his pants, given that he'd had an erection since the minute he'd spotted her behind the blackjack table.

"No, thanks." She gave a rueful smile. "And I guess if I think about it, I doubt you've been saving your penis until you could see me again."

He actually had, though she would never believe him, not given her reaction to him so far. But he did tell her, "I've been saving a lot of things for you."

She just rolled her eyes, though her cheeks were unnaturally pink for a vampire.

Deciding not to push his luck, and needing to talk to Sergei, Michael pulled the tiny enamel box out of his pocket and put it in her hand. "I believe this is yours."

Her expression puzzled as she looked down at the elaborate box in her hand, and then her head snapped up, recognition in her eyes. "Michael . . . how . . . why . . . ?"

"I'll explain later. Just remember that I've never stopped loving you. Not for one minute of one day." He handed her his room key. "I'm in fifteen-twenty. Call or come see me anytime you want."

Katie didn't speak, but she did accept the card with a nod.

"And stay away from Rasputin," he told her, before moving down the hall and forsaking the elevator for the stairs. Five floors was nothing to a vampire, and he was in a hurry.

FIVE

"I know what he wants," Michael told Sergei, pacing in his hotel room. "Katie has the necklace. The one with the blood in it, the one Rasputin gave her mother."

Sergei was always so calm, sometimes it irritated Michael. Now was one of those times.

"Ah," Sergei said mildly. "That makes sense. That's how he knew Katie was here in Vegas. That vial contains the power to reveal the thoughts of the person wearing it. I imagine he'll try to get it back."

Michael stared at his longtime friend, sitting on the couch in his khaki pants and golf shirt, his stylish glasses sliding down his nose. "Yes, I imagine he will. And we have to stop him, damn it. I don't want him anywhere near Katie and I don't want him to have any more power than he already does."

"I agree."

There it was again. That annoying nonchalance. "Don't you even care? Don't you want this to end? We've been tailing this bastard for almost a century and you act like it's no big deal. Like it's been a drop in the bucket of time."

"It has," Sergei said with a shrug. "We're going to live forever, Michael. This is a job to me. And when Rasputin is dead or emasculated of his power, I'll find another one. There's no point in being emotional about it."

Michael stared at him in disbelief. "I am emotional about it. I'm sorry. This man manipulated the politics of our country, influencing our tsarina to the point that he probably contributed to the revolution. He has spent his life engaged in everything unethical and immoral he could get his hands on, including running a porn empire that abuses children. He disgusts me to the point where I cannot wait until he has breathed his last breath, and now he is trailing the woman I love, and I have no doubt he will stop at nothing to get the vial from her." He forced himself to unclench his fists. "I am emotional about it and I am not going to apologize for it."

"No one said you had to."

Michael scoffed, shaking his head. "No. No, they didn't. But tell me what motivates you . . . What are you passionate about? What the hell matters to you?"

Sergei just stared at him. "I'm not passionate about anything. And I'm glad I'm not. Look what it's done to you. You've spent ninety years saving yourself for a woman who just rejected you. I have no interest in that kind of pain."

It wasn't like he was particularly fond of it either. But he wouldn't take it back, and he didn't regret devoting his immortal life to finding Katie, even if she hadn't given him a warm welcome. He would never, ever regret loving her, and he would never *stop* loving her.

"Then I guess we can agree to disagree. I can't live without passion and purpose. I can't separate emotion from motive. Now, will you please go and make sure that Rasputin is nowhere near Katie? I need to sit and think. I need a plan to divert his attention from her."

"Sure." Sergei stood. "No offense, Michael. I'm not criticizing you."

"I know." Michael tried to give him a smile, but couldn't quite manage it. "You've always been much more mercenary than me, and you have the bank account to prove it."

He meant it as a joke, since his acquaintance with Sergei went back to the days when he had hired him to help execute Rasputin, before any of them had understood the world of the undead, and that Rasputin was one of them, a vampire. Their assassination attempts had been unsuccessful, and in the end had resulted in both of them becoming vampires themselves, but Michael knew Sergei had never been involved for politics or love of country. It had been for money, and Michael would never truly comprehend that.

"That's true. I admit it, and I'm not ashamed of it. If I'm going to live for eternity, I'm damn well not going to do it in poverty."

All Michael wanted was to live his life with Katie. Feeling a wave of sorrow and anger washing over him, he turned and headed to the mini-fridge in the hotel room. He had a few bags of blood in there, and he needed the distraction, the tinny taste of satisfaction in his mouth.

"I'll catch up with you later. Thanks. Thanks for everything."

He did owe Sergei a thank-you. The conversation had cemented for him that he would keep trying to talk to Katie until he got a straight answer from her.

She was his—his best friend, his soul mate, his destiny, his past and his future, and he wasn't going to rest until she agreed with him.

KATIE closed the door to her suite behind her and bent over, giving in to the weakness in the knees she'd been fighting against since she had first heard Michael's voice a mere hour ago.

Just sixty minutes had passed, and it felt like her entire existence, her comfortable, predictable immortal life, had been turned ass over tail. She never should have tempted fate by complaining about boredom, because this form of excitement was guaranteed to either break her heart all over again or make her vomit in her own mouth. Neither a pretty option.

And the most irritating thing of all was that she'd wanted all these years to tell Michael exactly what she thought of him and his deceptions, and she hadn't gotten one eloquent and scathing line of her speech out. All she'd done was snipe at him and fight with him over her damn room key like a couple of dogs with a chew toy.

It was all just wrong. So damn wrong.

Lifting her hand, she studied the enamel box, covered in a red-and-green floral pattern, the bottom a burnished gold. It had been her mother's, meant for storing her medicinal powders. Her father had brought it back from France for her, an expensive little trinket that her mother had kept on her vanity.

It had been left behind when her family had been removed from the palace. It was just one of hundreds of objects that had to be abandoned. Some had been more personal than priceless, others had been worth a fortune. That was why Katie had assumed Michael had sold them all.

This box, while not the most expensive of her parents' possessions, would command a fair amount on the open market. She would have thought it was long gone. It made her wonder what else Michael was holding on to that belonged to her family.

And why had he chosen to return it to her?

He had also seemed surprised to see her wearing her mother's necklace.

Katie walked into her suite and set the box down on the coffee table, staring at it. Why was Michael really in Las Vegas? How the hell had he found her?

Then there was Rasputin . . .

There were answers out there, and she wanted them. Not even bothering to change out of her work clothes, Katie pulled the room key Michael had given her out of her pocket and stared at it.

If he had more of her family's treasures, she wanted them back.

She wanted answers to nearly a century of questions.

And she wanted to see that he felt some measure of remorse for seducing an innocent young girl just to use her and toss her away.

Maybe she'd never get the latter, but she was going to harass him until he gave her the former.

M ICHAEL went to answer the door, hoping Sergei had some reassuring news for him. He was no closer himself to a decision as to what to do about Rasputin and Katie's necklace, and despite Sergei's detachment, he could use someone to bounce thoughts and ideas off of.

Except that it wasn't Sergei standing in his doorway. It was Katie.

"Hi," he said, pleased despite the sour look on her face. "Come in." He held the door open wide and fought the urge to smile. God, she was so beautiful. It amazed him that one woman could have so much inner and outer beauty. He had missed her so much, and he just wanted to drink in the sight of her.

He wanted to touch her as well, but he didn't want to lose a hand.

She walked into the room, arms over her chest. "Explain why you gave that box to me."

So she wasn't going in for any chitchat or social niceties. That was just fine with him. They needed to talk. Maybe she even needed to yell at him or hurl a vase at his head. Whatever. He'd take it. He would bleed for her if it meant she would look at him the way she used to.

"I gave it to you because it's yours. Or technically, it's both yours and your brother's. I would have given it to you years ago if I had known where you were."

Leaning against the closet door only a few feet into the hotel room, she eyed him. "Why? Why didn't you just sell it along with everything else? You could have gotten a decent price for it."

That confused him, and he leaned on the opposite wall, sticking his hands in his pockets so he wouldn't reach for her. "Why would I do that? It's your family's. I took it out of the palace so that when I saw you all again, I could return it to your parents. When I heard what had happened, I . . ." Michael paused, his throat tightening. "I thought you were dead. So I kept it for me, as a way to keep a part of you, but also on the hope that somehow you had escaped. When I heard that bodies for you and your brother were never found, I was so relieved, I can't even tell you. I looked for you. But I couldn't find you."

Now Michael did reach out and stroke his hand down her rich brown hair. "I can't tell you how hard it's been, hoping like hell you were out there somewhere, but not being able to find you. I've always thought you were alive, but it's maddening not to know for certain, to not see you for myself."

She moved out of his touch, her hand coming up to stave him off. "Wait a minute. Are you saying you didn't intend for us to die? That you just meant for us to be imprisoned?"

It took him a second to digest her words. Then he stood up straight. Oh, God, so that's what she thought? "Sweetheart, what are you talking about? I didn't mean for you to die, I didn't mean for you to be imprisoned. I was trying to protect all of you."

Her cheeks had gone pale, her green eyes wide. "But I

saw you that day they took us. You were with the men down the hallway who were ordering our removal, the men who were commanding the guards to haul us out like common criminals."

No wonder she was so angry. She thought he had betrayed her family. "No, no. That is not what happened." He gestured to the room. "Please, come sit down. Let's talk. Let me explain."

She did, albeit reluctantly, dragging her heels on the carpet. Katie sat on the edge of the small sofa, her hands on her knees. "I'm listening."

He sat on the coffee table in front of her. "You know that as a distant relative of your father's I was involved in politics. I was also one of the principal players in the plan to assassinate Rasputin in the year before the revolution. Of course, at the time, we didn't understand his immortality, so we were unsuccessful. But we wanted him removed to prevent his influence over your mother. It was obvious to most of us that as an empire we were headed for turmoil and upheaval, and we wanted to avoid that. We wanted to transition peacefully to a governing body. But as you know, that isn't what happened. So I ingratiated myself to the Bolsheviks as someone who would support them, so that I could protect all of you. That was always my primary goal—to protect you. And of course, to do what was best for Russia."

Katie shook her head. "I don't know what to believe. I thought, when I saw you looking so chummy with those men, that you had betrayed us. I don't know if I can believe that you didn't now, after all these years of being so convinced of that."

Michael put his hands on her knees. "Baby, why would I? My God, I loved you. Still do. Do you understand that? I *loved* you, and wanted to spend my whole life with you. I wanted you to bear my children and grow old with me. You know your father disapproved of our match, that he wanted you to marry a grand German

prince. And you know that I was willing to disregard
that, to ruin my career and political aspirations by elop-
ing with you."

He would have done anything to be with her. He still
would. Rubbing his thumbs over her knees, he leaned
closer to her, breathing in her floral scent, sighing at the
pleasure of feeling her, seeing her after all of these years.
"My Maria, I love you. Then. Now. Always."

Running his finger over her soft, plump lower lip, Michael stared at her as her eyes grew moist and a single tear
rolled down her cheek. He wiped it with the pad of his
thumb. "They were going to kill you immediately, that
very first day, but we got them to agree to your contain-
ment at Ekaterinburg instead. We had our own guard pos-
ing as one of them. It was never supposed to end the way
it did. When I heard . . . I wanted to die, too."

"How did you end up a vampire?" she whispered.

Grateful she wasn't yelling at him or accusing him of a
pack of lies, Michael answered, moving his hands to her
shoulders, her hair, to anything and everything he could
touch. His tactile memories of her were reawakening as
he rediscovered the feel of her skin, the angles and curves
of her arms and shoulders. "After one altercation with
Rasputin, I was dying. Our man, the guard we sent to
Ekaterinburg, was a vampire. He turned me. That's why I
hoped you might still be alive. I thought maybe somehow
he had saved you."

Her eyes went wide. "Nick? Was it Nick you sent?"

"That wasn't his name, no. Why?"

"Because it was a guard in that room who saved Peter
and me. He was a vampire and he turned us. I can't
imagine there could be two vampire guards in the room.
We've been living with Nick all these years. Changed
our names, moved away, got jobs. He's been like a big
brother to me."

While part of Michael ached that he hadn't been there
for Katie, that he hadn't been the one to acclimate her to a
new life as a vampire and help ease her grief over losing

her family, he was glad she'd had someone with her. And was profoundly grateful that she hadn't died in that room.

"I'm glad he was there for you. And I'm so, so sorry for what happened to your family, for what you've endured. I failed you, and for that I'm sorry." Michael dropped his head, fighting the very unmanly urge to cry.

Katie stared at the top of Michael's head, and she wanted desperately to believe him. If he hadn't betrayed her, then it was all okay. Not that she had lost her family, but that she had given her heart to this man. Thoughts and emotions were a muddled mess in her mind, and she still had questions, still had doubts, but she had to touch him. It had been so very long and she ached to run her fingers through his hair.

He sighed when she did, brushing an errant lock off his forehead and trailing her fingers across his temple.

"It was horrific," she told him in a whisper. "Until the very end, my father didn't believe it would happen. He was the proverbial lamb being led to slaughter. I knew. I could see it in their faces, knew it the second we walked into that tiny room. What else would they be doing? But there was nothing I could do. I tried to hide Peter, but it was useless, and as I lay dying, I hoped I would descend to Hell so that I could meet you there and spit in your face when I saw you."

Michael's hand tightened on her knee, and he glanced up at her from under his long black eyelashes. "You always did say exactly what you were feeling. I'm glad we were both spared that particular conversation over fire and brimstone."

Katie gave a small smile, the tears in her eyes blurring her vision. "The box? How did you get it?"

"I pocketed what I could before the palace was ransacked."

She nodded, still not sure what to believe, but at the moment, she no longer cared. She simply wanted to be in Michael's arms again. "Kiss me, Michael."

He gave her a look that was so filled with love and passion, Katie almost glanced down to see if he had seared her clothes off.

"I'll do anything you want," he told her.

What she wanted was to have sex with him, and somehow she didn't think he was going to object to that.

SIX

KATIE wanted to make the first move, wanted Michael to understand that despite the doubts and confused thoughts rattling around in her, she wanted him. She wanted to just let go and sink into the comfort of his arms around her. But she hesitated when he didn't just reach forward and kiss her, and she wasn't sure why. It wasn't like she had been shy about her sexual feelings for Michael when they were young. In fact, he had tried to be noble and hold off until they were married, but she had tempted him to the point that he had given in—with great gusto.

But maybe now, after all this time, she needed him to take the first step to bridge the gap of a century.

"Do you remember the first time?" she asked him in a whisper.

His eyes darkened as his fingers moved further up her thighs in delicious circles. "Of course. It was after some elaborate dinner party for a foreign diplomat, a German, and it made me jealous to watch you being trotted around the room by your mother as she introduced you to a handful of German eligibles. Men she deemed worthy of your hand in marriage, unlike me."

"All I wanted was to be with you, talking, laughing. You always made me laugh, Michael. We shared the same sense of humor. Every single one of those men she introduced me to were wrong, completely wrong for me." Katie put her hand over his, stroking him in kind as he caressed her. "Only you were right for me."

The intensity in his eyes made her shiver. Gone from both of them was the vibrancy and naïveté of youth, but the connection, the love, was still there.

"I'm sure that jealousy was part of why I gave in that night," Michael said. "I had wanted so desperately to wait because I wanted you to understand I respected you above all others. I loved you as a wife, forever." He gave a rueful smile. "But it was a constant battle, you know, between the desire to hold you in my arms, our bodies giving each other pleasure, and the need to wait until we were legally married. That night I couldn't resist what you offered so sweetly and passionately."

"I couldn't wait anymore. I wanted to be yours, and it was lovely," Katie whispered. "You took your time, did all the things that you knew I would like, so that I was ready."

"I wanted it to be good for you."

"It was."

"For me, it was the most special night of my life." Michael cupped his hands around her cheeks and moved his mouth softly over hers. "Until now."

Katie closed her eyes as he kissed her, his lips a delicate brush over hers. God, she had missed him. Missed this feeling. No man had ever been able to arouse as much honest, raw desire from her as Michael had. It was just a kiss, a light and innocent press. She knew already that he could talk her into anything sexually, and she knew that was the advantage, the benefit, of being in love. Sex had been physically gratifying with other men, but never the same. Never the same as looking up at a man as he filled her, her heart sighing with sweet, earnest love.

"Tonight I have what I thought I'd lost forever," he told her, his voice a warm tickle against her ear. "And I want to show you how much I love you, how I've never stopped loving you."

Katie didn't know what to say, how to articulate the emotion that had lodged itself in her chest, but she didn't have time to speak before Michael scooped her up into his arms and stood.

"Let me make love to you, angel."

Like she was going to say no to that? Katie slipped her arms around his neck. "You are more than welcome to make love to me as long as you'd like."

She meant that most sincerely. "You don't even need to ask."

Michael gave a soft laugh as he carried her to the other side of the room where the bed was. That was the convenient thing about a hotel room—it only took sixty seconds before she was lying on her back on the comforter, and Michael was tugging her clunky work shoes off.

He peeled her socks off, too, running his fingertips along the bottom of her feet. Then, before she could protest that it tickled, Michael was lying beside her. "I've missed the feel of you." He breathed in deeply. "The smell of you." His tongue trailed across her bottom lip. "The taste of you."

Katie sighed, closing her eyes to enjoy the feel of his caress across her stomach where her shirt had ridden up, indulging her senses in the nearness of his masculine body, the sound of his breathing, the feel of his soft hair beneath her fingertips. He started to undo the buttons on her white shirt, and Katie shifted onto her side, opening her eyes to see him. It was a given she was a little biased, but she thought he was gorgeous. Princely, ironically enough, with his long nose, chiseled cheekbones, and striking eyes. He had been a Russian prince, though unable to offer the grand political alliance her parents had craved for her. But he had been regal and charming.

Now, the way he was staring at her, lust lit in his expression, his every movement, he was more intense than charming, but just as confident, aristocratic. When he finished opening all the buttons on her shirt and cupped her breast, Katie pressed into his touch, the simple contact kicking the warmth between her thighs up a notch.

"I haven't been with a woman since you," he told her.

She stopped thinking about how good it felt to have him stroking her nipple through the satin of her bra. "Excuse me?" she asked blankly. He couldn't possibly mean . . .

"I haven't had sex since that last night we were together."

"Are you serious?" That stunned her. She couldn't even fathom an adult male going all those years without sex.

"Yes. In my mind we were still together. I was being faithful to you."

Katie didn't know what to say, and tears clouded her eyes. That was the most romantic, yet strangest thing any man had ever said to her. "Wow, I don't know what to say."

Because she couldn't exactly say the same in return. Not that she'd been racking up the bed partners, but there had been a few. All futile attempts to banish the memory of Michael. Encounters that had shown her that while the body could easily be satisfied, the heart and soul were greedy little bitches—they wanted what they wanted and wouldn't take any sort of substitute.

"You don't have to say anything. I just wanted you to know."

Then he left no time or ability for her to answer when he pushed back her bra and took her into his mouth. Katie arched into the touch, gasping when his teeth lightly skimmed her nipple. Before she could blink, he had her shirt down her arms and off, the bra following suit.

He licked and sucked both breasts, his tongue rolling around each nipple in tight, teasing circles. It was delightful, each flick of his tongue tip sending a warm jolt through her, the ache of desire grabbing a hold of her body and squeezing tighter. Katie moved restlessly against the pillows, letting her hands fall to her sides.

"You're so beautiful," he murmured. "The most beautiful woman on the planet."

"Don't exaggerate," she protested, even as she flushed with pleasure at his words.

Michael looked at her in a way so intense, so loving, so sexy, Katie lost her ability to breathe.

"Oh, I'm not exaggerating," he said as he undid the button on her black pants.

"Maybe a little?" Katie let her eyes slide shut when his hand slid down into her pants to cup her panties, his thumb so close to where she wanted him to touch, yet painfully far away.

"No," he said, at the same time he pulled his hand away. "You are beautiful. Stunning. Gorgeous. Amazing. Tell me you believe me."

Lamenting the loss of his touch, moved by the sincerity and depth of his words, Katie nodded, unable to force the words out of her tight throat.

"Good."

Then Michael pulled her pants and panties down in one swift motion, tossing them on the floor. The cool air hit her equally cool skin and Katie shivered, from both the breeze and anticipation. He brushed his hand over her, gently pushing her legs apart and then his mouth was on her.

Katie couldn't prevent a moan from slipping past her lips. Dammit, that felt so good, just the slow and leisurely slide of his tongue over her, up and down, warm and sensual. It felt decadent to just lie there and have him coaxing a languid pleasure from her, her eyes drifting closed. He worshipped her with his tongue in a nice easy rhythm, occasionally dipping inside the moist heat of her body, before showering more attention on her tight clitoris.

It was amazing, to think that this was real, that they were here together, after all this time. It had a surreal quality, like a soft rumpled fantasy, like the whisper of a long-lost memory winding through a lonely mind. She had never thought to be with Michael again, this way, his fingers on her thighs, his mouth expressing his love in an intimate physical gesture that left her floating in pleasure.

When she started to feel restless, her ankles moving on

the bed, her back arching, when the need to either orgasm or shift positions became frenetic, Katie grabbed Michael's head and dug her hands into his hair. "Come here," she told him.

"Why? I'm enjoying this." He gave another lingering lick.

Oh, she was, too. "But I want to touch you. At the same time you're touching me."

Michael raised an eyebrow. "Are you saying . . ."

She shot him a grin. "Yes." As much as she loved him offering such delicious devotion to her, she wanted to run her hands over his hard body, taste his flesh, take him in her mouth and give him as much pleasure in return as he was giving her.

Michael squeezed Katie's thighs, his erection responding to her saucy smile by growing hard enough to cut glass. A hundred years was a long time to go without sex, but that wasn't the only reason. Not only was she damn beautiful, she was sexy and passionate as well. He had always appreciated her enthusiasm, and it turned him on beyond anything to know that she wanted him, that she enjoyed sex as much as he did.

"Well, I'm not stupid enough to say no to that," he told her, shifting his position on the bed.

His tongue had barely slid across her clitoris when her fingers gripped the bottom of his cock and her warm mouth covered him. Michael groaned, closing his eyes against the wave of pleasure that crashed over him. God, that felt amazing. Each stroke, him on her, her on him, back and forth, over and over, shoved him deeper into ecstasy. There was nothing but the two of them, in that moment, bodies entwined, flesh to flesh, soul to soul.

When it became too much, when he was too close to losing it, Michael pulled back and moved quickly before Katie could protest. She was wiping her moist lips, about to voice a protest, her eyes heavy with desire, when he moved between her thighs and pushed into her.

She gasped. He groaned. Michael paused, savoring the

sensation of throbbing in her tight body, his tongue thick, body covered with a hot sheen of sweat. "Oh, Maria, he said, unable to force her new name past his lips. "You feel . . . so good."

It wasn't unique or romantic or prizewinning, but he was incapable of thinking beyond simple words, reduced to nothing but sensation. Michael started to move inside her, and when she lifted her hips to meet him, nails digging into his back, he thrust harder, faster.

Katie was tearing into his flesh, body arching up, cries careening and desperate, spurring him on, before she startled the hell out of him by sinking her fangs into his shoulder. He paused inside her, erection full and swollen, her heat surrounding him, as she sucked his blood, the pull of her teeth an erotic walk across his veins.

Never, in his entire long life, had anything felt as amazing and sensual and all-consuming as the feel of her in him and him in her simultaneously.

She fell back against the pillow, lips crimson from his blood. "Oh, I'm coming."

So was he. "Come for me," he demanded even as he felt her orgasm in its beginning quiver, her muscles contracting around him.

"Yes!" she said, squeezing his back even tighter.

Michael let go, stopped trying to make it last, and just pounded into her, his own orgasm joining hers in a hot, frantic blending of their bodies.

"I love you." she said.

A hundred years of anguish disappeared for him instantly. "I love you, too."

MICHAEL lay in bed with Katie, content to just hold her against his chest. He was thirsty, and would enjoy a good glass of blood, but he had no desire or ambition to get up and leave the warm bed. But Katie started fidgeting, her hand repeatedly moving over her neck and collarbone.

"What's the matter?" he asked her.

"This necklace itches like crazy. But I don't want to take it off. I know it's stupid, but I really want to wear it."

Michael shifted so he could see. Her skin beneath the chain was no longer alabaster, but an angry red, almost like a burn. Vampires didn't get skin rashes, so he knew it had something to do with the power of the vial. This could be his opportunity to get the necklace away from her without her being suspicious. He didn't want it leading Rasputin to Katie, but neither did he want to reveal the whole of what it was, unsure of what her reaction would be.

"It looks like it's the chain that's irritating your skin. Why don't I take it and get a new chain for you?"

"Oh, okay, that's sweet of you." She turned her head and smiled at him. "Do I have to take it off or can you just go buy a new chain?"

"It's kind of a funny shape, sweetheart, I think I need to take it with me to make sure I can fit the chain through the hole."

"Good point." Katie reached up and took off the necklace. She squeezed the egg and sunburst before carefully handing it over to him.

Michael set it on the nightstand beside the bed and told her, "I'm very happy. I hope you are, too."

"I am."

"I want to be with you." He pulled her closer, wanting to feel her whole body caressing the length of him.

"I want to be with you, too."

"Do you believe me about the past? Do you trust me?"

Katie hesitated slightly. "I want to."

He did not like the sound of that. "I'm telling you the truth. If we're going to be together, you need to accept it."

Hell, he wasn't trying to be stubborn or a jackass, but if they were going to build a future together, they had to put the past to rest. They needed to heal the hurts, and the only way to do that was to trust each other. He trusted her, believed in her feelings and her intentions, and he needed the same in return. It had been so long that he'd been without her, he needed to know that she was in this for real, for the long haul.

Katie couldn't believe Michael was going to ruin the perfectly blissful moment of lying in bed together, satisfied and in love.

But he clearly was.

"Well?" he asked.

"Michael, don't push this." Katie turned onto her side so she could look at him. "I just had my whole perception of what happened turned upside down. Of course I still have doubts and fear and hesitation. I think that's perfectly natural given what has happened."

She didn't want to think about this, worry about the future. Making love to Michael again had been so satisfying, physically and emotionally, and she just wanted to savor the sensation, the perfect moment of contentedness she was living in.

Because when she started to think, doubts crept in. It was a lifetime of misperception—or so he told her. If she started analyzing, wondering, she wasn't sure if she could trust him. Hell, even saying he hadn't been with another woman wasn't logical if she dissected it. That could just as easily be a lie as well, and she didn't want to be forced to confront that.

"So what are we supposed to do? How long am I supposed to wait until you decide you trust me? And what does that even mean . . . '? How can we have a relationship when you think I'm a complete asshole?"

She sighed. So much for not having to confront the situation. He was going to be irrational. Fabulous. "I never said you were a complete asshole. I said I want to believe you. I'm trying to believe you. I just need some time and some reassurance. Is that so much to ask for?"

He sat up in bed and tossed the covers off. "I have no idea how to do that. And while I understand what you're saying, and I know you've been hurt—so have I." Michael swung his legs around and put his feet on the floor. He glanced over his shoulder at her. "I don't know how to be with you and know that you don't believe me. That you want to believe me, because you love me, but that even any small part of you could suspect I'm the kind of man who would betray my lover and her family . . . I just can't be comfortable with that."

Katie pulled the covers over her bare chest, a chill rushing over her body. "What are you saying?"

"I'm saying that you're either with me one hundred percent or you're not. That if you need time to decide what is right and what is wrong and how you feel, I think you need to do that separate from me. I can't be with you, fall in love with you all over again, and yet be waiting for the other shoe to drop. Do you understand? I can't be wondering all the time if today is the day you decide I'm a scoundrel and leave me."

She did understand that. She just didn't like it. Because she couldn't give him what he was asking for.

"Michael, I want to, believe me, I do. I just can't right now, not yet." She ran her fingers down his strong and muscular back. "My heart was shattered into a thousand pieces. I can't glue it back together overnight."

Katie fought against the tears that were threatening, unable to swallow past the sudden tightness in her throat.

He half turned. "And I understand, I do. But I guess I need to protect myself as much as you need to protect yourself."

She watched him stand up and put on his boxer shorts, not looking at her. "So what does that mean? Where does that leave us?"

Michael ran his fingers through his hair, his expression troubled but determined. "It means that I'm giving you the space to decide what it is you believe, what it is you want. I'll leave Vegas." He rummaged around on the dresser across from the bed, writing on the hotel notepad before turning back to her. Holding up a key, he said, "When you're ready, use this key. Here's the address."

The pad of paper and the key sailed through the air and

landed on the comforter in front of her knee. She picked the pad up and read an address in Birmingham, England. Katie fingered the key, running the tip of her finger across the jagged edge, not sure what to say.

"I . . . I love you," she finally said, letting the tears she'd been trying to contain push forth.

Michael sighed. He leaned over and kissed her forehead. "I love you, too. More than anything in this world. When you're ready, come to England. Until then, I bid you adieu, my love. I'm going to take a shower."

"So this is good-bye?" She gripped the notepad and the key tighter.

"This is good-bye. Until you decide otherwise."

Then Michael turned and went into the bathroom, closing the door with a soft click.

Katie sat on the bed, still rumpled and warm from their lovemaking, and wondered why it was that her past emitted such a loud echo that she could no longer hear the future.

SEVEN

AFTER she pulled on her work clothes from the night before, Katie fought back the tears as she slunk back to her room, keeping her head down so she didn't have to make eye contact with anyone walking the hallway in the opposite direction. When she got to her room, she called Nick, hoping he hadn't gone to bed yet.

"Hey," she said when he answered. Then promptly burst into tears.

"What's wrong? Are you okay?"

"No. Can you come over?"

"Of course."

He was there in two minutes and the instant Katie saw his big, steady form crowding up her doorway, she launched herself into his arms and let the tears turn into sobs. It was so damn unfair that she could have Michael walk back into her life and yet be emotionally unable to hold on to him.

"Shh, it's okay." Nick patted her back and led her into the room, closing the door behind him. "What the hell happened?"

Soaking his T-shirt with tears, Katie lifted her head.

"Do you remember how I told you I was engaged? And how he betrayed me? Well, my ex-fiancé just showed up in Vegas."

"Oh, geez, I'm sorry, sweetie. Was he horrible to you?" Nick's dark eyes were filled with concern. "I can tell him to stay away from you."

Nick was a bodyguard and huge. The sight of him intimidated most men, but in this case it was ironic that Michael had technically walked away. Katie didn't need Nick to threaten him to keep his distance, which somehow made it all the worse.

"No, he wasn't horrible to me. He explained to me what happened, that he wasn't responsible for turning us in to the revolutionaries. He said he has been looking for me all these years. And I want to believe him, I do, but it's so hard. I trusted everyone in those days, and it was stupid and naïve." Katie stepped back and wiped her eyes. "I'm afraid to be hurt all over again."

"Wait a minute. You thought he turned your family in? When you told me he betrayed you I thought you meant that he had cheated on you."

Katie frowned, sniffling. "I never said he cheated on me."

"I just assumed that's what you meant. Why would you think he turned you in? What is his name?"

"Michael St. Markov. And I thought he did because he was there, that day, in the palace, looking like he was BFF with the Bolsheviks."

Nick's jaw dropped open. "Oh, my God, are you serious? Markov was your fiancé? Oh, baby, no, no, he did not turn you in. He was trying to prevent them from killing your family by being sympathetic to them so he could have a position to negotiate leniency from. He was the one who hired me to be there in that room. I was supposed to let him know if anything happened, but there was no time. They shot all of you, I turned you to vampire, and then we were on the run. I thought it was best to hide our location, our names, from everyone, including him. But I didn't know about you and him . . . I had no idea."

Katie wasn't sure if she should jump up and down for joy or if she should find a way to kick herself in the ass. "Are you sure? But why did he have my mother's enamel box?"

"Yes, I'm sure. Did you ask him about the box?"

"He said he pocketed it before our possessions were stolen and sold to save it for me."

"That sounds reasonable to me. I'm sure he risked a great deal to pilfer that. If he had been caught, it wouldn't have been good for him."

Katie put her hands over her eyes and pressed above her eyebrows. God, she had a headache. "So, why is it that I can hear you say it and believe you, but I doubted him?"

Nick gently pulled her arms down. "Because you've been hurt. That's understandable. Ninety years is a long time to have pain simmering. But the question is, do you want to be with him? Do you still love him?"

As if she'd ever stopped. "Yes, I do." The tears renewed and she had to stop speaking to choke them back. "But I've blown it."

"How did he leave it?"

"He told me if I wanted to trust him, to have a future, that I should meet him in England." She pulled the address and key out of her pocket and held them up. "I guess this is his house."

"Then I guess you need to book yourself an airline ticket and go to England."

"Do you really think I should?" Katie bit her fingernail.

"I know so. But what do you think?"

Katie felt a surge of hope rise up in her. She loved that man, with all of her girlish and now very much adult heart. "Tally ho, I think that I'm going to England."

THE necklace was off Katie. Rasputin clenched his fists in frustration. He had felt it the minute she had removed it. The power was gone, the glow of his matching vial diminished, the connection he'd felt to her life force, the sweet pulsation of her blood through her veins, gone.

"Sergei!" he shouted, climbing out of his bed in the suite of rooms they had taken. He cast a cursory glance at the woman next to him, snoring lightly in a sleep so deep it was subterranean. Between the alcohol she had consumed and the blood Rasputin had taken from her, not to mention multiple orgasms, she would be out for hours.

"Yes?" Sergei appeared in the door, not even blinking at the state of the disheveled bed, the naked woman, or the dried blood from his lover that Rasputin had smeared all over his chest, lips, and hands.

"I have to go out. When she wakes up, get rid of her."

Sergei raised an impassive eyebrow. "Kill her?"

Rasputin rolled his eyes. "No! Don't be so damn dramatic. I meant call her a fucking cab and send her home."

"Oh, okay. Absolutely."

As Rasputin started pulling on his clothes, Sergei stood in the doorway, just staring at him, eyes unblinking behind his glasses. The man was a total freak, and Rasputin wondered if it was time for a new assistant. Either that or get him a prostitute. Maybe that would loosen him up.

"Do you like women?" Rasputin asked him as he tugged on a T-shirt that smelled like sweat. He could go dig through his suitcase for a clean one, but it seemed like too much effort. "Or do you prefer men? Or are you just asexual?"

"I like women, sir. In theory."

That made Rasputin laugh. "Go out and get laid, Sergei. I'll catch up with you later."

Right now he was going to find that little bitch Katie and figure out what the hell she had done with his vial of vampire blood.

TWENTY-FOUR exhausting hours later, Katie found herself staring out the window at what was clearly a storage unit in an industrial park. "Are you sure this is right?" she asked the cab driver.

Something was wrong. Why the hell would Michael live in a storage unit?

"It's right. Unless the address you gave me was wrong." The cabdriver looked irritated, like he was tempted to grab his money and toss her out into the street so he could be on to the next fare.

Katie reread the address out loud just to make sure.

"Yes, this is it."

"Okay." Not sure what to do, Katie paid him and climbed out, grabbing her overnight bag. She stared at the building and fought the urge to cry.

She was tired and desperate for a drink, having ignored the urge to feed in her haste to get to England. Michael had checked out of the hotel before she could talk to him, so she had booked a ticket and set out, assuming when she got here she would find Michael. She didn't have a phone number for him, and now she wasn't even sure why the hell she had just assumed this was an address for his house, or that he would be there.

Adjusting the floral duffel bag in her hand, Katie decided to go to the office and ask about Michael. Hell, for all she knew he owned the storage facility. There was an ancient woman sitting hunched over a desk, her eyes magnified by her thick glasses as she shuffled through a sheaf of papers.

"Excuse me. My boyfriend is Michael St. Markov, and I believe he has a storage unit here. He gave me this address and a key." Katie pulled it out of her purse and held it up. "Could you tell me which unit is his?"

"It would be my pleasure, young lady." She tapped the keys on the computer keyboard in front of her, then squinted at the screen. "Number sixteen. One of the big ones. Just head on down the first row. It's at the end."

"Okay, thank you so much."

Katie clutched the key and headed out, grateful for the cool temperatures and overcast sky of England. She wasn't used to daywalking, and even though it was early in the day, the fierceness of a Nevada sky would have irritated her eyes and skin. In England it was manageable, and she followed the numbers down the aisle until she found sixteen. Setting her bag down, she opened it and stepped inside the cool, dark interior. There was a light switch on the wall, but she didn't need it, a benefit of her vampiric vision.

What she saw in the unit made her stop barely a foot in the door, eyes rushing over objects, heart full, tears coming freely and without restraint.

"Oh, God," she said, running her hand over the desk closest to her. It was her father's, where he used to sit and pen letters of importance to diplomats and to his advisors. On it was stacked a pile of books.

Katie sifted through them and retrieved the one that was flat and wider than the others. She flipped it open and swallowed hard. It was her sketchbook. She had been seriously lacking in technical proficiency, but she had loved to draw, and her mother had insisted on lessons. In it were poorly done sketches of her sisters standing in the garden, their hair streaming down their backs, smiles of laughter on their faces.

Running her finger over the paper, over those who had been her flesh, so irritating as only siblings could be, but so dear to her, she whispered, "I've missed you. I hope you are at peace."

She was.

Looking around the large room, every inch filled with furniture, objects, and personal effects belonging to her family, some valuable, others purely sentimental, Katie was at peace. She didn't know how Michael had accumulated all of it, but he had. He had done it for her, salvaged what he could of her childhood and her family and kept it in storage for the day he found her.

It was the most beautiful gesture she had ever experienced, and as she picked up a Fabergé egg and rolled its glossy form around her hand, its intricate patterns just as bright and wondrous as the day it had arrived at the palace, she knew that she would spend the rest of her life with Michael. That their love was as simple and pure and priceless as an artist's egg.

And she was in danger of crying again, and she didn't want to. She had a plane to catch.

So she ran her fingers over the egg, the sketchbook, one last time, then backed out. She locked the door to the unit carefully, then went to find a cab.

The man she loved was somewhere between England and Las Vegas, and she was going to find him.

EIGHT

MICHAEL knew he shouldn't interfere, that he should leave it alone and let Katie live her own life without him, if that's what she chose. But even after checking out and heading to the airport and flying to New York, he couldn't stop himself from turning around and returning to Las Vegas and the Paris hotel and getting himself another room. He'd then asked the front desk to call her room for him, but she hadn't answered. He stared at the desk clerk, debating a minute before asking to be connected to Nick Stolin's room.

It had only been two days, and he was doubting his ultimatum. Did it really matter if Katie didn't entirely trust him? That would reappear with time. And wouldn't it be better to be with her, nurturing that trust, than to be alone and miserable? He had intended to go back to England, but in the end he'd had to return to Las Vegas, hoping for an opportunity to talk to Katie.

"Hello?"

"Hi, is this Nick?"

"Yes." The voice was suspicious. "Can I help you?"

"This is Michael St. Markov. It's been a long time,

hasn't it?" He wanted Nick to understand that Michael knew who he was, despite the name change, and that he was friend, not foe.

Surprise was in Nick's voice. "It certainly has. I hope all is well with you."

"I'm doing alright. I was hoping you could tell me where Katie is. I'd like to speak to her."

There was a pause, and then Nick said, "Katie went to England to find you. Haven't you seen her yet? She called me yesterday to tell me she had landed."

"What? Katie's in England?" The desk clerk shot Michael a look of reprimand, but he didn't care. "Where the hell did she go?"

"To the address you gave her. It's your house, right?"

"No, no it's not." Michael was equal parts elated and appalled. If Katie had gone to England, then surely she wanted to work things out, and that made him ecstatic. But she was currently halfway around the world, which frustrated the hell out of him. "Can you give me her cell phone number?"

"Sure. And can I just say that maybe you two should have exchanged numbers before you both went running off after an argument?"

"Duly noted." Michael gestured to the desk clerk for a pen and paper, which she handed to him with a frown of disapproval. Whatever. He would give her a tip before he headed to the airport. Jotting the number down, he tore the top page off the pad.

"And Nick? I owe you a lot of thanks. For saving my life. And a huge thanks for looking out for Katie all these years. I'm glad that even if I wasn't there, she had someone on her side." That meant a great deal to him, more than he knew how to express. If something had happened to her . . .

But it hadn't, and he wanted to focus on the future.

"Not a problem. Now call her."

"Absolutely." Michael hung up the desk phone and said

thanks to the clerk. Then he pulled out his cell phone and dialed as he strode toward the elevators so he could retrieve his things from the new room he'd been given when he had rechecked into the hotel.

"Hello?" Katie said, sounding breathless.

He stopped walking and closed his eyes. Just the sound of her voice was such a pleasure, its sensual tones easing the stress that had tautened his muscles. "Hi," he said. "It's me, Michael."

"Hey." A different expression seeped into her voice, one he thought was pleasure, and maybe a little shyness. "Where are you?"

"In Las Vegas. I just found out you went to England. Can we talk, are you busy? I want to apologize for leaving things the way I did the other morning."

"It's okay, I understand. And I want to apologize, too, for not trusting you. I should have known . . ."

There was a pause, and he could tell she was crying. "Oh, honey, it's okay, it is. It was so much new information all at once, it was overwhelming. I should have given you the time you needed. I want to give you all the time you need, if you'll still let me. I want to be together, and the trust can be rebuilt."

Michael stood in the lobby of the overblown casino and prayed that she would say yes.

"I want to be together, too."

Ninety years of pain, of worry, of heartbreak and loneliness, washed away under the rush of those simple words.

"And I do trust you. I went to the storage unit. Thank you, from the bottom of my heart, for preserving all of that . . . for giving me something of my family. It means more than I can ever express."

He was going to cry. He was going to cry right there in the goddamn lobby. Widening his eyes, he said gruffly, "You're welcome. I tried to steal what I could in the chaos, but most of it I bought at auction as pieces appeared on the market over the years. I had an advantage in that I knew what was a true piece and what was a fake since I spent so much time with your family. With you."

"My father would approve of what you did. He would approve of us."

The whispered words came both from his phone and from behind him, and Michael turned around in confusion. Katie was standing there, her cell phone up to her ear, a smile playing on her full lips.

Michael's jaw dropped, and Katie felt her smile splitting into an honest-to-goodness grin. "Hi," she said.

"I thought you were in England."

"Guess what? I just got back."

Then she couldn't speak as she was pulled up into Michael's arms and he kissed her, a passionate, open-mouth kiss that made ninety years disappear in ninety seconds.

"Will you marry me?" he asked, when he pulled back enough to let her catch her breath.

"Yes. Absolutely yes. Tomorrow if you'd like. Today even." Katie kissed him again, deliriously happy.

"Why don't we go upstairs and plan our wedding?" Michael said, with a look in his eye that had nothing to do with reception halls and bridal gowns.

Katie laughed. "I would love to. *I love you.*"

"God, I love you, too." He kissed the top of her head.

As they walked to the elevators hand in hand, she asked him, "Did you know Rasputin is in town?"

"Yes, that's how I found you. I have someone following him, and when I heard he was coming to Vegas to make contact with a bodyguard, his niece, and his thirteen-year-old son, I was hoping that it was you. So I followed."

Katie frowned at Michael as he hit the up button. She glanced over at a tottering older couple approaching the elevator. Lowering her voice to a level most humans wouldn't be able to decipher, she said, "He came here because of Nick, Peter, and me? Why? What does he want with us and how did he find us?"

"The necklace. He wants it. It's very powerful, Katie. It has the blood of every ancient vampire that is walking the earth. He has a matching vial, and with the two, he retains his immortality. He can also read the mind of the person wearing the vial. He's not really a vampire in the truest sense of the word, because while he craves and drinks blood, it doesn't sustain him. He needs the magic of the vials."

They were going up in the elevator and Katie pondered the information. "That's how he kept my brother from dying and made my mother think he was a miracle worker."

"Exactly."

"Why didn't you tell me when you took the necklace from me?"

"I just wanted to get it off you first to sever the connection with him, and then it didn't seem like a good conversation for such a romantic morning. I was going to tell you and ask for your permission to destroy it."

"Of course." Katie stepped off the elevator, reaching back again for Michael's hand. She wanted to touch him every minute of every day. "Do you think he's dangerous? Do we need to try to get the other vial from him?"

Michael shook his head. "I would love to, it would totally disarm him. Make him essentially human. But there's no way anyone can get that necklace off of him."

"You're probably right." Katie opened her door and turned on the light switch to flood the main room with artificial light.

She stifled a shriek when she saw Rasputin sitting on her couch. "Oh, Lord," she said. "What are you doing in here?"

"I want the necklace, little girl." Rasputin rose to his feet and gave her a flat, angry smile. "And don't play dumb. I know you've been wearing it and now you're not.

Where is it?" He moved menacingly to her. "Tell me or I will fuck up your shit quite thoroughly."

"Back off," Michael said, stepping between her and Rasputin. "Don't you dare threaten her."

Thinking on her feet, wanting to defuse the tension, Katie said, "It's in England."

His eyebrows rose. "Oh, really? And how is that possible since you had it here in Vegas two days ago?"

"I just flew to England and put it in a storage unit there with some other personal effects. I wanted to ensure it was safe, so I put it with the rest of my family's possessions. Millions of dollars' worth of items."

"You went to England for less than two days? Don't fuck with me."

Katie reached into her purse and pulled out her passport, stepping around Michael. "See for yourself. Stamped with the dates."

He yanked it out of her hand and stared at it, scowling.

"You can have the necklace if you want. I just wanted it as a memento, but it makes my skin itch. You'll just have to go get it."

"Really? You'll just give it to me?"

"Sure. Technically, I guess it was yours to start with, and you clearly want it. I'm not unreasonable."

Michael reached out and squeezed her hand. "That sounds fair, R."

Rasputin hesitated, then said, "Well, thank you, then. Apparently you didn't inherit your mother's greed. If you can give me the address, I'll be on my way."

"Sure." Katie pulled out the address. "I trust you won't take anything else out of the storage unit?"

"Of course not." He gave her a sly smile. "What kind of man do you take me for?"

One who was about to lose his power. Katie had her eye on his necklace. It was actually resting on top of his shirt, like he had been holding it as he waited for her to come home. The chain was a thin leather strap. He was obviously so arrogant he didn't think anyone could take the necklace from him.

"Just checking." She smiled back at him. "Congratulate me. Michael and I are finally getting married tomorrow."

"Well, that has to be the longest engagement on record. Congratulations. You know I've always thought of you as a daughter."

"Thank you so much." Hoping she didn't look as nauseated as she felt at the prospect of touching him, Katie stepped forward and held out her arms for a hug. "Let's let bygones be bygones, shall we?"

The old lecher didn't hesitate, but threw his arms right around her and pulled her straight up against his chest in an embrace that wasn't fatherly in the slightest. Katie could hear Michael making sounds of protest, but she hoped he would give her thirty seconds. Resting her head on Rasputin's shoulder—and praying she wasn't contracting lice—she pretended to enjoy the hug, while with her fingernail she snapped the string of his necklace. Another snuggle against his chest and she had the vial up her sleeve.

When she pulled back, Rasputin was grinning. "Well, this is a whole new era for us, isn't it? I'll be hanging around Vegas for a few weeks once I collect the necklace, so give me a call when the honeymoon phase has worn off. Hell, before then if you want."

"I will," she said, breathlessly, which was a good effect and not necessarily acting. Now that she had the vial, she was feeling equal parts triumphant and terrified he would figure it out.

"Get the hell out," Michael said, pointing to the door, and scowling to the point that it was a wonder he wasn't hurting himself. "And my wife will *not* be calling you."

"Okay, alright, fine, I'm going." Rasputin put up his hand and ambled toward the door with a grin. "Enjoy the wedding night."

He pulled the door closed behind him with a loud slam

and Michael strode over and clicked the deadbolt in place. "I hate him," he said. "He's a vile, disgusting human being. Or immortal being, if you want to get technical. How could you willingly put your arms around him?"

Katie grinned and held up the vial. "So that I could take this."

Michael looked at his fiancée in amazement, before bursting into laughter. "No way. Sweetheart, you are good."

She laughed with him. "Now how exactly do you think we destroy these? Where is the other one, by the way?"

"It's in my room. Let's go right now before he figures it out."

Five minutes later they were in his hotel room staring at the two vials lying side by side on the dresser. "They look harmless enough," he said.

"Yeah. Mine is just a decorative egg, and that is a snake head. Hard to believe there is blood inside these."

"I guess we should just smash them and disperse the blood. Some down the sink. Maybe some where no one will touch it, like the ceiling. Down the toilet."

"Let's get to it." Katie laid toilet paper under the necklaces, then handed Michael the ice bucket.

He smashed the snake necklace, she the starburst and egg, and both cracked with relative ease from their vampire strength. Within minutes they had tossed what tiny portions of blood there were on the toilet paper into the toilet, and washed the rest down the sink.

"That's not a lot of blood for like a dozen ancients," Michael said, staring at the receding wad of toilet paper as it was sucked down into the hotel's plumbing.

"I guess a little goes a long way. Now wash your hands."

Trust a woman to be primarily concerned about hygiene. "Good idea."

They scrubbed all the way to their elbows, and Michael smiled at her. "Have I told you lately how much I love you?"

She grinned back at him. "Not for at least thirty minutes. I think you're due."

He leaned over and kissed her, both their hands still covered in suds in the sink. "I love you. Forever and always."

NINE

RASPUTIN was partying on the rooftop of the Venetian, with a motley assortment of vampires, most of them scantily dressed females. It seemed to be a primary source of entertainment for the locals to drink vast quantities of alcohol-laced blood, then roof-dive down into the fake canal below. The key, he'd been told, was to move quickly once you hit the water so that no mortal noticed your impact. They would hear a splash, turn, and then you'd be gone before they could interpret what they had just seen.

It sounded humorous enough, and Rasputin was bored and agitated waiting to leave the following night for his jaunt to England to recover the necklace. If the girl was lying to him, he was going to break every bone in her delectable body. After he had his way with her.

"Come on, R," said a brunette whose IQ probably equaled the diameter of her minuscule waist as she grabbed his hand. "Jump with me."

"I would love to," he told her, running his hand over her nipple and squeezing it.

She giggled.

Together they moved to the edge. Rasputin peered down at the canal. He wasn't sure how much of a thrill this was going to be, but he was willing to give it a shot. "After you, Rebecca," he told her.

There was the giggle again. "I'm not Rebecca. I'm Amy."

"Whatever."

She leaned forward like she was going to kiss him, and Rasputin moved toward her. Then the little bitch pushed him off the building.

"See you in a minute!" she called, laughing her fool head off as he tumbled down into open air.

Crossing his arms, Rasputin sighed. Maybe it was time for more sophisticated company. And while falling was mildly amusing, it was probably messing his hair up. He reached for his necklace out of habit, intending to hold it when he hit the water so he wouldn't feel the pain of impact as much.

But his necklace wasn't there.

Rasputin looked down at his chest, patting all over, a sudden panic arresting him. No necklace.

Then he remembered the hug from Katie a few hours earlier. Had she lifted it?

It hardly mattered. It wasn't on him, that was the important fact. He suddenly realized that he couldn't breathe, that he was feeling horrifically weak and mortal for the first time in a century.

A glance down past the rushing wind showed he was a second from impact.

Well, now that just totally sucked.

He closed his mouth and waited for the water, irritated as hell that he was going to die.

He hadn't even bought Katie a wedding gift, and how rude was that?

Then he hit and all thoughts shattered just as brutally as his mortal body.

TOTAL CONTROL

L. L. FOSTER

ONE

IMPATIENCE clawed through Brax, sparking fire in his every nerve ending. After his last bloody assignment, he required her total surrender to his will. Only her heated touch, her screams of fulfillment, would salve his turmoil and save his sanity.

The cursed talent made it far too easy to get lost in eternal blackness. Lately it felt as though the depravity soaked into his pores, worming its way into his soul.

Only the most complete possession of Cameo Smithson, body and soul, would save him.

He needed her.

Desire battled with his conscience until he heard the quiet opening of his office door. His smile was one of anticipation, satisfaction.

But inside his heart the apology burned. For his benefit, he'd bring her into his private hell. If he were a stronger man, he'd do as his uncle Amos had done, and disappear from society.

He couldn't. Knowing she was near proved an irresistible temptation.

Today he'd end the eternal wait.

For weeks he'd struggled with nonexistent patience, determined to give her enough time to acclimate to the new shift in their relationship, her new life, her new sexuality.

What they'd share would be electric and sizzling hot. It would feed him, and drain her, and only together would they both survive.

He would give her more than she'd ever experienced before. More than most could tolerate.

Cameo didn't yet realize she was his salvation, but he'd accepted the fact months ago. Now he had to coerce her into accepting it, too.

The door closed with barely a snick of sound. He felt her heavy pause as she surveyed him standing before the yawning hole in the wall.

"Brax?"

Her voice held that tentative, cautious tone that he'd expected, the tone she'd adopted since picking up on his sexual advances.

She was right to be wary; before long he'd strip her of even that small choice. Claiming her meant obliterating her reserve. She'd be totally vulnerable to him and his whims.

Forever.

Gathering his thoughts, he continued to stare out the gaping hole in the outside office wall. On the third floor of his expansive home, the giant cavity opened to his back-yard, showcasing a decorative pool, fountain, and manicured landscaping carefully arranged to look as if nature had designed it.

The upscale lifestyle helped him forget what he was, what he did, and worked to conceal his atrocious proclivities.

No one would believe that a wealthy, respected businessman would occupy his free time by demolishing brutish societal abnormalities.

Barefoot, he stood so near the edge that his toes hung over the broken bricks of the house's exterior. A stirring breeze wafted in; he heard the trickle of the fountain, the songs of birds.

The steep drop was such that it sucked the air from his lungs.

Keeping his back to her, he commanded, "Come here, Cameo."

He could almost hear her searching for a reply. He waited, muscles knotted, hoping for the right answer.

"I'd rather we sit down, okay?"

Something dark and destructive loosened inside him. She worried for him. His smile teased; he braced his hands at the top of the hole and leaned out, letting gravity drag at him, feeling himself grow weightless.

"Damn it, Brax," she snapped. "Move away from there right now."

Ah, so she tried a different tack. That was so like Cameo—adaptable, always in charge, always intelligent, thinking through possibilities and consequences.

He looked down at the yard below, and saw a few discarded bricks lying broken amid plaster dust. "I told you to come to me."

The seconds ticked by. When he heard no movement behind him, he turned. Staying close to the edge, he took in the tantalizing sight of her. Dressed in another of the proper but alluring business suits that he'd grown to associate with her unique style, she looked . . . exciting.

Like salvation.

In an effort to withstand him, she locked her hands on the back of the wing chair placed before his desk. It was where she'd normally sit to take dictation.

Her innocent, baby-blue eyes closed, denying him a sight he adored, a sight that gentled him against the ugly, corruptive influence of his life. The lips he'd so often dreamed of were now compressed.

Brax understood. She felt his compulsion—but she fought it. It was as much her ability to deny him, as her other attributes, that reeled him in.

Determined to test her, Brax centered his efforts, hardened his tone. "Cameo, you will come to me. Now."

Tensing her entire body, she shook her head.

God, but she stirred him on the most elemental levels. Her refusal caused his voice to drop to a husky whisper. "You know you want to."

A shiver ran over her. "I'm not an idiot." She opened her eyes, showing him stark pain and gutsy defiance. "You move away from there."

The display of contumacy perversely thrilled him; his pulse sped, his blood heated. "No, Cameo," he agreed, "no one would ever accuse you of lacking smarts."

When conquering others, he often got a frisson of excitement.

But Cameo conquered him—without even knowing it.

Satisfied with her reaction, he eased back mentally, freeing her from the grip of his power. She immediately sucked in a deep breath.

Still edgy with predacious excitement, Brax watched the lush rise of her full breasts beneath a buttoned-up blouse. The sheer material showed the lace, and the woman, beneath.

Lounging on the broken wall beside the yawning void, he studied her, taking in every nuance of her expression. "I need to locate a new contractor. As you can see"—he indicated the hole in his office wall—"I fired the last one."

She visibly struggled for composure. "But . . . I'd only just hired him."

He shrugged and waited for her to make a move.

Cameo took her time regaining her balance. Would she mention the compulsion to join him at the dangerous rupture of plaster and drywall? Would she acknowledge his attempt to use control over her?

Doubtful. Until Cameo understood and accepted his influence, she wouldn't address the issue at all.

After today, she'd be forced to understand.

Drawing herself together in an efficient and practiced

manner, she whisked aside the fallen plastic sheeting and seated herself in the chair.

Adopting a de rigueur posture, she crossed long, very shapely legs and placed her hands in her lap. The turmoil vacated her expression, replaced with query. "Why?"

Smiling at her façade of serenity, Brax moved to sit at his desk across from her. Other than his desk, and now the chair she occupied, plastic adorned everything in the room to protect it from the demolition debris.

Studying her, Brax sat back at his leisure. The ensuing conversation would no doubt prove a fun interlude before the trials he'd impress on her. "He didn't show up on time this morning."

"Did he have a reason?"

"Not one that he called with in advance." He loved how myriad emotions flashed through her expressive eyes. "Cameo, you of all people know that I won't tolerate that type of unprofessional behavior."

"You are strict," she admitted before turning very businesslike. "I'll compile a list of reputable and available contractors for you to peruse. I'll have it ready within an hour."

"That's not necessary." How long would it take her to catch on? How long would it take him to convince her?

"You intend to keep that . . . that . . ." She gestured toward the sign of demolition. *"That?"*

"Of course not."

"Well . . . surely you want it repaired sooner rather than later."

"By the end of the week, I'll have sliding doors and a railed balcony. The walls will be repaired, sanded, and painted." He was not a man without influence. Enough money could solve most problems. But it couldn't put a dent in his nightmare.

"But then . . . ?"

Anticipation heightened. "I'm taking care of it myself."

Her slim eyebrows nudged closer together. "You don't want me to handle it for you?"

Damn, but even her frowns brought about the start of a boner. Cameo's gentle, uncorrupted, moralistic ways made the perfect foil for his life of destruction.

His voice dropped, went rough but gentle. "Henceforth, Cameo, you will no longer serve in the capacity of my personal assistant."

She stared at him. "You're firing me?"

"I'm relieving you of those duties. Effective immediately."

Time stood still. For long moments, she said nothing, did nothing, didn't break the contact of their locked gazes.

Then her head tilted and she affected a look of mere curiosity—but he saw the hurt.

He *felt* the hurt.

"I see." A proud smile lifted the corners of her full lips. "I suppose I lasted longer than most."

Brax didn't move. If he did, he'd grab her, crush her close, absorb her into himself. "Understand Cameo, it's because you're different from anyone I've met that you've lasted longer." The tension inside him tightened.

It was a craving like no other.

For her.

He put his hands on the desktop. "That's also why you can't remain my personal assistant."

In a sudden burst of energy, she left the chair. She looked to be at a loss as she started for the door, but then turned back. "I guess I'm grateful you didn't have me hire my own replacement."

"I'll choose someone myself. I start interviewing tomorrow."

Anger and hurt showed before she cloaked herself behind a shield of indifference. "You have everything taken care of, then."

"No." Slowly, his desire for her a live, demanding thing, he left his chair and circled the desk. "Come here, Cameo."

Her mouth quirked. "Ah, but I don't take orders from you anymore."

"I'm afraid you do."

She said, "Ha!" even though he detected the many ways she strained to deny his lure.

Brax advanced ever so slowly. He hadn't planned to, but now he needed her to understand the altruism of his motive. "I could make this easier for you, Cameo, but I'm not going to."

"This?" Alarm took her back a step, and then she stopped and straightened her shoulders. "I don't know what you're talking about."

He couldn't look away from her beautiful eyes. "In the long run, it'll make you better able to accept certain things."

"What things?" She turned and moved closer to the door before again facing him. With her hands behind her on the doorknob, she cast a nervous glance at the perilous hole in the broken wall. "You didn't . . . didn't hurt the contractor, did you?"

Brax paused to study her. "You believe I'm capable of causing him harm?"

"Oh, most definitely." She didn't shy away from the disturbing eye contact. "You're capable of a great many things, not all of them good."

Even if she didn't comprehend the *how* or *why* of his actions, he *knew* she'd understood at least that much about his nature. And still she'd stayed with him, worked for him in an intimate capacity, for more than five years.

His respect for her amplified.

His desire thickened.

"You don't fear me." He made it a statement, not a question. His heart punched in time to the salacious images searing his brain, images of Cameo spread out beneath him, stripped naked, accepting him, all of him, in all the erotic ways he'd dreamed about.

"Sometimes I do." Her tongue came out to moisten her bottom lip. Her proud gaze never wavered off him. "A little."

"Please don't." He moved closer again, but to ensure

she wouldn't flee, he paused with several feet still between them.

If she did run, he'd catch her. They both knew it. He wouldn't let anything interfere now that they were finally coming to terms. Too much pent-up attraction and boiling chemistry demanded she face the harsh truth about him.

Choosing his words with care, Brax said, "It's true that, under the right circumstances, and for the right reasons, I'm capable of doing severe damage."

"An understatement."

Yes, she understood the core of him as a man. Amusement took him by surprise. Cameo possessed so much courage, and trusted him more than she knew.

He had an important point to make. "I promise you that anything I do to you, regardless of how you might feel about it at the time, will be for your own good."

Those words started her trembling; her chin lifted. "Since I'm not working here anymore, it's a moot point. I don't expect to ever see you again."

"Actually," Brax corrected, "you'll see more of me." She started to protest and he added, "In bed and out."

Her mouth went slack for only a moment before she laughed at him. "My God, your ego is incredible."

The insult didn't faze him because he knew the truth. He had to have her, and nothing would stop him. It helped that at least in this, she offered little objection. "You want me, Cameo. You have all along."

Panic edged in. "You're outrageous."

"It's okay, you know." He put his hands in his pockets, affecting a casual stance when in truth the animal side of him urged him to pounce. "I want you, too."

True anger flashed in her eyes. "You want anything in a skirt!"

"I have . . ." How could he elucidate such a complicated issue? "Because of my . . . genetic makeup, I have an elevated . . . sexual need."

"You have got to be kidding me."

Stubborn woman. She was getting ahead of him and

making a complex issue more difficult. "It's based on things you don't yet know about me. Things I will shortly explain."

"What?" she challenged. "About your sexual addiction?"

"No." God knew, there wasn't an easy way to disclose the truth. "Not an addiction, per se, but I do feed off corporeal exertion."

"Sex?"

With a shrug, he moved closer. "Soon, I'll feed off you."

She spun around to leave.

"Don't."

The single word froze her. Keeping her back to him, her spine taut, she whispered, "Or what?"

His every muscle rippled with eagerness. "You will likely regret it." Blood rushed to his groin; his erection throbbed. More softly, as a promise and a warning, he stated, "But I won't."

Her shuddering, indrawn breath brought a shimmer to her shoulders seconds before she attempted to jerk open the door.

Already knowing how he'd stop her, Brax stared at her shapely back from the proud shoulders, the narrowed waist, that lush, curvy ass. A conflagration of heat scorched him as he summoned his considerable concentration for a talent known only to an elite few, unimagined by most.

He shouldn't enjoy this, but regardless of his aberrant ability, he remained a man.

And he had lusted after her for a very long time.

Application of the productive method he'd devised exclusively for Cameo would, as usual, be devastating in effect. But this time, it would be without real harm—except maybe to her pride and modesty.

As he connected with her emotionally, she stopped. He took her feelings, distorted them for his own purpose, and gave them back to her.

It served the desired effect immediately; her back arched a little, and she clung to the doorknob as her knees weakened.

"Brax?" High and thin, her voice wavered.

"Shhh." He came up behind her, not physically touching her, but he needed to be close enough to smell her sexual excitement, to hear her every small breath. "It'll be easier on you if you don't fight it."

Trembling, her breath hitched, she gave up her tenuous hold on the door to slump down to the floor. Her beautiful eyes went unseeing, then closed.

She looked so sensual, so stunning, that Brax had to brace himself.

"Oh, God." She gave one small groan before biting her swelling lips. Shaking, her hands curled into fists, she dropped back against the door.

Brax came down on his knees beside her. He wanted to come with her, he was so excited, but that would be unfair to her.

When they joined, she'd be willing—unlike now.

"I could make this go so quickly," he whispered to her, "but . . . I'm a selfish bastard. I need to relish this, to watch you experiencing everything."

"No." Her face flushed and she tipped her head back, turning away from him. "Please. Make it . . ." Her back arched, pressing her breasts forward as she gasped. " . . . Make it stop."

"No, baby." He couldn't. He wouldn't. "Not just yet." He truly believed it'd be best for her to understand the depth and expanse of his power firsthand, but he couldn't stand it.

He had to hold her.

Drawing her into his lap despite her feeble resistance, Brax cradled her to his chest. "I won't touch you sexually, Cameo. It wouldn't be honorable."

As she panted without reply, her short, manicured nails dug into his biceps through the material of his shirt.

"Just relax. Accept it." *Accept me.*

"You . . ." She was unable to finish whatever insult she'd intended.

Stroking her back, Brax explained what was happening and why. "I know you've suspected that I'm different from other men. I've also known of your heightened awareness of me for a long time." He rocked her just a little as the pleasure built, receded, then came back stronger, racking her slender body.

Catching her chin, he forced her to look at him. "The truth is that I can manipulate people in numerous ways. This is only one of those ways, and I've saved it exclusively for you."

She cried out, her legs stiffening as she tensed hard in his arms. "You have to . . . to stop this!"

"Not yet." It'd be easier to talk to her now, with her defenses crushed. Once she came and, of course, regained her wits, he'd have his hands full with her embarrassment and anger.

Unwilling to have her climax so soon, he forced himself to retrench a little.

"You must be familiarized with the reach of my capabilities," he murmured.

She turned her face in to his chest and bit him on a deep, resonating groan.

Brax caught his breath at the sign of escalating passion; the sinking of her small teeth into his pec muscle damn near proved to be his undoing.

For his own sake, he had to finish this, and soon.

He tangled his fingers in her long, light-brown hair and drew her face back. "For some time now, I've been able to . . . assist with legal affairs. It's all very top secret, and no one knows how I gain confessions, and more."

Her lips parted on another wave of intense sensation.

He needed her to hear him. "Cameo, I've never told another soul, not even my sister, of what I can do."

She looked at him with her eyes wild and dark with need.

He touched her cheek. "Only you, Cameo."

Moaning long and low, she twisted tighter to him again. "Please, Brax. I can't bear it."

Her high heels had fallen off already, and he watched her toes curl, her calf muscles flex. Her trim skirt had ridden high on her thighs.

Thanks to his fingers, her hair tumbled loose from the elegant twist she'd worn. He liked her hair down.

He liked her ripe and wet with need.

"You'd be surprised what you can take." Once she accepted him on every level, he'd find great pleasure in exploring her sensual depths. He'd school her in an ecstasy she'd never considered.

Even through her blouse and bra he could see the pebbled stiffness of her nipples, knew they ached as if he'd been sucking on them, and his eyes closed on a stark visual. "I look forward to showing you."

She almost spiraled out of control right then. Her body jolting in small spasms, her breath rasping, Brax held her tight and absorbed the wave with her until it receded yet again. Tormented with her need, each pass of pleasure sharpened the yearning.

As sensuality consumed her, she looked wanton and Brax didn't have it in him to drag it out any longer. Much more, and he'd lose control himself. The scent of her arousal heightened his own. As he'd told her, he fed off sexual contact, using it to dissipate the darkness and strengthen his focus. But now, with Cameo, the effect was too potent, too dark and lush and hot.

Given that he shared it all with her, they were both in an agony of burning need.

She was every bit as passionate as he'd always suspected. All he'd done was unleash that passion—without a single touch—as a demonstration to her, a harsh lesson she'd never forget.

Now he had to finish his explanations and let her rest or they'd never get the bigger issues resolved.

"Understand, Cameo, nearly everything is heightened, if not entirely controlled, by emotion. Sickness and fear, tension and pain, and yes, the sexual desire you feel now, are based on an emotional level that I can manipulate through concentrated focus." He leaned down to breathe in the scent of her hair and flushed skin. Huskily, he admitted, "I focus on you a lot these days. No doubt you've felt the effects."

Whether or not she heard him, Brax couldn't be sure. She was so frenzied, writhing in his arms, tears tracking her cheeks, that rational thought might be well out of her control.

But he had to say it all anyway, had to share with her what only a limited few knew. "This odd ability is a trait within the males of my family, used throughout history mostly to assist in the greater good."

He traced two fingertips along her throat to where a pulse thrummed wildly. Passion left her skin dewy and soft; he badly wanted to taste her, to mark her as his own.

All over.

"There have been a few black sheep who've used the ability exclusively to take advantage of others, but they're few and far between—"

Suddenly crying out, Cameo interrupted his disclosure on the family tree.

He cupped her neck, supporting her while the racking orgasm vibrated through her. She tried to turn away from him, but he was self-centered enough that he wanted to see everything. "Look at me," he told her, "and I'll allow you to come."

For only a moment more, she refused, and then, with all her resistance shattered, she met his gaze.

Brax wallowed in the moment, triumphant and so very close to satisfaction. "That's it," he said, encouraging her, breathing with her. "Give me everything, Cameo."

Ripe with ever-coiling tension, raw sounds of need tore from her throat. Brax cuddled her closer, kissed her temple, and held her as the overwhelming release consumed her.

In his midthirties, he'd pleasured many women in many different ways. He'd taken, and he'd given. He'd used and been used. He enjoyed savage sex and tender lovemaking.

This was different.

This was Cameo.

This moment, the first of many, would always hold a special place in his heart.

When her cries finally abated and she went lax in his arms, panting from an excess of exertion, he smiled and again kissed her temple. "Now, Cameo, you are mine. There will be no going back."

CAMEO lay limp in his arms as she slowly regathered herself. Her brain felt too replete to function, her body too limp to move.

What had just happened, what he'd *made* happen, that wasn't her. It had never been her.

She understood his reasoning, she really did. If she hadn't experienced his ability, never would she have believed him. But each time he'd sent more sensation sizzling along her nerve endings, she'd known it was him. He only held her, a near-platonic embrace but for the look in his eyes.

And still, he'd turned her inside out with sexual excitement stronger than she'd known existed.

Her hair was in her face, her legs inelegantly opened over his lap. Tear tracks had ruined her carefully applied makeup.

God, she thought of how she'd screamed, even begged, and how much he'd enjoyed her response.

Through a haze of humiliation, she peeked at Brax and saw the satisfaction in his amazing golden eyes, the small smile he wore.

She lost it.

With no warning at all, not even a frown, she swung her palm up fast and hard, slapping his smug face with all the meager strength she possessed.

His head didn't move, but the smile disappeared real quick. His eyes flinched, his mouth firmed as a red handprint rose on his jaw.

"I take it you're convinced of what I can do."

"Yes!"

He eyed her furious expression with interest. "Feel better?"

Breathing hard in her ire, Cameo nodded. "A little."

His mouth remained grim, but she saw the smile in his incredible golden eyes. "Still pissed?"

Oh, she was angry alright, no two ways about that. But she was more mortified than anything. "Maybe."

After a very cautious hug, he said, "Then I'll give you a little more time before we talk."

About . . . his astounding ability? Or the fact that he wanted her physically? Or that she'd been fired?

The first left her incredulous. The second thrilled her.

The third was out of the question. Fire her? No, she wouldn't allow it.

She was good at what she did, and now that she knew how he felt, the idea of anyone else getting that close to him, tending all his personal and professional needs, didn't sit well with her at all.

How to change his mind, Cameo didn't yet know. He'd hit her with too much all at once, leaving her thoughts and emotions staggering.

Was it truly possible for a man to do what he'd done? For years, she'd suspected Brax of amazing things. He was by far the most intelligent person she'd ever met, keen witted and cagey, as proved by his bank account. He was also sinfully gorgeous, with inky black hair that contrasted sharply with gold-hazel eyes unlike any she'd ever seen except on his sister, Mercy.

But . . . mind manipulation? She'd never even heard of such a thing.

As confusing as it all was, she couldn't grasp anything beyond one mind-numbing fact: he'd easily used her, worked her, wrung her out—all without touching her except to hold her close.

Brax stood six feet, five inches tall and possessed laudable strength within a well-honed, muscular body. But he hadn't used height or brawn to bend her to his will.

He'd used his incredible mind.

Gradually her heartbeat slowed from its furious pace and her heated flesh began to cool. Brax continued to cradle her close, saying nothing. Her weight in his lap was insignificant to him.

Was she insignificant? What did he have planned for them now? Was she to *feed* his bizarre talent?

He'd claimed that he'd never told anyone but her about what he could do. Even living through it firsthand—she shuddered again in memory—didn't make it easy to accept. She had a thousand questions, but first . . .

"Mercy doesn't know about this?"

He smoothed a damp tendril of hair away from her face. "No."

That didn't really surprise her. Brax and his sister were closer than any other siblings she knew. After the death of their parents, when Mercy was ten and Brax had just turned a legal eighteen, he'd taken over raising her. He loved Mercy unconditionally, which was easy to do given that Mercy was so kind and smart and wonderful.

"So you want to protect her from this?"

"Yes." He watched her. "It's not an easy thing for most to accept."

"No, it's not." Maybe she needed to rattle his damned complacency a little. Sitting up in his lap, Cameo said, "If you ever again do that to me—"

"Without your permission," he interrupted her to say, and now his gaze burned.

Cameo scowled, but yes, she might allow him to make her feel those all-consuming things again, *if* he was with her every step of the way.

She raised a brow and said, "Promise me you won't do that without my very clear permission. I mean it, Brax."

His hand cupped the back of her neck. He stared at her mouth, then into her eyes as he murmured, "I can't."

Cameo barely had time to absorb his refusal before he drew her forward and ravaged her mouth with a starving kiss.

When he finally let her up for air, he was the one panting. "God, woman, the things you do to me."

Cameo couldn't believe him. She smacked his shoulder, this time lacking any real rage. "That's the pot calling the kettle black, isn't it?"

He smiled, drew in and let out a big breath. "I won't make a promise I might not be able to keep." His brows came down in a self-directed frown. "All men use the skills they possess to seduce and pleasure the women they want."

"You're not like other men."

He acknowledged that with a slight nod. "The thing is, you push me and tempt me. I'll do my best, but I'm only a man, and I've wanted you—"

"Just be quiet and let me think." She couldn't believe his audacity, but in a way, what he'd said was a compliment, as if she could take him beyond his own control.

"Look at it this way." A knowing, masculine gleam entered his eyes. "We've already established that I can't coerce you to do things you don't want to do. I can bend you to my will to a degree, but you are never fully under my control."

"It didn't feel that way to me."

"Because you want me sexually, too, I am able to . . . encourage you enough to give us both pleasure."

Except that he hadn't taken anything for himself. "You didn't—"

Knowing her thoughts, he interrupted her to say, "Watching you, hearing you, and breathing in your scent, it gave me great pleasure."

He waited a few seconds before asking, "Questions?"

"A million of them." Using his broad shoulders to brace herself, Cameo left his lap and stood before him.

He remained seated on the floor. "Well?"

Cameo shook her head. "Not this way, Brax. If you had any idea of payback of the sensual kind, you can forget it."

"I was afraid you'd say that." He reached down and readjusted his jeans over what looked to be a rather sizable bulge.

She tried not to notice the very noticeable erection beneath his fly. "Let's go to the kitchen, get some coffee, and talk—without touching."

Proud of the way she calmly stepped into her shoes, Cameo went to the door. This time he did nothing as she opened the door and walked out.

When she heard a thump, she looked back to see Brax's long, hard body sprawled on the floor, one leg bent at the knee, one forearm over his eyes.

"Brax?"

He didn't look at her or move in any way. "Go on. I'll join you shortly." He drew in another deep breath. "I just need a minute."

It was Cameo's turn to smile. Feeling magnanimous and, in some evil feminine way, powerful, she said soothingly, "Take all the time you need."

The feeling lasted all the way through coffee preparation. But when she sat down at the table alone and started to think, she also worried.

Many women had tried to tie down the magnificent, wealthy, and influential Brax Jardine. He'd accepted sexual favors from them, escorted them to necessary social events, but nothing more ever came of it.

She wasn't a hag, and her figure was more than okay, but . . . she knew she wasn't in league with the women he usually gravitated to.

Unlike them, she could never settle for half measures or temporary pleasures.

Her fingernails tapped on the tabletop as she waited for Brax to join her.

Brax wasn't a liar. If he said he'd confided only in her,

then she believed him. What that made her to him, she couldn't know.

But as soon as he got himself together and joined her, she'd damn well ask him.

TWO

BRAX walked in wearing jeans, a white shirt, a thick black watch, and nothing else. They were the same clothes he'd had on earlier, only they were more rumpled now.

At the sight of him, Cameo's breath caught. His broad shoulders filled the doorway. He was so much man that he sent her to blushing all over again.

He planted his big feet apart and just stood there, watching her, taking note of the heat in her face she was sure.

Neither of them moved.

His eyes narrowed the smallest bit. "I like your hair down and loose like that."

Reminded of her tousled state, Cameo touched one long lock hanging over her shoulder. She was not a woman used to "cutting loose," in either attitude or dress. "For work, it'd be inappropriate."

"You aren't working anymore." And with that, he strode in and poured each of them a cup of coffee.

Anger sabotaged her planned inquisition. "Oh, I'll be working—just not for you."

He halted in midmovement, going still in the way of a

startled bear. It wouldn't last. Agitated bears attacked; they did not retreat.

But Brax was a silent, very contained hunter. With a steady hand, he set both cups of coffee on the table and seated himself. "I want you with me, not working elsewhere."

She was so startled, she forgot to be mad. "What do you mean, with you?"

"Here." He sat back, his relaxed posture deceiving. "In my house. It's plenty big enough."

"Can't argue that. You could house a football team with ease. But I won't be a kept woman."

His mouth quirked. "Don't be puritanical. I fired you to avoid conflict of interest because I want you here, in a completely different capacity."

Completely different capacity. "That's so romantic." She picked up her coffee. "But I want my independence. That means maintaining a paying job."

"I—"

She sat up straighter in warning. "If you offer to pay me for services rendered, you'll be wearing the coffee."

He eyed her hold on the cup and must have decided it was an idle threat. "Mine is yours."

"No, yours is yours."

"I want to share."

"Talk to Mercy. Maybe she'll take a gift or two."

Frustration brought him forward. "You are being deliberately antagonistic. Why?"

He couldn't be serious. "Are you kidding?"

Going for a different tack, he glanced at her breasts, then her mouth. That one quick glance, and Cameo felt the stirring of new interest. Or . . . wait!

Through her teeth, she warned, "You better not be using your wiles on me."

"My wiles?" He shook his head. "You want me, I want you. You can't deny that."

Still, she didn't quite trust him on this. "Did you or did you not just provoke me with your mind?"

"Not." He reached for her hand and held it when she would have pulled away. "I looked at you the way any man in lust looks at a woman, and you responded in kind. We have a megadose of chemistry going on here."

Oh God, she felt it. Knowing everything he'd recently forced her to experience didn't help. Still sensitive in key places, the memory of sizzling sensations almost brought them right back.

She jerked her hand free. "I said no touching."

"Then don't accuse me of using amped-up means to seduce you." He pushed back from his chair and loomed over her. "I don't need help to have you screaming with pleasure."

"Brax . . ."

He leaned closer, bracing his hands on the seat of her chair, caging her in. His mouth was so close, she could almost taste him.

"There are so many ways I want to take you, Cameo." His lips brushed hers on a path to her throat. "So many ways I've thought about having you, night after night."

"Oh . . ."

"Sometimes hard." He put a damp, open-mouthed kiss to a very sensitive spot between her neck and shoulder. "Sometimes easy." His teeth grazed her skin, making her tingle. "But always deep and hot and—"

She shoved up both hands to halt him. "Unfair practice, Brax." A deep breath refilled her starving lungs with oxygen. "You know I lack your experience."

He took one of her hands and brought it down to his fly. "I'll share my experience with you. Right now."

So fast that she nearly toppled over in her chair, Cameo pushed back. She managed to land on her feet; the chair wasn't so lucky.

They both ignored it.

Again, their gazes locked and it was so fierce, it had her heart punching double time.

Think, Cameo. You had questions. Yes, she did. "Why me? Why now?"

Brax retreated to lean on the kitchen counter. In the stainless-steel-and-granite kitchen, he looked right at home, just as solid and sustainable as metal or rock.

He crossed his arms over his chest. "You defy me."

Her spine snapped straight in affront. "This is a game? I'm a challenge for your ego?"

"My ego is healthy enough that challenges are unnecessary." His close observation burned over her, lingering in key places on her body. While looking at her breasts, he murmured, "My emotional mastery has, so far, proven overpowering."

"Mastery?" she questioned with a raised brow. Yes, the man had a very healthy ego.

"Whenever I've chosen to trigger an unconscious response in a person, largely against a criminal element so corrupt that it blackens all others in its vicinity, I've succeeded without fail."

"Criminals?"

"One thing at a time, honey." He eased closer to her. "With you, I sensed that you had some strange power to resist me. Don't get pissed, but I've subtly tried to encourage you to do things you didn't want to do."

Things clicked into place. "Today, when you ordered me over to that awful, gaping hole in the wall . . ."

"You refused, and I couldn't encourage you to my will."

"You almost did," she whispered. "It scared me. I didn't want to get that close to the drop, but the urge to do what you said was almost overwhelming."

"Almost," he reiterated. "But you rejected my mental coercion. No one else has ever managed that."

Oh God, this was so confusing. "Have you . . . coerced others to their death?"

Something flickered in his gaze. He looked down, gathering his thoughts before facing her again. He spoke slowly, willing her to understand. "There are a lot of evil people surrounding us, Cameo."

"I know that."

He shook his head. "I'm not talking ordinary criminals. Thieves, liars, bullies—they infest the earth. They disgust me, but I accept them as a part of our society. But there are beings that are more craven and malevolent than you could ever know. And sometimes, even with a confession, our legal system is helpless against them."

Her chest hurt. "Is that a yes?"

He searched her gaze before giving one firm nod. "Yes."

Shock took her back a step.

He didn't reach for her, but Cameo saw the urgency rushing through him.

Tone harder, harsher, he said, "A child molester, Cameo. He'd tortured two sixteen-year-old boys. It was only when he got so involved in murdering one of them that the other was able to escape."

Sickness twisted in her stomach, burned her throat. She pressed a hand to her heart, trying to contain the vicious thumping. "You were certain of all this?"

"The sick fuck took videos. Yes, I was absolutely certain."

The depravity of it stole her breath.

Jaw clenched, eyes clouded, Brax said, "I saw it in his face, Cameo, the complete pleasure he took in causing them pain. He enjoyed it too much to ever quit. There'd be no reform for him. Ever." His gaze flashed back to hers. "Do you really want society to falter and turn him loose again?"

Understanding the agony he'd experienced, not just this time, but as a course of his life's calling, altered her perspective. "What did you do to him?"

Pulling back, expression guarded, he whispered, "You don't need details."

"Yes, I do." If she was going to enter into this . . . alliance, she needed to know everything.

A deep breath expanded his chest, making him look bigger, more dangerous, when he was dangerous enough on a daily basis. "He savagely broke his neck while trying to hang himself."

The torment was there in his eyes, showing what it cost him to fulfill his heritage. He did what he had to do to protect others, not because he was twisted or evil, but to stop the evil from striking again. Accepting it all, accepting *him*, her nervousness faded beneath a rush of empathy. "I'm so sorry, Brax."

"No." Sudden rage darkened his expression. "*Fuck no. I don't want your goddamned pity!*"

But she wasn't afraid anymore, and her gentle smile was a buffer in the face of his anger. "It's called understanding, and you have it whether you want it or not."

Lunging forward, he caught her arms and jerked her up to her tiptoes, flush against his hard body. Hanging there in his grasp, the disparity in their sizes was more evident than ever. He stood a foot taller than her, large boned and layered in solid muscle. One of his hands would easily span the width of her back. His forearms were larger than her calves.

And she felt . . . protected.

Safe from the ugliness in the world.

His mouth came down on hers, his tongue raping her with a fierce hunger. Cameo didn't fight him. She wouldn't have sex with him yet; for her, it was still too soon to switch to that level of intimacy.

But if this brought him comfort, she was more than willing.

Putting her small hands to his heated chest, she stroked over bulging muscles.

He set her away from him as quickly as he'd grabbed her. Breathing hard, he stared at her in disbelief. "Damn you."

When she said nothing, he let her go and stepped a few feet away. "Let's get this straight. All I need from you is release."

He sounded distant, harsh and determined.

"Sex will help you?" Before making any final decisions, she needed to comprehend this odd code, and the nuances behind surviving it.

His nod was slow, as if he disbelieved her calm. "It's always been that way in my family. When we find the right woman, she can . . . save us."

To Cameo, that certainly sounded like more than just sex. "And if you don't find the right woman?"

His giant shoulder lifted in a failed attempt at nonchalance. "A few have gone insane. It's sometimes too much, trading emotions with psychopaths, committing sins in the name of humanity."

Many things began to click into place for her: the veil of secrecy that always cloaked him, the "businessmen" who'd left a private meeting in much worse shape than when they'd arrived, and the women.

So many women had come and gone during the years since she started working for him. She was not a prude, and she did her best not to judge others.

But his treatment of them, even with their willing participation, had seemed so callous, as if he saw them all as disposable pleasures.

"What?" Brax asked. He touched her swollen mouth with unspoken apology. "I can see you thinking."

She caught his wrist and drew his hand away from her. She couldn't think while he toyed with her. "All those women you've been with."

"What about them?"

"They were . . ." She laughed at the absurdity, but said it anyway. "Treatment?"

He cupped the side of her face. "I've occupied myself with agreeable women to feed my emotional reservoir. I know how that sounds, Cameo, so don't try to hide your disbelief." As if he couldn't help himself, his thumb brushed her bottom lip again. "I want you to understand it all."

"I do." But it wasn't easy. Knowing what he could do made her feel exceptionally vulnerable. Not only was he physically powerful, but he could control her mind, too. It left her very uncomfortable—and strangely excited.

The odd but combustive combination kept her heart beating too hard and left a slow burn churning deep inside her.

He'd fulfilled her—and yet, he hadn't.

"The use of coercive persuasion on another can strip the controller of his own emotions, leaving him raw and burned out. Only that free, utterly replete sensation during and right after release allows me to recharge internally."

"That sounds suspiciously like a convenient, male-contrived excuse to have a lot of sex with a lot of different women." The way he kept staring so intently at her mouth, it was a wonder she could speak coherently.

"There's nothing convenient about it." His eyes narrowed, looking at her with a near-tactile potency. "The truth is that hot, gritty sex helps me regain my perspective on life." He bent and kissed her very gently. "But for some time now, it hasn't been enough. Because of you."

"I have never openly judged your promiscuity."

His large hands settled over her back, using subtle pressure to bring her closer. "No, but by your very presence you provoked me and showed all other women as lacking."

The import of her next question made it impossible to look at him directly, so instead Cameo stared at his chin. "Will you continue seeing other women, too?"

One big hand lowered close to her derriere. "If you and I come to an agreement, I'll have no need of other women."

Her heart pounded so hard, it was a wonder he didn't hear it. "The agreement being?"

He kissed her again with a tenderness that made her want to consent to anything. Staying so close that she felt surrounded by him, he said, "I need total release, Cameo, the oblivion that comes only from losing myself in a woman's body. To obtain that, you must be accessible to me. Always. Here when I want you, ready when I am.

Agreeable to all my sexual needs." His mouth brushed hers, and his voice thickened with desire. "Whatever those needs might be."

"But—" That made her sound like a sex slave. And God help her, she wanted to agree. "I . . . I can't blindly agree to that, Brax. I don't know if . . ."

"If what? You'll want me to do the things I'm dying to do to you?" He held her face, stared into her eyes. "Understand, Cameo, I can ensure that you are always ready, even anxious, when I am." His tongue traced her upper lip, sank in soft and slow past her lips to play with her tongue, then retreated. "That's already been proved to you. I promise I will always make you as wild, and agreeable, as you need to be."

That was part of what scared, and excited, her. "I . . . I don't want to be manipulated."

His eyes locked on hers. "I guarantee you that when I manipulate you, you will love it."

Caught in his spell, Cameo felt herself sinking beneath his persuasion despite her better sense.

Until the clearing of a throat shattered the spell.

Brax reacted so quickly that before she could blink, Cameo found herself shielded behind the protective wall of his hard body.

She felt his rigid preparation to attack—and a second later, the faint shifting of those impressive muscles as surprise replaced rage.

"Uncle Amos? What the hell are you doing here?"

A very deep, whisky-rough voice said, "Interrupting, obviously."

Cameo peeked around Brax to see a man even more intimidating and impressive. He was of a similar height to Brax, with that same inky black hair and startling golden eyes. But on this man, an edge of savagery showed as bright as a badge.

Age had added another layer of sturdiness to his frame and flicked silver highlights through the hair at his temples. A nasty scar cut through one eyebrow. The knuckles of both hands were bloody, and . . . the right side of his shirt dripped blood.

Cameo shoved around Brax. "You're hurt."

With stiff movements, the man pulled out a chair and talked about her as if she weren't there. "She's observant."

"More than you'd realize." Acting as if a bleeding relative were a routine thing, Brax got out a dishcloth, dampened it in the sink, and handed it to the man. "I didn't see your approach."

"With your surveillance?" His rude grunt conveyed much. "It's lacking."

"Not for most. And family is always welcome."

Cameo looked at them both. The gist of their conversation was that his family would have an advantage over other less-talented humans. She almost rolled her eyes. "How did you get in? The entire house is secured." As a routine part of her duties, she'd seen to that herself.

Brax rolled a shoulder. "A locked door wouldn't stop one of my relatives, any more than it would stop me." Then he gestured at the intruder. "Cameo, meet a long-lost relative, my uncle Amos."

The absurd formal introductions mixed with the macho disregard for bleeding wounds irritated her. "You're both ridiculous," she snapped. And then to Amos, "How badly are you hurt?"

Again he ignored her to speak to Brax. "Got a medical kit? I'm going to need stitches."

Cameo stiffened, but refused to be daunted. The man looked ready to pass out. Maybe he was in shock. She pushed aside his very large, roughened hands and lifted his blood-soaked shirt.

Both men reacted with raised brows.

The sight of gore and torn flesh just beneath his right armpit and over to his ribs didn't turn her squeamish, but they did invoke her sympathies. Gently, she prodded along the deep gash. More blood oozed out.

She reached back and took the cloth from Brax. "I can't be sure, but it doesn't appear that you've cut deep enough to affect anything vital." Mopping away most of the blood, she continued to examine him and his torn flesh. "You'll need more than stitches. Probably antibiotics and strong pain medication—"

"No pain meds, honey." Brax took the crimson-stained cloth from her and tossed it in the sink. "They don't mix well with our psyches."

That made her blink, but she supposed she could understand it. Anytime she'd ever taken pain meds, they'd made her loopy. Being that Brax and his uncle were more . . . visceral than most, an added effect made sense. "Aspirin, then?"

Brax turned to Amos. "What do you think, Uncle? To take the edge off?"

Amos surveyed Cameo with the same probing absorption he might have reserved for a two-headed frog or some other absurd freak of nature. "I'd prefer whisky. And if you can tear yourself away, I could really use that med kit, too."

"I'll be right back." Without another word, Brax headed out of the kitchen.

Straightening, Cameo admonished Uncle Amos with her sternest frown. "Are you two serious? Pain meds won't do, but a good stiff drink works just fine?" To her mind, the last thing Brax's uncle needed was alcohol thinning his blood or blurring his reactions. "I think this is more of your male-inspired logic."

Using alarming leisureliness while somehow taking her captive, Amos leaned forward. The glittering animus in his eyes urged Cameo to flee—but she couldn't get her legs to work. Inside her, panic swirled and churned in a dizzying ebb and flow; she fought it back with sheer force of will.

Yes, he was big, bloodied for reasons unknown to her, and more intrinsically wild than any man she'd ever met. He looked angry at the world, and perturbed by her in particular.

Her first impression had been shock and apprehension,

but she'd seen his injuries and caring for him had taken precedence over everything else.

He was Brax's uncle, so surely he posed no danger to her. Brax wouldn't have left her alone with him if doing so put her in peril. Right?

Amos didn't smile, but something showed in those fathomless, inhuman eyes of his, some very sardonic amusement—at her expense.

Even sitting, his extreme height put him on a level with her, and he used that to his advantage. His disquieting, probing scrutiny made her heart punch and her pulse leap.

Nearer and nearer he came, until his nose touched her cheek. His hot breath warmed her skin; his whisker-rough jaw brushed her hair, along her jaw.

Was he *smelling* her?

For only a moment, his eyes closed.

Her chest ached from holding her breath and fighting off the urge to scream.

Amos didn't move his hands; he kept them relaxed, one at his side, the other curved over his injury. But somehow his thighs now caged her in. The scent of blood and danger clung to him—

"What the fuck?" Brax dropped the med kit on the table with a clatter. With an arm wrapped around her waist, he snatched her back. Glaring at *her*, he said, "Make some more coffee, will you?"

Now that she was freed from Amos's mystical shackle, her umbrage exploded. Brax wanted to chastise her? Of all the . . .

Cameo folded her arms. "No, I will *not* make coffee, and don't you dare use that tone with me. If you'll recall, I don't work for you anymore."

Brax had turned to his uncle, but with her antagonistic gauntlet thrown out there, he slowly pivoted back around to her.

A strange foreboding came over Cameo. But damn him, she would not cower in his presence.

Incredulous, indignant, Brax stared down at her through

eyes gone molten. One eyelid twitched. A muscle in his jaw tightened.

Admittedly, it unnerved her to have two powerful, enormous men scrutinizing her in such minute detail, but she didn't want them to know it so she didn't retreat.

Pointing a finger at Amos, she said, "He started it, and all I did was wait him out."

Brax's jaw hardened more. Through his teeth, he said, "I know what he did, Cameo. Given who he is and how you fawned over him, it's understandable."

Her shoulders snapped back. She was so . . . well, hell, she was hurt. She'd expected Brax's trust, his defense, and instead he continued to accuse her. Regardless of his strange powers or special gifts, she would not be anyone's doormat.

No matter if she already loved him.

Her smile wouldn't fool anyone, but Cameo donned it anyway. "I see. Well, I'm glad that was all made so clear to me. I'll leave now so that I don't accidentally *fawn* over anyone here again."

Neither man moved.

Had she really expected him to apologize and beg her to stay? Yes. She'd been a fool.

Cameo forced her chin up a notch. "Good-bye, Brax. I'm certainly glad we were able to clear up so many things so thoroughly."

It would have been a good parting shot if both men hadn't spoken at the same time.

Amos said, "Leaving isn't an option, sweetness, not anymore."

At the same time Brax said, "Forget that, Cameo. You're not going anywhere."

One look at their hard-hearted expressions, and Cameo knew they meant what they said. They intended to keep her here—one way or another.

So okay, maybe she wasn't able to fend off the panic after all.

THREE

BRAX put her in a chair. Literally.

He wanted to apologize, to explain, but first he had to attend to his uncle. Amos might be blowing off the severity of the injuries, but he'd had enough of his own to gauge the damage and the pain involved.

He hadn't seen Amos in almost five years. That he'd shown up now screamed *imminent danger*.

In a rightful snit, Cameo wanted to leave. After regaining her courage, she started to rebound from the chair. Brax restrained her with a swift, almost negligent thought.

Yes, she had the ability to fend off his influence in some instances. But not where it concerned her safety.

Wincing as he examined his uncle's injury more closely, he said to Cameo, "Try to relax, honey. You'll be more comfortable if you're not fighting so hard."

A low growl and renewed struggle were her only responses.

Brax sighed. "Let me take care of Amos and then I can explain everything to you. Trust me. Everything will be okay."

Pride brought about her complacency, but he sensed the turmoil boiling inside her.

Even under his physical persuasion, her thoughts remained clear and concise. "You're not a dummy, Brax. You know that you just shot a million holes through any type of trust."

True enough. It'd be like starting over, except . . . well, Cameo was smart. So far she'd shown more tolerance and acceptance than he'd ever dared hope for. When he told her of the necessities—

"She's not going anywhere, boy. You've seen to that. Do I really need to bleed to death while you ruminate over soothing her?"

As Amos spoke, his gaze bored holes through Cameo. Brax understood because his initial reaction to her had been the same, and it had only grown stronger through the years. She alternately fascinated and entranced with her candor, openness, and independence.

Cameo always presented herself without artifice. What you saw was the real deal.

He'd gone through a five-year process of observing her idiosyncrasies, learning the level of her compassion and intelligence, growing closer to her.

And in that time his desire for her became inexorable: *He had to have her.*

So yes, he understood the depths of Amos's curiosity.

But his uncle's blunt apperception didn't help alleviate Cameo's growing distress. Not that Amos would care about Cameo's finer sensibilities. He'd stopped caring a long time ago. His lack of deference to females was in part why he'd retreated from the world.

Amos couldn't deny his heritage, but neither could he find the right woman to help soften the ever-corroding edges of his domestication.

It was safest for Amos, and everyone else, if he kept to the outskirts of mainstream society.

Only his uncle Torne was more savage. And no one had seen Torne in a decade.

Aware of Cameo's unwavering attention on him, burning his flesh, pricking his conscience, Brax threaded a needle.

"I've chosen her," he said to his uncle while intending for Cameo to hear, too. "She's mine now."

"You think I didn't know that?" Amos's gaze flickered over Cameo in that unsettled way of his. "You really put her through her paces first, didn't you? It's a wonder she can sit upright."

The sound of Cameo's gasp rebounded in the stainless steel kitchen.

"Don't sound so scandalized, honey." Though his uncle's sensual observation pricked his covetous instincts, Brax bent to the task of mending his flesh. "He didn't see anything."

Being contrary, Amos said, "I see plenty, if not first-hand then secondhand."

Brax scowled at his uncle, then glanced at Cameo. The color in her face told him he had better explain. She was such a refined, private woman that having her sexuality out there on display would cause her to withdraw from him more than anger or indignation ever could. "After a time, as we age—"

"By *we*, you mean your family?"

"The males of my family, yes." Brax possessed capable medical skills, but his uncle's injuries worried him. He'd lost a lot of blood. "As we age, our other senses become heightened, almost extreme. Sometimes even painful. You'd be surprised to learn—" He paused on that thought and took a moment to glance at her with speculation. "Or maybe not. You've been refreshingly open-minded so far."

The compliment didn't soften her one iota. "My open mind is closing fast, so I suggest you finish this fascinating tale."

Hiding a spontaneous grin, Brax went back to stitching. Though the needle pierced Amos's ravaged flesh again and again, he never made a sound. "There is a lot that can be deciphered through scent and taste." Another glance showed hot color washing her face and neck.

"He did *not* taste me."

Again Amos flickered—and almost smiled.

"I'd have already killed him if he had." Family or not, no one touched what was his. And Cameo, regardless of her acceptance of the fact, was his.

Cameo pulled back in apprehension over such a dire statement.

Amos continued to study her, no doubt absorbing her reaction to the implied threat. He understood Brax's perspective, and if Amos ever found the right woman for himself, he'd feel the same.

"My point is that arousal leaves a distinctive scent clinging to a woman's body." Thinking about it heated Brax anew. Cameo might have been satisfied, but he remained on a razor's edge of need. "I kept you at the heights of stimulation for an extended period. Not that the length of time matters. Anytime you're aroused, the males of my family will know it." He paused to give her a level look. "And when with me, you'll usually be aroused."

"Then my answer is no!"

Lacking any real apology, Brax said, "I'm sorry but it's too late for that. I want you too much to give you up."

"Ohhh . . . just . . . shut up, Brax!" Breath strangled in Cameo's throat as her color deepened more. "Not another word from you. I mean it."

Brax couldn't say the exact emotion evoked by her impudent commands, but whatever it was, it pushed him to assert his claim completely, and soon. When he made her his in every way, she would learn the proper way to deal with him.

It might take an all-day session of lovemaking, but then he could explain to her that *no one* spoke to him in that tone or dared to order him about, not even the elders. People unrelated to him sensed that much just by his presence.

And yet, while held immobile by the sheer strength of his will, Cameo dared much.

Her gumption proved a trust she might deny. She understood his capabilities, so if she truly feared him, she would be smart enough to hold her tongue.

Knowing that, despite everything, she still felt safe with him reassured Brax that he'd made the right choice. He would never hurt her, or allow harm to come to her, and she instinctively knew that.

It would take a confident woman to match him, and Cameo's strength was an asset. She only needed to temper it with him.

But then, her demure attitude on all things carnal also added to her allure. That she saved all her fire and passion for him stirred his primitive nature.

"And you," she said, redirecting her venom to Amos. "You can just put away your lethal stares and unspoken innuendo. I don't like it. I don't like you."

"And yet," Amos said, "you would have tended my wounds."

Most of her body remained still, but not that stubborn chin. She lifted it in challenge. "I'm not inhuman. I wouldn't watch you or anyone else bleed to death."

"Intriguing."

"Isn't it?" Brax saw Cameo's confusion and decided to elucidate. "It was your complete disregard of Amos's demeanor that enthralled him. Even though you felt threatened and afraid, you fawned over his injuries."

Amos's gaze moved over her. "It's unheard of for a woman to approach me without invitation."

Cameo's expression did not bode well for understanding. "I approached you only to help, not for any other reason."

Stubborn woman. "Cameo, I know you weren't coming on to him, and Amos wasn't coming on to you." He looked at Amos and, with steel in his tone, said, "Were you?"

"I have no use for women."

Right on cue, Cameo said, "Huh. And here Brax has so many uses for them."

Deciding he'd do better to smooth things with Cameo after he had her alone, Brax asked his uncle, "How long will you be here?"

"I need new weapons and tech. Then I'll leave."

Thinking of the severity of his injuries, Brax shook his head. "You should at least eat and get some sleep, maybe leave in the morning."

"The woman has distracted your judgment."

"The woman," Cameo said, "has a name."

Ignoring her, Amos finally turned all his attention on Brax. "There's no time for resting when innocents are at stake. The wound is fresh."

"Well, of course it is," Cameo said. "What's significant in that?"

Brax sat back on his heels. "It means that the one who attacked him is in the vicinity."

One corner of Amos's mouth tipped. It was the closest he ever got to a smile these days, and it wasn't pleasant or reassuring. "I can almost feel his breath on the back of my neck. I don't want to lose my focus on him."

Finished with cleaning and stitching the wound, Brax added antibiotic ointment and gauze. He stood. "I'll get you what you need."

"I have a question."

They both looked at Cameo, Brax curious as to her query, and Amos with impatience.

"If you knew trouble followed you, why did you come here?" Her baby-blue eyes never wavered from Amos's toxic stare. "Why run the risk of getting Brax hurt, too?"

Brax held up a hand before Amos could speak. "She doesn't yet realize what an insult that is."

"Amos got hurt," she pointed out with a shrug in her tone. "Are you claiming you're better at this than he is?"

Temper fraying, Brax fought for a moderate tone. "I'm saying that a paltry wound would be no reason to avoid conflict."

Amos slowly stood. "I didn't know Brax had a female of importance here."

Cameo's brows lifted. "So there's another kind of female?"

"Yes." His level stare withered her bravado. "There's the kind that doesn't distract him." And then to Brax, he said, "Handle your woman."

With a nod, Brax freed Cameo from the cerebral tethers—and barely caught her swinging palm before it made solid contact with his face.

God Almighty, but she must have been exerting a lot of energy to do that, to move as quickly as she had the moment she regained free use of her limbs.

Disapproving, Amos watched while Brax struggled to physically control her without hurting her. She fought in enraged silence without concern for injuring herself, her movements fast and frenetic. Her bones were so fragile and her muscles so slight that Brax knew inadvertent harm could easily befall her.

Before that could happen, he caught her up close, slamming her back to his chest. He trapped her by wrapping both arms around her, pinning her arms down, and hugging her body tightly to his.

She still said nothing, but fury hummed in every line of her petite body. She had to know it was useless, that his strength far exceeded hers, but still she fought him, laboring against his hold.

"Settle down now," Brax soothed.

"Go to hell."

Damn, he hadn't expected a physical confrontation from any woman, much less this woman. That his uncle witnessed it all didn't help. "This is absurd, Cameo."

"I *told* you I didn't want you to do that to me without my permission. I was very clear."

"I thought you only meant sexually—"

Her renewed struggle cut off that explanation. "Can't we agree to conversation instead of battle?" he asked.

She twisted again. "Since you don't respect my wishes, I can agree to leave and never see you again."

The mere suggestion of such a thing obliterated Brax's

more civilized temperament. He tightened his hold until she had no choice but to still completely. His mouth touched her ear as he breathed, "Unacceptable."

Playing mediator, Amos moved to stand right in front of her. "Understand, Cameo, he held you here because it's dangerous for you now, too. The man I'm chasing is a fan of sexual slavery. I found his hideout, a half-buried shack at the back of abandoned property. At the time he kept three women captive there." He touched Cameo's chin. "They were not faring well under his attention."

A new anxiety stiffened her spine. She stopped fighting. "Sexual slavery?"

"He had them chained at the ankles with heavy, rusted shackles. They were naked, dirty, hungry, and . . . marked."

Silence ticked by until Cameo whispered, "Marked?"

"Branded." Amos slashed a hand through the air. "He treated them worse than animals. They'd been used piteously, repeatedly. His appetites are not . . . normal."

Cameo's breath turned shallow and fast.

"Other than a dirty mattress on the floor, they had nothing. Their surroundings were wretched. I was deciding how best to free them when I was attacked from behind." He touched the back of his head. "A woman bludgeoned me with a shovel, knocking me down and stunning me."

"You hadn't sensed her approach?" Brax asked.

"I was concentrating on him." His mouth quirked. "I wanted the bastard decimated."

A fine trembling of fear replaced Cameo's fury.

"Luckily," Amos continued, "the bitch's loud screeching helped me recover my wits just as she struck with her knife. It was meant for my throat, but I leaped up and back, and she caught my midsection instead."

Horror widened Cameo's eyes and made her body go limp. "You could have been killed."

Instead of restricting now, Brax offered comfort. She pressed back closer to him, thrilling him, reassuring him that somehow they'd work through the difficulties.

Loosening his hold so that he could stroke her arm, he bent down and pressed a kiss to her temple.

"I believe the woman was his wife, and that she's working with him in his twisted sex torture." Amos's scowl darkened with disgust. "That somehow makes it sicker, right?"

"Very sick."

"The cretin broke from my spell when he heard her yells. He withdrew a gun. I was already bleeding like a slaughtered pig, so I made my way back to my car."

"You don't have the same level of talent as Brax?"

"He does," Brax said, fascinated by the way Amos now related to Cameo. His uncle rarely spoke with women anymore, and never would he explain himself to a female. But her easy acceptance of the unbelievable went a long way toward earning trust. "His talent is more refined than mine."

"I've been at it a few years longer." Amos searched Cameo's face, and Brax saw the moment that she drew him in.

He opened completely to her.

"I could have stayed and finished him off, but it's difficult to concentrate on two people at once, especially when injured. One of them at a time would have been no problem at all."

"Or both of them, if he hadn't lost so much blood." Unable to resist, Brax smoothed back Cameo's hair. He loved touching her. Soon, he'd touch her everywhere. To Amos, he asked, "What do you want to do now?"

Cameo pushed away from Brax and moved to Amos's back. She stretched up on tiptoe to touch the back of his head, examining the wound there. "You have quite the goose egg. Are you sure you're not concussed?"

Her gentle touch left Amos floundering for a heartbeat before he turned to face her with a frown so fierce, Brax half expected her to scurry back into his arms.

She didn't.

Amos was as bemused by that as Brax. He ignored

Cameo's question and addressed Brax's instead. "Soon as I reached my car I called the police and alerted them to the situation."

"Or most of the situation, anyway." They never shared their own involvement with local police. It was too risky.

Amos nodded. "I heard the sirens even as I was driving away. He won't have time to move the women to another spot. They'll be saved."

Cameo touched Amos's chest, above his injury. "Thank you for that."

His frown deepened more. He propped his hands on his hips. "The point is that whether he understands my talent or not, he knows now that I did something to him. And he knows that I'll be back for him. There's no place for him to hide, so his only recourse is to try to get to me first."

"That's what you wanted?"

"I'm tuned in to him, so I can find him again with little effort. But until I have him, anyone who's been in contact with me had better be on guard. You're best protected here."

Cameo shivered. "I've decided to stay." She looked past Amos to Brax, and added, "For now."

To himself, Brax clarified, *forever*.

Satisfied, Amos went to the counter and poured himself a drink. He tossed it back, winced, and then poured another. After two more sips, he dug into the back pocket of his jeans and withdrew two wrinkled snapshots. "I got these with my Polaroid before the bitch blindsided me."

He tossed the photos onto the table.

Wide-eyed and silent, Cameo crept to the table to look.

Brax absorbed her emotion and experienced her confusion. "The photos are insurance, honey, in case we're ever implicated."

"The people I work for insist on them." Amos drank a little more.

"You work for someone?"

Brax hadn't gotten quite that far in his disclosure. "For

more than a century my family has worked with high-level government officials within elite force units."

"Not the police?"

"More exclusive than that."

"With more leeway," Amos added. "We don't answer to anyone. We just report what we've done." Ringing with sarcasm, he added, "We save the taxpayers a lot of money that would be wasted on official procedure."

"Many crimes that go unsolved, well, that's us, Cameo. The murder and mayhem stops and that's all we care about."

Holding her breath, Cameo touched the photos, turning them for a better view.

Knowing what she'd see, Brax stepped up behind her, bracing his hands on her shoulders. It was always painful to be pulled into the blackness of a depraved soul. Like an oily sheen, it clung, stunk, and clogged cleaner thoughts.

"Dear God." Cameo's shaking hands went to her mouth. She closed her eyes for a moment, swallowed convulsively.

"If I don't get him," Amos told her, "he'll do this again and again. More women will be hurt, and most will never recover."

Agreeing, she said, "We have to do something."

"We?" His heart almost stopping, Brax jerked her around to face him. "Amos will handle it, and if need be, I'll help."

"But what should I do?"

Dear God, was she trying to push him past his control? *"You,"* he stressed with iron in his tone, "will keep yourself safe from harm."

That stubborn frown of hers appeared.

It took all Brax had not to shake her. "Understand me, Cameo. I will never allow you to be involved in any of this. Never."

"Allow me?"

His jaw clenched. "You are a beautiful woman with a

generous, innocent spirit, and I plan for you to stay that way."

She chewed that over before saying, "The women in your family—"

"They are protected, cherished." And the ones who knew of the inherent influence understood. "The talent only affects the males, never the females. What nature started, I will continue."

She pulled free of his hold and tried another tactic. "I understand what you're saying, and you're right—to a degree. But Amos is injured and can't concentrate, so of course you'll help him." She turned a frown on Amos. "Don't argue. You need Brax."

Brows lifted, Amos said, "Perhaps."

She turned back to Brax. "And you already said that you need me to help you stay clearheaded."

Damn it, he did not want to have this discussion in front of his uncle. Refusing to look at Amos, Brax leaned down close to her. "My need of you is limited to a sexual environment. That's all."

Her eyes narrowed and a lethal edge entered her tone. "That's all?"

Why did women excel at twisting a man's words? "You know what I mean, woman, so don't try to provoke me."

Her arms folded beneath her breasts. "I will not be a paramour, Brax."

"We agreed you would be what I need you to be."

Her mouth fell open. "I agreed to nothing!"

Amos lifted his drink and leaned back on the counter, waiting to see the outcome of their skirmish.

Brax took a step closer to Cameo. "I could settle this right now."

Anger brought her nose to nose with him. "You could—in the short term. But in the long run, if you expect me to stay here—"

Brax waited.

"—then I want my job back."

Well. That unexpected reply took him back. He'd expected demands, but not that she be allowed to continue in her position of personal assistant. "Impossible."

"Why?"

How dare she continue to challenge him in front of his uncle? "Sexual harassment?" He stared at her hard. "I don't want to be sued."

He expected fireworks over the blatant sarcasm. He expected another slap.

She surprised him.

Stoic again, she said, "Fine. I get that." She moved closer still, put a hand to his chest. "Then I guess you'll have to marry me."

FOUR

THE look of shock on his face didn't encourage Cameo. That Amos spit out his drink was annoying, too. Was marriage so unheard of?

She still had a lot to learn about his strange emotional aptitude and family dynamics, and there was no time like the present.

"So." Trying not to sound hurt, she crossed her arms and propped out her hip. "Your family doesn't believe in marriage?"

"We do, but . . ."

It was a rare thing to see Brax Jardine falter in any way. He was such a take-charge guy, a natural-born leader, and superbusinessman, that to see him blank-faced seemed almost comical.

"But?" Cameo prompted. "You don't want to be saddled with me long term? Is that it?"

"That's not it at all."

"Well, come on, Brax. Something has you flopping about like a fish out of water."

Brax frowned, but remained mute.

Cameo sighed—until she felt Amos's heavy arm drape her shoulders.

"Few women," Amos said, "know what we're capable of. And those who do know had to be . . . heavily coerced into marriage. But you, well you're Little Miss Fearless, aren't you?" He chucked her under the chin.

Cameo got hung up on a single word. "Coerced?" She didn't like the sound of that at all.

"Erotic coercion." A devilish twinkle came into Amos's golden eyes. "Women can become addicted to the complete fulfillment of their appetites." He leaned closer and whispered, "Their sexual appetites."

Though Cameo frowned over Amos's attitude, she could see his point. Already she yearned for more of what Brax had shown her.

She turned her gaze on Brax. "So he can tell me this, but you can't?"

"It is a sensitive, personal conversation."

She'd give him that. But right now they didn't have the opportunity for privacy. Not with that deranged monster lurking about. "Get a grip, will you, Brax? If we're going to be married, I'll expect coherent conversation."

He straightened in umbrage and spoke through his teeth. "I *have* a grip."

"About time." She put her hands on her hips as she faced Amos. "So we're all in agreement. You'll wait a few hours to eat, rest up, and then when you leave, you'll take Brax with you."

"You're a little tyrant, aren't you?"

"Apparently I'm the voice of common sense." She looked at each man in turn. "Agreed?"

"Fine by me," Brax said. "As long as I have a few hours before we start the hunt."

Amos shrugged. "I could use a bath, something to eat. And a change of clothes wouldn't hurt."

Cameo nodded in satisfaction. "Great. Now do you need any further assistance?"

"With what?"

"Preparing your bath? Finding clothes? Locating those weapons and whatever 'tech' you say you need?"

Bemused, Amos shook his head. "I'm quite self-sufficient."

"Everything you need is downstairs," Brax told him. "Including a bathroom."

"Wonderful." She moved to Brax's side. "Then perhaps Brax and I could continue our talk in private."

"I see why she served as personal assistant." Mocking her, Amos gave a bow that made him wince, then said to Brax, "Just point me in the right direction."

Brax dug in his pocket, removed a set of keys, and tossed them to Amos. "Turn right at the bottom of the stairs, then go to the far end of the basement. Behind the bar in my gym, in a hidden panel."

"I take it no one uses the gym but you?"

"True." His big hand clasped the back of Cameo's neck. "Most never enter the basement without me accompanying them, and then it's to the theater or game room. Mercy's been there with her new husband, but they weren't into anything."

"Mercy's married?"

"Happily, yes. And expecting a baby." Brax grinned. "You'll like Wyatt. He has very strong emotion for her."

Cameo rolled her eyes. "It's called love."

Brax's brows pulled together. "For Wyatt, it goes beyond even that."

Amos nodded in understanding. "There's love, and then there's something more."

"I suppose you're right." With a sigh, Cameo realized that she wanted the something more, but would settle for love. Actually, she'd settle for marriage.

She loved Brax enough for the both of them. And if she truly made him happy and gave him what he needed, why would he ever need to look elsewhere?

"Ready?"

Drawn back to the present, she smiled and nodded.

"Some might even say anxious." She realized how that sounded and stammered, "That is, I have a lot of questions."

Amos chuckled as he headed to the basement.

They'd taken only a few steps when Brax stopped and kissed her. "Thank you."

"For?"

"Amos hasn't had reason to laugh in a very long time. He's hovering on the abyss of oblivion, holding on by sheer, indomitable will. But that can only last him so long. He needs laughter, and love." Brax cupped her face. "You astounded him as much as you astound me."

"Is that a good or bad thing?"

"It's an unexpected thing. And for men who can pick apart others by their emanation of emotion, it's nice to get the unexpected on occasion."

And with that, he scooped Cameo up into his arms.

Taken by surprise, Cameo grabbed for his neck to hold on. "Brax, what are you doing?"

"I need you. Now. Yesterday and tomorrow. We'll talk after." He started for his bedroom.

"After?"

"After I've sated this inferno of lust." His stride was long and sure. "Know now that it's going to take some time."

Understanding how badly Brax wanted her had a singular effect on Cameo. Her own desire ignited. She wanted him so badly . . .

Or did she?

Wondering if he influenced her, Cameo pulled back to look into his eyes, and warned, "I want this, too, Brax, but no . . . tricks."

Without a word, he bounded down the long hallway, his face set, his gaze hot.

Her body burned with every step he took. "Damn it, Brax, I mean it." She caught a fistful of hair at the back of his head to get his attention. "Don't persuade me with your blasted talent."

Undisturbed by her insistence, Brax pushed through his bedroom door, carried her to the bed, and came down over her. He rose to his knees and pinned her arms to either side of her head.

Staring down at her with such smoldering intent, he was so big, so impossibly overwhelming, that Cameo felt more vulnerable than she ever had in her life. "Brax?"

His gaze moved over her, and he shook his head with disbelief. "The wonder of it all, sweetheart, is that I haven't influenced you now at all." His gaze came back to fasten on hers. "And still you want me so much that it's tearing me apart inside."

He hadn't manipulated her? But . . . but she'd never been an overly sexual woman. It didn't make sense.

Still, she believed that Brax wouldn't lie to her. "Oh."

He closed his eyes a moment. "It's taking all I have to keep this civil."

Civil? That should have alarmed her, and instead it thrilled her.

"I want to do everything to you, honey. Right now. Whether you're ready or not."

"I think I am ready."

"Don't!" He worked his jaw. "That doesn't help, damn it. Now just be quiet. Don't move. Let me . . . do this right."

He hadn't yet said if he'd marry her, but Cameo couldn't see pushing the issue at the moment. He looked agonized, frenzied, and that was as aberrant as him being tongue-tied. It just didn't happen to the awesome Brax Jardine.

"All right."

Her agreement amplified his heat. He released her wrists, and when she stayed still, he went to work on the buttons of her blouse. Big as he was, he had astonishing dexterity, and the tiny pearl buttons opened with ease.

He spread the blouse wide and looked at her lace-covered breasts. Breathing deeply through his nose, he trailed his hands over her throat, her shoulders, and around her breasts to her rib cage. When he reached the top of her skirt, he wedged one hand behind her and unfastened the hook.

"Lift up."

It wasn't easy with him stationed over her, but Cameo managed to raise herself enough for him to slide down her zipper. The position thrust her pelvis up hard into his bulging erection. They both took a moment to absorb the sensation of that.

After releasing a breath, Brax scooted farther down her body, and rather than remove her skirt, he reached up beneath it. His hot palms smoothed over her nylon-covered thighs.

"I prefer stockings," he told her as he worked the pantyhose down her hips.

"Tough." Cameo did her best to keep her voice even under the escalating stimulation. "They're too much trouble."

A half smile curved his mouth. "Maybe I'll just keep you naked and it'll become a moot point."

He had to be kidding, but just in case, she said, "Not on your li—"

The nylon ripped apart in his hands, startling her. "Brax!"

"Shhh." He pulled the shredded material down to her knees and reached back up for her panties. "You have on too damn many clothes."

She would have denied that, except that his hot palm settled over her sex and it was nearly enough to set her off.

"Easy," Brax whispered. "Slow down."

"I . . . I'm not sure I can."

He looked into her eyes and stroked her experimentally.

"Oh, God." Her breath caught and her muscles clenched, causing her body to bow.

Brax smiled—and removed his hand. "I need you naked." He took care of that with little help from her, and before she could resettle her racing heartbeat, he had her stripped down to nothing.

It was an irregular thing for her to be naked in front of a man, and her embarrassment would have been extreme except for Brax's reaction.

Kneeling beside her on the bed, he locked his hands behind his neck and just looked at her. His nostrils flared, his jaw worked. Those beautiful eyes of his blazed with a thousand emotions and raging need.

Still not touching her, he whispered, "Open your thighs."

Seeing the effect she had on him made Cameo feel so powerful. It wasn't easy for her to display herself, but Brax's life was never easy, not with the gift he had, so the least she could do was give him this pleasure if that's what he wanted.

Slowly, she scissored her legs open.

His biceps bunched, his pecs tightened. His chest labored. Voice rasping, he ordered, "Show me everything. Bend your knees for me."

Biting her lips to help quell her timidity, Cameo drew her legs up, then let them fall open.

Brax sucked in a deep breath, struggled with himself for a few moments. And suddenly he broke.

It was unexpected, a little scary, and it caught her up on a whirlwind of exhilaration.

He bent down and opened his mouth on her inner thigh, sucking, biting a little, softly eating his way over to her sex.

Cameo held her breath, but he bypassed over to her other thigh, then up to her hip bones and her belly, her ribs.

She felt consumed. In a barely there voice, she said, "Brax?"

He reached up for her breasts, caressed them, and then held them together as he kissed and licked his way there, teasing all of her flesh.

He remained fully clothed, and she wanted to protest

that, but then his mouth covered her nipple and it was unlike anything she'd ever felt.

There was nothing subtle in the strong way he sucked at her, the hungry way he fed off her. And the more he took, the higher her need soared.

She held his head to her and without meaning to, begged for more. "Brax, *please*."

He moved to her other breast and at the same time, rested one big hand on her belly.

Somehow, it was enough.

The stimulation of her nipples spread out everywhere, pooled between her thighs, and she started coming.

Still feasting on her, Brax moaned against her breast, and that was a keenly pleasurable sensation, too.

When the orgasm abated, Cameo lay there stunned, unable to comprehend how or why it had happened—unless he'd lied to her and manipulated her by other means.

"You are amazing," he told her. He sat up again, his chest billowing with his breaths as he stroked her body. "Perfectly amazing."

She swallowed hard. "Did you . . . ?"

"No. I swear." His gaze sought hers. "Did you want me to?"

"No." She licked her bottom lip. "I just . . . I don't understand."

"You're incredible." As if it were nothing at all, he slipped two fingers between her legs and tested her wetness. "Damn, Cameo."

Electricity shot through her again. "No, wait." The sensations were too sharp, almost painful. "I need a minute."

"Sorry." He started leaning down, and in a growl said, *"Can't."*

He kissed her belly again, pressed both fingers into her, stretching her, filling her. The incredible stimulation froze them both.

Urgent now, Brax caught her hips and turned her so that he had better access to her. He parted her sex, licked her deeply, and then closed his mouth over her. He made a sound of sublime pleasure, and that proved enough to send Cameo reeling.

"Brax!" She arched up as another climax spiraled through her, but this time when it ended, he didn't stop. She cried out, tried to ease away from him and the too-intense feelings on her already sensitive flesh.

He didn't allow it.

His sharp teeth nipped, his rough tongue lathed, and far too soon, discomfort changed to the most blinding gratification. She was almost there again when Brax jerked away from her.

Through a haze of lust, Cameo watched as he ripped his shirt off and shoved down his pants and boxers.

Eyes widening, she rose to her elbows. He was . . . well, bigger than she'd imagined.

He found a condom in the nightstand drawer and rolled it on with experienced ease.

"Um, Brax . . ."

He spared her a quick glance. "It'll be fine, Cameo. I promise."

"I should have guessed," she said nervously while still eyeing his erection. "I mean, you're so blasted big everywhere."

He made a choking sound. "I know you're far from experienced, but you'll take me, honey. Trust me."

Her heartbeat hurt inside her chest. Her skin tingled. Her body ached.

Trust was there, as was love so bright, it outshone her misgivings and nervousness.

She opened her arms to Brax, and he came back to her in raging urgency.

His thick, muscled thighs opened her legs even more. His weight bore her into the mattress. She felt the head of his erection at her opening, prodding, and then Brax kissed her so deeply that she couldn't think. Heat infused her, surrounded her. She smelled Brax's wonderful scent, tasted the heat of his mouth, felt the sleekness of his muscles under her palms.

Behind her closed eyelids, lights exploded—and then he pressed into her with one solid thrust.

The shock on her body had her arching hard. Her shout of mingling discomfort and carnal satisfaction was muffled by the thrusting of his tongue, his deep, hot kiss.

He kept still, letting her get used to the size and girth of him while pinning her down, claiming her. And all the while he continued to kiss her, to touch and stroke her body. Her muscles clenched involuntarily and he moaned, shuddered.

Wanting to accept him, to ease him, Cameo slowly lifted her legs around his lean waist and locked her ankles.

He cupped her face, kissed her some more before lifting up to look at her. His bright gaze searched her face. "You're alright?"

Cameo stroked his midnight hair and loved him so much it hurt. "I'm filled with you. I'm better than all right."

The gold of his eyes smoldered. "I need you so bad it's killing me. I can't be easy. I'm sorry."

Cameo smiled at him. "I'm ready." And she was. As overblown as it seemed, she wanted him. Again. Maybe she always would, with or without his influence.

"I could make it easier on you."

"No. This is ours, Brax. It has to be real."

He closed his eyes on an internal battle and lost. Taking her mouth again, he began driving into her. The maelstrom shocked her and drove her toward release. He kissed her throat, her shoulder, and just as he came he reared back and slammed into her, growling out his release.

The near-violent upheaval left Cameo panting. He hadn't hurt her at all, but never in her life had she imagined sex to be so all-consuming, so wild, so feverish.

Still on straightened arms over her, Brax said, "That's a start."

A start?

He pulled out and stood by the side of the bed. "Turn over."

Cameo blinked. Her skin still tingled, her nerve endings all buzzing, her mind nearly numb. "Surely you aren't . . ."

"Done? Not even close." He got out another condom, changed up, and then caught her hips to flip her over. "Up on your knees, baby."

She was too speechless to reply or to protest when he pulled her up himself. His big hand smoothed over her derriere with appreciation.

"Beautiful." This time he sank in easier, slow and deep.

The hair on his chest brushed her back. His hands dipped under her, one to ply her nipples, the other stroking her sex. Her clitoris was still swollen, and he very gently touched a fingertip to it.

Cameo moaned. How she could still respond, she didn't know, but Brax knew what to do to get her with him again.

When he donned a third condom, she didn't even bother protesting. Of course, she was so sluggish, so drained, that speech would have been a bother. Not that he seemed affected by any of it.

He pulled her atop him and then helped her sit up on his abdomen, letting her lean back on his knees. His hands on her breasts, lightly rolling her sensitive nipples, he ordered, "Lift up, honey, so I can get inside you."

Whimpering at the thought of another explosive climax, Cameo closed her eyes and slowly elevated herself.

Brax positioned his erection, waited until she opened her eyes and looked at him, then said gently, "Sit down."

Her eyes closed again as she slowly sank onto him.

He held her hips, helping her, urging her. "It's deepest this way, Cameo." His hands clenched a little, betraying his need. "All the way down, honey. Do it." His breath caught as she settled onto him.

She groaned and collapsed back against his bent legs.

"That's it." His voice was gruff, uneven. "Just relax and let me enjoy you."

Relax? She was on fire again, her every nerve ending

sparking from erotic stimulus. Words were beyond her; she could only moan and pant and do as he asked, trust in what he needed and wanted.

This time Brax did everything, and as usual, though she remained mostly lax and exhausted, he brought her with him to another ripping release.

Already half-asleep, Cameo barely noticed as Brax moved her to his side on the rumpled sheets, smoothed back her hair, and pulled the bedcovers over her. She felt his kiss to her forehead, and his smile.

Seconds later, as the bed dipped and Brax left her, she thought that she should probably say something. But instead, she faded into peaceful, utterly replete oblivion.

FIVE

AFTER freshening himself and redressing, Brax found his uncle in the kitchen again, this time at the stove cooking. Amos wore a clean pair of jeans and nothing else. So many scars, old and new, crisscrossed over his shoulders and back.

For a man who'd just been badly wounded, he didn't move with caution. As he scrambled eggs and fried bacon, he showed no signs of discomfort or weakness.

"That smells good."

Amos glanced over his shoulder. "I figured you'd be hungry when you came back downstairs. I cooked plenty."

Brax moved to the stove. "What made you think I'd come back down?"

"I'm here. And you're curious." Amos handed over the spatula and moved to the counter to drink some orange juice. "Besides, I can't picture you napping the day away. No matter what."

Brax grinned. "Switched to juice, huh?"

"The alcohol took the edge off, which is all I needed. I don't want to blur my judgment."

The bacon was almost done, so Brax took down a plate. "Why don't you sit and let me finish this?"

Without a word, Amos moved to the table. "The little lady sleeping?"

"Yeah."

"You going to marry her?"

"We'll see." Brax stirred the fluffy eggs. "I don't want to rush her into anything."

Amos snorted. "Like you have a choice? From what I saw, she did all the arm twisting."

Brax grinned again. Damn, but he felt good. Great. Cameo was more than he'd ever expected, more than he'd ever hoped for. "You like her?"

"Depends."

Taking the frying pan off the stove, Brax asked, "On what?"

"On whether you can be with her and keep your perspective." He propped an elbow on the tabletop. "She seems fine enough, and God knows you've got a bad case for her. But if she throws you off your game, then I think you'd be better to end it now, while you can."

Brax was already shaking his head. "Too late for that."

Amos studied him, then snorted. "I suppose we'd better hope for the best, then, huh?"

Toast and butter were already on the table, so Brax dished up the eggs and bacon and joined his uncle. It was a little after noon, but he didn't expect Cameo to show herself again for an hour or more. He'd worn her out—by necessity and design.

He'd needed her to regain his focus, and he'd wanted her to sleep so he'd have some time to talk with his uncle.

They each ate a few bites before Brax spoke. "I think she's the one for me."

"I can see it. Reservations already stated."

Brax shook his head. "If anything, she calms me so I can better concentrate."

"Your uncle Torne felt the same about a woman—until

she changed her mind and walked out on him. She couldn't deal with his duty, and he couldn't deal without her. Took him years to put himself back together."

"You've seen him?"

"Briefly, a few years back. He looks like hell." Amos considered that, and restated himself. "Like hell with a purpose. He's a machine, hard-bodied and clear thinking, but without much compassion left. I'm not sure how much longer he can go on like that."

A tightness settled into Brax's chest. He fashioned a cynical smile. "Then I better not let Cameo go, right?"

Amos shrugged. "For what it's worth, she doesn't strike me as the type to turn tail and run when things get rough."

"As they always do with Jardine men." Sooner or later, Cameo would witness the residual effects of his talent. She'd see him cut and bleeding as Amos had just been. She'd see him in a blind rage, intent on destruction.

She'd see the worst of him.

"You can't deny your heritage. Some have tried and failed." Amos finished off his food. "She's a tough one, but I've learned that with women, you just never know. I suggest you not marry her until you're damn sure. Marriage complicates the hell out of things. It gets all kinds of legalities involved."

Given their lifestyles, the Jardines always shied away from the legal system. Too many questions, too-close observation, was never a good thing.

"When do we leave?"

Amos glanced at the clock on the wall. "A couple of hours, I guess. I already got the weapons and tech equipment ready. Now that I'm fed, I figured I'd catch a little sleep, too."

Judging by Amos's haggard appearance, he could use more than a little sleep, but Brax wouldn't push him. It was a huge concession for Amos to admit he could use his help—and he had Cameo to thank for that. "That's fine. I have some business to attend anyway."

"Wake me at two thirty. I'll be ready to head out by three."

"Sure thing."

After pushing back his chair, Amos clapped Brax on the shoulder. "I'm assuming you have a guest room in this palace?"

Because he was proud of his home, Brax grinned. "I'll walk you up. I'm heading that way for my office, anyway." The dishes would wait for later. Normally the housekeeper came in for them, but in anticipation of settling things with Cameo, he'd given her the day off. Same with the gardener and pool guy.

Since Amos had brought trouble right to his front door, he was doubly glad not to have extra people around. And thinking of extra people, he'd give his sister a call to check in, before she decided to drop by.

Half an hour later, Brax was at his desk, balmy air drifting in through the hole in his wall, when Cameo appeared in the doorway. He felt her presence before she spoke, and looked up, taking in the voluptuous sight of her.

She looked like a woman well loved, soft and sleepy and sated.

Interesting. Brax sat back and laced his hands over his midsection. "Hey."

Light-brown hair tumbled in disarray around her shoulders, half hiding her heavy eyes. She'd pulled on her clothes, but they were messy, the blouse untucked, her legs nude beneath her skirt.

"Hey yourself." She sauntered in with new sensuality, her bare feet making no sound on the floor. Nodding at the wall, she said, "That has to be fixed, sooner rather than later. It's a hazard."

"Agreed." Brax tracked her every movement, and was pleased when she came to sit on the edge of his desk.

He didn't reach for her.

She didn't reach for him.

Tilting her head, Cameo smiled. "I woke up a little while ago, and I've been thinking."

A sliver of apprehension pierced his contentment. He kept his expression remote. "About?"

The corners of her mouth lifted in a sly, sanguine smile. "About the fact that I'm going to continue serving as your personal assistant."

Relief eased his taut muscles. Before that moment, he hadn't realized just how sexy confidence in a woman could be. "Is that so?"

"It is." She leaned in a little, deliberately displaying her cleavage for the first time since he'd met her. "I don't want you hiring another woman who'll be in my way, and I can't see you working comfortably with a man."

Jealousy? This was about her not wanting another woman around? "I will be faithful to you."

"Sure you will." Her smile turned lazy. "But I'm still going to be your assistant."

The phone rang, keeping Brax from saying anything more on the subject. He started to reach for the phone, but Cameo beat him to it.

As if her position as his number one employee had never been interrupted, she said in a businesslike tone, "Jardine residence. Cameo Smithson speaking."

She waited, then smiled at Brax and crossed her legs. "Mercy, how are you?" Nodding, she said, "I see. Well, I hope it gets better. Brax is right here. Did you want to speak to him? Sure thing. You, too." She handed the phone to Brax with the mouthpiece covered. "I'm going to go shower while you talk to your sister."

A tantalizing visual sprang into his mind. He'd love to join her, but his sister waited. Cameo knew he'd never ignore his sister. "Tease," he complained.

She kissed his mouth very gently, and then left the room.

After watching her seductive exit, Brax took a moment to draw in a calming breath. Given how Cameo kick-started his libido with no more than a familial peck, she was definitely the woman for him, the one he wanted around for the long run.

But as Amos had pointed out, the Jardine males had

more considerations than other men. He wanted Cameo to be happy, and until he knew he could give that to her, he wouldn't cement their relationship legally.

Putting the phone to his ear, he said, "I was going to call you in just a few minutes. How are you?"

"Like I told Cameo, I'm tired."

To give his sister all his attention, Brax closed the file on his computer. "You're not getting sick, are you?"

"I'm getting fat." Mercedes sighed. "The pregnancy is really starting to show, and not just in my waistline. I am so lethargic, it's nuts. And to top things off, I think I ate too much this morning and now I feel yucky."

Worry brought Brax out of his chair. He strolled to the hole in his wall and looked out at the grounds. "Describe *yucky*."

"It's nothing, Brax. Just . . ." A shrug sounded in her tone. "Yucky."

"What does Wyatt say?"

She laughed. "My dear husband doesn't say anything. He's in a big meeting today and no way am I interrupting that just to tell him that I'm—"

"Yucky." Brax narrowed his eyes at a line of bushes at the back of his property. Had something just moved? "Maybe you should call your doctor."

This time Mercy huffed. "You are such a mother hen. I'm sorry I said anything. Seriously, Brax, I am *fine*."

Definitely, something moved. Perhaps an animal—but perhaps not. "What do you have planned today?"

"Nothing much. I'm staying home to work on some jewelry designs, that's all. Why?"

"I don't want you out driving around, not if you're not feeling well."

"Brax, you're being ridiculous. I am not incapacitated."

"You're pregnant, and I'm very excited about being an uncle. So please, will you take it easy and call the doctor if you don't start feeling better?"

"I will absolutely call the doctor if it's necessary. I promise."

He supposed that'd have to do. Brax thought of his baby sister now married, soon to be a mother, and warmth spread all through him. "I love you, Mercedes."

"Right back at you." She hesitated, voice tentative, and asked, "Speaking of love . . . what's going on with you and Cameo?"

Surprised that Mercedes had held off this long without grilling him, Brax grinned. They were close and shared most everything, but never had Brax talked to her about his love life, and never did she ask.

Cameo was different, and Mercedes knew it, but he still wasn't going to spill his guts to her. "I'll tell you everything as soon as I figure it out. Now I've got to go. Take it easy, and don't forget to call if you need anything."

He hung up on her exasperated *"Brax,"* and gave all his concentration to the bushes on the perimeter of his property. He saw nothing more than a possible flash, maybe of something metal, maybe of nothing at all.

He didn't take chances, not with this, not with Cameo in the house.

Before he went to investigate, he decided to have a chat with Cameo. She needed to understand what he expected of her, at least as far as security was concerned.

She was still in the shower when he walked into one of the upstairs bathrooms, breathed in the thick steam, and pulled back the curtain.

Head back, water streaming over her bare breasts, she remained oblivious to him.

Brax wanted to curse the bad timing of things. He needed to spend every available moment with Cameo. That's what he'd intended before Uncle Amos had shown up with a psychotic lunatic likely trailing him.

To him, Cameo looked so beautiful, but it wasn't just her slender body, her soft skin and womanly allure. It was everything about her—her intellect, her sense of responsibility and honor, her caring nature, and the way she reacted to him both emotionally and physically.

She looked asleep on her feet, basking in the warm caress of the water. It turned him on.

Hell, she could do nothing and he'd be turned on.

"I wish I could join you."

She didn't jump as he'd expected her to do. She didn't even open her eyes. She just smiled. "Why don't you?"

"Sadly, I have something more important that has to be tended to."

Those beautiful blue eyes zeroed in on him. "Tell me."

She showed no modesty, and that surprised Brax more than anything. Not that she had reason to hide her body. He was already hard just looking at her. But she'd always been so circumspect, so modest.

Maybe it'd wait after all . . .

A thunderous boom shook the house, jarring everyone and everything. Cameo faltered, slipped on the wet tub floor, and would have fallen if Brax hadn't scooped her in close to his chest.

Snarling a curse, he shut off the shower and snatched up her towel. "Get dressed. Hurry."

She wrapped the towel around herself with haste. "What was that?"

On his way out the door, Brax said, "That was an idiot, sealing his fate."

EVEN through the thick smoke and the stench of sulfur, Brax saw that the office was in ruins. Scraps of paper floated in blackened air. Glass from cabinets littered the floor. Plaster dust mingled with smoke.

Amos charged in behind Brax. "What the fuck happened?"

Hands on his hips, seething with fury, Brax used the toe of his boot to nudge aside a chunk of broken pipe. "I'm not going to investigate right now, but I'd say a homemade bomb was somehow lobbed through the opening in the wall. It looks like a powerful firework, stuffed inside a can with sharp debris."

"Effective." Amos spoke loudly over the splintering peal of smoke alarms. "My guy is trying to lure us out."

"It's tricky, though." Brax went out in the hall to a central control board and shut down the alarms. Silence fell like a dark curtain of doom. He dropped his tone accordingly. "How does he know we won't just call the cops on him?"

Still wearing only a towel, Cameo said from behind them, "He's probably far enough away that he can run if the police show up."

Seeing her there in the damp towel and nothing more, Brax stared with disbelief. She looked . . . too damn sexy with her wet hair and dewy skin.

Amos coughed and turned his back on her.

Burning possessiveness crushed Brax's calm. That she would show herself to his uncle like this infuriated him—until he noticed the trembling of her bottom lip. He had to remember that his world was not the same as hers.

He inhaled a calming breath. "Uncle Amos, why don't you go get ready before the bastard slips away from us? I'll join you downstairs in just a minute."

"Right." Amos disappeared with alacrity.

Brax saw the shadowing fear in Cameo's eyes as he approached her. "It'll be okay."

Her gaze searched his with incredulity. "Brax, your home was just *bombed*."

Damn it, he did not want her to get spooked. If she did, she might not want to stay with him.

And he couldn't let her go.

With an arm around her, he steered her back to his bedroom. He had little time to spare, but he couldn't leave her like this. "Let's get you dressed. Then I'll take care of everything."

"I don't have any other clothes here."

"We'll take care of that tomorrow."

"After you annihilate a lunatic today?" Her raw laugh quivered with trepidation. "Do you really think it's that easy?"

Giving himself time to choose his words carefully, Brax took her towel, hung it over a chair, and took one of his own shirts from the closet.

"Trusting me should be easy because I'd never harm you, or allow you to be harmed." As he would a child, he pulled the soft cotton T-shirt over her head and worked her arms through it. It hung on her like an oversized dress, half covering her knees.

"You promise?"

He held her face and made a solemn pledge. "I swear to you, Cameo, I will care for you. Always."

She slowly nodded. "All right." Her arms went around him in a ferocious hug. "Go, then. Do what you have to do. But Brax? Please be careful."

God, her concern touched his heart and made him ache with tenderness. "I'm always careful. Now promise me the same."

She leaned back to smile at him. Her voice steadier, she said, "I keep reminding you that I'm intelligent, not foolhardy."

"It's a fine quality." He patted her backside. "You look very tempting in my shirt."

She held out the material. "I'm lost in it, but thank you anyway. It'll do for now while I dry my hair."

"Get whatever you need and take it downstairs. The smoke isn't as stifling there. I'll come back as soon as I can and then I promise to get everything cleaned up."

"As your assistant, that's my job. I'll make some calls."

Agreeing with a nod, Brax walked with her while she gathered her clothes, her purse, a blow dryer, and a brush.

When they got downstairs, Amos was waiting impatiently at the door. He wore all black and had a leather bag in his hand. "He's here, I feel it. Let's go."

Before Cameo could start asking more questions, Brax kissed her. He touched her cheek, kissed her again—and left without a word. He'd already said what needed to be said.

He'd asked for her trust, so he'd just have to trust in return. She'd be there when he got back.

She had to be.

UNTIL Brax returned, Cameo planned to keep very busy. She would launder her clothes, put on makeup, eat, and make phone calls to repair the damage from the bomb. She would eat up the time with errands to give herself less time to think, less energy to worry.

Nervous about another bomb, she steered clear of the windows as she carried her washables into the laundry room. Along the way, she checked the security monitors. Outside Brax's expansive home, nothing stirred but an occasional bird.

And still her heart pounded too fast and hard.

With the example she'd been given today, it would be hell loving Brax Jardine. But what choice did she have? Giving him up now would be impossible.

When the phone rang, it startled Cameo so badly she gasped aloud. Hand to her heart, she went to the receiver, checked the caller ID and then picked up with a smile of relief. "Mercy. Hello."

"Shh, Cameo, I don't want Brax to know it's me."

"He's not here right now." She heard something in Mercy's tone and went on alert. "What's wrong? Are you all right?"

"I'm sure I am, but . . . I'm having some unusual cramps and it . . . well, it scares me." She sniffled, as if fighting tears. "I'm just so emotional lately and I keep thinking that if something *is* wrong with the baby . . ."

"I'm sure everything is fine." As she spoke, Cameo pulled on her wrinkled skirt under Brax's shirt, stepped into her shoes, gathered her purse, and found her keys.

Normally her first move would be to call Brax. But this time she knew exactly what he was doing, and she hesitated to interrupt him, never mind his staunch rule that Mercy always came first. "What can I do? Where are you?"

"I'm glad Brax isn't around. I don't want to worry him, or Wyatt for that matter. I definitely don't want either of them to see me being such a . . . a woman."

On her way to the front door, Cameo repeated again, "Where are you?"

"I'm at my apartment," she said, and then in a rush, "but I already called my doctor and he wants me to meet him at the hospital. Just as a precaution so he can check things. My cab should be here any minute, but . . . I don't want to be there alone . . . just in case."

"Of course you don't." Holding the phone to her ear, Cameo checked the monitors again and saw that the grounds were clear. There were no bogeymen lurking behind the trees or waiting to pounce on her. "Try to relax. I'll find you at the hospital as soon as I get there. I'm already on my way."

"Don't rush. I'm sure the doctor will keep me waiting for a while. You know how these things work." Mercy took a breath. "And Cameo? Thank you."

"I'll have my cell on me if you need to reach me. Try not to fret. I'll see you in just a few minutes." She hung up, unlocked the front door, secured it again, and then hurried toward her car. Brax would be very upset with her for not calling him, but knowing where he was and what he faced, combined with Mercy's request that he not be told, made her decision easier.

Out of the safety of the house, it took all Cameo's concentration not to run. But she was afraid that if she did, if she gave in to the fear, she'd be lost in total panic.

Brax was so calm about it all, but for her, dire threats and evil beings were brand-new and quite horrifying.

A breeze stirred the air, dissipating the scent of smoke from the homemade bomb and ruffling the drying tendrils of her loose hair. She seldom wore her hair down, and she absolutely never went out in public dressed so ridiculously, but these were extenuating circumstances.

On her way to her car, she tried to listen for any sounds of pursuit. She heard only gurgling water from the enormous fountain and the rustling of leaves from sturdy branches in tall trees.

After checking the backseat for unwelcome occupants, Cameo unlocked her car and got in. Immediately she started the ignition. Not until she left the long driveway and turned onto the main street did she start to relax.

It was only a ten-minute drive to the hospital, eight if she hurried. Now that she felt secure again, she said a quick prayer for Mercy and the baby. Having no children of her own, her knowledge of pregnancy pains was sorely limited. But one thing was certain—if the doctor said there was a problem, she'd call Brax immediately, regardless of the job at hand. His sister came first with him, definitely before a vile creep.

Her thoughts had just veered to Brax and Amos's safety, and she was wondering if they had found the man yet, when suddenly an older, slightly beat-up sedan showed in her rearview mirror. Why it alarmed her, Cameo couldn't say. Maybe because Brax resided in an affluent neighborhood and disreputable cars were seldom seen. Maybe because of everything that had happened that morning.

Whatever the reason, her instincts jangled and fear soured her throat. Swallowing convulsively, her every muscle clenching, she held the steering wheel tighter as the car closed the distance between them.

There was no one else on the road. The grand houses were all set so far back, shielded from passersby with thick, meticulous shrubbery, that no one would see her if the unthinkable happened.

The sedan roared up closer behind her, and Cameo braced herself, unsure what would happen, what she should do.

Suddenly the car lurched forward at full speed. It clipped her back left fender. Cameo tried, but she couldn't keep the car from spinning out of control.

Her scream resonated within her brain, but never left her tight throat. Before she could draw in a necessary breath, the car careened off the road and collided with a sturdy oak at the end of a very long, isolated driveway.

The air bags deployed with a painful, smothering blast.

Her ribs hurt. Her throat hurt. She tried to slap the air bags away but couldn't. A trickle of blood trailed down from her forehead. She didn't even remember hitting her head.

Struggling to get her bearings, Cameo groaned—and the door jerked open. Dazed, sick to her stomach, she turned her head toward the intruder.

A maniacal-looking woman, hair and eyes wild, laughed with glee. "Gotcha!"

Horrified, Cameo tried to shrink back, but she couldn't. Dizziness pervaded her entire body.

The woman seized her arm in a deliberately painful grip. After cackling another laugh, she backhanded Cameo hard. "Stop squirming around, you bitch. I've got you—and I'm not letting you go." She flashed a lethal blade in Cameo's face. "Now get your ass out of the car. We have some fun ahead of us."

Was this the woman who had cut Amos? Was that the same knife she'd used?

Cameo didn't know what to do. Terror held her in its grip, and her mind refused to function rationally. She had to do something. She couldn't just go with the woman.

But what?

As the woman yanked her from the car, she tripped and went down on her knees on the hard ground. The jarring pain helped revive her.

Cameo looked around and saw only trees and the occasional entrance to a long driveway. She was on her own here.

That knife flashed in front of her face again, spurring her to instinctive action. She jerked free of the woman's hold and scrambled back as fast as she could. In the process, she tripped up the other woman as she tried to grab for her.

When a few feet separated them, Cameo jumped up

and ran. Her head pounded with every step, but she didn't slow. She headed back the way she'd come. She hadn't driven that far before she was forced off the road. If she could just make it back to Brax's house, she could barricade herself inside. His home was like a fortress.

The woman screamed and threatened her, but she'd be damned before she'd willy-nilly leave with a nutcase bent on torturing her.

As Cameo raced up the road, she prayed for another car to come. She prayed for Brax to somehow know her predicament, to save her. She saw the end of his driveway and pushed harder.

And then she got tackled from behind. She hit the ground hard and felt the knife slice along her upper right arm. It wasn't a deep cut, more like a thin scratch, but it hurt. And still she fought—until a gun pressed into her ribs.

Her entire body ached.

If Brax didn't find her, she knew she'd end up dead.

Or worse.

SIX

IT took a little more than half an hour to track their prey. He had moved from Brax's backyard, but he'd left a trail, and he hadn't gone too far. Amos had known that the man remained nearby. They found him about a mile away, in the backyard of a mansion, cowering behind a pool house. The fool didn't realize that once Amos had tuned in to him, his instincts would guide him right back.

Brax motioned for Amos to circle around the yard from the other direction. If the man ran, they'd have to chase him, and even though the main house was a good distance from the pool, pursuit might draw attention. As long as they trapped him where he now hid, they'd be completely concealed—free to handle matters as necessary.

Together, they closed in, tightening the space around their quarry. Brax saw the sweat streaming down his face and neck. He huddled low to the ground, his back against the outside structure, a gun squeezed in one hand while he ruthlessly chewed his bottom lip.

Brax tipped his head to study him. Fear robbed him of any menace. He looked like any other man, albeit dirtier, more panicked. Few would guess him capable of executing extreme torture on innocent women.

Brax could smell his anxiety, could nearly taste the blackness of his being.

He waited until he knew Amos was near enough to control things, then stepped into the open to draw the man's attention. The idiot lumbered to his feet but got no farther than that before Brax snatched his control.

He was weak, very weak. Not a nice or honorable man, but did he have the fortitude to carry out immeasurable torture?

Brax had a moment's doubt.

Motionless, his gun hand held out, the man's expression froze with austere terror.

Brax said nothing. This was Amos's kill, and never would he poach on that unless absolutely necessary.

It wasn't.

Amos moved up to the man with an anticipatory smile.

"How accommodating of you to come looking for me." He circled the man, each pass sending acrid terror burning through the man's veins. "What is your name?"

"It's . . . it's Bradley."

"Bradley what?"

"Bradley Edgers."

Brax felt the fear accumulating, as did Amos, until it consumed the man's thoughts.

"You know, Bradley, I'm not used to that type of consideration." Amos smiled. "Especially from a miserable worm who would hurt innocents. Thank you for making it easier."

The man wavered on his feet, but he couldn't fall; Amos didn't allow it. The man was held in his grip as surely as if Amos had tethered him.

With a look of pure scorn, Amos dropped him to his knees, bowed his back painfully. "But you know, Bradley, you aren't the only one I want."

The man whimpered. "Belle isn't here."

Amos moved to stand in front of him. Unconcerned with the aimed weapon, he braced his feet apart and crossed his wrists behind the small of his back. In a voice eerily gentle, he asked, "Where is she?"

The man's mouth trembled, moved, but no words came out.

Amos tsked. "I can kill you easily, you know. Fast, clean." He stepped on a twig and it snapped. "Just like that, Bradley."

Tears filled the man's eyes and overflowed to stream down his ashen face. It sickened Brax to see such cowardice after all the pain he'd inflicted.

"Or," Amos said, studying him without an ounce of sympathy, "I can make it agonizingly slow with enough torture to make you beg for death. You know about torture, don't you, Bradley? I'm sure you can imagine what I'll do to you—and how much I'll enjoy it." He waited a heartbeat. "Maybe even as much as you enjoyed torturing those women."

"No, *please*." Though Bradley couldn't move, he openly sobbed. "It wasn't me."

Impatient, Brax wished Amos would get on with it. They'd already been gone too long, first in locating the exact position of the man without alerting him to their pursuit, and now this ridiculous banter. He wanted— *needed*—to return to Cameo. For reasons he couldn't understand, he felt a great deal of unease.

"I saw you," Amos pointed out. "You were there with them, tormenting them, taunting them."

"No."

"And I saw the women, what you'd done to them."

"No," Bradley denied again. "I mean, it was me, but I did it for *her*."

Amos stilled in the process of removing his Polaroid camera. "You mean for Belle, your wife?"

A very bad feeling came over Brax.

The man shuddered, but otherwise couldn't regain use

of his limbs. "Yes, yes, for her. Belle is the one who gets off on it. It doesn't matter to me. I only do it for her, to make her happy."

With the same cutting force of a heavy leather whip, Amos's voice slashed through the quiet of the day. *"Where is Belle?"*

Brax's phone rang at the same time that the man started confessing.

"She . . . she was watching the front of your house from down the street."

Oh, God. Brax snatched out his cell without checking the number. "Cameo?"

"No, Brax, it's me, Mercy."

Intuition cramped his muscles. "What is it? What's wrong?"

"Nothing, I hope. I wasn't feeling well and I went to the hospital—but I'm okay, Brax. So is the baby. The doctor says I have food poisoning, if you can believe that, so they're keeping me, but it's not serious. Just uncomfortable." She sucked in a weak breath, her voice thin with worry. "It's Cameo I'm worried about. I called her and she agreed to meet me here but she hasn't shown up. Before we hung up, she said she was already on her way, but it wouldn't have taken her more than a few minutes to get here, and she's . . . not."

Icy control crept over him. "Maybe she's held up in traffic."

"I hope so, but I've called her cell a couple of times and she's not answering. Brax, she told me she'd have her cell with her. I'm . . . scared."

Brax felt himself expanding with rage. Protecting his sister was an instinct he couldn't shake even at the worst of times, so he said simply, "I'll take care of it, I promise. Don't worry."

Unwilling to waste any more time, he disconnected the call and turned back to Amos in time to see him haul the man up by his shirt collar.

"We have to move," Brax said, watching as Amos dragged Bradley along. "Tell me you can track her."

"She cut me." Amos gave one sharp nod. "Of course I can. Let's go." He headed for the street, but stopped in his tracks.

Brax turned on him. "What?"

"This way. Back to your house." Amos turned and started running across the massive backyards, forcing Bradley to keep up. "We have to hurry before Belle gets away."

"She already has Cameo?"

"Yeah." His long legs ate up the distance. "And she's planning to kill her."

CAMEO fought off the lightheaded feeling as the woman jabbed the gun into her spine.

"Open the door."

She couldn't believe the woman had brought her back to Brax's home. Fingers numb, she punched in the necessary code and the door unlocked.

The woman pushed her. "Let's go."

Grateful for anything familiar, praying Brax would finish his business and return soon, Cameo went inside. "What are you going to do?"

"I'm going to have some fun. Now that you're alone, I plan to enjoy you."

"I'm not alone." Very slowly, her movements cautious, Cameo turned to face the woman. Insanity shone in her eyes and in her wicked smile of anticipation. She fought back a shudder. "Brax will be back soon."

"Wrong. Wrong, wrong, wrong," she sang. "Bradley will shoot him and the other one, too, and then he'll join us. We'll have all the time we need to play."

"Play?"

Keeping the gun pointed at Cameo, the woman withdrew the knife from her belt loop. "Do you know how I brand them? I heat my knife, and then carve my initials into them."

"You . . ." Cameo's mouth went dry. "You tortured those women?"

"Bradley helped—with my instruction." Her smile showed surprisingly straight, white teeth. "Bradley doesn't have my imagination."

Remembering those awful photos, Cameo's stomach revolted and she nearly threw up. For a single second, rage burned brighter than her fear. "You miserable, sick bitch."

The woman's brows came down. "You'll call me Belle, or nothing at all. I won't tolerate insults from you."

Incredulous, Cameo shook her head. "How could you bear to do that to those poor women?"

Belle examined the blade of her knife. "You know what bothered me about torturing them? How they looked at me." Her piercing gaze leveled on Cameo. "How you're looking at me now. Like I should stop it just because I'm female." She came closer. "You know how I can fix that?"

Cameo said nothing.

"I can take out your eyes before we even start."

No, Cameo thought. *No, I won't die like this.* She glanced at the gun, held steady and sure. She looked at the knife, long and thick.

She would not be a coward. That's exactly what Belle wanted—and she wouldn't give it to her. "You go ahead and keep hemorrhaging your vile threats. It won't matter in the end when Brax gets you. And my God, the things he's going to do to you . . ." She mustered a credible, sneering laugh. "I could almost feel sorry for you, except you deserve every bit of it."

Belle turned red with rage. "I told you, Bradley killed him."

"Oh no. Bradley couldn't even control you, could he?" Cameo taunted. "Do you really think he'd be able to stop a powerful, determined man like Brax? Never. Brax has already taken care of him, and now he's on his way back here. He's going to make you very sorry for touching me."

"Shut up!" Belle screamed. She glanced beyond Cameo to the long hallway, and then the stairs. "Go. Up that way."

"Why?"

The knife flashed out, pricking the skin of her waist. Cameo cried out and stumbled back a step.

Thrilled with her spontaneous reaction, Belle grinned. "Because I said so. Now get up there before I cut your pretty face."

Seeing no alternative, Cameo headed for the stairs. Her skin crawled at the sensation of having a demented maniac at her back. She could hear Belle breathing, almost feel her thinking, planning, all of it obscene.

Each step added to her anxiety until the need to run almost overwhelmed her. Only the certainty that Belle would shoot her kept her in control.

"The room we bombed," Belle said. "Take me there. I want to see my handiwork."

Cameo's thoughts shifted this way and that. The office was now in shambles with debris everywhere. Maybe that would afford her a better means to escape. Perhaps she could use a chunk of broken glass or splintered wood as a weapon.

She opened Brax's office door and a breeze carried new smoke into the hallway, making her choke and cough.

Belle chuckled. "Look at that! Bradley did a great job with that bomb, didn't he?" She prodded Cameo's back. "It's too bad your man wasn't still in there when the bomb exploded. Instead of papers everywhere, it'd be little pieces of him."

Her laugh was enough to make Cameo ill. She eased into the room, her eyes quickly scanning everything, looking for any means of assistance. There were a lot of possible weapons about—but with that unwavering gun aimed at her, did she dare try anything?

Cameo was weighing her odds of survival when she heard the faintest sound.

Belle didn't notice. She was too busy enjoying her destruction—but renewed hope surged inside Cameo.

It was Brax. She just knew it. Somehow, in her heart, she felt his presence. A sense of security eased some of her blind panic and rampant fear. Brax would not let her be hurt.

But a few seconds later, it wasn't Brax who stepped into the room. It was a stranger with glassy eyes and inflexible movements. Though he said nothing, his bizarre gaze clapped onto Belle like a lifeline. In his right hand was another gun. Stiff-legged, he came farther inside.

"Bradley!" Belle stepped over rubble to reach him, but when he didn't open his arms for her, she slowed. "What is it? What's wrong with you?"

He still said nothing. Beads of sweat poured down his temples and matted his light-brown hair. His eyes were so wide that the whites showed all the way around, amplifying his dilated pupils.

And Cameo knew. Brax controlled him.

Fascinated, she watched as Bradley raised his gun— and aimed it at Belle.

"Bradley?" she snapped as she stumbled back a step. "What the hell are you doing?"

He caught her arm with his other hand and yanked her up close to him. He shoved the gun hard against her sternum. Tears mixed with the sweat.

As the macabre scene unfolded in front of her, Cameo backed up, horrified, relieved, and sickened.

"Bradley!" Belle struggled in earnest—and the gun fired.

In the high-ceilinged office, the sound was so loud that Cameo flinched, but she couldn't look away. Belle's shocked expression faded to blank dismay, and she slowly sank to the floor amid broken glass and shattered wood. Blood oozed from her midsection like a blossoming flower until it soaked through fabric and began to drip over her side.

Big, imposing, and in control, Brax came through the doorway. His booted feet squashed everything in his way as he made a beeline for Cameo. She was still reeling from witnessing the loss of a life, but Brax stopped in front of her and in rapid order examined her many minor injuries.

His hands were gentle as he pushed back her hair to see her face, stroked along her arms, each leg, over her back and belly. "Talk to me, Cameo. Where are you hurt?"

"I'm . . . I'm okay," she told him.

As if he needed to collect himself, his eyes closed for a moment. With tender care, he lifted her into his arms and briefly pressed his mouth to her forehead. "God, sweetheart, I am so fucking sorry."

Cameo touched his face. "Don't be. You saved me."

"I'm taking her to the hospital," he announced to Amos, who had just joined them in the room. "She might need stitches."

"She's okay?"

Cameo spoke up. "I'm definitely okay, and I'm not going to the hospital." But mention of the hospital reminded Cameo of why she'd left the house in the first place. "Mercy is there, though."

"She's fine," Brax told her. "She called me when you didn't show up."

"The baby?"

He frowned at her, but little by little, his face relaxed into an expression of wonder. "Everyone is fine except for you."

"And Belle." Her gaze went to the zombielike expression on the man's face. She shuddered. "And him."

Voice hard, he ordered, "Don't you waste a second of remorse on either of them."

"I won't," she promised. "It's just . . . unsettling."

Brax groaned, hugged her, and then carried her out of

the room, down the hall, and into his bathroom. He set her on the edge of the tub while he dampened a towel. "Let me see your arm."

Dutifully, Cameo held it out to him. He cleaned away the blood with incredible care.

She looked at her skin, at the angry red cut, but really, it was nothing more than a bad scratch. "I don't need stitches."

Unconvinced, Brax continued to clean and inspect her arm until, finally, he nodded agreement. "Maybe not. But it has to hurt like hell."

It did, but given how stoic Amos had been over his injuries, she felt compelled to say, "It's not too bad."

Brax rinsed out the towel and then started on her face. "Damn," he said when he uncovered the small cut caused by the wreck. A wealth of emotion shone in his golden eyes. "You're going to be black and blue."

"Maybe Amos and I will look related."

When he didn't laugh, Cameo wished for a way to soothe him, to remove that horrible guilt from his face.

"Brax, I am *fine*, I promise." She didn't want to look weak, but she couldn't help giving him a small truth. "I really just wish you'd hold me."

His gaze shot to hers.

"I'm not physically hurt," she said again, "but inside . . . I'm still shaking so badly." Her voice wavered, then broke on a thin, high note. "I've never been so scared in my entire life."

With a growled curse, he gathered her close, lifting her off her feet and back into his arms, rocking her, hugging her close. "You're safe now, Cameo. Safe. I swear it."

"I know," she said with tears in her voice. "Because I'm with you."

For long minutes, he held her like that, still rocking her, kissing her every so often.

A knock sounded on the door. Amos stuck his head in, looked at her with concern, and frowned at Brax. "It's done."

Brax nodded. "Go ahead and call it in."

"What's going on?" Cameo asked.

Brax went into the bedroom and sat on the edge of the bed with her. Matter-of-factly, as if he spoke the truth rather than a fictionalized story, Brax stated, "Bradley and Belle broke in after throwing that pipe bomb into my office. They terrorized you. You and Belle were struggling. Bradley meant to shoot you but accidentally shot Belle instead. Filled with remorse, the miserable fuck threw himself out the hole in the wall and ended his own life."

Cameo could only stare at him. She swallowed. "Did he really . . . ?"

Brax smoothed back her hair. "Yes, baby, he did."

She accepted that—but she didn't want to see it. "This is going to be tricky for you, isn't it? I mean, you've never had this happen in your home before."

"No."

She had really screwed up everything. "If I hadn't opened the door and let her inside—"

"Thank God you did." He put his forehead to hers. "It made finding you fast and easy. Once I knew you were in danger . . ." Words failed him and he hugged her tight, so tight that she gasped. "God, Cameo. I thought I'd go crazy. I don't ever want to feel that again."

She stroked his broad, solid back and absorbed his incredible strength. "Belle thought you were dead. She thought Bradley had shot you."

"He might have," Brax said against her hair, "if I were an average man."

For an altogether different reason, tears stung Cameo's eyes again. "But you are oh so extraordinary." She pushed him back to see his face. "And you are mine."

He went still. His eyes glittered. "Yes."

Breathing too hard and fast, Cameo said, "Marry me?"

Seconds ticked by, and his mouth quirked. "Yes."

The tears she'd held back suddenly spilled over. "Really?" She laughed around her tears. "You mean that?"

Using his thumbs, he brushed her cheeks. In the gentlest voice she'd ever heard from him, he said, "I can go on one knee if you want."

Feeling like an utter fool, she started crying in earnest. "Brax, I am so sorry that I didn't immediately call you when I knew Mercy was unwell. As your personal assistant I know that's the number one rule—that Mercy always comes first . . ."

He interrupted her to say, "I love my sister, Cameo, you know that. But as my wife, you'll need to know that my number one rule has changed."

She took in a shuddering, hiccupping breath. "To what?"

"I love you."

Her heart skipped a beat. Her mouth opened, but nothing came out. Finally, one hand to her mouth to stifle the near-hysterical giggles, she managed to say, "That's a rule?"

Brax slowly nodded. "I love you. I need you. I want you with me always. And from now on, that's the only rule you can't forget."

EPILOGUE

POSITIONED near the fireplace, trying not to grin like a sap, Brax stared out at the room at large. He enjoyed seeing the family dynamics at play in front of him. To announce his and Cameo's impending nuptials, they'd invited everyone over. In six months, she'd be his wife. He was anxious to have her tied to him legally, but to give her the wedding she wanted, he could show some patience.

His brother-in-law, Wyatt, hovered over Mercedes, still worrying about her even though she'd gotten through the food poisoning and was now radiant with her pregnancy. Every couple of minutes Wyatt kissed her, and he continually touched her swelling belly in a protective gesture. He'd be a great dad. He was already a terrific husband. And as a brother-in-law, Brax couldn't be more pleased.

Mercy hovered over Amos, thrilled to get to know one of her uncles better. Amos had at first chosen to stay around just in case any problems arose with the police over Belle and Bradley's deaths. After their story was accepted, Brax talked him into extending the visit for his engagement announcement.

It was still a little startling to see Amos circulating with polite society. Wyatt was rightfully wary of him, and Mercy was fascinated by him. For his part, Amos didn't quite know how to deal with either of them—though he had no problems relating to Cameo. Already the two of them had formed a very special bond.

Brax liked having Amos around, finding assurance that he wasn't yet a lost cause.

And Cameo . . . well, she amazed him more each day. Flitting from one relative to another, serving drinks and hors d'oeuvres, she made a beautiful hostess. He couldn't look at her without wanting her, but he did his best to temper his need when in polite company.

After her ordeal she'd had several sleepless nights, and though more than two weeks had passed, faint bruises remained on her delicate body. Brax still trembled whenever he thought of how close he'd come to losing her.

To help her put it in the past, Brax had seen to the removal of all reminders. It had cost him extra for the rush job, but his office was not only repaired but remodeled. All smoke damage had been removed from inside his home, and damage to the lawn and landscaping caused by Bradley's fallen body had been spruced back up. Now, only the horrible memories remained, but Cameo was strong, one of the strongest people he'd ever met.

As if she knew his thoughts, she set aside the tray and came to him with a knowing smile. Brax straightened from his relaxed posture against the mantel. The love in her eyes never failed to set his heart racing.

When she reached him, she straightened the collar of his polo shirt, smoothed her hand over his chest, and then went on tiptoes to kiss him. "You're showing remarkable restraint, Brax."

He curved his hand around her waist and growled low, "You have no idea."

"I love you, so yes, I have all kinds of ideas."

"God, woman, what you do to me . . ."

"Tonight," she whispered, "you can show me." She patted him. "But don't forget that tomorrow morning you have a meeting with the press to talk about your new benefit." And with that, she left him to mingle again.

Brax smiled with incredible pride. Cameo had gone through hell because of his special ability, and she still declared her love for him.

She was the perfect personal secretary, the perfect hostess. The perfect woman—for him.

UNDEAD MAN'S
HAND

ERIN MCCARTHY

ONE

SAMANTHA Keller knew she was going to die.

She was fighting it, but it was harder and harder to keep her eyes open, and her defensive kicks and blows were getting weak, ineffectual. Her body felt paralyzed, the sharp sting in her neck pinning her against the wall, the dizziness rolling over her in waves, the pain mingling with fear, regret, horror.

Funny how she had only meant to help. It would have been cruel to walk away from those pleading, innocent eyes. Even as her legs shook and her fingertips went numb, her brain couldn't quite wrap itself around the irony of what was happening. This couldn't be the end, but she knew it was.

As an agonizing pain ripped through her abdomen, she tried to scream but couldn't, her voice frozen, even as the high-pitched voice laughing rolled around the alley and in Samantha's pain-soaked consciousness.

Hearing the gurgle that came from her own mouth, she closed her eyes and waited to die.

* * *

"FOR every season there is a purpose, and in Vegas it's murder."

Jordan Waters stifled a groan as Shawn Marshall, another detective on the Metro Police force, slapped a file down on her already overburdened desk. "Thanks for that daily inspiration. You going to put that on stationery? How about a calendar?"

"I should. Three hundred sixty-five days of death in the desert."

Exhausted from yet another night crawling through a crime scene, Jordan could only offer Shawn a heavy eye roll. "Brilliant. It will be an Internet hit."

"You going to open the file I gave you?"

"Nope. I can't deal with another victim. I haven't even gotten lab reports back on the first three, and I'm ticked that Thomas left and dumped this in my lap." It was Jordan's first serial killer case and it was kicking her ass. The sick bastard was draining women of their blood and then displaying their bodies in the gruesome pose of being nailed to the ground with a stake.

"This isn't your boy's work. We've got ourselves a male victim, body found in the lot behind the Venetian hotel, head found in the Dumpster. Witnesses say he fell of the roof, but that doesn't explain his missing head."

"Decapitation? Nice." Jordan picked up the file and shoved it back at Shawn. "So take this back, then. We can't take on another case, you know that."

"Tell that to the chief, girlfriend. It's you and me on this one."

Now she did groan. "No, I'm not doing it." There weren't enough hours in the day to handle her workload, not that she had much choice, really. It was a token protest and she and Shawn both knew it, but it made her feel better to bitch.

Shawn continued like he hadn't heard her. "The victim has been identified by the name of R, thirty-five years old, a Russian émigré."

"R?" Despite her exhaustion, that made Jordan look

up with a smirk. "Like the letter? Since when is that a name?"

"I guess it's some kind of Russian gang thing. I don't know. No one seems to know his last name, and no one in his little circle of pals seems cut up that he's dead. It looks like a straightforward retaliation kill."

Shawn was rocking on his heels, his hand in the pocket of his ugly dress pants. Why he insisted on wearing pleated pants, Jordan would never understand. Not that she had any room to talk. Being knee-deep in death every day didn't exactly call for high fashion, and it had been months since she'd gone shopping or gotten a manicure. It didn't look like she would be doing so anytime soon, either.

"So you deal with it, Shawn. I haven't been to bed in two days and I have a crazy bastard out there who is shortening his time between kills that I want to catch." Which was why she had no life, and why it had been a year since she'd had sex, not that she was keeping track. It was a brutal combination, being surrounded by death with a total lack of intimacy and sexual release in her life, and Jordan knew she was getting edgy.

But she couldn't stop murder, and she couldn't pull a man out of her desk drawer. God help the poor guy if she could, because she would probably wear him out and use him up before she was finished with him, she was wound that tight.

Since a male distraction wasn't going to appear anyway, she stared at the glossy crime scene photos spread on her desk and tried to get into the mind of a killer. Three women, all in their thirties or forties, successful and attractive in life. Yet all three gruesome, pale, and waxy in death, sightless eyes wide open in shock, their chests gored from the impact of a wooden stake, their arms and legs askew as they lay in their macabre crucifixion. The last victim, thirty-three-year-old Samantha Keller, had thick long hair, and it had been caught by the violence of the stake and jammed into her abdominal cavity, pulled taut from the impact and forcing her head to tilt at an odd angle, as if she were puzzled. A ribbon of dried blood from internal bleeding trailed from the corner of her mouth to her chin.

When you laid the photos side by side, you could see that as the killer's confidence grew, his impact of the stake was lower and lower. The first kill had the stake right through the heart, with instant death. Each subsequent kill was farther from the heart, and presumably the coroner's reports would show they had lived for several agonizing minutes while the killer enjoyed their suffering. Jordan had seen a lot of murder, but never like this, never in this sick display of twisted humor, this utter revelry in the power of torture. It made her gut burn and her palms sweat. God, she wanted to catch this bastard.

"Well, it sucks to be you," Shawn declared. "I haven't slept either, you know. And don't you think it's strange that we have yet another homicide in such close proximity to a casino? That makes victims found at the Ava, the Bellagio, and the Venetian in how many months?"

Jordan rubbed her temples, trying to ease the tension that was on the verge of tripping off a migraine. "Yeah, but you just said this isn't our serial killer's work, so it's just a coincidence. Our sicko's victims are all female." Another puzzling point. A few months prior, there had been a series of murders with the same curious result—all the victims' blood had been drained from their bodies. But those had all been men, and the killings had stopped as quickly as they had started. Neither she nor the detective who had been on that case could decide if they were related to the current body count or not.

There was a knock on the door and Jordan called, "Come in." If it was news of another murder, her head was going to explode.

It was Detective Andrew Baldwin, and thank God, he was waving a piece of paper in his hand. "We got an ID on the kid the kitchen lady told us about."

That was the best news Jordan had heard in two days. The Bellagio had security cameras sweeping the service alley where Samantha Keller's body had been found, and they had seen several staff members from the hotel smoking out there on the video throughout the night of her death. The entire kitchen crew had been questioned. Everyone claimed not to have seen anything suspicious, and as far as Jordan could piece together, no staff had been outside alone, but had always had at least one other person with them. But two different women had mentioned that frequently a kid was playing in the alley at night, unsupervised, and had suggested that maybe if there was a murderer on the loose, his parents should keep him inside.

While initially it had seemed like the kid could be a potential witness, no one seemed to know who he was, and it had quickly become another dead end.

"You did? How the hell did you do that? And who he is?"

"One of the busboys said the kid is the cousin of a blackjack dealer at the casino named Katie, and that he thought maybe the kid's dad was a security guard. We found the dealer named Katie, who denied the kid would be outside at night by himself, but she gave us the dad's name, who agreed to let us talk to the kid, as long as he's with him."

"Excellent. When can we do this?" Jordan was standing up, sore muscles, growling stomach, and fatigue all forgotten.

"I said you and Shawn would be there at ten tonight, so in an hour. Only don't get your hopes up. Chances are the kid didn't see anything, and even if he did, I have my doubts about how reliable he'll be."

Andrew was frowning, and Jordan didn't like the look of that.

"Why?"

"Because the kid's autistic."

Jordan stopped groping in her drawer for her car keys and stared at him. "Oh, shit, you're kidding me."

"Afraid not."

"How high functioning is he?" She knew there was a

massive range for autism and she prayed this kid fell on
the lower end of the spectrum.

"I have no idea, I didn't see him. I guess you'll find
out, though."

"How old is he?"

"Thirteen."

At least that worked in their favor. Too young to be de-
vious and lie to them to cover his own butt, and old
enough to know what he saw and be able to communicate
it. In most cases.

But who knew what they'd get out of this kid. "What's
his name?"

"Peter Stolin. The father's name is Nikolai Stolin.
They're Russian immigrants."

"Really?" Jordan looked at Shawn. "Like your retaliation kill. What a coincidence."

And Jordan didn't like this many coincidences.

TWO

NICK Stolin glanced at his watch. He turned to Ringo Columbia, the other bodyguard who had been assigned to patrol the casino with him while Mr. Donatelli played the tables. "I have an appointment, can you cover for me for thirty minutes?"

Ringo eyed him from under his stringy dark hair, sucking hard on his cigarette before removing it from his mouth and blowing the smoke in Nick's direction. "What, like out of the goodness of my fucking heart? I don't think so."

God, Nick hated Ringo. He was a waste of oxygen, a slimy, selfish cesspool of a human being, or vampire, in this case. Working with Ringo every night taxed Nick's patience and made him constantly question if it wasn't time for a career change. But after a hundred years as a guard, Nick wasn't sure what else he was qualified for.

"I'll give you fifty bucks." It should be a good incentive, enabling Ringo to sneak off and buy his special drink of choice, blood laced with heroin, and then finish it off with a cocaine chaser. By the time Nick came back from talking to the cops, he had no doubt Ringo would be flying.

Even though it wasn't his problem, he couldn't say he

liked aiding and abetting an addict, but Nick knew he should cooperate with the police. Let them talk to Peter and see they weren't going to get any information out of him, and be done with it. That was a key rule to being a vampire. If you appeared on mortals' radar, deal with it swiftly and calmly, then let them forget about you.

"Done," Ringo said. "Where are you going anyway?"

Nick cast a steady eye around the casino floor, making sure there were no vampires or any outward signs of danger before he left. Donatelli hadn't moved from the blackjack table, and he had a blonde hovering near his left arm. Everything looked status quo.

"I'm going upstairs to check on Peter." Not the whole truth, but not a lie either.

Ringo's eyes narrowed. "My wife is watching Peter, you don't need to check on him."

Kelsey Columbia's ability to truly monitor Peter was dubious at best, but since babysitting for vampires was hard to come by, even in Vegas, Nick had settled on the arrangement with her. "I just need to discuss something with Peter."

"You're not running up there to fuck my wife, are you?" Ringo asked, raising his cigarette to his lip and smiling with a feral menace Nick found disturbing. "Because I will kill you."

Nick had zero interest in Kelsey, who was arguably the female version of Peter—erratic, vague, a poster child for bipolarism in vampires. But he wasn't about to let Ringo think he could intimidate him. "You mean you'd *try* to kill me," Nick told him calmly. "You'd never be successful."

He outweighed Ringo by seventy-five pounds, had a century of training, experience, and blood drinking behind him, and he would kill before he was killed. No questions asked. "But no, trust me, I have no interest in your wife. I would never think to interfere in your unique relationship." Unique was a good word to describe a couple that alternated between abusive behaviors and obsessive all-consuming devotion to each other.

Nick was no expert on marriage, and unfortunately couldn't even precisely recall the last time he'd had a woman, vampire or mortal, in his bed, but he knew he didn't want that mess Ringo and Kelsey called love in his life.

"Good." Ringo's shoulders relaxed a little. "How'd you get stuck with that kid anyway? He's one weird little dude."

As if Nick would ever tell someone like Ringo the story of the night he had turned Katie and Peter. The crying, the gunshots, the blood, the instant decision to save the two young adults who had haunted Nick every day since. It was a private tale of horror that he told no one, least of all a self-absorbed junkie.

"Of course he's odd," Nick said, evading the question. "He is technically over a hundred years old and yet he resides in a thirteen-year-old boy's body." The consequences of which had never occurred to Nick in those spontaneous seconds when he had chosen to try and save the little duke and his sister. Futile to worry about it now—it was what it was.

Ringo shook his head. "Yeah, that would fuck you up. Think of all the twenty-five-year-olds you'd want to bang, and you look like a kid to them. That would suck . . . your only choice would be, like, fourteen-year-olds who don't know what the hell they're doing or some pervy older woman who wants to mother you and molest you all at once."

And on that note, Nick was leaving. Someone like Ringo would never understand that sexual frustration was relevant and part of Peter's problem, yes, but it was a small piece of a complex puzzle of emotional issues. Nick didn't even come close to understanding Peter himself, though, so there was no reason Ringo would or could.

"I'll be back as soon as I can. Thanks." Nick adjusted his suit jacket and turned to head for the elevators.

Ringo's hand closed around his arm.

When Nick gave him a pointed look, Ringo just smiled. "Payment up front, my friend."

"Friends, we are not," Nick told him with a hint of steel, shaking Ringo's arm off. He didn't like to be touched. But he did pull out the money and hand it to him. "Don't let anyone kill Donatelli while I'm gone."

Ringo laughed, pocketing the cash. "Don't worry about it. You may be the big brawny silent Russian who looks scary, but trust me, I *am* scary."

"Then we are the perfect partnership," Nick said sarcastically and walked away. He didn't want to be associated with someone like Ringo, and yet, that was his destiny, this was his life. He was a vampire and a bodyguard, who had made a career of working for amoral men.

The thought made his blood breakfast burn in his gut.

It was with relief for the distraction from his thoughts that he spotted Katie and her fiancé, Michael, coming toward him on the casino floor. Saving Katie had never given him a moment's regret. The story they gave everyone was that she was Nick's niece, even though nothing was further from the truth since she was royalty and he was the son of a serf. She had taken his last name for simplicity after her turning, and for a century he and Katie had gotten along, even as she had chafed at the restrictions he had tried to put on her over the years. She was a normal, witty woman who was glowing with happiness now that she had been reunited with her girlhood lover.

"Hey, where are you going?" she asked as she reached out and gave him a hug.

Katie was one of the few people Nick didn't mind being touched by, but sometimes even her easy invasion of his space unnerved him. He forced himself to hug her in return, then took a step back. "Up to my place. The cops are coming to talk to Peter." He shook Michael's hand as he greeted Katie's fiancé. "How's it going?"

"Good. Great." Michael smiled at Nick, then at Katie.

But she was making a face. "Sorry about the cops. They caught me off guard when they asked me about Peter, and I figured if people had already ID'd him and connected him to me, it was better not to lie."

"It's fine." Nick didn't like it, but he didn't think it would be an issue. "You know how Peter is. He won't tell them anything that makes sense and they'll let it go."

They shared a sad moment of silence, the two people who had cared for Peter and watched him descend into mental illness.

"Yeah, you're right. But let me know if it doesn't go okay." Then Katie smiled again. "And now Michael and I are going off to pack. Last night was my final shift at work for three weeks, I can hardly believe it. We're going to Paris, Nick! I'm so excited."

Katie and Michael were leaving for three weeks to get married and honeymoon in Paris. Nick was deeply happy for the woman he had spent a hundred years looking out for, and thought of as a surrogate daughter. "You should be," he said, feeling a smile tug at the corner of his mouth. "It's not every century a girl gets married."

She laughed, tossing back her thick, rich brown hair. "This is the only time for me, I can tell you that. And we're going to be married until Michael dies."

Her fiancé raised an eyebrow. "What makes you think I'm going to die before you? Or die at all for that matter? I am a vampire."

"Statistically men die before women, even in the vampire world. I think it's because they engage in more dangerous activities than women. So I'm just assuming you'll probably die before me."

"As long as it isn't soon and you don't plan to kill me."

"I might tear you up, but I would never kill you."

Uh-oh. They were getting a look in their eye that Nick recognized as one that usually led to sex, so he said, "Stop by and say good-bye before you leave. I've got to go."

Then he got the hell out of there and headed toward the elevator. Bad enough they were a constant reminder of how lonely he was, he didn't need to think about his total lack of a sex life, too. Most of the time he could ignore it, and he had significant willpower. Plus he could honestly say that there weren't many women he encountered in his job guarding Donatelli that even tempted him. The majority of them floating around the casino or with Donatelli were bubble-headed or trashy, neither of which appealed to him.

But he was a man, and he was feeling a bit, well, in need of release.

If he did encounter a woman he found attractive, he might have trouble controlling himself.

Which he realized the very second he stepped onto the elevator and met the green eyes of a petite redhead. Well, petite to him anyway, given that he was six foot five, but she was probably an average height for a woman. Her gorgeous rich auburn hair went to her shoulders, cute little freckles dusted across her nose and under her eyes, and the sleeveless summer shirt she wore showed off the creamy smoothness of her fair skin. He could smell her blood, sweet and juicy as it coursed through her veins, her heart beating strong and steady in her chest.

She was beautiful, stunning. Sensual and alive and intelligent looking.

Lust slammed into him so unexpectedly that Nick briefly paused while stepping in, needing a second to recover himself. "Hi," he said, before turning and taking the appropriate front-facing place on the elevator.

"Hi," she said in return, her voice a little huskier than he expected, and unfortunately, sexy as hell.

Nick hated those Minnie Mouse voices on women, and this one was the furthest thing from it—she had the voice of a forties film star, the sound sliding over him and grabbing onto his balls and squeezing. Damn, he was in trouble, especially since the woman was clearly with a man.

"What floor?" the guy asked, adjusting his pants under his ample gut.

"Tenth," Nick said. "Thanks." How could this woman be with this guy, who was clearly a decade older than her and in desperate need of a gym membership? Maybe they were co-workers, going to some business meeting or event. They were both wearing black dress pants and carried jackets over their arms. Then again, how many business meetings occurred at ten o'clock at night?

"That's where we're going," the guy said, raising his arm to smooth his thinning hair and revealing a giant sweat stain in his armpit. "All these floors and we're going to the same one. Weird."

"It's called a coincidence," the woman said to him, then turned to Nick and rolled her eyes, her irritation with her companion cheering Nick up.

He gave her a smile even as he realized there were no meeting rooms on the tenth floor, just suites. Then again, they could be doing who knew what, and what difference did it make, because the elevator doors were going to open and Nick was never going to see her again.

The doors did open and the guy said to the woman, "What room are we going to?"

She gave Nick one last look, naked curiosity in her eyes, before glancing down at a paper in her hand. "Tenthirty. Is that left or right?"

Oh, shit.

Nick said, "It's left. And that's my room."

He had a sinking feeling he knew who the gorgeous woman was.

She gave him a sharp look as they clustered outside the elevator. "Really? Are you Nikolai Stolin, by any chance?"

"That would be me, though I prefer Nick." He stuck out his hand. "I take it you are from the police department?"

"Yes." The woman took his hand and gave him a firm shake, her expression curious. "I'm Detective Jordan Waters and this is Detective Marshall. Thank you for your cooperation."

Jordan was an intriguing name for an intriguing woman. She was so very feminine in appearance, yet she was a homicide detective with an androgynous name. Nick's interest only increased, and he had to force himself to focus on the subject at hand. "Sure. I doubt Peter can be any help to you, but I'm willing to let you try. It's my understanding these were quite brutal killings and if we can help, we're happy to."

He took the hand Detective Marshall was now offering, glad to know this wasn't Jordan's lover. He gestured toward his suite. "Shall we?"

Jordan nodded. "So Peter is your son? And he's thirteen?"

"Yes." That was their story, anyway. "I told the other detective that Peter is autistic. The things he says don't always make sense to the average person, even though they make sense to him."

"And you live here? Where does he go to school?"

"Yes, we live here. It's convenient for work, and my employer pays for my accommodations. I'm a personal bodyguard. And Peter is homeschooled with a tutor."

The look she gave him told him her opinion on the fact that he was raising a child in a casino. But he couldn't tell her that Peter was no child, but a hundred-year-old vampire trapped in a pubescent boy's body.

"Could he have been in the alley behind the casino kitchen three nights ago?"

"It's possible," he admitted. "We try to take precautionary measures but Peter is sneaky and he likes to wander."

"We? Who is we?"

But Nick was already opening the door to his suite and he could hear Kelsey singing off-key to a pop song, the lyrics highly sexual. Embarrassed, he stepped in and called, "Kelsey, I'm home. For that meeting I told you about."

Ringo's wife appeared in view, wearing a very tiny red bikini. "Oh, shit," she said. "I totally forgot. We were going to the pool."

Peter was sitting on the couch, wearing swimming trunks with sharks on them and a UNLV T-shirt. He had been a sickly mortal child, and even though he'd been thirteen when he'd been turned, he had been slight, look-

ing more the age of nine or ten. It was occasionally unnerving to see him still in that child's body, but with the
eyes of a man, and it had that effect on Nick now as he
recognized the very manly appreciation for Kelsey's bikini in Peter's expression.

A glance back at Jordan Waters showed her frowning,
deep grooves in her forehead.

Something told him this interview wasn't going to go
well.

THREE

JORDAN didn't consider herself judgmental, especially when it came to raising children. She always figured she had never walked in those shoes, being childless herself, so who was she to criticize when a kid was running loose in a restaurant or a parent lost patience in a public restroom?

But she couldn't help but think that the Stolins weren't doing their kid any favors by having him living in the false glitz of a casino, homeschooled without any interaction with kids his own age, and heading to the pool after ten on a school night.

And Mrs. Stolin? Good God.

Jordan stared at the brunette in the bikini—which one half turn of her skinny body revealed to actually be a thong—and felt an instant female dislike for her. Maybe it was because for a few sensual shared moments in the elevator, aware of Nick Stolin's flattering assessment of her, conscious of the spark that flickered between them, she had remembered she was a woman. She had actually contemplated flirting with him, and if the kid had no information, she would be free to do whatever she wanted with

Nick without it being a conflict in the case. That had all raced through her head in two minutes, shocking her, considering she hadn't really glanced at a man in months. But there had been something about his brawn, the soulful brown eyes, the way he stared at her . . . Even now her inner thighs felt warm at the memory.

But this dingbat in a bikini was his wife? That was just all sorts of wrong, and made him nothing more than a pig for checking her out so avidly.

Not to mention that looking at the pale skin of the thin brunette, her muscle tone amazing, Jordan was painfully aware of the doughnut—okay, two doughnuts—she had eaten an hour earlier.

The woman was babbling. "I'm going to go ahead and go swim my laps, Nicky. You know I hate cops. It's because it was their fault I OD'd, you know. If I hadn't been worried they were going to take my stash, I wouldn't have shot it all up and ended up flatlining. I know it was a long time ago and I'm clean now and everything, but cops still creep me out."

Was she serious? Jordan felt her eyebrows head north and she glanced at Shawn, who looked equally flummoxed.

"I think they have a few questions for you, Kelsey, since you were with Peter the night in question. It will just take a minute, don't worry." Nick's voice was calm and reassuring, and he picked up the beach bag that was laying on the coffee table. "Here, put your cover-up on and have a seat on the couch." He handed her a gauzy shirt, and she actually obeyed.

He turned to the boy, who had his feet crossed on the coffee table. "Peter, this is Detective Waters and Detective Marshall. They just want to talk to you."

Peter stared at his father blankly.

Great. Jordan had a feeling this was a complete waste of time. She took the seat in the easy chair that Nick offered her and decided to start with the wife. "Mrs. Stolin, are you with Peter every night?"

The woman just stared at Jordan, much like the kid. Feeling her frustration increase, she was about to repeat the question, when Nick interjected.

"Oh, Kelsey isn't my wife. She's my babysitter." He gave an apologetic shrug. "I'm not married, and I work nights. It's not easy to find an overnight sitter, and Kelsey doesn't mind the odd hours. Sorry for the confusion."

Well, at least it made the once-over he'd given her in the elevator flattering again instead of creepy. She could also see that raising an autistic child alone on the Strip when you worked nights would be something of a challenge. But it seemed like there could be better options than this woman if you looked a little harder.

She tried again. "Okay, then, Kelsey, are you with Peter every night?"

"Yes, except for Sunday and Monday, Nick and Ringo's nights off."

"Who is Ringo?"

"My husband. He works with Nick."

Jordan turned to Nick, who was hovering next to the couch. "Is that how you met Kelsey and decided to hire her?"

He nodded. "Yes."

"And how long have you been in Vegas?"

"Five months."

"And how long in the U.S.?"

"Five months. We came from Odessa with my employer."

Jordan was willing to give him the benefit of the doubt, then. It couldn't be easy to relocate halfway around the world, and it seemed logical that you would seek a babysitter from a co-worker. She had a thought. "Does Peter speak English?"

"Of course." Nick looked offended. "I speak English, don't I?"

"Yes, very well, actually," she said. "You only have a hint of an accent." And he was looking at her again, with naked interest, and she was responding, her nipples hardening, her long-neglected body stirring to life, and she suddenly couldn't remember what she had been about to ask, which irritated the hell out of her.

Shawn saved her. "So last Tuesday, that's three nights ago, were you with Peter?" he asked Kelsey.

"Yes."

"What time?"

"Uh . . . I guess on Tuesday their shift was eleven to seven, so that's when I was here."

"Did you leave the room at all?"

She shifted on the couch. "No."

Well, that was clearly a lie. Jordan recovered herself and gave Kelsey what she hoped was a reassuring smile. "The kitchen staff saw Peter in the alley, so we know you weren't with him all night. It's okay, just tell us the truth so we can piece this together."

Kelsey bit her lip, which was bloodred from her lipstick. "I went down to the slots for just a half an hour. Peter went with me and sat at the milkshake place in the casino, where I could see him. He was reading."

Jordan turned to the kid. "Did you leave when Kelsey wasn't looking and go outside that night?"

"Maybe I did, maybe I didn't," the boy said, and then he laughed.

It was an eerie, unhappy sound, and instantly Jordan was reminded of her brother Bill, who had suffered from schizophrenia and had killed himself at eighteen. A sweat broke out between her breasts and on her upper lip as she remembered all those nights of trying to reason with him, only to have him spout random nonsense and give her that creepy, all-knowing laugh.

"Why did you go outside?" Shawn asked.

Peter's laugh cut off. "To eat boogers, where no one will yell at me."

Jordan's stomach flipped at that. She could look at homicide photos and keep her lunch intact, but oddly, the thought of eating mucus made her feel sick. "Ah, I understand," she said, in a soft, soothing voice. "We all have things we like to do in private."

"Yes, we do. In the dark." The look Peter gave her, his eyes inky black as they dropped down to roam over her body, his mouth raised in a smirk, startled her. If he had been an adult, she would have thought he was hinting at sex, at masturbation. But he was just a kid. Even though thirteen put boys securely in the hold of puberty, they weren't sophisticated or experienced enough to make witty innuendoes about sex. At least she didn't think they were.

Shifting on her chair, uncomfortable and not sure why, she said, "Did you see anyone out there in the alley with you?"

He shook his head. "Just me. And my shadow." Then he smiled, revealing small, crooked teeth.

Jordan glanced at Shawn. He seemed to be of the same opinion as her. This was a dead end. "Okay, well, thanks for talking to us, Peter." She smiled at Kelsey. "And thank you for your cooperation. You're free to go swimming now if you want."

Kelsey grinned and hopped off the couch. "Yay!" She turned to Nick, "Can we?"

"Sure." He checked his cell phone. "I have to go back to work. Keep an eye on him."

"Always." Kelsey stretched, threatening to expose her petite breasts. "Come on, Pete, let's make waves."

Jordan was relieved to see that the bikini held its place behind the see-through cover-up that shouldn't ever bother to call itself a cover-up.

"Okay." Peter stood up and fiddled with the strings on his swim trunks. "I need a drink first."

There was a pause where Kelsey looked to her employer for approval, which Jordan thought was an intriguing dynamic. The babysitter clearly thought of Nick Stolin as the man in charge.

Nick said calmly, "Of course you can have a drink, just no caffeine. Kelsey will get you something downstairs."

Jordan admired his control, his serenity with the situation. She wasn't so sure she could handle a child like Peter day in and day out. She certainly had failed Bill miserably. "Do you like Sprite, Peter? I have a bottle from the machine in my purse if you want it. I haven't opened it yet."

Nick knew exactly what Peter wanted and it wasn't a soft drink. He wanted blood, his appetite always more voracious than Peter's or Katie's, and he shook his head at the detective's offer.

"Thanks," Nick said to Jordan. "But he wants one of those fruity drinks they serve at the bar without alcohol."

Another lie, always a lie. Nick wanted to sigh, but there was no point. There was blood in the fridge, but he wasn't sure how long the two detectives planned to stay, and it was too risky to have Peter drink it around them. Nick trusted that Kelsey could figure something out. She had blood in her apartment, and there were dozens of vampires roaming the Paris at any given time who might have a nip on them. He hoped she wouldn't let Peter live-feed because it always made him excitable. He got flushed and giddy and talked nonstop for a day after he took blood directly from a mortal, and Nick didn't feel like dealing with it tonight.

He was pissed off, and he wasn't sure why. But he suspected it was because he knew he and his dysfunctional little family looked weird as hell, and if he asked Detective Jordan Waters out, she would flat-out say no. Which frustrated him to no end.

Kelsey and Peter left, and the male detective excused himself to answer his cell phone, stepping into Nick's kitchenette.

"I'm sorry Peter wasn't more help to you," Nick told Jordan. "I'm not even sure if he really was in the alley or not." When Nick had gotten home from work that night,

Peter had already been asleep, so he hadn't said anything to him about being out of the hotel, though he probably wouldn't have. He knew Nick would frown on his slipping away from Kelsey.

"It's okay," she said. "It was worth a shot." She stood up and slid her black purse over her shoulder, the emerald-green shirt she was wearing bunching up and revealing her bra strap. "Thanks for letting us question him."

"Sure." Nick stood with his hands in his pockets and debated going for it. Just asking her out. What difference did rejection make? If she said no, he would be in the exact same position he was in now—alone. But if she said yes . . .

"It must be hard for you, raising Peter alone, working nights. Where is his mother?"

"She died. A long time ago." Longer than Jordan could possibly fathom.

"I'm sorry." Her voice had softened and her eyes were sympathetic. "You must miss her."

He had to be somewhat truthful, not wanting to own the grieving widower persona. It felt too dishonest. "We were not together when she died, though I was of course sad for Peter. But what about you, are you married?"

She gave a rueful smile. "No."

"Boyfriend?"

"No. I'm married to the job."

They were standing closer to each other than two normal strangers would, and Nick smelled her blood again. He ached to taste her, to sink his fangs into her neck, into her breasts, and draw her sweet life force into him. He wanted to kiss her lips and run his tongue all over her creamy white skin. "Do you ever date?"

"Not very often." Her voice was low, quiet, but coy.

He decided he had nothing to lose. "So you would say no if I asked you out?"

"Why don't you ask me out and see?" she said, voice growing huskier.

Nick smiled. Maybe she was actually going to say yes,

and that made his mouth dry and his body hard. "Would you like to go out, Jordan? Maybe for a drink and a movie? You seem like an interesting woman and I would like to get to know you a little better."

"I should say no," she said, her eyes darting to her pre-occupied partner. "But I'm not going to."

"Why is that?"

"A couple of reasons. I need to get a life and I can spare time for one date. And I'm attracted to you."

He liked her boldness. "What a coincidence. I'm attracted to you, too."

"Normally I don't like coincidences. But in this case I'm willing to accept it."

So was he. Nick smiled. "Are you free tomorrow? I don't have to work until eleven. We could meet at say, eight?"

"Sure. Do you want to meet in the lobby?"

"That will work. See you then. And have a good night."

"Thanks, you, too." Jordan tucked her hair behind her ear and turned back to her partner, who was still on the phone. She gestured to him to head for the door.

In another minute they were gone, and Nick headed back to work in a much better mood than he had left it in.

"WELL, that was a total bust," Shawn said after he hung up his phone and stepped into the elevator with Jordan.

"Yeah," she said, distracted, wondering why the hell she had just agreed to go out with Nick Stolin. It had all the makings of a Very Bad Idea.

"What a fucked-up trio, I'm telling you. That chick was missing a few IQ points."

"And clothes."

Shawn laughed. "Now that I didn't mind, though she was a little too skinny for my tastes. I like some curves to hold on to."

"TMI, Shawn, seriously."

"And what about that kid? He seemed more like a head case than autistic to me. And I could swear he had a boner. Did you notice that?"

Jordan turned to stare at Shawn in disbelief as the elevator descended. "No, I did not notice that. Why would I? Christ, you're a sick man."

"I'm not the one with a boner! How does that make me sick? And I guess you can't blame the kid . . . he's at that age, regardless of his mental capabilities, and he has a smoking-hot babysitter with her ass cheeks hanging out."

"I don't even want to think about it." Ass cheeks, boners, death, why she had agreed to go out on a date with a man ripped with muscles . . . Jordan didn't want to think about any of it. She just wanted another doughnut.

"And the dad, I mean, come on. What is he thinking, hiring that chick?"

"I don't know. It must be hard to be new in a city, working nights like that. I bet she's a bargain babysitter, and he probably only makes peanuts himself."

Shawn held the elevator door open for Jordan. "You're just defending him because you're flattered he had the hots for you."

Jordan bristled. "He did not have the hots for me."

"Unh-uh. He basically fucked you with his eyes. But okay, you pretend you didn't notice."

"Okay, I did notice, but come on, you know me. I would never let that cloud my judgment." At least she never had in the past. Arguably going to dinner with Nick Stolin was a bit murky.

"Did he ask you out?"

Jordan winced. "Yes. How did you know?"

"I've got eyes. I've got ears. You said yes, didn't you?"

Damn it, was she blushing? Jordan hadn't done that since middle school. "Yes, and I don't want to hear one word about it. I'm serious. You give me shit, and I will hurt you."

"Like I would ever give you a hard time." Shawn gave her a mock look of innocence. "I wouldn't dream of it.

And if you want to get bounced by the bouncer I figure that's your business."

"Wow, thanks." Jordan rolled her eyes in annoyance, even as she wasted a tiny second wondering how exactly it would feel to have a guy like Nick Stolin inside her. The heat in her cheeks increased, and it wasn't from embarrassment this time.

"So what now?" Shawn said, his thoughts clearly not on sex and on the case, which was where Jordan's should be. "We've got no witness. It's going to be weeks before we can get DNA results back on the skin found under Samantha Keller's nails, since the lab is always backed up, and the coroner's report only told us what we already knew. She was killed, then drained of all her blood via a wound in her neck, presumably some kind of needle, though I can't imagine how freaking long that would take. I mean, how did he not get caught draining them like that?"

"I don't know. Logic would say he moved them after death, but the coroner says the stakings were wounds inflicted prior to death, and the blood loss at the scene where the bodies were found would indicate that. So all we can do right now is go back to trying to connect the victims to each other, to establish a pattern. Talk to family and friends, pull Samantha's cell phone records." The problem with a case like this was that the casino area was full of strangers, people who had never crossed each other's paths before and had no connection other than their trip to the Strip. Of the three victims, two had been local, one had been from Seattle in town for a bachelorette party, and they didn't appear to have any connection to each other at all.

"I think he's just an opportunist," Shawn said. "He grabs whatever woman is by herself when no one is around to witness him snagging her."

"That's not usually a serial killer's MO, but I don't know, I'm inclined to agree with you. The victims were not the same physical type at all. We had the average-height, very athletic Latina; a short, slightly overweight blonde; and a tall, fair-skinned brunette."

"Maybe he's going for every type intentionally," Shawn said, as they headed into the parking garage. "Or maybe he just snags what he can."

"I don't know . . ." Jordan stopped at the car and waited for Shawn to unlock it as they talked over the roof to each other. "I can't get in this guy's head at all. Most killers who display their victims don't actually want them found right away. They want to visit them, spend time with them in their death. His victims are found right away because they're in such public venues. And why casinos? Does he work in a casino? Are you right, does he just step outside, see a woman by herself, and go for it?"

"But with a stake in his pocket?" Shawn made a sound of disgust and got in the car.

Jordan followed suit. "We're missing something."

"We're missing a lot of somethings."

"These were not stupid women. They were all middle class—two professionals, one married with children. They weren't just hanging around an alley behind a casino at midnight by themselves. None of them had had enough alcohol in their bloodstream to be intoxicated, including our bachelorette party attendee. He's tricking them somehow, flirting with them, luring them off, don't you think?"

"Like he's hitting on them in bars and they step outside with him for a smoke or something?" Shawn pulled out into the stifling traffic and heat of a Friday night on the Strip. "God, I hate this fucking traffic."

Jordan barely heard his bitching. She thought they might be on to something. "Yeah, I think maybe so. He is charming, good-looking, harmless. They chat in the bar, she steps outside with him a few times during the night to smoke, which seems harmless because presumably other people are around and they're right outside the casino. By the end of the night, she feels comfortable and lets him walk her to her car. Did any of them smoke?"

"I don't know. And what about their friends? Wouldn't

their friends have told us if the victims were talking to some guy?"

"Not if she talked casually to several guys, or she just spoke to him when she was outside smoking, and not if we didn't ask."

"So you don't think he's just grabbing these chicks off the street? We didn't see any of the victims talking to any guys on the security camera footage."

Which had amounted to all of about ten minutes. With the cameras sweeping and the women moving around they had very little actual footage of the women's interactions in the casinos.

"No, I don't think he's just grabbing them off the street." Jordan wasn't sure why, but her gut was telling her he earned these women's trust in some way first. "Why else would they willingly be in a dark place with a guy they don't know?"

"Are we sure he doesn't already know them?"

Jordan squeezed the handles of her purse in her lap. "No. No, we don't know that. Shit, Shawn. We need to reinterview the friends the victims were with the night they died."

"What we need is some goddamn DNA."

"DNA won't do us any good without a suspect."

"Can't you just let me delude myself for a minute that he's already in the system?"

Jordan smiled. "Yeah, right."

"Alright, I'm dropping you off then I'm going home. I want to get naked with my wife tonight."

Like she needed to know that? "You need to work on that verbal vomit problem you have. I don't want to hear about you and your wife having sex."

"What? It's not like I got specific or anything, so deal with it. What are you going to do tonight?"

"Nothing."

What she was going to do was spend the entire evening wondering why she had agreed to go out with Nick Stolin.

And trying to convince herself that absolutely under no

circumstances would she have sex with him on the first date.

When she was pretty much certain that unless he proved to be a complete freak, she was going to wind up in bed with him.

A year was just too long, she was just too on edge, and he was just too hot.

He hadn't popped out of a desk drawer, but he had been virtually handed to her, and Jordan was smart enough to take him and run with it.

FOUR

"YOU'RE going to meet the detective, aren't you?"
Nick paused on his way out the door and turned to meet Peter's accusatory glare. "Yes. Why?"

"You said you'd take me to the movies this week and now instead I'm stuck with Kelsey while you nail the cop."

Nick was never sure which was more disturbing— Peter's delusional, vapid ramblings, or his lucid moments as a hundred-year-old man in a thirteen-year-old's body.

"You can go to the movies by yourself, I don't care."

"It's not whether *you'll* let me go or not, it's that the theater people won't let me in." Peter's face twisted in anger. "I'm not *old enough*."

And there was nothing either of them could do about that, and the guilt weighed heavily on Nick. "Kelsey will be here in five minutes, she'll take you."

Peter clicked the TV off and tossed the remote down on the coffee table. "I'm an emperor, the rightful tsar of all Russia, and I have to be chaperoned by a vampire who can't find her ass with both hands."

Nick glanced nervously down the hall at the elevators

and ignored the comment about being royalty. It wasn't like Peter could reclaim his throne or get a different body, and Nick could sense Kelsey's vampiric presence and knew she was about to appear. "Kelsey's also about to come down the hall and can probably hear you. You'll hurt her feelings."

Crossing his arms over his chest, Peter pouted. "I don't give a damn."

"Alright, fine." Nick didn't have the patience for it. "Stay here and whine or go to the movies with Kelsey. Do whatever you want."

Peter smiled. "I will."

Nick didn't like the look on Peter's face. It was an indicator that he would try to ditch Kelsey, but Nick had to work later and he didn't want to cancel his date with Jordan. Peter was an adult, and frankly, Nick was tired of catering to his bad behavior and trying to keep him out of trouble. Peter was his responsibility, but he couldn't control him any more than he could protect him.

"Good night." When he got to the elevators, they opened and Kelsey stepped out in a hot-pink cocktail dress.

"He's in a mood, isn't he?" she asked with a bright smile. "I could hear his nasty thoughts from eight floors down."

"Yes. Sorry."

"No biggie. I'll take him downstairs and bribe the guard to let him play poker in the private room. Peter likes that."

Nick felt the tension in his shoulders increase. "That's illegal."

"Duh," Kelsey said, looking at him like he was a moron. "So what? We don't have the same rules as mortals, and we can get out of anything. We don't show up on camera, and we can move faster than the mortal eye can see. We get to do what we want."

The problem was, Nick never got to do what he

wanted. If he could, he would quit his job and start his own private security firm. He was really tired of walking his own moral fence by working for guys like Donatelli, and he wanted to be his own boss. He also wanted to go back in time and be anywhere other than that room in Ekaterinburg, but those were futile wishes. Peter was his creation, and his responsibility.

But at least, maybe for one night, he could actually enjoy the company of an attractive woman.

"Alright, thanks for watching him, and just don't get in any trouble, okay?"

"Never," she said breezily.

When Nick got down to the lobby, he spotted Jordan at the same time he smelled her. She wore a vanilla-scented perfume, and it hit his nostrils right as he saw her leaning against the back of a couch checking her cell phone. Dressed in dark jeans, boots with a heel, and a tank top, she looked casual and sexy as hell. He was almost immediately in front of her before she glanced up.

"Geez, you startled me," she said, snapping her phone shut and standing up straight. "I didn't hear you coming toward me at all."

"I move light for a big guy," he said, with a smile. It amazed him all over again how truly beautiful she was, and now that he knew what she did for a living, he was even more intrigued. Weak women didn't interest him, but Jordan seemed to be that attractive combination of very feminine, yet strong and decisive.

"I guess you do," she said with an answering smile. "So, how are you? How was your day?"

Since he had slept for most of it, it had barely existed, but he just shrugged. "Okay. Peter is a little cranky tonight. How was your day?"

"Oh, I'm sorry Peter is out of sorts. That must be hard. My day wasn't great either. I can't really talk about the case, but let's just say, it isn't going well. That consumes my days and my nights lately."

"Do you enjoy your work? Why did you choose police work?"

She paused. "You know, people ask me that all the time, and I always give the pat answer. Because I like putting away the bad guy. And that's true. But you know, it's a control thing . . . doing my part makes me feel like I have more control over life. Not doing anything to make the world a better place makes me feel helpless. Does that make sense?"

"Yes," Nick said. "Yes, it does." It was why he had stepped in front and taken the bullets meant for Katie and Peter. It was why he struggled now to find purpose.

Then Jordan gave a rueful shrug. "I should feel guilty for being here with you, you know, but I really needed to clear my head and take a step back."

"Well, let's help you do that then. Are you still interested in seeing a movie?" Nick crammed his hands in his jeans pockets because he suddenly had the overwhelming urge to touch Jordan. He wanted to run his fingers through her rich auburn hair, brush his lips over her mouth, slide his hands down her body. He wanted to bite her, feel her hot blood in his mouth, with an intensity that shocked him.

He didn't really ever have the desire to touch mortals, and he didn't live-feed anymore. That he wanted to do both was unnerving.

Denying himself had been a mistake. He should have taken more time to slake his sexual and vampiric appetites over the past few years.

"Sure. I already ate so I think we can skip dinner or a drink, if you don't mind. That way we can get in a movie and you won't be late to work."

"I don't mind not eating." Since he didn't eat anyway. "We can walk to the movie theater. And it's ladies' choice—we can see whatever you want."

They talked as they walked, chatting about the usual things—career, family, likes and dislikes—that you did when you were getting to know someone. Nick was intrigued listening to her, and startled at how much they actually had in common, their taste in music, movies, and books.

She was just as voracious a reader as he was and listing obscure titles to each other kept resulting in him saying, "Read that," and her exclaiming, "Oh, my God, no way."

They discussed a couple of books in depth, and then Jordan asked, "Do you have any other hobbies?"

"Not really," he told her as they approached the movie theater. "I like to work out, but other than that I don't really get out of the house much."

"I'm sorry," she said, with a knowing look.

He shrugged. "It is what it is. I love Peter, you know, and that makes it easier."

"Of course you do. I can see that. I had a brother who was schizophrenic, and it's love that gets you through those days when they're so irrational you just want to cry."

"I'm sorry, that must have been hard on your family."

"It was. Lots of tears of frustration and sadness."

Nick smiled. "I'm not a big crier."

She rolled her eyes. "Of course you're not, Macho Man."

Giving a short laugh, he shot her a side glance. "But seriously, thank you for understanding. There are rough days, especially now that my niece is gone. I raised her as well, and she's getting married in a few days and I miss her. She kind of balanced out our odd little household."

"You raised your niece, too, and she's old enough to get married? Wow. How old are you?" Then Jordan wrinkled her nose as they got into line to buy tickets. "God, that was rude. Sorry. I think my social skills have gotten rusty."

"It's okay. I'm a guy, we don't worry about our age as

much as women do." Plus he was a hundred and twenty years old and still looked the way he had the day he'd been turned. He wasn't overly concerned about a number at this point. "I'm thirty-eight." It was a reasonable age to explain his guardianship of Katie in earlier years, and was close to the thirty-three he'd been when he'd been turned back at the beginning of World War I.

"Really?" She looked surprised. "You look like you're barely thirty to me."

"Hardly," he told her, enjoying teasing her. "Look at these crow's-feet." He pointed to his undereye. "And I'm going gray at the temples."

Jordan scrutinized both his skin and his hair and then smacked his arm. "Oh, please. You don't have a single wrinkle, and if you are going gray it's one random hair. You look better than me and you're ten years older than me."

"You look amazing," he said, dropping his eyes to her soft, plump lips.

She sucked in her breath, her eyes darkening. Her voice grew husky. "That's because I'm wearing makeup. And clothes. It all goes to hell when the concealer and the 'suck it all in and push it all up' bra and panties come off."

Nick gave in to temptation and brushed her hair back off her face. "I have no doubt you're being ridiculously hard on yourself. You're gorgeous, with a great figure."

"I'm not fishing for compliments, I swear. And I also swear to you that I have muffin top."

"What's a muffin top?" he asked in bewilderment.

"It's when your fat hangs over the top of your jeans. I have that because my only other hobby besides reading is baking. I probably eat my body weight in baked goods in a month. Hell, a week."

Nick had moved his hand to the small of her back, and she hadn't protested. He felt nothing but smoothness below her shirt, nothing like what she was describing at all. "If you're trying to scare me off from touching you by fabricating horror stories of what I might find, it's not going to work. Unless you don't want me to touch you, then you just need to tell me you're not interested, and I'll respect that."

"Oh, I want you to touch me, I'm just warning you," she said with an honesty he found incredibly refreshing. "You work out, I don't. You've got a six-pack and I just drink a six-pack."

"I think you worry too much."

Jordan laughed. "Yeah, no kidding."

"And I wish we weren't still standing in this damn line, because I really want to kiss you, and I'd prefer not to do so with twenty people watching us."

"Wait until we get inside," she told him. "It's nice and dark."

He sincerely loved the way this woman thought.

JORDAN was being super forward, and she didn't even care. There was something just so *hot* about Nick Stolin. The man was ripped, so tall and brawny that he made her feel tiny and very feminine when he was standing next to her. He had a sly, closed-mouth smile that did interesting things to her inner thighs, and he looked like he wanted to eat her one bite at a time. Plus he was an avid reader, had raised his niece and his autistic son alone, and he wanted to kiss her.

Sold.

She knew herself, and when she made up her mind nothing could stop her, and she wanted to sleep with Nick. A fling was just what she needed, a passionate, pleasant distraction. It was unbelievable to her that she had managed to suppress her physical urges for an entire year, because they were exploding at the moment.

They had been in the theater only five minutes when

Nick put his hand on her knee, stroking with his thumb, distracting her from the previews that were playing.

Another three minutes and he whispered in her ear, "Jordan."

"Yeah?" She turned to see what he wanted and barely had time to catch a breath before his mouth was on hers.

Oh, my. It took a second to recover, but then Jordan sank into the kiss. In the dark theater, his shoulder brushing hers, it was perfect. Sexy, skilled, the kind of first kiss that confirms the attraction you're feeling is legitimate and is going to go to good, happy places. He had a firm, demanding mouth, but with a strange, unexpected tenderness that left her breathless.

Nick pulled back and she stared into his brown eyes in the dark theater, and everything feminine and emotional and romantic in her just melted. It stunned her, the way want and need and the desire to be touched just rolled over her, and when he bent his head again, she met him eagerly and with passion. She kissed him with all her pent-up frustration and need, and he took her lips in kind, his arm pulling her tightly against him.

God, he was so big and hard and masculine, and if Jordan hadn't been in public, she would have crawled right onto his lap. Which further shocked her. She wasn't a lap percher; she was a detective, one of the guys, and there was nothing Barbie about her. But while she was still tough and independent, this man tugged on her softer side.

It was with both regret and relief that she pulled back, breathing hard. He looked the way she felt—drowning in passion and overwhelmed by it.

Nick squeezed her lower back, then turned to the screen.

Jordan did the same, staring at the images flickering in front of her with no idea what the hell she was looking at.

She should walk away. She should get up out of the theater and just leave, to shake this feeling of vulnerability that had suddenly stolen over her. It would be smart, logical.

But her butt stayed stuck to the seat, and she knew she wasn't going to do it.

FIVE

ANGIE Martin paused at the traffic light, wishing she had skipped that last glass of wine at dinner. She wasn't exactly drunk, but she had a healthy buzz and had a feeling she shouldn't be driving. Contemplating turning back into the parking lot of the casino and calling a cab, she saw movement to her right.

Doing a double take, it took her a second to process what she was seeing. Then she realized it was a kid, running at breakneck speed, shirtless. He stumbled over the curb, weaving erratically toward her car.

What the hell?

She idled, suddenly sober. He looked like he was barely in double digits and she knew it was past ten o'clock. Why was he running around the streets of Vegas by himself?

He came right up to her car and knocked on the passenger window. Worried, maternal instinct kicking in, Angie rolled down the window.

"What's wrong? Are you okay?" she asked.

His eyes were panicked, and he was breathing hard. "Please help me," he said. "I got away, but he's coming after me!"

The words collapsed into a sob and Angie didn't hesitate. "Get in, I'll help you. Who's after you?"

Opening the door, the boy climbed in, and Angie could see that he wasn't wearing shoes and his cargo shorts were sliding down off his hips, unbuttoned, revealing the waistband of his underwear. He had dark circles under his eyes and dried blood on his chin and chest.

Oh, my God. "What happened?" she asked, appalled.

"Go!" he begged, locking the door.

Shock wore off, and she pulled her foot off the brake and hit the gas. "I'm taking you to the police station."

"We have to get my mom," he pleaded. "He left her there."

"Who?" Not sure what to do, Angie pulled over to the side of the street and tried not to panic.

"My stepdad. Please, she's in that parking lot over there, and I think . . . I think she's dead." The boy burst into tears.

Oh, Lord. Angie's heart started to pound and she reached for her cell phone, only to find it wasn't sitting in its usual spot by the gearshift. Damn it. "We need help. We need to go in the casino and call for help."

"Can't we just check on her first? I can't just leave her there! What if he comes back?"

Angie pulled the car into the parking lot he was pointing to. "Show me where." She wasn't about to leave the kid alone with his mother in case the stepfather did come back, but neither did she want to be standing there if he showed up. She would position her car in front of the woman as some kind of protection, and she would find her stupid cell phone and call the cops.

"Right here." He pointed to the shadowy end of the lot, by the garbage Dumpster.

Great. Sick to her stomach, Angie slowed her car, cautiously scanning the ground, and felt around the backseat for her purse. Her phone had to be in there.

"She's not there!" he wailed. "He must have come back."

And before Angie could even react, the kid had opened the door and jumped out of the still-moving car, stumbling to the blacktop.

Jesus. She slammed on the brakes and parked the car. "Get back in here!"

Her fingers found her purse and she grabbed it, got out of the car, and ran after the kid, who had disappeared behind the Dumpster. "We need to go get help!"

The blow to the back of her head sent her pitching forward, the pain exploding behind her eyes, in her hands, and on her bare knees under her skirt as they made contact with the asphalt, and she lost her hold on her purse.

The stepfather was back, was her stunned thought as she struggled to focus her eyes and make her body move.

She tried to stand up, nausea climbing up her throat, but she was yanked backward onto her butt by a strong grip in her hair, pulling it so hard her head tilted up and she had a clear view of the Dumpster. A woman was in front of Angie, thin and pale in the murky glow of the streetlight. She wore a short pink cocktail dress, her long black hair sliding over bare shoulders.

"What . . . ?" Angie asked, confused. This woman didn't look injured in any way. Fear for the boy began to shift to fear for herself, the hairs on the back of her neck rising, a cold shiver sliding over her, a hot anxiety flooding her mouth.

The pressure on her hair roots was causing her eyes to water, blurring the figure in front of her, but she didn't need to see anymore when the woman said in a reassuring, high-pitched voice, "Don't worry, it will only hurt for a second, then you won't remember anything."

Oh, God. Angie went wild, trying to escape the hand holding her, not caring if she lost every hair on her head or the layer of skin off the backs of her legs. She had to get away. Every instinct in her said to run, that she was in danger, and she swatted at the person behind her, trying to rise to her feet. An arm whipped around her middle, the skin cool and clammy, the hold so tight that she wheezed, trying to suck in air.

"This is boring," the woman said. "I was winning at blackjack and I want to get back. Text me when you're done."

Then the woman disappeared. A sharp sting on Angie's neck made her scream, and as she felt pain infiltrate every inch of her body, the sensation of having all her insides drawn up and pulled out of her, she started to pray.

NICK shouldn't do it. He shouldn't even suggest it. He didn't know if Peter and Kelsey were in the suite, and he had to be at work in thirty minutes. It was too much, too soon, and he was going to offend Jordan.

But he still heard himself say to her as they lingered in the lobby of the Venetian after the movie, "Do you want to come up to my place for a drink?"

Jordan hesitated and Nick was about to retract the offer, when she said, "Well, I *want* to."

The look on her face, the way her eyes bore into him, made it clear what she was referring to, and Nick felt his body respond.

Then she added, "But is it really such a good idea?"

If she could be honest and direct, so could he. "I don't know. It is certainly what I want."

"Oh, trust me, I want it to. But I'm a cop, Nick. I know there is nothing smart about going up to the room of a man I just met, especially one who is huge and trained as a bodyguard."

Ah, so that was what was bothering her. Personal safety. Being smart. Funny enough, she didn't look the least bit afraid of him. "I can assure you that I'm not going to hurt you, but words are meaningless I know. Do you think I'm dangerous?"

She shook her head slowly, swinging her purse gently back and forth between her hands. "No. I don't. I have a radar, you know, from all my experience. I can spot a weirdo at twenty feet. A pedophile at five. That still doesn't mean I should trust you. It's possible I could be wrong."

Nick brushed that gorgeous auburn hair off her cheek and met her steady gaze. "I guess we have two options then. We'll make plans to meet in public again and you leave, or I can help you feel comfortable and you can stay."

"How are you going to do that?" she asked, the corner of her mouth going up in a sly smile, her eyes sparkling.

God, she was sexy. Even as she was telling him she shouldn't sleep with him, she was flirting with him. "We could go to your place instead, so you're on your own turf. Would that make you feel better?"

She paused, then shook her head. "No. Because then I would be isolated from others, unlike here in the casino, and then you would also know where I live."

Logical, he'd give her that. But he wanted her badly enough that he wasn't about to give up without exhausting all their options. "Okay. We could stay here then and you can have total control over me."

Her eyebrows shot up. "Oh, yeah? And how exactly would I do that?"

The idea had just popped into his head, and now it had a strange appeal to it. Nick wanted Jordan to stay, and he wanted her to trust him. "You're a cop. You can cuff me."

Now her jaw dropped. "Are you serious? You would let me put you in handcuffs . . . for real?"

"Yes. Then you can do as much or as little as you want. Leave after a few minutes or stay all night. It's up to you. Everything will be yours to control."

"Oh, really?" Her shock shifted to intrigue and she gave him a curious look. "Do you do this frequently? Let women handcuff you?"

"I've never done it. It's never even occurred to me before. But the truth is, we can spend months getting to know each other before you're comfortable being alone with me, and I don't have that kind of patience at this point in my life."

"That I definitely understand. I'm fresh out of patience myself. So say I come upstairs with you . . . are you going to call me tomorrow?"

She was definitely direct and the question had curiosity in it, nothing more. "Yes, I will call you. I have a ton of baggage, a kid, and a lousy job, and I should probably spare you the horror of getting involved with me, but I am feeling just selfish enough that I will call you. I want to see you again."

"Everyone has baggage. It's unavoidable. I'm not exactly quality relationship material myself."

"So what do you say we don't worry about that and just enjoy the moment?" Nick could learn to do that. He worried too much, was weighted down by responsibility, by concern for what the rest of his long, immortal life was going to be like. He just wanted a little bit of pleasure, physical and emotional, no matter how brief.

"I think that's a damn fine idea," Jordan said. Then she grinned. "I'll cuff you before we get on the elevator. Good thing I still have them in my bag from work. I don't usually go out on dates with them."

"Given my job, it would have never struck me as odd, trust me." Nick gestured in the direction of the elevator and followed Jordan when she started walking.

"You're a personal bodyguard?" she asked. "What does the guy you work for do?"

"He's an Italian businessman." And vice president of the Vampire Nation, but he couldn't tell Jordan that. "He owns a lot of real estate."

"I thought you said you came from Odessa with your employer. What was an Italian doing in Odessa?"

It pleased Nick that she had clearly had paid attention when he spoke. "That was my former employer—a Russian businessman. I came here with him, and then unfortunately he was killed."

"Really? That's awful."

"Yes, it was. He was a horrible human being, but I suppose even he didn't deserve to die. At least it wasn't on my shift. That would have been embarrassing."

Jordan laughed. "Nice. Hey, don't you have to work tonight?"

They had reached the elevators and she was fishing around in her purse.

"Oh, I'm not going to work tonight." Nick faked a cough. "I'm sick."

Her tongue slid across her bottom lip as she looked up at him in amusement. "Shame on you. Shirking responsibility."

"I never do." Not in a hundred years. "Tonight I am." Nick stuck his hands out in front of him, wrists together. "And I'm not going to feel the least bit guilty."

JORDAN couldn't believe Nick had made the offer for her to cuff him, but she wasn't going to say no. With his hands mostly unavailable, she knew she wasn't in any real danger from him should he prove to be something other than the nice guy she thought he was.

It was good to take the precaution, and hell, a little bit sexy. But she trusted her gut—he was lonely, like she was, and burdened by responsibility. It was in his eyes, a mirror image of hers, though his were laced with a sadness she didn't think she had. Tonight, it was clear they both just wanted to forget. To talk, to kiss, to enjoy themselves, wherever that might lead.

"Shouldn't you make sure Peter isn't home? I'd hate to scare him by having his father walk in wearing handcuffs."

"Yeah, I should, though I suspect Kelsey is running around with him. They talked about going to the movies, too. But I also need to call off work."

He fished his phone out and made the quick calls while Jordan checked her own phone to make sure no one was trying to contact her.

"Done," he said. "I never call off work, so they were fine with it. And Peter isn't home—Kelsey is letting him look at the fountains outside." He smiled at her. "We're good. Cuff me."

A shiver raced up Jordan's spine at the sound of his voice. "I hope no one gets on the elevator with us," she told him as she clicked the metal rings around his wrists. "They'll assume you're a criminal and be terrified."

"They'd probably be more terrified if we told them the truth."

Jordan laughed. "You're probably right. I'm not sure how normal this is," she said as they both stepped onto the thankfully empty elevator.

"I don't suppose that either one of us has a normal life in the strictest sense," Nick told her, giving her a small, rueful smile. "You spend your days with dead bodies and chasing down killers. I have, well, not exactly a white-picket-fence lifestyle either."

"We belong on the Island of Misfit Toys, don't we?"

Confusion clouded his face. "What is that?"

"Oh, it's from a Christmas cartoon, an island where all the toys that don't fit into a standard of perfection go to live since they won't be given as gifts to children for Christmas. Like a wagon with a square wheel."

With a soft laugh he said, "I imagine that is a fairly good description of me and my life. A wagon with a square wheel."

They stared at each other briefly before he leaned forward and kissed her. Jordan knew he was going to and she welcomed it. As the elevator shot up, she gave in to the gentle yet passionate kiss and slipped her hand around the back of his neck. She had to go way up on her toes to reach his mouth, and his confined hands were trapped between their bodies, brushing at her abdomen.

God, he could kiss. And she had missed this, the right

to touch someone, the invasion of her personal space, the hardness of a man's body pressed close up against the softness of hers.

The elevator dinged and the door opened. Nick stepped out and grinned at her. "My room key is in my back pocket. I think you're going to have to get it out since I'm, uh, helpless here." He held his bound hands up in the air.

Oh, darn. She was going to have to dig in the denim back pocket of his jeans. "I'm a professional," she told him briskly. "I can handle it."

Since it was more fun to do it from the front, she reached around his hips and patted both pockets. One was smooth while the other was lumpy. Tempted to linger on the smooth one, she resisted and slid her fingers into the other pocket. Of course, the position meant that her whole body was brushing against his chest and thighs, and it was a pleasant side effect. The bump in the one pocket was obviously his wallet and she extracted it, pulled out his room key, then tucked it back in, efficiently and without squeezing his backside like she really, really wanted to.

She held the key up. "Told you I was a professional."

Nick's eyes were jet black. "That's a little disappointing."

"Good things come to those who wait."

"You don't really believe that, do you?" Nick asked, his voice low, sexy. "I think I've learned that the only thing that comes to those who wait is more of the same. If you want something, you have to go for it."

Jordan had never articulated it herself, but she did feel the same way. Passivity got you nothing in life, not even peace or contentment. You had to reach out with both hands for what you wanted and take it with gusto. She hadn't been doing that; she'd been drowning under dead bodies and paperwork. "Trust me, I'm going to go for it."

"Yeah? I can't wait."

Neither could she. "Guess that means neither one of us gets a gold star for patience."

"A gold star or you? I think only a fool would choose the star."

Jordan laughed and opened the door to Nick's suite. "After you."

He strolled in, shooting her a smoldering look over his shoulder as he went into the living room. "Do you want a drink or anything? I'm not sure what I have in the room but I can order from downstairs."

"No, thanks. I don't want a drink." What she wanted was him, naked, not on a platter, but on a bed. She wanted to climb onto his strong, broad body and fill herself with his hard erection. The intensity of the thought shocked her, but not enough to dissuade her.

She took a step toward him and her intent must have been clear on her face, because Nick's eyes widened.

"Come here, Jordan," he said, slowly, carefully, his hands dangling uselessly in front of him in the handcuffs.

She did, reaching her hands out as she approached to wrap them around his neck, kissing him hot and hard and with all the pent-up passion she felt. Nick kissed her back, using the tips of his fingers to tug on her shirt and pull her closer, then undo her pants.

That was skill, taking down a zipper with handcuffs on while sliding his tongue inside her mouth. Then he was walking her backward, hands on her opened waistband, legs on either side of hers, his mouth doing seriously wonderful things. Her back hit the wall of the entryway, knocking a gasp out of her at impact. He was strong, even without real use of his hands, and damn it, that was so sexy.

Moisture flooded between her thighs, and her nipples were tight and aching, so Jordan wrapped her thigh around his in an open invitation to do whatever he wanted.

He did, yanking at the neckline of her shirt, exposing her flesh to her bra. Nick bent forward and kissed her neck, the cleavage, the rise of each breast, while Jordan gripped his impressive biceps and enjoyed the pleasure surging through her.

"I don't know how good I'll be at this under the constraints," he said as he maneuvered two fingers inside her jeans. "But I'm damn well going to try."

He stroked along the slickness and Jordan moaned quietly.

Nick's dark eyes bore into her. "You're very wet."

"It's been very long," she told him, letting her eyes flutter closed and her head loll against the wall as he moved inside her, hooking his finger in a way that had her groaning softly. "The restraints don't seem to be holding you back. My God, that feels good."

His lips were on her chest again, kissing and licking and sucking. With his tongue, he had managed to shove one of her bra cups down and he was flicking the tip of his tongue over her nipple. "You taste so wonderful," he said. "And I have to warn you . . . I'm a biter. I can't help it. It turns me on."

"Oh, yeah?" In the past it had never done much for Jordan but the idea of Nick taking a little nip at her sounded exciting. "Where are you going to bite me?"

"Here," he said, scraping his teeth lightly across the swell of her breast.

"Really?" she asked, not sure if she would like that or not but distracted by his finger stroking deliciously inside of her.

"Yes."

Then his teeth put pressure on her flesh and Jordan gasped at the sharp sting of pain. But before she could protest or pull away, the shock of discomfort gave way to a flood of ecstasy. The squeeze of his mouth on her shot through her entire body like an electrical current, causing her muscles and limbs to tremble and squirm and pulse like she was having an entire-body orgasm.

Jordan couldn't breathe or make a sound, her eyes rolling back into her head, fingers fluttering uselessly at the back of Nick's neck. She had never felt anything so amazing in her entire life. When the pressure increased just a little on her breast, Nick also pinched her clitoris, and Jordan let out a cry and came in the most explosive orgasm she'd ever experienced.

Wow.

She clutched at him, bit her lip, and sank into the pleasure.

SIX

NICK continued to stroke Jordan through her powerful orgasm, but he forced himself to extract his fangs
from her flesh. If he pushed it, let too much of her sweet,
juicy blood roll over his tongue and down his throat, he
would lose control and do things he shouldn't do. Like
take her harder than a vampire ever should a mortal. Or
drain too much of her blood, leaving her weak and disoriented.

He didn't want to do either of those things to Jordan,
and he wanted to be as close to normal with her as possible. But he hadn't been able to resist tasting her, and it
had met every expectation, satisfied every one of his taste
buds, every inch of his body. Licking his fangs to taste the
lingering tangy sweetness, Nick watched Jordan's explosive pleasure.

He had done that to her.

He had made her come like that, her eyes dilated,
breathing frantic, legs spread, inner thighs slick and juicy
from her desire, and that satisfied him as profoundly as
the taste of her lifeblood. Most vampires had mind-reading
skills, but Nick had always been lacking in that particular

talent. For him, it was like a dull buzz, random words or thoughts that were so disjointed he couldn't even determine the person who was having them, but when Jordan had walked into his suite, he had heard and almost seen her thoughts like she had broadcast them in high definition. She wanted him inside her, and knowing that had been all he needed to push her against the wall and sink his fangs into her flesh.

Now he wanted to feel the completion she had craved as well, so he pulled back, running the tip of his fingers across her bottom lip as she trembled and panted, her green eyes wide and glassy.

"Come to my bedroom," he said.

"I would love to." Her tone so emphatic that he groaned.

The honesty of her passion was very pleasing to him, very arousing. It was probably a good thing that he was wearing the cuffs. He was feeling rough and raw, and the restriction would force him to maintain control.

Nick gave her a deep, probing kiss, then said, "Follow me."

In his room, he closed the door and pushed the button in to lock it. Then he lay down on his bed, with his hands over his head. "Be gentle with me."

Jordan gave a soft laugh as she came toward the bed, peeling her shirt off and tossing it on the floor. She wiggled out of her jeans, giving him a fabulous view of soft flesh and womanly curves before she crawled onto the bed. "Should I turn the light on?"

"It's up to you," he told her. He didn't need the artificial light to see in the dark. He could see fairly well without it. Just another side benefit of being undead, and at the moment, he could even see the goose bumps on her chest as she leaned over him, one leg on either side of his.

"Then I'm not going to bother. It will take too long."

Jordan's thin and nimble fingers were already on the fly of his jeans, and then she had them undone and his erection out and in her warm hand with an efficiency Nick fully appreciated. She stroked him with just the right speed, just the right pressure, and he relaxed, enjoying the lazy pleasure the movement gave him.

"There's a condom in my pocket," he told her before he could become so distracted he totally forgot. He had no need for the latex to combat either disease or pregnancy, but it would reassure her since he couldn't tell her the truth.

Jordan kissed his jaw, her hand still moving over him, her breasts brushing over his chest. "Good idea."

Wishing he could feel her bare flesh completely on his, he said, "And once you have that, take off my clothes."

"Even better idea."

It had been far too long since he'd felt a woman's touch, and Jordan unrolling the condom over his erection had him wanting to sigh. She gave a little squeeze and he did expel air, his desire acute and aggressive.

"Take my pants off," he told her, his voice rougher than he intended, but he was feeling the impatience of not having his hands free. Without the cuffs, he could have already disposed of his clothes and been buried deep inside her wet warmth.

"In a hurry?" she asked with a smile as she tugged down his jeans, her breasts brushing against his thighs, hair tickling his abdomen.

"Fuck yes."

She laughed, a sweet, delightful, sexy sound, and Nick felt a vulnerable tug of emotion. He had missed these things—intimacy, laughing in bed, sharing hot passion with a woman. Then again, he had never met a woman like Jordan, a woman who said exactly what she was thinking and exactly what she wanted, and he was very attracted to that. It was the reason, aside from her beauty, that he had noticed her after ignoring women for so long, and he wasn't surprised when she shoved his T-shirt up to expose his chest.

"I just had to see it," she said. "Touch it." Her fingers

ran all over his flesh, tracing the definition of his muscles, her thighs straddling his, her soft inner thighs resting teasingly on his erection.

Nick kissed her, nipping lightly at her bottom lip. "Does it meet your expectations?"

"Oh, it surpasses them," she assured him, her head bobbing in the dark room. "You're a rock from head to toe."

"Especially below the waist," he told her, lifting his hips to drive home the point. "Ride me, Jordan."

"With pleasure." She shifted, then thrust herself down onto him.

They both groaned, Nick squeezing his eyes shut at the feeling of her, tight and slick, wrapped around him. She moved slowly up, then down the length of him, resting her hands on his chest. It was delicious, exquisite, painful in its slowness. Nick was caught between wanting to savor her, wanting to draw out the delight, and wanting to pound himself into her with staccato thrusts.

She moved on and on, in a slow erotic tease, her breathing a series of pants and sighs, her breasts just out of his reach.

Nick tried to grip her waist, tried to move her up and down on him faster, but he couldn't get enough of a palm spread with the handcuffs, and he wound up even more frustrated. He slid his finger down her clitoris, hoping to encourage her to pick up the pace, but she only pushed his finger away.

"Too much," she said. "I don't want to come yet."

Lifting his hips only resulted in her coming to a complete stop. "Are you doing this or am I?" she asked, her eyes languid with desire.

"I am." Nick jerked his wrists apart, breaking the steel handcuffs with his vampiric strength and gripping her hips firmly.

"How the hell?" she asked, looking at him in astonishment. "Those are impossible to—"

Her shocked words were cut off when Nick pulled her down onto him at the same time he lifted his hips. The erotic collision had her saying, "Oh! Oh, wow."

Nick did it again, harder, and again, building a rhythm that within seconds had Jordan yelling in ecstasy. He loved that sound, loved the feel of her soft flesh within his fingers, loved the impact of their bodies together, the way she slammed down onto him each time he dropped her hips. Twisting his head, he bit the flesh above her knee and sucked hard, drawing a mouthful of blood past his lips.

Jordan screamed, her body pulsing on his as she had another orgasm, just as intense as the first. Her fingers squeezed his chest, her inner muscles milking his cock, and Nick joined her, letting go with his own shout as he came with her.

He probably had a dozen or so years of sexual release in that orgasm, and he throbbed into her, locking eyes with her in the dark, not sure if she could see him or not, but wanting that connection.

She collapsed against his chest, breathing hard. "Oh, my God. That was . . ."

"I hope you're going to say *amazing*." Nick swallowed hard. "Because it was for me."

"Definitely." She stroked his chest, her hair soft on his shoulder. "And I cannot believe you broke those cuffs. I don't know whether to be flattered or freaked."

"A man who wants a woman can break just about any-thing," he told her, hoping she wouldn't reflect too long on the fact. It hadn't been wise to do that, but he hadn't been rational at the time. Hell, he still wasn't feeling ra-tional, because he was thinking that he would do anything to have a real, honest-to-goodness relationship with Jor-dan, which he knew was impossible.

Yet he suddenly really very much wanted to try.

"And maybe you could unlock me now," he said, kiss-ing the top of her head gently. "If you don't mind."

"I don't mind," she said, peeling herself off his chest.

"Do you want me to leave, then? I don't want to make things awkward with Peter."

"No, I want you to stay." He did, desperately. "Please stay. I want to make love to you again after a quick nap." Nick reached out and drew his finger down her cheek. "Please say you'll stay."

Looking down at him from under her long, mink-colored eyelashes, Jordan didn't hesitate. "Okay. I'd love to stay."

A minute later she had him uncuffed and was settling in alongside him on the bed. In another sixty seconds she was asleep, her naked body snug beside his, her foot draped across his leg. Nick pulled the covers over both of them.

He didn't sleep at night, but Nick was content to lie there for the next two hours, stroking her hair, her back, her hip, enjoying the feel of her warmth, the sound of her breathing.

It had been too long since he had shared these intimacies, and he was ready to invite them back into his life with the most beautiful detective he had ever seen.

JORDAN woke up to Nick gently shaking her shoulder and saying, "Jordan, your phone just rang."

"Hmm?" she mumbled, her mouth thick, body warm and satisfied. She scooted a little closer to Nick's bulk under the covers and started to drift back to sleep.

"Jordan . . . it said it was Shawn on your cell phone screen. If your partner is calling you at two in the morning, maybe you should answer it."

Damn it. Jordan pried her eyes open. Nick, sitting up in bed, his back on the headboard, was holding her cell phone up in the dark. The backlight illuminated the missed call from Shawn. Her phone chimed, indicating Shawn had left a voice mail.

Sighing, she sat up and took the phone from Nick. "Thank you. How did you even hear that? I have it on low."

He just shrugged. "Light sleeper."

And phenomenal lover. Jordan smiled at him, running her fingers over his chest with her free hand while she pressed the appropriate buttons to listen to her message.

Shawn's voice was clipped. "Where the fuck are you? We've got another body down by Caesar's. This one is only a couple of hours old. Meet me down there."

All the warm and fuzzy aftermath of sex dissipated. "Shit." Jordan deleted the message. "I have to go, Nick."

"What's wrong?" He tucked her hair behind her ear.

"Another murder."

The shock on his face gave way to understanding. "Oh, no. I'm sorry. Here, I'll walk you out." He threw the covers back on the bed.

"Oh, you don't have to get up," Jordan protested as she crawled out of bed and searched the floor for her clothes.

"It's just rude to lie in bed and watch you leave. I'll walk you out," he repeated, leaving no room for discussion.

Jordan had to admit there was something pleasing about that. A lot of men would see nothing wrong with staying in bed, and truthfully, she didn't either, but she liked the inherent gentleman in Nick.

He had his clothes on faster than she did and, scooping the broken cuffs off the nightstand, he dangled them in front of her, the corner of his mouth turning up. "You might want these back."

Jordan gave a small laugh. "Thanks."

Despite the fact that her mind was already leaping ahead to the addition of a fourth victim to her case, Jordan appreciated that it was comfortable leaving Nick's suite, his hand on the small of her back in the dark.

"I'll talk to you soon," she said at the door.

His eyebrow shot up. "I'm walking you to your car."

"Oh." Jordan was so used to being independent that it had never even occurred to her. She was about to protest, then decided she liked the concept, and his company. "Thanks."

They were quiet on the way down, but Nick always

found a way to touch her—a hand on her back, brushing her waist, touching her hair, kissing the top of her head.

"I'll call you tomorrow," he told her when she was sitting in the driver's seat of her car, engine on. He gave her a soft kiss. "Be safe."

"Thanks," Jordan said, staring at his face, puzzled.

This felt natural, normal, right.

And that was confusing, to say the least.

But she shoved those thoughts aside as she pulled out of the garage.

Murder called, and that always trumped romance.

NICK stood next to his bed and tenderly kissed the bruise on Jordan's shoulder after he pulled her shirt off. "I should stop doing this to you," he said, feeling guilty. It wasn't the only bruise she had from his bites.

He had made love to Jordan almost every day for two weeks, and he'd bitten her repeatedly. It was such an intense and pleasurable joining, and the blood heightened it for him, and he had to say it seemed to have the same effect on Jordan. But that didn't make it right. The bruises were evidence that even though they both enjoyed the sensations it created, he was hurting her.

Which was a horrible metaphor for what he was going to do eventually anyway. Nick knew this relationship couldn't last long-term, not when he was a vampire with a laundry list of secrets, and Jordan was mortal.

"I like it when you bite me," Jordan said, her soft lips tickling his ear as she whispered. "I like *you*, you know. More than I can say."

Breathing in her vanilla scent, his mouth now on the peak of her breast, Nick knew that he had no ability whatsoever to step away, to protect Jordan's feelings, or even his own. He wanted her, this relationship, too much. He had fallen in love with her, and even if they had to crash and burn at some point when the truth became too difficult to hide, Nick wanted to enjoy it while it lasted.

"I like you, too. So, so much." He wanted to tell her he loved her, but he didn't want to overwhelm her. And truthfully, if she answered in kind, he would be overwhelmed.

But they both felt it, he knew that. They had fallen in love over long talks and passionate nights, and for two people used to being alone they seemed to be in agreement not to really discuss it, but to just enjoy it.

A door slammed down the hall. Peter.

A nice reminder of reality.

"I feel funny staying here with Peter home," Jordan said again, like she did every night.

"He's just going to the bathroom," Nick said, lifting his head and brushing her hair off her cheek. "He has no idea you're here."

"Yeah, but . . ."

Nick undid the zipper on her jeans. "But what?"

"Maybe." Her eyes fluttered closed as he slid a finger down inside her briefly. "Shit, that feels good. Maybe we should try to introduce Peter to the idea of us as a couple. Maybe we should take him out on activities. I know you do that when I'm at work, but I'd like to be a part of that, to get to know him."

No, he didn't. Nick didn't take Peter on any excursions during the day. He and Peter were usually asleep, but he let Jordan believe that he was a superdad who was taking his kid to museums, and that made him feel guilty.

Which he didn't want to dwell on at the moment. He just wanted to enjoy being in love. "We can do that."

"I don't want to insert myself into your life if you don't want me to . . ." she said, sudden doubt in her voice.

Nick cupped her cheeks. "I want you in my life. I'm in love with you, Jordan." It was crazy and stupid and bound to give him no small amount of pain, but it was the truth.

"Oh, God," she whispered. "I'm in love with you, too. How is this possible so fast?"

Jordan willingly lay back down on his bed when he gave her a little nudge of encouragement.

He shook his head. "I have no idea, but I'm so glad I met you."

And although there were many lies between them, those were his two truths—he was glad he had met her and he loved her most desperately.

The smile she gave him as she opened her legs to accommodate him lit his body and his soul on fire. "Likewise, I'm sure," she said.

Then they both forgot to talk.

SEVEN

JORDAN couldn't believe she'd fallen asleep in Nick's bed again. It had been a bad idea to spend the night making love to him when Jordan had to be at work at eight for a meeting with the powers that be to discuss their serial killer. Given that she'd passed out for hours after sex, she was clearly behind on her sleep, and it would have been smarter to stay home and get a good night's sleep. But it had been Nick's night off from work, and it had been impossible to resist those brown eyes staring at her like she was the most beautiful woman on the planet, or to stay away from those giant hands that did magical things to her insides.

Yet she needed to go home and shower before work, so she reluctantly slid out of bed as quietly as she could. Nick was sound asleep and she didn't want to disturb him, so she got dressed and moved softly into the hallway.

She was moving through the dark living room toward the door when the voice came out of nowhere, causing her to jump.

"It's about time you left."

Jordan swiveled and saw Peter sitting on the couch,

still dressed, a portable movie player in his lap. "Oh, you scared me."

"Good," he said sullenly.

Embarrassed to have been caught sneaking out of Nick's bed by his son, Jordan gave a nervous laugh. "Sorry to disturb you. Are you watching a movie?"

"Yes." He hit a button repeatedly, turning up the volume so that she could hear the sound of explosions. "I've been watching a movie while you have sex."

Peter wasn't even looking at her, but the matter-of-fact way he said the words, and what he said, caused Jordan to frown. A flush spread over her face. It was the truth, that's what she had been doing, but to hear it come from the mouth of a thirteen-year-old made her uncomfortable.

"I'm sorry, I don't think your dad realized you were awake." Jordan didn't know what else to say, and she glanced back at the bedroom, wondering if she should wake Nick up. "Most kids your age are asleep at five in the morning."

"So you mean if you had known I was awake, you wouldn't have fucked my dad? You only do it when I'm asleep? Is that a rule that makes you feel better about coming over here to get fucked every night?"

Jordan had seen a lot as a cop, had heard all sorts of language and encountered kids way too young to be acting the way they were. But those were punks, lost kids from nasty environments, not the child of the man she was very possibly falling in love with. Hell, had already fallen in love with. She had meant that when she'd said the words to Nick.

Now Peter's words temporarily robbed her of her speech as she stared at him in shock.

He was calling her a slut. He was a child and he was calling her a slut.

"Your dad and I are dating," she managed to say. "What happens between us is our business."

Peter hit a button on his video player, then turned it around so she could see the screen. The sound of heavy breathing and moaning filled the dark room as a couple moving aggressively in sex appeared on the screen. Oh, shit. Jordan gripped her purse tighter and swallowed hard. She was in over her head here, and it wasn't her place to say anything to this kid. She was going to have to tell Nick, though, and then Peter would hate her more than he clearly did already.

"I'm leaving," she told him, feeling mildly nauseous as her eyes fell back on the tangled limbs. "Have a good night."

"Wait. Don't you want to see him come on her face?"

What thirteen-year-old said things like that? How did he even know what that meant? Profoundly disturbed, Jordan didn't say anything. She just walked out of the suite and closed the door behind her. Leaning against it, she took a shaky breath and swallowed hard.

She had just asked Nick to let her become more involved in his life, more involved with his child, because she wanted a real, long-term relationship with him.

But she didn't know how to deal with Peter, and she suddenly doubted her own maternal abilities.

None of this was any good, and she felt a little sick to her stomach.

IT didn't get any better when she was sitting across the desk from her boss and Shawn.

"You know what this looks like," Shawn told her, his expression grave. "We have a witness ID-ing Kelsey Columbia at the scene of Angie Martin's murder."

Jordan rubbed her forehead. "So what does that mean, Shawn, really? You know as well as I do that Kelsey is not capable of carrying out these crimes. She's not physically strong enough. And you know that very rarely are serial killers women."

"So why was she there? On that night? In that parking lot?"

"Because she's weird. Who the hell knows? She was probably going to gamble."

"Maybe she did it with someone else. Maybe she's part of a serial-killing team."

Jordan wasn't going to touch that. If Shawn was going to guide this discussion around to Nick, which was ludicrous, she wasn't going to lead him there. He'd had to go there himself.

Their boss, Jim Shapiro, had been sitting there silently behind his desk, his fingers steepled in front of his face. An average-sized man, he had a quiet, steely intelligence. "Did you know that Nick Stolin's former boss, the man he came to the United States with, was killed?"

"Yes, he mentioned it." Squeezing her fingers tightly together in her lap, Jordan wondered what that had to do with anything. She studied Jim's face, but his expression was closed.

"The boss, a Russian named Chechikov, was found dead outside the Ava casino and hotel with all his blood drained from his body. The fourth and final victim of last summer's spate of murders."

Uh-oh. "Really?" Jordan said, keeping her voice even, despite the sweat that kicked up between her breasts and the jump in her heart rate.

"Yes. You didn't know that?"

"No, I had no idea. Nick has never mentioned his name, though I'm not sure I would have recognized it anyway."

"Nick's a big guy," Jim said. "He could easily overpower those women."

It was the logical direction to take. If Jordan were sitting on the other side of the desk, she would say the same thing. But she knew it wasn't Nick. She knew that it wasn't possible that he could fool her like that, that underneath his gentle and tender demeanor could lie a cruel, calculating monster.

Having spent nearly every night with him for two

weeks, she was convinced she would know if he was something other than what he seemed. Nick was a great guy. He couldn't be a killer. He wasn't a killer.

Besides, she had an ace in the hole. "Nick was with me the night of Angie's murder."

"He was with you?" Jim asked, eyes narrowing, hands shifting ever so slightly. "What time?"

"All night. From just before eight P.M. until I got the voice mail from Shawn just after two saying the victim had been found." It was a rock-solid alibi and she knew it. The coroner had placed time of death between ten and midnight.

Jim stared at her. Shawn shook his head and sighed.

Then her boss said, "Alright. We need to pay a little visit to Kelsey Columbia for some questioning." His cell phone buzzed and he glanced at it. "Hang here for a minute, I'm going to take this in the hallway. I'll be right back."

Jordan let out a breath when Jim walked past her and out the door. Sweating profusely, she unbuttoned and peeled off her blazer. To hell with how unprofessional it might be sitting in the office in a cotton cami, she felt sick to her stomach, and her hair was growing damp. She didn't know what any of this meant, but none of it sounded good. What was the connection between the first round of male victims drained of their blood and this second round of murders of women?

"Jordan," Shawn said, his voice appalled.

"Hmm?" Distracted, Jordan glanced up.

"What the hell happened to you?" Shawn's hand ran down the length of her arm and then he pointed to her chest above her bra.

"What?" Jordan glanced down and realized he was seeing her bruises. The marks from where Nick bit her during sex. Her cheeks went hot. "Oh, that's nothing. I fell down the stairs and you know I bruise easily."

Shawn had gone pale, and now his voice was grave, concerned. "Jordan, come on. That's a classic battered woman's line. You've only been seeing this guy a few weeks."

"It's not like that." She didn't want him thinking that she was a victim or that Nick was capable of violence. She also didn't want to demean what true battered women endured, but neither did she want to tell Shawn the truth. It was private, something just between her and Nick that made sense in the heat of passion but in the harsh daylight probably would seem strange to someone else.

Now Shawn got angry. "For Chrissake, if he's hurting you, dump him. Don't protect him."

Noting that Shawn's hand had involuntarily reached under his jacket and was stroking his gun, Jordan sighed. "Shawn, I appreciate your concern. But seriously, lay off, okay? He's not hurting me, at least not the way you think. It's a sex thing."

Her partner's eyebrows shot up. "Excuse me?"

Jordan stared him down defiantly. "He likes to bite me during sex and I like when he does it. It's very erotic. Like an animal claiming his mate."

There was an extended silence where they just stared at each other, and then Shawn made a sound of disgust. "That's the weirdest fucking thing I've ever heard."

"Then you need to get out of the house more. As far as kink goes, this is pretty mild. Or better yet, mind your own business."

Though she was still sweating moisture by the gallon, Jordan picked up her blazer and slipped back into it. She didn't want to answer similar questions from Jim. Not when she had enough to explain already.

WHEN Nick woke up it was the following night. He had pushed it, staying up all night making love to Jordan, then falling asleep at about five, so he hadn't heard her leave. Still groggy, he shuffled in his bare feet and boxer briefs to the mini-refrigerator in his kitchenette for a bag of blood.

Peter was already awake and drinking a bag out of a juice tumbler.

"Good morning," Nick said.

"Good morning, fuck face," Peter said, giving him a sneer.

"You continue to be charming as usual." Rubbing his hand through his hair, Nick frowned at Peter. "What's your problem?"

"I just hate your girlfriend, that's all. I don't know why she has to be here every single night. Oh, wait. I know why. Because she's blowing you, that's why she has to be here."

Nice. Nick chose to ignore the sexual slurs. "She's not bothering you."

"Yeah, but how long before she decides she wants to be involved in your 'son's' life? How long before we have to start going to museums and the shows together as a happy little family? I'm not doing it."

That troubled Nick, too, he had to admit. Hadn't Jordan mentioned that very thing the night before? She wanted to get to know Peter, share Nick's life with him, in its entirety. But the reality was, she couldn't share most of his life.

He was a vampire and she couldn't know that.

How the hell had he ever thought he could have a normal relationship with Jordan? There was no explaining Peter long term, no explaining his own lack of aging, their inability to move around during the day.

He had chosen to ignore all of that. Now he cared a great deal about Jordan, and they were both going to get hurt.

"I'm not going to make you play happy little family, don't worry." He couldn't stomach the deception or the stress of worrying what Peter might say. Nor did he want to draw Jordan further into a relationship that couldn't last.

"I think maybe it's time for me to leave," Peter said. "Go off on my own. You can tell your cock-sucking cop that your kid ran away and she can comfort you."

Nick grabbed a bag of blood out of the fridge and glared at Peter. "You need to stop insulting Jordan. I'm not going to tolerate that. I'm serious."

Peter just stuck his tongue out at him.

"And as for leaving, we've discussed this before. What kind of life is there for a person everyone thinks is a thirteen-year-old boy? You can't get a job, so you won't have any money. Even if you had money, no one is going to rent you an apartment without parents. And you'd probably get in trouble for not being in school. I'm sorry, I know it sucks, but your options are limited."

"I need a girlfriend," Peter said morosely. "A woman in her thirties who will want to have sex with me or adopt me, or both. I can't stay here with you any more."

Nick drank his blood quickly, then licked the remnants off his lips. "You can do whatever you want. You're a grown man. I've just been trying to help you." Though he did not want to think about the kind of woman who would get her rocks off screwing around with a boy she thought was still preadolescent.

"You really mean that? So like if I said I wanted to go out tonight without Kelsey, you wouldn't freak out?" Peter rocked back and forth on the stool at the breakfast bar and looked slyly at Nick.

"I don't think it's a good idea, but I can't stop you." Maybe Nick needed to recognize that. He couldn't control Peter. His life was his, to screw up however he wanted. Nick was weary and ready to wash his hands of all of it.

"Cool." Peter hopped off the stool. "Cancel the sitter, I'm going out."

NICK was dressed and ready for work an hour early, sitting around watching TV, worrying about Peter running around the Strip by himself, worrying about Jordan and how he had involved her in his abnormal life, and worried about Kelsey, who had neither answered her phone nor shown up for work at ten like she was supposed to. He had also texted Jordan twice and she hadn't answered him, which was odd. He was used to their daily communications, and he was feeling melancholy and missing her.

When the doorbell rang he assumed it was Kelsey, until he realized it was a mortal as he moved to answer it. He could smell blood. Jordan's blood.

A smile tugged at his mouth. This was a pleasant surprise.

"Hi," he said, when he opened the door. He leaned forward and gave her a soft kiss. "I'm glad to see you."

Jordan kissed him back, but her lips were stiff. When Nick looked closely at her, he saw her expression was troubled, the circles under her eyes pronounced. Her arms were wrapped over her chest.

"Are Peter and Kelsey here?" she asked as she moved into the room. "We need to talk."

Nick stopped short. That was not a good tone in her voice. "No, they're not here," he said cautiously. "What did you want to talk about?"

Jordan dumped her purse on the coffee table and flopped on the sofa. "God, I have no idea how to broach this subject. But do you really know what Peter is doing when you're not around? I mean, do you ever check to see what's on his computer or DVD player? Does he have a cell phone?"

Of course he didn't check those things. Peter was an adult vampire, such as that was. "Why do you ask?" he said, avoiding the question.

"Because I caught him watching porn when I left this morning."

Nick almost sighed in relief. Here he'd been thinking Jordan was going to break up with him, and it was just more oddities from his alleged son.

"Oh, I see. Well, boys will do those things."

She frowned. "Don't you care? I mean, this was explicit. And he seems to have picked up some questionable language from watching them."

"It's natural for a boy to be curious. But I'll speak to him about it." He'd speak to Peter about not bringing out the porn in Jordan's presence. As far as him viewing it, he had no say over that, even though he had personally never gotten the appeal of pornography.

Jordan stared at him for a long minute. Nick tried to sit down next to her, but she wouldn't scoot over, so he perched on the coffee table and took her hand. "Hey, is something else wrong?"

"This is none of my business and I'm not a parent, but I think you need to recognize that autistic or not, Peter is at a pivotal age, Nick. I don't think porn and Kelsey are the best influences for a young boy."

"I appreciate your concern, but I have it under control."

She gave a sound of exasperation. "No, you don't. Peter asked me if I come over here every night to get fucked. Any thirteen-year-old who is saying that is not under control."

He shouldn't be surprised, but it still made him angry that Peter was speaking like that to Jordan. Before Nick could answer, though, Jordan continued.

"And Kelsey is going to be taken in for questioning for the latest murder. She was spotted in the area where the victim was found." Jordan rubbed her hands over her face. "They think you and Kelsey are a serial-killing team."

"What?" Appalled, Nick sat up straight. "You know that's not possible! I would never kill anyone."

"I know it's not possible because I was with you the night of the last murder. I was in your bed." Jordan held her hair over her ears, tucking hard before dropping her hands. "But do I really know what you are capable of? I don't know."

"You know me. Granted, we haven't been together that long, but what we have is real, honest. You know that, Jordan. I am in love with you." Idiotic or not, he most definitely was.

She shook her head. "I don't know what I know. Something's not right. Your boss was murdered, too."

Nick couldn't believe she was serious, that she was really implying that she thought he had something to do with Chechikov's death. "He was a man who made a lot of enemies in the business world. It's not surprising he was murdered. I had nothing to do with that."

"Yeah, but most businessmen aren't drained of their blood. Like these women are." Jordan shot him a look. "Are you really even Russian?"

"Of course I am! Why would I lie about that? Especially to a cop who can do a background check on me very easily."

"I don't know. But why is your English so flawless?"

Nick hesitated. How much of the truth should he tell her? "Peter's mother spent a lot of time with her English grandmother. English was her preferred language." That was the truth, even if Nick had never had any contact with the tsarina.

"Why don't you ever eat?"

That question came out of left field. The hours they saw each other were so unusual that Nick hadn't thought Jordan had noticed he never ate anything. "Umm, I eat. Obviously." He patted his stomach and lifted his brawny bicep. "Jordan, what's really going on?"

"That's what I want to know," she whispered. "Who are you? Why does your son watch porn? Why are you connected to these murders in any way? Why do I like it when you . . ." She swallowed hard. "Bite me."

Nick stroked her hand and tried to stay calm. They were reasonable questions. "It's just possessive, that's all, a small form of domination. If you don't like it, I'll stop."

"But I do like it. A lot. That's what I don't understand. It can make me orgasm . . . Why? I've never experienced that before."

The look on her face was alarming. She was staring at him like he was someone she had never seen before, like she was actually afraid of him.

"Nick, do you really care about Peter?"

"Of course I do."

Suddenly she stood up, shaking her head. "I'm leaving. I can't see you anymore."

Then he knew that he was going to have to tell her the truth. The whole truth. Nick grabbed her arm. "Wait. Jordan, please, let me explain." He wasn't one to use vampire glamour all that often, but he did now, using a subtle mind influence to guide her back to the sofa. She slumped down and just stared at him, eyes huge, breathing heavy and frightened.

"Just listen to me, okay? I will tell you everything, from the beginning."

Nick had never bothered to turn the lamps on in the room, and the only illumination was the glow of the Vegas strip from his living room window. It cast a pale gleam across Jordan's face, and he sat down across from her on the coffee table again. Digging his nails into the denim of his jeans, he took a deep breath.

"Peter is not my son. Peter and Katie were supposed to be assassinated with their whole family in Ekaterinburg, and I was one of the guards standing post at the door. I was to make sure they didn't try to escape. That was not something I had signed on for. Being a guard, protecting those in power from other grown men, yes, I could do that. Killing insurgents I was capable of. But standing there and watching children being gunned down? I hadn't intended that . . . I couldn't stomach it." Nick swallowed hard. "I can still smell that room. It was damp and acrid and two of the girls were crying. The others were stoic, dressed in their expensive and impractical clothes. Their mother cursed the gunmen, and their father, the tsar, he looked as though it could not actually be happening. That's how I felt . . . this is not happening.

"Then the bullets started flying, spraying the family left to right and back again and there were screams and cries and the loud ricochet of the bullets, the scent of sweat, fear, fresh blood. What the guards hadn't realized was that the little girls were wearing all their jewelry sewn into their clothes, which repelled bullets, sending them back . . . And when you have bullets bouncing around in a windowless room that is fifteen feet square, they hit everything, including those pulling the trigger. I stepped into the room, in horror, to try to stop something, anything, and I saw that Peter and Katie were still alive, crying and cowering in a corner, wounded and covered in blood."

Nick rubbed his jaw, amazed that the image, the horror, was still as fresh today as it had been a hundred years earlier. But then, he had never told anyone the story, and he kept it tightly locked in a corner of his mind most of the time. "To see a young girl, blood sprayed across her lovely gown, bits of brain and flesh from her family stuck to her face, her brother wrapped in her arms, it was the most appalling sight I had ever been witness to, and I acted on instinct. I stepped in front of them and took a bullet. And as I went down, landing on her, I told her to play dead. To both play dead.

"They took us out with the other bodies and tossed us on a cart and took us into the woods. They were building a fire to burn the bodies, just two guards, and I overpowered them and had the children run into the woods. I caught up with them, and we escaped and moved west to start over, with new names, new lives." Nick shrugged. "But there are emotional scars that have not faded as the physical ones have."

Jordan leaned forward, touching his knee. "I . . . I'm sorry. That's horrible. When did this happen? I know there was a lot of fighting in Chechnya a few years back."

Now for the even harder part. "It happened in nineteen eighteen."

Her face went blank. "Excuse me?"

"Nineteen eighteen. During the Russian Revolution."

"That was almost a hundred years ago!"

He nodded. "You have heard of the last tsar of Russia, Nicholas, and his wife, Alexandra? And her son, who suffered from hemophilia? That is Peter, and his parents. Katie is his sister Maria . . . like I said, we've taken new names, new identities."

Jordan stood up so quickly, she bumped Nick with her knees. She dropped her purse, but grabbed it off the floor and strode across the room.

"Where are you going?"

"I'm leaving. I'm not going to sit here and listen to you make up stories. I felt sorry for you for a few minutes and it was just bullshit!"

"It's not bullshit." Nick caught up to her and tried to take her hand. "It's all the truth. I can tell you anything about that night, anything about the family that you want to know."

Jordan yanked at her hand but couldn't get it free from his grip. "Let. Me. Go. There is no fucking way you can be over a hundred years old."

He held on, knowing she could never escape, not with his strength, and he needed her to hear everything. "I can be if I am a vampire."

She stopped struggling. "Oh, my God," she whispered. "You're a whack job! I can't believe I thought for one minute I could be falling in love with you."

It was a logical conclusion, that he was insane, but it still wounded his feelings. Nick said carefully, "No. I'm a vampire."

Jordan was shaking her head, her efforts to free herself renewed.

But Nick continued quickly. "That's how we survived the bullets. I knew I would survive because I was already a vampire. I landed on the children and bled into their open wounds, turning them. I was trying to do the right thing, save their lives, but I didn't think about the fact that Peter would be forever in a small boy's body, that he would mentally grow to a man yet still be the size of a thirteen-year-old. It's made him difficult to deal with, mentally unstable . . . He craves blood more than normal vampires."

Jordan was grappling in her purse with her free hand, and Nick wasn't surprised when she pulled a gun out. "Let me go."

But he was still stupidly hurt. "Jordan . . . I'm telling the truth. I don't eat. I sleep during the day. I drink blood. But I am still the same man you knew and were falling in love with. Just with . . ." He bared his teeth, displaying his fangs for her to see. "A few differences from the average mortal man."

That was a mistake. She went pale in the dark room, swaying a little on her feet.

He wanted to hold her up, but she struggled against him, so he gave up and let her go, the gun still pointing at him. "You can shoot me to prove it. I won't die."

"I'm not going to shoot you. I'm just going to leave." Jordan gave him one last look of disbelief and horror, then stumbled out the door of his suite.

Nick punched the wall, creating a two-foot hole in the drywall.

That probably could have gone better.

EIGHT

KELSEY Columbia stared at the picture in front of her and then at the detective who had shown it to her, the same man who had come to Nick's room a few weeks before. Kelsey recognized this woman smiling up at her from the photo, and Kelsey had just figured out what the little vampire was doing.

Ringo always said she was slow on the uptake, and she guessed she was because she'd been clueless as to what was really happening, which made her just the worst babysitter ever.

"I've never seen her before in my life," she told the detective, uncomfortable with him standing in her suite, wishing Ringo were home. Cops made her nervous, especially ones who thought she had anything to do with murder. Ringo wasn't afraid of cops. Her husband wasn't afraid of much of anything, except maybe his drug supply drying up.

"Two different people said they saw you in the parking lot in front of the Dumpster a mere thirty minutes before this woman was killed there."

"So? I went outside to smoke. I was playing blackjack

all night at the Ava. They can tell you. They know me there, I'm there almost every night."

"So you're saying you didn't see her? You didn't see anything suspicious at all?" He gave her a hard stare.

Kelsey crossed her fingers behind her back. "No. I didn't see anything at all."

"Are you protecting someone?"

Ack. Was he a mind reader? Kelsey didn't think mortals could do that. She widened her eyes and blinked. "No. Of course not."

The detective sighed. "Alright, but if you remember anything, anything at all, give me a call. And keep in mind, we may be back with more questions. This is a dangerous killer on the loose and we want to catch him, understand?"

Kelsey nodded solemnly. "That's all I want, too."

She walked the detective to the door, waited until she heard the elevator start down with him, and then grabbed her purse and headed out herself.

Time to have a chat with the little vampire.

"I can't believe you went to question Kelsey Columbia without me," Jordan said to Shawn in a shaky voice, feeling doubly betrayed.

She had come racing downstairs after talking to Nick, terrified she was going to cry, desperate to get to her car, when she had spotted her partner.

The guilty look on his face said it all. "You're off the case, Jordan. I'm sorry. You're too close on this one. You know that."

"No, I don't." Shit. The tears were there, blurring her vision and making her furious. Jordan blinked hard, needing to control them, wanting to hold the floodgates on her emotions closed, despite the pressure building up behind them.

The man she had thought she was falling in love with

was either insane or playing some ridiculous game with her.

God, it was just horrible, crazy, ridiculous, weird. He wanted her to believe he was a vampire and that his thirteen-year-old son was actually over a hundred years old.

And the biting . . .

Jordan actually gagged at the thought of what that meant, and she clapped her hand over her mouth and squeezed her throat shut to stave off vomiting. Here she had been letting him do that, nip at her, and she had been aroused by it, thoroughly enjoying it, and it was part of some sick fantasy on his part that he was a goddamn vampire. It was sickening.

He'd had fake fangs in his mouth.

"What's the matter with you?" Shawn asked. "You look like you're going to hurl."

"I am." Glancing frantically around the lobby, Jordan spotted the restroom and set off at a fast walk.

After she tossed the contents of her stomach into the toilet, Jordan broke all her personal rules about touching any surfaces in a public restroom and slumped down onto the floor, her back to the door. Wiping her mouth and her clammy forehead, she tried to get a grip on herself and her emotions.

Her cell phone buzzed. Pulling it out with shaky fingers, she saw it was a text from Shawn.

Hope you're ok. Had to leave. Sorry about the case . . . talk later.

Nice. Not only had they thrown her off the case, Shawn hadn't even bothered to wait around to see if she was okay. Of course, six months ago, she would never have thought twice about either reaction. It was appropriate for her to be removed from the case, she recognized that intellectually. And she had never needed nor courted sympathy and compassion.

Something had shifted in her the last few weeks with

Nick. She had enjoyed and appreciated having someone thinking about her, expressing concern for her, displaying such obvious pleasure at her presence.

This sucked. To be given something she hadn't even really realized she had been missing, and then to have it yanked away, to have their brief relationship revealed as a mockery, was shocking and severe.

Dragging herself off the floor, Jordan splashed water on her face at the sink, avoiding looking at herself in the mirror. She didn't want to see the pain in her own eyes. After washing her hands, she left the restroom, wondering what she should do. She could go to the office and do what? Stare at pictures of dead women on a case she wasn't allowed to investigate anymore?

Or she could go home and pace.

Neither option sounded like fun and she was in no hurry to get to her car, so she lingered in the lobby by the side door that led to the parking lot.

A cool hand touching her arm startled her, and she whirled to see who it was. Peter was smiling up at her.

"Hi," she said to him warily. Glancing around to see who he was with, she willed herself to stay calm if she had to see Nick. It looked like Peter was alone, though.

"Hi," he said. "I'm sorry about before. I said mean things and I shouldn't have."

"Okay, thanks." Jordan studied his face. He looked a little pale, dark circles under his eyes, probably from his odd sleeping patterns, but he looked sincere enough to her. Then again, Peter was a hard person to read. His eyes were deep and emotionless. "Where's Kelsey?"

He shrugged. "I don't know." Then he just turned and walked out the doors and toward the parking lot.

Jordan watched him for a second, stunned, before she followed. "Hey! Where are you going?" she demanded, catching up to him. She might think Nick was nuts, but that didn't mean she didn't feel a responsibility for the safety of his child.

"I saw something out here from my window. I'm going to look at it."

Debating whether to call Nick or not, Jordan frowned and stayed in pace with him. Peter couldn't possibly have seen anything from his window on the tenth floor, but she wasn't about to point that out. Peter seemed more child-like again tonight, less the snide kid who had gone for shock value and more the vague, simplistic boy she had first met.

Peter bent over where the sidewalk met a row of hedges that hid the air-conditioning units. "Look," he said.

Impatient, Jordan knew she was going to have to do the inevitable, and she pulled out her cell phone. Hoping to avoid actually speaking to Nick and make Peter do the talking, Jordan found Nick on her contacts list.

"Look!" Peter said again, more urgently.

"What is it?" Jordan asked, glancing down at the side-walk, convinced she wasn't going to see anything. What she saw made her squeeze her phone, pressing the send button instinctively, her knees buckling. "What the . . ."

There was a wooden stake on the ground, just like the ones that had been found in the victims. Glancing around, she didn't see anyone in the area, and she told Peter, "Don't touch it, please."

But suddenly not only was the stake in Peter's hand, he had her down on the ground and the stake up against her chest. The shift from standing to lying on her back on the concrete was so sudden and unexpected, Jordan couldn't focus her eyes or catch her breath. But she knew he was leaning over her, felt the press of the wood on her chest, smelled the sickening sweetness of his breath as he laughed.

"You didn't see that coming, did you?"

Blinking hard, her head ringing from the blow when she had hit the ground, Jordan tried to process what was happening, refocus, understand how a child could have knocked her off her feet.

"They never do," he added. "I can look very innocent and helpless when I want to." A grin crossed his pale youthful face. "Of course, I didn't try very hard to do that with you, did I?"

Despite not really understanding what the hell was going on, Jordan's training and instinct kicked in. She rolled, anticipating freeing herself of Peter's weight and being able to spring up.

Instead, his arm shot out and her maneuver was halted so quickly it felt like she'd run straight into a brick wall. Trying to move, sweat breaking out all over her body, Jordan let out a cry of frustration. My God, it was like he had dropped a car on her instead of his hand and arm. Panicking, she struggled harder, looking up to see if it was really him, Peter, a child.

It was. But what she also saw made her freeze.

He was leaning over, and he had fangs. Like the ones Nick had shown her that she'd thought were fake.

It wasn't possible.

But then the sharp sting on her shoulder set her to action and she started screaming. A hand clamped over her mouth, and Jordan fought against the tugging force dominating her with all her strength and will.

K ELSEY glanced around the parking lot frantically. She'd seen Peter leave the hotel with the policewoman, the one that Nick liked. That wasn't good.

She smelled the scent of fresh blood to her right, and she ran toward it. He must have taken her behind the hedge, so despite sinking into the grass in her expensive heels that Ringo didn't know she'd bought, Kelsey squeezed through a hole in the bushes and found the little vampire down on the ground, feeding from the woman.

"Stop it!" This wasn't the way to live-feed from mortals, without their permission, without giving them pleasure in exchange. The cop was convulsing, her arms

flailing around as she tried to pry at the source of her torment. "Peter, no!"

Peter glanced up at her, his eyes disdainful, but he
didn't lift his fangs from the woman's flesh.

"I know what you did," Kelsey told him. "You killed
those women. You told me that woman came willingly
with you, that you were just feeding, nothing more, and
you lied to me." She was hurt by that. Here she had been
babysitting him for months and he couldn't even tell her
the truth?

Though she guessed that a vampire who was actually
murdering women wasn't all that honest.

Peter pulled his mouth back, his lips smeared with
blood. "I told you the truth. She did come willingly with
me. They all did. Then I killed them . . . so what?" His
hand pressed harder on the cop's mouth when she started
to moan and cry out. "It feels amazing, taking their blood
over and over again, until they're begging and crying, then
dizzy and disoriented, their eyes losing focus. In the end,
they look so confused when the stake goes in that it makes
me laugh."

Kelsey hated confrontation. She did not want to do
this. But she was going to have to. The little vampire was
sick and twisted, and she could not let him keep doing this
to helpless women.

Poop. Kelsey closed her eyes briefly, giving a nice big
mental call to Ringo for help, before she kicked off her
four-hundred-dollar heels and moved forward.

NICK dove for the phone when he saw it was Jordan,
despite knowing he shouldn't really answer his cell
when he was working. Ringo shot him a curious glance
but didn't say anything as they stood behind Donatelli in
the private poker room.

"Hello?" There was no response on the other end.
"Hello? Jordan?"

He heard what sounded like her saying "What the?" but she wasn't talking into the phone. Then the very obvious sound of the phone dropping came, and Nick just knew that something was wrong. He wasn't sure how he knew that, but every cell in his body was vibrating. "Jordan? Are you okay? Answer me!"

Donatelli turned around, cards in hand, and frowned at him. "Who the hell are you talking to?"

"My girlfriend . . ." he said, pulling the phone away from his head and glancing at it to make sure there was still a connection. "Something's wrong, I think she's been hurt."

"Well, go outside and deal with it. You're distracting me."

"Sure, of course. I'm sorry, Mr. Donatelli." He was moving toward the door when Ringo slammed into him. "What the hell . . . ?"

Ringo had a look of both terror and rage on his face as he bolted around Nick. "Kelsey. She just called me mentally. Something is very wrong . . . she's in trouble."

"Is everyone leaving?" Nick heard Donatelli complain, but he didn't bother to answer.

"Something is wrong with Jordan, too. She called me then clearly dropped the phone, and something tells me they might be together. Can you tell where Kelsey is?" Nick felt his suit jacket for his knife. He was strong enough to take any mortal, but sometimes a little extra encouragement was needed to persuade a criminal to leave. Usually between Nick's brawn and a flash of a weapon, they ran before he had to take any real action. He glanced around the lobby, wishing he hadn't let Jordan leave earlier like that, upset and confused.

Nick didn't know what he would do if something had happened to her, but it wouldn't be pretty.

"She's in the parking lot," Ringo said.

They both ran, Nick following Ringo, who seemed to sense where his wife was. When they burst through a row of bushes, what Nick saw stopped him flat in his tracks.

Jordan was on the ground, waxy and pale, lying completely still. He ran over to her but drew up short when he saw what else was going on a few feet away from Jordan.

Peter.

What he was doing absolutely stunned Nick as he dropped to the ground to check if Jordan was alive. Even as he frantically rushed his hands over Jordan, checking for damage, listening for the sound of her breathing and the pumping of her heart, Nick couldn't believe Peter capable of such a heinous thing.

But he obviously was. Peter was struggling with Kelsey, pressed on top of her, and he had clearly been on the verge of raping her until Ringo had attacked him at the same time Nick had dropped to check on Jordan.

With a primal growl of rage, Ringo lit into him, dragging him off his wife.

Knowing that was being taken care of, Nick focused all his attention on Jordan.

She was still alive, though barely. A rush of relief shot through him.

"Jordan, honey, it's okay, I'm here. Everything is going to be fine," Nick said, cradling her head in his hands, smoothing her hair back as he whispered in her ear. "You're going to be okay."

But even as he said it, he could hear her heart rate slowing, could feel in the coolness of her skin and see in her waxy pallor that she was struggling. Peter had taken a lot of blood, more blood than Jordan could survive the loss of, and the angry and raw bite marks on her shoulder made Nick furious at the same time he felt sick and helpless and overcome with grief. Jordan's eyes opened, dazed and glassy from pain.

He wanted to turn her more than anything he had ever wanted in his entire long life. The thought of Jordan dying, eternally still, her life cut short while she was in her prime, while he lived on and on to no purpose, horrified him. But he couldn't make that choice for her. He had made it for Katie and Peter, and he never wanted that kind of power over another human being again. Immortality was a burden to some, a gift to others, and he felt strongly that it was each person's choice to accept or reject it.

The last time he had seen her she had been shaking her head at him, upset and disgusted with what she had thought was a made-up story on his part about vampirism. He didn't know if she could understand now how true it had all been, or if she was too hazy from the loss of blood to comprehend what was happening, but he had to try.

She surprised him by saying, "Nick . . . I'm dying, aren't I?"

His heart squeezed. "You've lost a lot of blood, honey. I can try to rush you to the hospital for a transfusion."

But he knew it would be too late. She had been almost entirely drained of blood. He couldn't even believe she was conscious, but her eyes were already fluttering shut again, her arm slackening against his leg.

"Or I can make you a vampire like me," he whispered into her ear. "So you won't die. But only if you want to . . . Eternity is a long time, Jordan."

Searching her face for any sign that she had heard him, Nick knew he was running out of time. He wasn't sure if he could let her die. Yet he wasn't sure if he could turn her without knowing she had consented in some way. As the vital seconds ticked away, Nick shook her a little, getting frantic.

"Jordan, do you want me to turn you . . . yes or no?"

Her chest rose slowly as she sucked in a labored breath, then with eyes still closed, she said, "Yes."

Relief flooded him, but Nick wanted to be sure she had actually spoken, and that he hadn't just heard what he wanted to. "You want to be a vampire so you don't die?"

"Yes."

It was even quieter than the first, but he had still heard it, and Nick didn't waste another second of precious time. Shifting her head into his lap, he raised his wrist and sliced it wide open with his fangs. Once he dribbled a bit of blood onto Jordan's lips and into her mouth, she started to drink on her own, and Nick closed his eyes and tried to quiet the fear that was still coursing through his veins from the thought of this woman dying, being gone from him and this life forever. He wouldn't have been able to handle that, he was certain, and while he had no idea if she would forgive him, if she would want to be with him in this new life, he was selfishly grateful that she had consented.

As she sucked more aggressively, strength gaining, the tug and pull of his blood out of his body sharp and satisfying, Nick glanced over at Ringo and Kelsey, wanting confirmation that Peter was contained in some manner.

Ringo had the other vampire on the ground and he was standing up, breathing hard, a knife in his hand. It was then Nick realized Peter had been decapitated, his dark eyes wide and empty, blood spilling over the gravel. Ringo met Nick's stare.

"He was raping my wife. He tortured and murdered four helpless mortal women," Ringo said, his hard tone brooking no argument. "He had to die before he hurt anyone else."

Nick just nodded. He had spent a century wishing the best for Peter, never thinking he could be capable of such evil. If he had gone that far astray, then Ringo had every right to take justice into his hands and execute Peter.

"Is she okay?" Ringo asked, gesturing to Jordan as he wiped his bloody knife on the bushes behind them to clean it off.

"She will be," Nick said, already hearing Jordan's heartbeat growing stronger, her fingers starting to grip his arm as she sucked.

He spotted Kelsey huddled in the corner, leaning against the air-conditioning unit and hugging herself. "Kelsey, how about you? Are you okay? I'm so sorry Peter hurt you . . . I had no idea he was capable of any of this."

Kelsey nodded, her hair falling in her eyes. "I know. I didn't know either. And I'm okay." She shrugged. "These things just seem to happen to me, but I'm always okay."

And Jordan would be okay, too. She had to be.

NINE

JORDAN moved her hand in front of her face again in Nick's bathroom, amazed at how sharp the movement could be, at how pale and perfect her skin was. The scar she'd gotten on her forearm from falling out of a tree house at age ten was gone. Even in the dark, with no light on, she could look down and see the water spots from her shower on her naked skin.

She was a vampire.

The inconceivable, preposterous story Nick had told her had been the truth.

And Peter had been the killer she'd been searching for.

She didn't know how to think, to feel, to process all of it, so she focused instead on the purity of her milky white skin, the intensity of her vision, and the force of her new strength.

With one quick movement, she snapped Nick's toothbrush into two pieces.

Jordan was staring at the broken plastic in awe, and a little bit of satisfaction, when a soft knock came on the door and Nick slipped inside.

"Are you okay?" he asked, those big hands sweeping her bangs off her forehead.

He was gentle, always so gentle with her, and now that she knew his secret, knew his strength, she was even more amazed, touched by the softness of his touch. Not trusting her voice just yet, she nodded.

"I'm sorry," he said.

"For what?" she managed, stepping closer to him, wanting the warmth of his body, the shield of his bulk next to her naked skin.

"For what Peter did to those women, for what he did to you . . . I had no idea, Jordan. Absolutely no idea."

"I know," Jordan reassured him, moving her hands to his shoulders. She could see the torment in his eyes, knew as surely as she would have died had Nick not intervened, that he'd only been trying to do the right thing. He'd had no knowledge of Peter's true depravity. "I'm just glad to know the case is essentially closed. We'll never officially find our killer on paper, but I'm glad no other woman is going to be hurt by him."

Part of Jordan balked at what Nick had told her, how Ringo had taken justice into his own hands and killed Peter, but she had to wrap her mind around this new reality. It had been the best way to handle the situation so Peter couldn't continue to murder when there was no possibility of traditional means of prosecution.

"I don't know how I'm going to tell Katie about this. She's due back in a couple of days."

"Maybe she already understands that Peter was no longer the boy she knew as her brother. You said she avoided his company."

"That's true." Nick kissed her forehead. "But what about you? Us? Is there still an us, Jordan?"

Now that all the secrets were gone, all the oddities explained, Jordan had no reservations. "There is if you want there to be," she told him, brushing her lips across his, closing her eyes to savor the passion his kisses always sparked in her.

"Oh, I want," he said, looking down into her eyes. "Are you okay with being a vampire? I wanted you to have a choice, but I'm not sure that you understood totally what you were getting into."

Even as the whole concept of the undead threatened to overwhelm her, Jordan was nothing if not prosaic. "This sure as hell wasn't in my plans, and I have more questions than hairs on my head, but it's okay. Standing here naked in the bathroom being kissed by the man I love, or being buried? No contest, Nick. Don't take on any guilt for this . . . and let go of the guilt over Peter. It wasn't your fault, none of it was your fault."

He sighed, his fingers squeezing her upper arms. "Thank you. And we can do anything you want, you know. We have the world, and eternity, at our disposal. I just want to be with you, to enjoy ourselves."

Jordan sighed, wrapping her arms around his neck. "Eternity with you sounds amazing. But let's just start with tonight. Hold me, Nick. Love me."

"That will be the easiest thing I've ever done in my whole life."

There was something fabulous about knowing that she was not alone, that she had someone to share her time, her heart, her thoughts with. Someone who had seen murder himself, who understood what her life and her job were like. "Hey, are you calling me easy?"

Nick laughed softly into her hair as he nuzzled her ear. "You said it, not me."

"I should refuse to have sex with you," she said, even as she tilted her head back to give him better access to her neck.

"Mmm-hmm," he said, like he didn't believe her for one second.

Hell, she didn't believe it herself, especially when his fingers teased her nipples.

Then Nick suddenly pulled back. "I love you, Jordan."

"God, I love you, too." Jordan stiffened as soon as the

words were out of her mouth. "Can I say 'God' now that I'm a vampire?"

Nick's mouth turned up in a smile. "You can say whatever you want."

"Then I say take me to bed and bite me."

New York Times bestselling author

LORI FOSTER...

"Writes smart, sexy, engaging characters."
—**Christine Feehan**

"Doesn't hesitate to turn up the heat."
—*Booklist*

"Delivers everything you're
looking for in a romance."
—**Jayne Ann Krentz**

So don't miss...

Causing Havoc

Simon Says

Hard to Handle

Available now from penguin.com

HER DESTINY CAN'T BE DENIED.

SERVANT:
THE ACCEPTANCE

THE SECOND BOOK IN THE SUPERNATURAL URBAN THRILLER SERIES

BY LORI FOSTER WRITING AS
L. L. Foster

Gabrielle Cody has accepted her destiny—for she is fated to destroy all evil. But she wasn't prepared to see Detective Luther Cross ever again. He's the beacon of reality in her life, the one thing that makes her feel human, like a real woman.

But Gaby must resist involvement with Luther now, for she is protecting streetwalkers. Her life of retribution is far too dangerous, and this time, it's not just their hearts that won't come out unscathed.

penguin.com

Also by
USA Today Bestselling Author

Erin McCarthy

A Date with the Other Side

Haunted house tour guide Shelby Tucker gets hot and bothered when she stumbles upon sexy, naked Boston Macnamara. She knows he's no ghost, though he does make her weak in the knees.

"Sexy, sassy...filled with humor."
—Rachel Gibson

penguin.com

My life…
My love…

My Immortal

By *USA Today* Bestselling Author
ERIN McCARTHY

In the late eighteenth century, plantation owner Damien du Bourg struck an unholy bargain with a fallen angel: an eternity of inspiring lust in others in exchange for the gift of immortality. However, when Marley Turner stumbles upon Damien's plantation while searching for her missing sister, for the first time in two hundred years it's Damien who can't resist the lure of a woman. But his past sins aren't so easily forgotten—or forgiven…

"*My Immortal* is truly a passionately written piece of art." —*Night Owl Romance*

penguin.com

M174T1107